Come Away With Me

Pat,

Thanks so much for critiquing this book; it's better for your having done it.

Enjoy the voyage again.

Harry McIntyre

Come Away With Me

Harry McIntyre

iUniverse, Inc.
New York Bloomington

Come Away With Me

iUniverse books may be ordered through booksellers or by contacting:

iUniverse
1663 Liberty Drive
Bloomington, IN 47403
www.iuniverse.com
1-800-Authors (1-800-288-4677)

ISBN: 978-1-4502-0809-3 (pbk)
ISBN: 978-1-4502-0811-6 (cloth)
ISBN: 978-1-4502-0810-9 (ebook)

Printed in the United States of America

iUniverse rev. date: 1/27/10

ACKNOWLEDGEMENTS

My very special thanks to Marie Trotignon for her moral support and critiquing skills, to Patrick Lettenmaier for his nautical and syntax critiquing, to Robert Ross, Ethyl Winters, and Jo Olafson for their syntax critiquing and support. **Come Away With Me**

Chapter One

Rodger McCauly sits slump-shouldered in the chair beside Dr. Smith`s desk as he lets his doctor`s proclamation sink in. "A year to live, if you take care of yourself." *Why did I let this happen? Why didn`t I come to him sooner when it was treatable? And just when I was planning retirement to pursue my lifelong dream of sailing to Tahiti.*

"Where do we go from here, Doctor?" Rodger asks lifting his chin off his chest and looking directly at Doctor Smith.

The doctor, a kindly, soft-spoken man, looks at him sympathetically, "Go home, Rodger, and get your affairs in order, do what`s most important to you, tell your wife and your family about your predicament. I`ll be available at all times, and we`ll know when it`s time for you to be hospitalized. Tuberculosis isn`t an easy ending, but with medication and hospice sevices, we can keep you reasonably comfortable and not communicable.

* * *

The taxi wheeled past the entrance sign to the Des Moines, Washington marina, and screeched to a stop. Helen Davis jumped out, leaned down to pay the driver, and then hoisted a bulging sea bag across her shoulder and headed toward the dock. Even at middle-age, she had a spring to her step, and a body language that shouted "I`m in charge."

At the end of the dock, a Tahiti Ketch, *Sea Witch* painted across her transom, bobbed gently in her moorage slip, and beside her, a still handsome, but gaunt, middle-aged man waited. His seaman-type clothes still had that "new look." His blue, loose-fitting turtleneck shirt made him appear even thinner. Sailor dungarees, needing to be washed a few times to lose their shiny look; a Greek fisherman`s cap, not having developed a proper crush and lacking a sweat-line at the brow, completed the faux sailor image. A briar pipe hung loosely from his lips as he watched the woman`s descent down the gangway, the woman who sold him the ketch, the woman who will be his skipper for the voyage to Tahiti.

Rodger arrived early, as he wanted time alone with the Sea Witch; time to get acquainted with his new boat before setting out on what would be his biggest and last adventure. Rodger let his gaze slide over the thirty-one foot ketch, its white hull trimmed in navy blue at the waterline. The two masts rising above the deck, stained mahogany and set off by white sails flaked on their booms. The hardware, all in good repair, and all lines nearly new. *A classic boat built by a real craftsman. She`s obviously been well maintained with a lot of nautical miles left in her.*

It all began when Rodger saw the Tahiti Ketch for sale in the Seattle Times. Maybe it had to do with the fact he had just come from his doctor`s office where he`d been told the tuberculosis was getting no better, that he had a limited time to live, a limited time to do all the things he had wanted to do with the rest of his life. The advertisement with its reference to a Tahiti ketch brought the painful thought he would never realize his life-long dream of sailing to Tahiti. *But why not,* he asked himself? *This just might be a boat I could single-hand.* He responded to the advertisement.

At their meeting, Rodger had been surprised to discover the boat`s owner was a woman; one obviously quite knowledgeable about boats and sailing. It didn`t take long for her to realize, Rodger was not. "I don`t think you have the experience needed to pull this off," she`d cautioned once he`d confided his plan to her. "I`m afraid you couldn`t handle this craft by yourself. It`s not a single-hander for an amateur"

Rodger`s disappointment was immediate and keen, but he accepted her assessment. Disheartened, he turned to leave when she stopped him. "Look, Rodger, buy my boat and I`ll throw my skipper services in free; I`ve always wanted to sail to Tahiti."

"I may not survive the journey," Rodger reminded her.

She`d passed it off with a wave of her hand, "That we`re going to die is a given; how and when is the unknown. My late husband, Clyde, used to say, *Death is the sugar of life. It makes each day we live that much sweeter*. Let`s just do it." The determined set of her jaw told Rodger the decision had already been made as far as she was concerned.

* * *

He now watched this woman approach, a woman he scarcely knew. A small twinge of misgiving stirred within him. *If only my family understood,* he thought. *If only they could have been here to wish me Bon Voyage.* A nervous attempt to light his pipe sent him into a spasm of coughing. He leaned against the gunnel of the boat until the coughing subsided. The doctor had said to get plenty of fresh air. *If fresh air is what it will take, I`ll certainly get my share in the next few months.*

"I see you beat me here," the woman said as she paused beside the ketch, and then slung her seabag aboard. "Ready for the big adventure, Rodger?"

Rodger glanced across the bay; its surface ruffled by a gentle breeze, the blue sky laced with marestail clouds, and a morning temperature in the sixties prompted him to say, "This is *a* great day to start our voyage... yes, I`m ready."

She instructed Rodger to go below and start the small diesel engine. It would get them out of the marina and into the shipping lanes where current and wind would launch them on the first leg of their journey.

Rodger responded dutifully and soon returned as the engine idoled smoothly. Uncleating the bow and stern line, he pushed them away from the dock, and the Sea Witch was on its way to Tahiti.

Standing at the tiller, Helen remarked, "In these light winds we'll use the mainsail and the engine until we get to Point-No-Point. Then we'll douse the engine when we pick up stronger winds at the tip of the Kitsap Peninsula and add the jib and mizzen sail. August is the best month for these waters, and crossing the Pacific Ocean should be a great adventure. By the way, can I call you Rod or Rodg instead of Rodger? That sounds so formal."

"Sure, just call me Rodg; nearly everyone does. Is there anything that I should be doing? I want to pull my weight and be a good First Mate even if you do have to teach me everything a First Mate should know."

"Well, you could make the skipper a cup of coffee. There will be plenty to learn and do later on, believe me."

Rodger went below to the small galley and lit the gimbaled, oil-burning cook stove. By the time the coffee was ready the salon was a toasty warm and begun to feel like a place two compatible people could share the eating, cooking, and lounging, all basically in the same space. Sleeping was another thing. He would sleep forward in the v- berth and she would sleep here in the salon on the hide-a-bed divan.

Rodger carried the two mugs of steaming coffee up the stairway to the cockpit to find Helen lost in reverie. Stopping short he studied her for a moment. *She's attractive; at her age, the auburn hair is probably tinted, but it sets off her green eyes well. Her ruddy complexion gives her a bit of an Irish look.* "You're lost in thought," Rodger ventured.

"Yes." Helen`s cheeks flushed, "I…I was here on the Sea Witch, but in my mind Clyde was at the helm."

"Oh," offered Rodger gently, "that`s easy to understand. I hope this trip will be all right for you."

"It will be, I just need a few days under my belt to get past the what-ifs. By the way, Rodg, you can bend on the jib and hoist it. The wind's picked up earlier than I expected, then you can shut the engine down and raise the mizzen sail."

"I can shut the engine down, but how do you bend on a jib?" asked Rodger as he carefully handed Helen her coffee.

"I keep forgetting what you don`t know. Take the tiller and my coffee cup and I'll show you how to bend on a jib." Going forward to the bow with the sailbag in her hand she shouted back to Rodger, "Hold the course at 320 degrees while I fasten the metal hanks on the forward edge of the sail to the forestay. Then I attach the halyard to the top of the sail and run it up the mast and cleat it off." She stepped back with hands on her hips, "That's called bending on the jib, and now I`ll raise the main sail and the mizzen sail that are already in place resting on their booms."

She retrieved her cup of coffee from Rodger before taking over the helm. "Notice the sails are luffing or in shore lingo flapping. We're headed directly into the wind, so I`ll fall off the heading about 15 degrees. Now, take each of the lines connected at the bottom corner of the jib, main, and mizzen sail and run them right-hand around the wenches located on the gunnels." Rodger took the lines, following Helen`s instructions. "Tighten the winches and see what happens."

"Ah ha! The sails have filled with air and stopped flapping or I guess I should say luffing?"

"Notice the boat has picked up speed as the sails draw air."

"Wow!" Rodger could feel the boat surging forward, like a gazelle set free. With the sudden silence of the engine, he now was able to hear the lapping sound of waves on the hull, and the sound of wind in the rigging and sails. "This is great."

"I agree! Now, let`s do something about lunch."

"Give me your empty cup, Skipper; I`ll go below and prepare it." As Rodger took out the ingredients to make sandwiches, a spasm of coughing overcame him. He sank weakly onto the nearby divan to regain his composure. As he sat quietly he thought *how intelligent is my decision to run off without any more explanation than the one page letter I left Irene. Given the circumstances of my health, I tried to explain my need to fulfill this dream. However, I did tell her I`d call from my first port-of-call to answer any questions she might have. There will be questions as this has been my big secret, but I didn`t want to give her a chance to talk me out of it.*

Ours hasn`t been an ideal marriage, but I`ve always been a good provider for her and our three sons. They`re adults now seeking their own pathway through life, and there are the seven grandchildren who will satisfy her need for family. Actually, she`s been running our mortgage company quite nicely since my health problem, and Junior has stepped into my job. So, all in all, everyone seems to get along without me very well… almost too well. Of course they`ll grieve when I give in to the tuberculosis. But I need this adventure! It may shorten my life, but so what? It`s not like I`m making this trip alone, but I wonder why I was reluctant to mention in my letter the skipper is a woman?

This fact brought him back to the moment. Finishing the two sandwiches, he added a couple of bottles of beer and chips to the tray. Climbing the steps to the cockpit, he placed the tray within Helen's reach, "I hope this meets your expectations, Skipper."

"It looks scrumptious, Mate. Take the tiller after you open your beer, and I'll freshen up a bit before I dive in." Helen rose from her place by the tiller to go below, "We`re on a heading of 330 degrees, so stay as close to that as the wind allows. If the sails start luffing, just fall off the heading a little until it stops. We must sail off the absolute direction of the wind by at least 15 degrees to keep the sails full. You'll get the hang of it pretty soon," Helen added with a grin as she disappeared down the hatchway.

Rodger sat at the back of the cockpit with the tiller in one hand, and a beer in the other. Surveying the shoreline, he marveled at the beauty of Bainbridge Island and the Kitsap Peninsula. He had spent most of his life in this part of the Northwest and had walked some of these very beaches as a young man. The location of the homes that were spaced along the shore was usually determined by by the height of the ground behind the beaches edge. If the bank was low, older houses appeared sprinkled with a few new, larger homes. If the bank was high, evergreen trees prevailed.

Naturally, the best property was built on first and development had started here about a hundred years ago. The newer homes on choice property usually meant a cabin had been torn down to accommodate the new home. Rodger had played with the idea of a retirement home along this stretch of beach on the Kitsap Peniinsula, but that was before his doctor`s proclimation.

Foot-high waves now predominated the surface of the water that were created by the 10-knot wind coming directly out of the north. The boat lay over noticeably and was picking up speed. Slowly moving the tiller, he could feel the boat`s response and thought, *It`s as if I had a living, cat-like animal by the tail.*

This sailing is far different from any of my previous boating experiences. At the end of my arm is this pulsing, surging, dynamic thing in rhythm with the water and the wind. Sailing is so wonderfully different from power boating, I can hardly believe it.

Helen appeared in the stairwell, "Well Mate, how do you like sailing on a day with good wind, lots of sunshine and the temperature in the 70`s?"

"Where has this been all my life? I just love it!"

"Good, because you're in for a whole lot more of it before we get to Tahiti." Sitting down beside Rodger, she turned her attention to lunch, "This sandwich is excellent; I'm glad you know your way around a galley, I can take or leave kitchen work. We'll trade off of course, but it's nice to know there are some decent meals in store when I'm not doing the cooking." After taking a swallow of beer she continued, "I assume you were able to get the list of supplies I gave you."

"Yes, but it took some doing over the past few days. I got everything on the list; even salt water soap. There's a lot of preserved meat aboard, but I'm hoping we will have fresh fish now and then."

"Oh we will, with any luck, but you have to be prepared for the worst. Clyde and I were out two weeks once and never caught a fish." Helen stood and walked toward Rodger, "I`ll take the helm now while you eat your lunch."

Rodger exchanged places with Helen. "Really? he replied. "I had no idea fish were that scarce."

"They didn't used to be, but that was before the dams on the spawning rivers and tributaries were built. Also commercial pollution and large trawler boats sweeping the bottom took a great toll. Japan and Russia can take credit for much of that carnage."

"What a shame, but maybe we'll luck out. I'd really like a more varied diet than canned meat." As Rodger sat eating his lunch, he let his eyes scan the passing scene. "The wind picking up, the waves higher, and hull speed seems to be increasing."

Helen smiled, "You know Rodg, you're talking and acting more like a sailor even in this short time. In fact, you even look more like a sailor with some color in your face. Even your eyes look more alive."

"Wow! Maybe I've missed my calling all these years. Perhaps I should have been a sailor instead of a mortgage broker."

"So that's what you did for a living, sounds like something I`d have no interest in. But what do I know about the banking world? I was a physical education teacher before I married Clyde."

"Really? Do you and Clyde have children?"

"No. I was the typical old maid schoolteacher. I didn't marry until I was nearly fifty and beyond my childbearing years. Clyde and I only had ten years together, but he taught me to be a sailor. I only sold the boat because I couldn't comfortably single-hand it, and there never was anyone to crew for me; I'm enjoying this as much as you are."

Helen stood at the tiller basking in the comaraderie of the moment, "Look, there`s Point-No-Point ahead to port, and by the looks of the water up there, I'd say we're in for a stronger wind as soon as we round it. The wind often blows down Admiralty Inlet like liquid flowing in a funnel, and the current can run up to four knots."

"You don't look like an old maid school teacher, Skipper," replied Rodger refusing to give up this intimate conversation. "I'd say you look more like a mature athlete of some outdoor sport: perhaps sailing, swimming or skiing."

"I'll take that as a compliment, Rodg, but don't emphasize the word mature too strongly; I'm not ready for the scrap heap yet. I figure I have ten active years left in me; then I'll play at the sedentary life." Helen stood a little taller obviously enjoying Rodger`s compliment combined with the glorious weather and the joy of sailing once again. She had missed the smell and soft sting of salt-laden air hitting her in the face as she stood at a tiller with a deck beneath her feet.

Even though the sun felt good on her skin, it wasn`t shortsleeve or tanktop weather yet. That would come when they were a thousand miles farther south. They`d be off the coast of California and into warmer weather by then, and shorts and polo shirts or tank tops would be the uniform of the day. For now it were long pants and long sleeve shirts, perhaps with a sweater or windbreaker in the late afternoon or early evening.

Rodger began to feel the formality of their relationship easing into friendship. Then continuing, "I retired because of my Tuberculosis. I wish I could say I had ten active years left, but it would take a miracle, as my doctor has given me only a year. Actually, I'd settle for one good active year. That would get me to Tahiti; then I'd be ready to play at the sedentary life, only mine will really be sedentary."

Helen was silent for a while, and then her voice softened, "Who knows, this trip might just be the making of you." This comment created a lull in their conversation as no response was required. Rodger stood silent and savored the positiveness of Helen`s remark.

As they approached Point-No-Point, the huge expanse of open water they`d been on opened up even wider. Rodger remembered reading somewhere this was a meeting place of the ocean water coming down the Straits of Juan de Fuca and the ocean water coming down the inside passage between Vancouver Island and British Columbia. It flows south another fifty miles on an incoming tide and fills Puget Sound all the way to the state capitol at Olympia.

Helen became intent on her task at the helm and stood as they neared Point-No-Point. "Rodg, when we round the point we`ll need to be on a compass setting of 240 degrees, and we`ll be on a starboard reach. If we aren't ready for the change, we could get a knock-down and we sure don't want that."

The water ahead showed small breaking waves a distance off shore indicating shallow water causing Helen to swing the bow to starboard in order to skirt the point even wider. She shouted, "Slack off the mainsail, we don`t want the rail to go underwater."

Once they were at the point, she swung the bow to port to the new heading while Rodger tended the sails. When they were on an even keel again Rodger ploped down beside Helen who had seated herself next to the tiller. "O.K. Skipper, I can guess what a knock-down is, but a starboard reach... what is that?"

Helen smiled at Rodger`s question, "When the wind is coming over the starboard side of the hull, which of course puts your sails to port, and you`re holding that course for a while, you`re are on a starboard reach."

"I don't know Skipper, there`s a lot to learn in just the vocabulary of sailing. I`m beginning to feel like I've never been on a boat before, which isn't true."

"Cheer up mate, give it a little time. If I use a word or phrase you don't understand, ask me. After all, none of us is born with a vocabulary and now we use thousands of words."

Rodger, satisfied with her explanation, sat looking at the passing beach scenery. Spotting Hansville coming up to port, he marveled at the growth of residence since he was there last. It had been a popular salmon fishing area for as long as he could remember, and had its own boathouse with Kicker boats to hire. He remembers the thrill of being launched down their marine railway into the swift current that always seemed to be running one way or the other. Reflecting on Helen`s last remark he responded, "Your point is well taken; I`ll just be patient, learn, and enjoy. I`m glad you`re an experienced teacher as you're going to get an opportunity to use all your skills with me."

Rodger stood to get a better view ahead. He continued to scan the beach scene to port and noticed the cabins and permanent homes started to dwindle as the low land behind the beach started to rise in elevation until it came to the promentary called Foul Weather Bluff. This was all familiar to him as he had fished for salmon here over the years renting one of the seaworthy fourteen-foot kicker boats with a single-cylinder engine amidships that was only capable of six knots of speed, but adequate for salmon trolling.

Turning to face Helen he asked, "Where do you plan for us to stay tonight?"

"Port Ludlow will be a full day`s run, and it's only an hour and a half ahead of us if this wind holds. If not, we'll motor in anyway and find moorage for the night. We have a choice. We can use the guest dock or just drop anchor in the bay." Helen turned to look at Rodger instead of the path ahead, "What would you like to do, Rodg? It's your boat."

Rodger thought for a moment, "I`d like to drop anchor and see what it's like to be isolated on a boat over a period longer than a few hours. Tomorrow night we can look for dockside moorage. How does that sound?"

"Sounds like a plan, Mate." Helen returned her attention to the water ahead. "By the way, did you notice the current is going the same direction we are? It adds to our total speed. Being close-hauled, our hull speed is about six knots. So, if the current is four knots and the hull speed is 6 knots, we are moving over the land below us at 10 knots. That's excellent time for a sailboat."

"I feel like we`re doing twice that speed," replied Rodger as he sat on the bench seat with his back to the cabin bulkhead. "By the way, what does close-hauled mean?"

"Close-hauled means you have winched down the jib, main, and mizzen lines as tight as you can without burying the rail in the water."

"Thanks," said Rodger standing. "I think I see Port Ludlow ahead; your navigating is right on target, Skipper. By the way, I`ve noticed the current seems to divide here and part of it is going to port."

"That's because we`re passing the mouth of Hood Canal. It`s a natural fjord shaped like a giant fish hook eighty miles long and up to two miles wide, and it takes a lot of water to fill it. A few more minutes and we will be beyond the rip tides, whirlpools, and roiling water caused by the entrance. If you look ahead you can see relatively flat water in the bay at Port Ludlow."

Rodger followed Helen`s instruction, then turned and looked at Hood Canal. "I see a floating bridge a couple of miles down the canal that looks to be a mile long. I guess that`s the joining link between the Kitsap Peninsula and the Olympic Peninsula." Not waiting for conformation he added, "It's been a wonderful day, Skipper."

"It's only the beginning, Mate!"

Chapter Two

Sitting at the drop leaf table in the salon, Helen studied the navigation chart detailing the harbor at Port Ludlow, their first port of call. Rodger, stationed at the helm scanned the waters ahead for obstacles. He liked the powerful feeling of having command of this nine-ton vessel. It made him feel like an intricate and all-important part of the whole sailing phenomena. In this state of euphoria he relaxed at the tiller and lets his mind wander back to his former life. *I wonder what the family's reaction is to my letter. There will be phone calls today from Irene, to our three sons at the least. They`ll be concerned because I`m ill and running away to attempt this monumental adventure, which they`ll consider foolhardy and suicidal. Being in good health and a knowledgeable sailor is one thing, but they know I`m neither. I wonder if they`ll try to stop me by alerting the Coast Guard, or police, or both? But what would the charge be…dementia?*

I told them in my letter I had arranged for the previous owner to act as Skipper, companion, and nurse, if a nurse is needed. Does this sound like the act of a demented person? They`ll probably assume the previous owner of the Sea Witch is a man, as few woman own sailboats or sail for that matter. When I keep my promise to make a phone call at our first port-of-call, the truth will be known, if I identify Helen as the skipper. This could make Irene angry enough to try to stop me.

Rodger looked up at the tell-tales near the top of the mainsail to be sure the sailing attitude of the Sea Witch was correct. Satisfied, he scanned forward on their path ahead for obstacles. Finding none he reverted to his reverie. *What happened to Irene and me? After thirty years of marriage how and why did our relationship deteriorate over the past few years?* We *started out like most couples, happy, in love, seeking the good life, which included children, a home, a place in the community, financial security. We`ve had it all, but now after thirty years we`re no longer lovers, only friends. Is that the way of marriage? I`ll have to give Helen`s identity issue more thought before I make that phone call. If I don`t go ashore at Port Ludlow I won`t have to make it, will I?"*

Helen appeared out of the companionway, "It looks like the wind is slackening; it usually does once you`re past Tala Point. I`ll take the tiller while you start the engine, we`ll do better now under power."

"Aye, aye, Skipper," replied Rodger, thankful to be interrupted from his train of thought.

Turning the tiller over to Helen, he went below to coax the engine into life. It was a get- down-on-your-hands-and-knees kind of job. Priming the engine, he pushed the starter and the engine sputtered to life. When he returned to the cockpit, Helen brought the Sea Witch facing into the wind; he then moved quickly to uncleated the halyards and drop the sails.

"Good job Rodg, stow the jib in the sail bag and we`ll leave it on deck attached to the deck cleat. Let`s flake, or fold, the mainsail and mizzen sail on top of their booms. Take the tiller, I`ll show you how to use the sail line to wrap the mainsail to the boom." She stepped aside to make room for Rodger to take the tiller. "That puts it out of the way and ready for use tomorrow. Now you do the same with the mizzen sail."

The wind had died completely by the time they entered the bay that lay beyond Tala Point. Port Ludlow appeared to be a good choice for the night and finding a place to drop anchor was no problem. Helen carefully guided the Sea Witch through a maze of larger boats and settled for a spot a hundred yards off shore. Rodger`s gaze swept the harbor and surrounding area teaming with people, boats, and condominiums.

"August is the prime month for the boating crowd in the Northwest," explained Helen, "brings them out in full force."

"It`s only five o`clock," commented Rodger. "I should have time to take a row in the dingy before dinner. By the way, what do you have in mind for dinner?"

"That`s your department Rodg. Whatever you want to fix is what we`ll eat. I told you, I don`t really like to cook and I`m not a fussy eater. If you`re out for a row in the dinghy you might try your hand at fishing; these bays usually have bottom fish, if nothing else."

"Great idea! We`ve a small pole on board, so I`m off to catch dinner."

Rodger abandoned his sweater almost immediately and now removed his T- shirt exposing his slender, pale upper body. *Maybe the warm sun will combat this demon in me,* he thought. *If I can just stay positive about this thing, I think I can prove the doctors wrong. They say a year if I take care of myself, meaning mostly bed rest. Yet, today has been glorious and I feel more alive now then I have in months. Even if they`re right, I`ve had today. Death, you really are the sugar of life; today is so sweet.*

As he rowed the small dingy off shore a short distance, he took in the sights and sounds about him. Music waifed from a large sailboat as he rowed past and a couple waved to him as they sat in their boat`s cockpit enjoying a drink of some kind. The rhythmic splash sound of the oars dipping into the water reminded him of the sound of a slow moving window washer on an automobile`s windshield. The smell of kelp arose from a kelp bed near a point of land jutting out from shore ahead of him. The sun was still high enough in the sky to be visible above the trees covering the hills that surrounded the harbor.

After awhile with only a bullhead to show for his efforts to catch a fish he noticed a commercial fishing boat moored at a dock with a crowd of people standing near its stern. He decided to row over and investigate.

* * *

Helen moved quickly about the cabin stowing her gear in the spaces she knew so well. Because Rodger put his gear in the forward berth area, she could see that he meant for her to have the divan in the salon for sleeping. The galley, small but adequate, took up the rest of the space except for a passageway leading to the small diesel engine under the cockpit floor. The drop-leaf table in the middle of the salon was the catchall for maps, books, etc. and most importantly, a place to prepare and serve food. At the end of the day it was moved out of the way to make room for the hide-a-bed divan to be opened for sleeping.

Helen leaned back on the familiar divan and remembered when she and Clyde had shared this salon. They had been a happy, compatible couple and life had been good until his sudden heart attack. Suddenly all her plans had been shattered and she was alone. Of course her family had been there to give her support, but eventually they returned to their lives and no one had taken Clyde`s place… that is until now. Her mind came to rest on Rodger. *He`s basically a very decent sort of guy forced to look at the end of life's journey too soon and asked, "Is this all there is?" Deciding to squeeze the most he can out of the last few months of his life, that`s where I came in. It was a spur-of-the-moment decision when I offered to skipper the Sea Witch to Tahiti; I could hardly believe what I heard myself saying. I decided to stick with my offer, but occasionally I`ve had second thoughts. Is this a way of joining Clyde sooner? Drowning, I`m told, isn`t a bad way to die and in a storm at sea would certainly be a dramatic conclusion to my full and satisfying life.*

Rodger pulled the dinghy alongside the Sea Witch and carefully lifted a freshly cleaned, three-pound salmon aboard. After tying the bowline of the dinghy to the stern cleat on the transom of the Sea Witch, he stepped aboard. "Is there anyone aboard you likes fresh salmon?" When Rodger received no answer he headed for the cabin. "Hello, anybody home?" Poking his head inside, he found Helen lost in thought; staring off into space.

Coming out of her daydream she asked, "What`s that in your hand?" she exclaimed. "It looks like an honest-to-goodness edible fish."

"My dear lady, this is the pride of the Pacific Ocean, a king salmon."

"Did you catch it?"

"I`m sorry you asked; I was hoping you would assume I did. Actually, I bought it for two dollars off one of the fishing boats. They had such a small catch they decided to sell to the locals instead of going to the fish buyer. After catching only a scrap fish, I decided to ensure we had fish for dinner."

"Well, Rodg, I`m pleased with your decision; I`ll do my part and enjoy it."

"If I cook it on the barbeque, it will taste better grilled and we can really doctor it up with sauces and spices. I guess the barbeque fits in that piece of hardware connected to the gunnel near the transom. Gunnel, transom; now if that language doesn`t sound nautical, nothing does."

"You know, Rodg, I`m going to make a sailor out of you yet. By the way, I`m up for an Old English 800. I`ll drink beer and you cook dinner, how does that sound?"

"What`s wrong with this picture?" Rodger laughed as he reached into the cooler, handed her a beer, and retreated to the galley.

Climbing the steps topside, Helen decided stretch out on the foredeck and enjoy the early evening solitude. The harbor noises diminished as workers were now on their way home. Boaters appeared busy going to the showers and cleaning up for the traditional cocktail hour preceding dinner. The rhythmic lap of the waves on the hull and the strong beer lulled her into a welcome nap after a busy day.

Rodger assembled the barbeque over the stern of the boat, filled it with briquettes, dowsed them with starter fluid, and lit it with his propane lighter. Satisfied with the briquettes, he retreated to the galley to prepare the salmon. Cutting off its head, he split the fish down the middle, laying it lay out like two extended hands and placed it on a bed of aluminum foil twice the dimensions of the fish. He then cut a dry onion and a lemon into thin slices and carefully placed them on the open fish. Tucking the edges of the aluminum foil up so it would hold liquid, he went topside to place it on the barbeque.

While the fish cooked, he opened a loaf of French bread, wrapped it in aluminum foil, and added it to the grill. After seasoning the cooking salmon with a mixture of spices blended for seafood, he closed up the aluminum foil making it into a caccoon. Then making a green salad, Rodger selected a Riesling wine and put it on ice in the small icebox. He decided to scrape carrots, wrap them in aluminum foil, and place them on the grill also.

Returning topside to add the carrots to the barbeque Rodger noticed Helen stretched out and dozing on the foredeck. *She is really quite a gal,* he mused. *She`s not nearly as domineering or dogmatic as she seemed at first. I hope she`ll be able to put aside Clyde`s ghost. Being on board the Sea Witch seems to have brought back memories of their sailing days together; I`m sure they were happy ones.*

Rodger settled into the cockpit where he could periodically inspect the salmon on the barbeque. Leafing through the ship`s log, he determined to know more about the Sea Witch and her beginnings. It seems Eli Johnson, a professional boat builder near Tracyton, Washington, had built her in 1947.

It said John Hanna had drawn the plans for a Tahiti Ketch in 1923 and an unknown number of them had been built between then and the late forties. The plans that came with the Sea Witch showed her to be 31 feet long from stem to stern with a 10-foot beam. She draws four feet of water and weighs in at nine tons. Massively built with solid oak keel, stem, and frames, she`s fir planked, with spars all of solid spruce and carries 470 square feet of sail.

"Oh, she`s a solid oceangoing boat, for sure," he`d been told by the marine surveyor who Rodger`d hired to do the marine survey before he bought her.

Rodger had to admit he was first attracted to the Sea Witch because she bore the design name of his intended destination, Tahiti. According to the surveyor, the design was called the Neptune for the first twelve years of its existence, but later changed to Tahiti when it caught the fancy of backyard boat builders worldwide. *This is not a boat,* it occurred to Rodger, *it`s a ship because of its design and the way it handles.*

Helen stirred, and raised herself on one elbow. "How`s dinner coming, chef? I think I`m about ready to do justice to your `fresh caught` salmon."

"Well, if you`ll set the table and pour yourself a glass of wine, it should be ready by then."

"You`re in charge," replied Helen as she made her way back to the cockpit, and descended down the ladder to the salon. Putting up the sides on the drop leaf table, she moved about the salon quickly as one adept at living aboard. After setting the table, she poured herself a glass of wine.

Chapter Three

After dinner Helen cleaned up, while Rodger sat on deck and smoked his nightly pipe. *Hopefully our relationship will be growing each day with this adventure,* he thought. *It`s so challenging for both of us. If my health improves, I`ll see Tahiti. If Helen survives the ghostly return of her husband, she`ll see Tahiti. If the weather stays favorable and the Sea Witch is as seaworthy as she appears to be, we`ll see Tahiti. If the authorities don`t stop us for whatever reason that Irene might trump up, we`ll see Tahiti. So many ifs` and only time will tell which ifs` will be satisfied.*

Finishing his pipe, Rodger checked the lines to the dinghy and anchor, then the mooring light on top of the mast. All seemed well. As he went below to the salon, Helen emerged from the bathroom. *Now comes the cozy part,* he thought. "Helen, I`ll use the head and then close the curtains to my forward bunk area, that way you`ll have the privacy of the salon."

"That should work, Rodg. I`ll go topside and check things there and enjoy the evening air."

When Helen returned Rodger was in his bunk asleep; it had been a full day for both of them. Helen stretched out her sleeping bag on the divan and went through her evening ritual at the sink. This didn`t match her accommodations at home, but in a way this was her second home. In her mind this was still her and Clyde`s boat even though she sold it to Rodger.

Rodger was the perfect one to buy the Sea Witch. His being at death`s door, it `s a win-win situation for me. If we make it to Tahiti it will be a great adventure and accomplishment, and if we`re lost at sea, I`ll join my beloved Clyde. For Rodg, it will be win-win, too. If we make it to Tahiti, he`ll have achieved his life-long fantasy. Iif we don`t make it, he won`t have to go through the awful final stages of tuberculosis. Helen lay there a long time staring at the interior paneling of the salon ceiling. She then became aware of the gentle rocking of the boat, and the gentle lapping sound of the waves against the hull. Finally sleep covered her like a favorite warm blanket easing her mind of what might lie ahead.

* * *

Rodger awoke first, taking a few seconds to get his bearings. The previous day came into focus causing him to smile at what they had accomplished so far. Rolling out of his sleeping bag, he pulled on yesterday`s clothes while thinking how good it would be to have a shower. Giving in to the pleasant idea, he grabbed clean underwear and socks, and then searched his pocket change for quarters. If this marina is like other marinas, there will be facilities ashore for showering and a laundromat. He quietly tiptoed through the salon noticing Helen, who looked so peaceful in sleep on the divan. After leaving a note, he cast off in the dinghy and rowed to the nearby dock.

It was 7:00 a.m. and only a few people were visible; mostly delivery workers. Rodger spotted the shower area near the harbormaster`s office. Finding an open stall, he enjoyed the warm water washing over his slender body. Taking advantage of the hot water to bath, shave, and shampoo his hair, he resisted a cold water wash down. Suddenly spasms of deep, body-wracking coughs reminded him of his illness, although he felt more alive now than he had in months.

Leaving the men`s shower room, he noticed two pay phones immediately opposite the exit door. *Should I or should I not make the promised phone call?* He decided he wasn`t ready to talk to Irene, thus giving her a chance to talk him out of his adventure, or worse still, have her call the authorities to stop him. *I don`t know if the authorities can do that, but I don`t want to take a chance. I`ll postpone calling for at least* *another day. In the meantime I`ll pick up the morning paper and head back to the Sea Witch.*

As he pulled alongside in the dinghy he could tell by the sounds and aroma from the cabin Helen was up and had coffee on. Tying the dinghy bowline to the stern cleat of the Sea Witch, he pushed it away from the Sea Witch to avoid the two bumping together. The hatch door was open and below laid his new home. "Hi," he called out, "I see you`re usurping my roll as chief cook and galley slave."

"When I discovered you abandoned ship, I knew if I was going to have my wake-up coffee, I`d better do the fixing. You look fresh, you obviously found a shower?"

"I did, and it was wonderful. It`s funny how our priorities change when we change our daily lives. I highly recommend the public facility located beneath the harbormaster`s office; I`ll even spring for the cost of a shower."

"How can I refuse an offer like that?" said Helen laughing. "Now, if I can interest you in my style of morning coffee, we can lay out our plans for the day. I`m thinking Port Angeles would be a good day`s sail assuming the wind is in our favor and we`re moving with the current."

"What`s the weather forecast?"

"The forecast is for temperatures from 48 to 72 degrees today with variable winds northerly at 5 to 15 knots with a rising barometer. The tide change is at 9:20 and we`ll have an outgoing tide."

"Sounds like a great day for sailing. It`s 8:05 now, and unless you take extra long showers, we should be on our way by tide change," said Rodger as he sat inhailing the strong aroma of the coffee he held to his lips. "M mmm, this is good stuff."

"I`ll take my coffee with me to the showers, you fix breakfast, and I`ll be back by 8:40. And by the way, I like my eggs over medium, my bacon well done, and my toast lightly buttered."

"Really?" Rodger chuckled as he sat with the paper before him. I *wonder how the market is doing this morning? Hmmm. Interest rates are falling; that`s good. A lot of people will want to refinance their mortgages, and that should make Irene happy.*

* * *

Irene McCauly paced the floor in the living room as she waited impatiently for her oldest son, Rodger, Jr. to appear. She had waited until breakfast time to call. *No sense in Junior having to put in a night like I`ve had. How could Rodger do such a fool-heardy thing? Imagine going off to Tahiti in a sailboat when he`s at death`s door. The only sensible thing about it is that he hired an experienced skipper to sail the `stupid` boat. I hate the ocean, I don`t like boats, and I prefer my water outings to be luxury cruises; not like Rodger.*

Junior`s car pulled into the long circular driveway lined with Rhododendrum bushes and roses. The house was a good example of the English Tudor style with a high gabled second-story roof and dormer windows with their own small gabled roofs. It wasn`t a mansion, but it was more than the average house. Quickly getting out, he slammed the car door and headed through the front door of the house on the run. "Mother, where are you?"

"I`m in the living room, dear." Irene was seated on the Louis V Loveseat. Both its elegance and that of the lovely Christian Dior negligee she wore reflected the luxury and good taste of the large, well-appointed room.

Junior, a larger man than his father with similar English features, could see the stress in his mother`s face caused by worry and lack of sleep. "Well, what`s the old man done this time? You said something about a boat and Tahiti over the phone."

"Here, read this letter he pinned to my pillow; I noticed it when I got ready for bed last night. I thought he was just late getting home from his day trip to Portland… instead this!"

Junior rolled his eyes as he read the letter and handed it back to his mother. "I can`t believe he would do this. Although, it`s not too far out of character for him. The flying lessons when he turned forty, the motorcycle when he turned fifty, and now this when sixty is just around the corner. Surely you`re going to stop him, if for no other reason than it`s suicidal?"

"That was my first impulse, however, after thinking about it, I wonder if we should honor a dying man`s final wish. I want what`s best for him, and the doctor has only given him less than a year to live. He`s approached me about the two of us sailing to Tahiti some time ago before he was ill. I told him, no way would I do that. I guess this is his way of getting what he wants with what`s left of his life."

"Yes, but he could be lost at sea, and no insurance for you for seven years if his body isn`t found. That`s a big ocean out there, and he`s not that much of a sailor. He could even die of tuberculosis on his way to Tahiti for lack of hospital care. It sounds like the act of a madman."

"Dear, it`s the act of a dying man, desperate to do this last life-fulfilling fantasy. Evidently, he`s willing to go out of this life violently, if need be. When he arrives in Tahiti, he said he`d send for me. I think I could handle his death happening at sea as well as I could handle it in a hospital or sanitarium; I`m no Florence Nightingale."

"It doesn`t sound like you need my opinion, Mother. It sounds like you`ve already made a decision."

"Yes dear, I guess I have. Now, let`s have some breakfast and then go to the office. Mortgage rates are falling, and business should be good."

* * *

Rodger started frying the eggs as soon as he heard the dingy bump against the hull of the Sea Witch. He quickly put the cooked bacon and toast on the table and poured two mugs of steaming hot coffee. By the time Helen started down the steep steps to the salon he had the medium-over eggs on two plates and half way to the table.

"Wow! I`m impressed. Are you sure you`re not too good to be real?"

"Well, I am working on perfection, but, I`ll admit, I`m not quite there yet. This is one of my better performances, so let`s eat and enjoy it."

After devouring every last crumb, they stowed the dishes in the sink until later. Rodger and Helen stood side by side in the ship`s cockpit and assessed the path they would take to weave among the boats anchored out in the harbor on their way to open water. Having mutually deciding on a path, Rodger started the engine, unflaked the sails, and raised them. As he raised the anchor, the Sea Witch started to move forward under its own sail power with Helen at the helm.

"I thought we would start the day by leaving the harbor under sail and using the auxiliary engine, if needed," half-shouted Helen as Rodger cleared the foredeck and secured the whisker pole. "It`s a good time to practice close-quarters maneuvering when we have ideal conditions in which to do it. When we get into the straits we`ll sail wing-and-wing if the wind continues from our stern. If it changes to a northwesterly, we`ll go on a beat at that time."

"O.K., I give up. What`s wing-and-wing?" asked Rodger with a ghost of a smile creasing the corners of his mouth, "and what`s a beat?"

"When the wind is from the stern, wing-and-wing means that the mainsail is extended on one side of the hull and the jib on the opposite side," Helen said, while she scanned ahead to avoid boats and buoys. "From the stern it looks like two wings."

"That makes sense, but the main has a boom to hold the bottom of the sail rigid when its out, but the jib doesn`t. How do you control it in that wing-and-wing position?"

"That`s where the whisker pole comes in. It`s like a small boom that we attach to the hardware called a cringle at the bottom of the jib and to a fitting on the mast. That way we get the most out of the sail."

"You asked about a beat," continued Helen, as she carefully maneuvered among the anchored boats on their way out the bay. "A beat is like we were trimmed yesterday when we rounded Point-No-Point remember? The jib, mizzen, and mainsails were winched down tight and we were heeled over up to where the rail or gunnel was nearly under water?"

"Yes, I remember the beat, and now I know what a whisker pole is for."

"We`ve worked our way out of Port Ludlow past Tala Point. Now we`ll take a course heading of 330 degrees, which is north, northwest. This part of Puget Sound is called Admiralty Inlet and leads to the Straits of Juan De Fuca." Helen checked the full, billowing sails. "The wind is holding and out of the southwest, putting it over our stern. We can sail wing-and-wing for now and change sail position or jibe as we round Pt. Wilson, which is a ways up ahead. The weatherman promises a temperature high of 72 degrees, which is ideal for the straits."

Occasionally a beach house or cabin is visible along the shoreline, but for the most part the land above the beach is hilly and covered mostly with evergreen trees. The Olympic Penninsula is to port and Whidbey Island is to starboard, on the route north. At this point the water pathway is from one to several miles wide due to the irregular coastline pitted with occasional bays and fjords.

"Let`s see, cringle is hardware, clew is the bottom aft corner of the sail and jibe is when the mainsail boom goes from port to starboard or vice versa."

"Right! Now, sit here by me and watch how I handle the boat wing-and-wing."

"Aye, aye, Skipper," he replied as he moved to the rear of the cockpit. "What time do you think we`ll get into Port Angeles?"

"I would estimate about five o'clock. That`ll give us time to clean up at the marina and walk the short distance to town. There is a Tai restaurant there I like and it may be our last chance to get a good restaurant meal for awhile. Neah Bay, our next stop, has only one restaurant and it doesn`t meet my standards."

The farther north they sail, the trees, mostly Douglas Fir, Cedar, and Madonna, come right down to the high tide mark where bleached driftwood in all possible shapes adorn the beach. Seagulls circle, dive, and feed on the herring balls that periodically appear on or near the surface of the water. Sport fishermen in small kicker boats follow and troll near the diving, screeching birds.

"This wing and wing is great, and the wind coming over the stern puts us on an even keel, doesn`t it?"

"That`s right mate, it`s unusual to be on an even keeel on a sailboat. Would you take the tiller for a while? I`d like to go below and clean up the galley, after all you fixed breakfast."

"Sure, but you`re the skipper and I expect to do the dishes, along with cooking the meals, and making myself generally useful."

"Well, Rodg, fair is fair. I`ll teach you all I know about sailing the Sea Witch, but I would like everything else to be an equal endeavor. We each share the helm and we each share the grunt work. You cook and I clean up. Is that agreeable?"

"Sounds good to me, Skipper. I`ll do my best to be a good student, as our lives may depend on it."

Helen retreated to the salon below and busied herself with the breakfast dishes. As she worked she thought *Rodger is all that he appears to be. Honest, energetic, friendly, and a man with a dream, unfortunately a dream with a time limit. How sad he can`t live to really enjoy Tahiti, assuming we get there. I sometimes feel so close to Clyde, like right now when I`m in the galley and the Sea Witch is sailing along without me being on deck. It`s like Clyde is up there at the tiller.*

"Hey Helen, would you put the coffee pot on? I could use a cup of your famous coffee."

Helen moved over to the open hatch, walked up a step and stuck her head out of the cabin to say, "Roger Wilco."

"What is this Roger Wilco jazz?"

"That`s a term from my Army days, which fits this occasion and probably a lot more before this journey is completed. Roger, means O.K. and wilco, means I will comply."

"You were in the Army?" Rodger questioned. "What else haven`t you told me?"

"I served four years in the army as a drill instructor for W.A.C.`s at one of the basic training centers during the Viet Nam debackle."

"I should have suspected," grinned Rodger.

"About the rest of my life, that will come on a need-to-know basis."

Chapter Four

Rodger stood at the tiller enjoying the day while he waited for his coffee and thinking *this is great, I can`t believe life can be this good. Especially with the depression I`ve felt after the doctor`s last pronouncement "six months to a year, so do what`s important to you." If this trip isn`t doing what`s important to me, I don`t know what is? I hope Irene and the boys will accept what I`m doing. I want their approval, but I don`t have to have it. I think I`m ready to make that phone call now when we hit port. I want to make this as easy for them as I can. However, I don`t know if I`m ready to tell them the skipper is a woman.*

As long as Helen and my relationship is platonic, I really don`t think it`s necessary to burden my family with that fact. Helen is becoming a real friend and our relationship has changed. However, no one likes a sick cat and that`s what I am, so I don`t see any change beyond platonic. She`s quite a woman I`m finding out, and I hope I can be as helpful for her as she is for me.

Helen emerged from the hatch with a mug of coffee in each hand. "Here`s your order Mate, do you want sugar?"

"No thanks, I`ll just stir it with my thumb."

Helen laughed, "Really?"

Rising to the occasion Rodger asked, "Have you heared that Northwest ballad?"

"As a matter of fact, I have. My father used to sing it to me when I was a little girl. He`d bellow out the line, *I can tell that you`re a logger,* *because you stir your coffee with your thumb.* Then I`d follow with the next stanza, *My lover was a logger, there`s none like him today. If you`d pour some gravy on it, he`d eat a bale of hay."*

"Such fun!" replied Rodger. "Maybe we should change that from Logger to sailor and have it for our theme song. By the way, have you noticed the wind has changed direction and is freshening out of the North? Maybe we`ll get to Port Angeles sooner than your E.T.A."

"I was just going to suggest that we go off wing-and-wing, Rodg. I`ll take in the whisker pole and let the jib work naturally. There, notice it`s slack now, so I`ll trim the jib sheet and let it fill. The list of the hull has changed now and we`re heeling to port. The wind is filling our sails differently now as both of them are out on the same side of the hull. With this position the sails are brought in much tighter, and the telltales on the upper part of the sail should be parallel."

"Hold it, Helen. Tell me about telltales again. I feel like I`m getting too much information too fast."

"Sorry about that mate, I keep forgetting what you don`t know. Do you see those two pieces of nylon yarn fastened near the top leading edge of the mainsail?"

Rodger leaned back to look at the telltales on the sail. "Yes, one is on this side of the sail and one is on the other, which we see only as a shadow."

"Right. Let me take the tiller and notice what happens when I fall off the wind a few degrees. See how the telltales are no longer parallel."

"Oh, yeah. The telltale on the backside is drooping while the other stays the way it was. What does that tell us?"

"It tells us that the sail isn`t trimmed right in accordance with the direction of the wind in accordance with the direction we`re steering the boat. The wind is not of equal velocity on each side of the sail. We either have to change the direction of the boat or we have to trim or ease the sail setting. However, you usually trim the sail to the wind because you have a destination and the bow is pointed the way you want to go."

"Boy, there sure is a lot to learn in this sailing business. I had no idea how much when I thought about sailing to Tahiti. What on earth would I ever do without you?"

"Frankly, Mate, you`d still be in Poverty Bay where we started."

Rodger winced and changed the subject. "I notice we`re off Point Wilson according to the chart. I guess a new compass heading will be needed."

A whole new body of water opened up ahead as they pass Point Wilson. They leave Admiralty Inlet behind and enter the Straits of Juan de Fuca. Fifty nautical miles northwest across this vast open water crossroads lies Canada`s Vancouver Island with the city of Victoria visible at its very southern tip. Compared to the smaller waterways of Puget Sound with its many islands and fjords, this large expanse of water is like an inland sea. The American and Canadian San Juan Islands lie to starboard and east of Vancouver Island. The Olympic Peninsula, with the stately Olympic Mountains towering over the Straits of Juan de Fuca, lies to port paralleling the Sea Witch`s journey route.

Cargo ships of the world pass each other with imports from the Orient and Europe coming inbound mostly to Seattle and Tacoma, Washington, and exports outbound, to provide a balance of trade, come from these same two seaports. Tankers from Alaska`s northern slope and the Mid East are in the shipping lanes too, loaded to the gunnels with crude and refined oil; they return empty. Cruise ships, mostly bound for Alaska or returning, like majestic floating hotels, are a recent addition to the parade of vessels. Pleasure craft of every description fill in the blank spaces on the open water, passing through the shipping lanes quickly, as they don`t argue with the commercial giants for right-of-way.

"Our new heading will be 290 degrees," stated Helen as she relaxed at the helm. "We`ll hold this setting until we clear Dungeness Spit. Then we`ll ease off to a heading of 250 degrees, which will bring us into the windward side of Edez Hook and into Port Angeles, now that the wind has changed from southwest to north."

"Are you ready for one of my famous Spam sandwiches and a cool Old English?"

"That`s music to my ears, Rodg. A few chips and a pickle would go well, Spam needs all the help it can get."

Rodger went below and spread out the food ingredients on the drop leaf table. In short order he had two sandwiches, two beers, two large dill pickles, and a handful of potato chips spread on a paper towel.

Balancing the tray of food and drink on his way up to the cockpit he called out,

"I`ll take the tiller while you eat unencumbered for a change."

"Thanks Rodg." Immediately making her way forward, she spread the lunch beside her on the foredeck making the most of the summer day. The cumulonimbus clouds overhead reminded her of mare`s tails the way they sweep across the sky. God`s handiwork fairly took her breath away. *This day makes up for a lot of gray days I`ve had this past year; maybe life is worth living after all. It`s great being back on the Sea Witch. It`s just too bad Rodger has tuberculosis as he really is a nice companion, and who knows what the future could hold?*

* * *

Rodger felt the pressure of the tiller in his hand each time the hull dove into the gentle swells of the straits. He checked the tell-tales, and they were parallel. He enjoyed the feeling of being in control of this nine-ton vessel and this feeling seemed to transfer to his feeling about his body and his physical well being. *This might be exactly what I need to fight this tuberculosis.*

"There`s the end of Edez Hook at eleven o`clock," called out Helen.

"What`s this eleven o`clock you're talking about?"

Gathering the remains of her lunch, she returned to the cockpit, "That`s army talk; here`s how it works. Think of a large clock face lying on the surface of the water and picture that the bow of the boat points to twelve o`clock. If I say look at eleven o`clock, then you would look off to the left of twelve o`clock to about where eleven o`clock would be on this huge clock face. Try it, see if you don`t see something at eleven o`clock."

"Oh yeah, I see what you mean. There`s a lighthouse on a narrow spit of land. Although, I would say it looks more like ten-thirty."

"Yeah, now!" replied Helen, playing along with the tease. "When we get within a hundred yards of the point change the heading to 250 degrees; that should bring us to the transient dock and an afternoon nap."

"Sounds like a plan, Skipper."

"Do you see that ferry dock in the middle of the shoreline?" asked Helen as she pointed straight ahead, and without waiting for an answer, "just to the left of it is the observation pier for the locals and the tourists and to the left of that is the transient dock. I`ll take the tiller while you start the engine; then we can drop the sails."

"Aye, aye Skipper."

As Rodger appeared back on deck Helen said, "I`ll bring the bow into the wind so you can drop the jib, mizzen, and mainsail. The engine will make this an easy, upwind approach. I've picked out a slip, so go forward and handle the bowline as we coast in. When you secure it, I`ll secure the sternline to the rear dock cleat, and then we`ll set up a spring line."

"I know how to set a spring line," stated Rodger eagerly.

Helen shifted into neutral and eyed the approaching finger pier in order to coast in close so Rodger could just step off at the right moment.

Helen held the course and watched the hull slide gently up to the finger pier. Rodger stepped quickly off the Sea Witch onto the dock, as Helen leaned over the gunnels with a stern line in hand to throw a double half hitch around the rear cleat. Rodger followed suit and moored the bow in the same manner.

"Well done, Mate; I couldn`t have done better myself," stated Helen as she stepped off the Sea Witch onto the dock.

"Thanks, Skipper. I`ll run a spring line now from the stern dock cleat to the midships boat cleat and back to the dock cleat. Then let`s go ashore, I`m really up for a walk. How about you?"

"I`m for that, but first, we`ll have to go to the harbormaster and get moorage for the night. I think they charge fifteen dollars here."

"I`ll take care of that while you talk to the people at customs. I see the two offices are side-by-side in the building beyond the ferry dock. By the way, where does the ferry go?"

"To the city of Victoria across the bay on Vancouver Island. Ever been there?"

"Yes, but I approached it from the south by way of Anacortes and through the San Juan Islands. That is a great trip, by the way."

"Let`s take care of the business at hand, and when you`re through I`ll meet you outside the Harbor Master`s office," replied Helen heading toward the customs office.

Rodger discovered the Harbor Master had left for the day so his secretary handled the transaction. They were set for the night with a checkout time of five o`clock the next afternoon. Rodger encountered Helen just as she walked out of the customs office. "What did you find out about leaving the United States?"

"It depends on our voyage plan. If we`re headed to Tahiti from the Washington coast we can go through customs here. If we`re going down the coast to California and then further south, we can use customs at San Diego."

"What is our voyage plan? I`ve been meaning to ask you, but there has been so many other things to consider until now, it didn`t seem too important."

"It`s up to you Rodger; this is your boat. My choice would be to hug the Pacific coast all the way to Peru and pick up the South Equatorial Current. That would take us to the Tuomotu Archipelago and Tahiti, which is one of the Islands. Another way would be to catch the North Equatorial Current out of San Francisco and head south of the Hawaiian Islands, but that way we have to contend with the Doldrums and the Equatorial Counter Current as we work our way south to Tahiti."

"Wow! This is an important decision. If you want to hug the coast to Peru, that`s what we`ll do. I`ve never been pleasure boating out of the Puget Sound or the San Juan Islands."

"Neither have I, Mate, but you said you wanted this to be an adventure."

"That`s true, but how do you know about the ocean currents and the doldrums and all that technical navigation stuff?"

"Clyde and I planned to take this trip to the Tuomotu Archipelago and Tahiti before he died. We read books on the subject and studied navigation so that we could do it. I`m just glad I was an equal partner with Clyde and didn`t leave all the planning and navigation to him."

"Me too," said Rodger as they headed up the sidewalk to downtown Port Angeles. "I`m with you all the way, Skipper."

"Thanks for the vote of confidence, Rodg. If we don`t make it, I`ll give you a refund on your ticket," bantered Helen as they walked along.

"I`m pleased to know I have such an ironclad guarantee." Spasms of coughing ended his gales of laughter at the acknowledgement by Helen of her limited expertise. The coughing did help bring their situation back into perspective. Helen reached out and took Rodger`s hand.

It was mid-afternoon and tourists filled the sidewalk. They walked hand-in-hand into this older part of town where the old stores had become new businesses that catered to the wants and needs of tourists. Coming to the Tai restaurant Helen had recommended, Rodger announced he had a phone call to make to his family back in Seattle before he ate dinner.

* * *

"Irene, this is Rodger?"

"Where are you?" Irene`s voice had a steel edge to it.

Rodger hesitated, but continued, "I`m in Port Angeles and everything is going okay. My health is no worse, the weather`s fine, and I`m learning how to be a sailor, not just a boater, a real sailor."

"Well, isn`t that wonderful," replied Irene. "I`m madder than hell at you, Rodger McCauley. I feel like the deserted wife and I don`t understand your sneaking around buying a boat and running out on me and the family."

"I had hoped for some understanding on your part Irene, but I I knew you`d never understand the depth of my dispair. I`m going to continue on my journey, Irene, with or without your approval."

Irene was silent for a minute, then said, "If that`s your decision, Rodger, there is nothing more to say. We both know your time is running out, and I`ve never had any Florence Nightingale tendencies. Call me when you start your ocean crossing."

Rodger sensed the difference in Irene`s attitude. "That may be awhile; we`re hugging the Pacific Coast all the way to Peru before we head into off-shore sailing. By that time I should be an accomplished sailor. My Skipper says I`m a good student."

"I imagine you are, Rodger." By the way, what`s your Skipper`s name?"

"Uh... Henry, my Skipper`s name is Henry, and I`ll call you before we leave Peru." he hurried on. "My feelings for the family haven`t changed. Tell the boys I love them and their families even though they`re angry with me. Someday, if they run into this kind of circumstance in their life, they may understand."

"Then I`ll say Bon Voyage to you and Captain Henry... and Rodger, don't pick up any mermaids."

"I`ll remember that Irene, good bye." Rodger put the phone back on its hook, breathed a long sigh of relief, and pondered his answer to Irene`s question, *what`s your Skipper`s name?*

* * *

"Well Rodg, did you make your phone call?"

"Yes, I called my wife as I had promised. First she was angry and when I told her I was determined to do this, she surprised me and wished us bon voyage."

"Really! What does she think about your traveling half way around the world with a woman, Rodg."

"Do you want the truth?"

"Of course," Helen replied studying Rodger`s facial expression.

"She doesn`t know, she thinks your name is Henry."

"Rodger! This could get pretty sticky somewhere down the line. I can just see her waiting at the dock in Tahiti."

"It`s a complicated relationship, Helen, it`s lasted this long only because neither of us had the courage to end it after the boys were grown. Habit is a strange phenomena; fear of the unknown enters the picture and unless the marriage is really uncomfortable, it`s easier to do nothing."

Helen walked over to Rodger and put her arm around his shoulder. That`s sad, Rodg. It makes me wonder if your health problem is your only motivation for taking this trip to Tahiti. Maybe this is your way of handling divorce."

"My God! I hadn`t made that connection... but there just may be the truth. If that`s so, this trip to Tahiti could have a double purpose."

Rodger began to pace up and down. "I think Irene and I should sit down and talk this thing out? If divorce is or isn`t the choice we make, I`ll feel better about this trip. I really don`t like being a runaway, that`s not my style under normal circumstances. However, what I`ve experienced of the voyage so far exceeds even my expectations; and you weren`t in my fantasy."

Helen stopped directly in front of Rodger. "I`m shocked, Rodg. I didn`t mean for my off-the-wall comment to lead to this."

"I know, but it fits. Irene and I have danced around this situation long enough. Actually, I`d feel a lot better about what I`m doing if we did talk it out and come to a decision about her and my relationship. Then I wouldn`t feel like a runaway."

"What are you going to do?" Helen asked as she started to walk along with Rodger who was headed back to the phone area.

"I`m going to call Irene back and tell her I`m flying home tomorrow. I`m going to tell her we have some decisions to make before I depart. I know this leaves you hanging; I suggest you return to your home while Irene and I work this out. We can get moorage here at the transient dock for up to two weeks. By then everything should be resolved, and we can be on our way. I know I`ll feel better about the whole trip if I do this. I won`t have this guilt feeling, plus it could put a new slant on our relationship." Rodger stood holding Helen`s hands in his and looking deeply into her eyes, "You are more than a skipper, Helen. More than a friend."

Helen looked pleased at Rodger`s remark. Then added, "I`m at a loss for words, but you`re the boss. If this is what you feel you must do, then do it. I won`t go home, I`ll stay aboard the Sea Witch, I`m comfortable there. I like the town of Port Angeles and this shouldn`t take too long. You can leave a phone message at the Harbormaster`s office to let me know when you`re returning, I`ll check there daily until I hear from you. I know this isn`t an easy decision, Rodg, but that`s life isn`t it? …just a series of tough decisions."

Chapter Five

The next morning Rodger stepped aboard the pontoon of the floatplane bound for Seattle. In less than an hour he would be landing on Lake Union and back into his former life. The view, as he flew over the Straits of Juan de Fuca, the lower San Juan Islands, and northern Puget Sound, would normally be breathtaking, but today he was lost in his thoughts and emotions. His mission was to sit down with Irene and decide if their marriage had come to an end. If it had, what was the best way to deal with that? Was divorce the answer, legal separation, doing nothing? His ultimate goal was to spend his last weeks or months of life enjoying his adventure as best he could. He would soon know one-way or another.

Leaving as he had on his voyage seemed like a good idea at the time, but now he`d had second thoughts. Now he knew he had to go back, face his family, and leave with their blessings, if possible. He had no intention of letting them talk him out of his adventure, but he had experienced some feelings he didn`t have when he started. These feelings put him on this plane today.

How could he have known the guilt he would feel regarding running away from his wife and family? How could he have known the joy of being a sailor on his own sailboat? How could he have known about the new hope he felt about the present and the future? Hope was something he hadn`t felt for awhile. And most of all, how could he have known how he would feel about Helen?

There`s Irene standing on the dock at the air terminal watching us land. Where do I begin? How do I explain what I`m feeling to my wife of thirty years from whom I feel so disconnected?

* * *

"Hello Irene thanks for meeting me."

Irene`s facial expression was dark, cold, and forboding, like a winter storm. "Hello Rodger, I didn`t expect to see you so soon after your first phone call last night. Did your conscience get the best of you? Is that why you called insisting on this meeting?"

Rodger stepped forward to touch her; she stepped away. Seeing Irene was in a no- nonsense mood he replied, "Yes, my conscience got the best of me. I hate the thought of having left without the family`s blessing."

"We would never have given it!"

"I guess I knew that and acted accordingly."

"So why are you here?"

"I want to talk to you about ending our marriage."

Helen sat silent letting Rodger`s words sink in to her consciousness. "Well… maybe it is time to put an end to this marriage, if you`re entertaining those kinds of thoughts."

"Let`s go somewhere where we can talk," suggested Rodger. "How about Benjamin`s? We can get a drink there."

"I guess that `s as good a place as any… and I need a drink."

Neither of them spoke as Rodger escorted Irene to their car in the nearby parking lot. Automatically going to the driver`s side of the car, he realized his mistake, walked back around the car, and held out his hand for the keys.

Sensing Rodger had now turned angry, Irene opened her purse and handed the keys to Rodger. "What else do you have to say that you couldn`t have said yesterday on the phone?

Rodger stared out the windshield, trying to find the right words. Coming up empty he blurted, "What if I told you my skipper is a woman, a woman to whom I feel very attracted to? Would that make a difference in your decision whether we go for a divorce or a legal separation, or do nothing?"

Shock sharpened Irene`s voice and distorted her facial expression into a combative expression. "Yes, that does make a difference. Is the feeling mutual …or is that any of my business? Surely she knows about your tuberculosis."

"I think the feeling is mutual, and yes, she knows."

"Boy, she must be as desperate as you are. Any more surprises I need to know about?

"No, that`s it." Rodger started the car and waited for Irene to speak.

Her expression relaxed, "Let`s just go home then. We can talk about it in the morning after you`ve had time to see the family and I`ve had time to think this out. The family will be over this evening for dinner."

Softening, Rodger replied, "That was nice of you to arrange dinner, Irene; I don`t want us to be enemies. We`ve had some good years together and we do have a great family; I want our family relationship to continue. I don`t have a lot of time left and I want to get the most out of it, that`s all. I don`t want to lie around in a hospital. This trip has been a lifetime dream and Helen is a total surprise."

With her anger and shock having reached and passed their zenith, Irene sat quietly for a moment while they traveled through the Seattle traffic to their home in Belleview. Finally speaking in a non-combative voice, "Life hasn`t been kind to you lately, Rodg, I know that. You`re the one who has had to live with the pain and isolation. I wish I could have been more help to you…more loving. In a perfect world, I would have been more helpful to you. I guess it just isn`t my nature. As I've said, I`d make a lousy Florence Nightingale."

"In a perfect world I wouldn`t be dying of tuberculosis at age sixty and we`d be living happily ever after," replied Rodger as he looked steadily at the road ahead.

Chapter Six

"That was fun with the family last night, wasn`t it Irene? Our daughter`s in-law were a little stand-off-ish at first; I guess they hope they won`t have to face this kind of dilemma a few years down the road. I assured them tuberculosis wasn`t a gene thing and the doctor says I`m not contagious, now."

"The grandchildren look upon you as a real adventurer with your own sailboat on the way to Tahiti. I saw no need to share with the family that your skipper is a woman whom you are attracted to."

"I appreciate that. I let you take the lead there."

"I`ve spent half the night thinking this through and I don`t want a divorce. A legal separation would take care of the estate and your will, assuming I will still your primary beneficiary. Go have your fling…if that`s what it develops into. And Rodger, I do hope you see Tahiti."

"Thanks Irene, I can live with that. Now, let`s call our attorney and get the legal wheels rolling."

* * *

The days passed slowly for Helen, and each day she asked at the harbormaster's office regarding a message from Rodger. Each day there was none. Helen waited until almost noon on day three before entering the harbormaster`s office. Diane, a woman Helen guessed to be about her own age, looked up from her desk. Pursing her lips, she gave a little shake of her head.

Sorry, Helen, nothing yet." Helen`s face must have registered her disappointment. Diane rose quickly from her desk and approached the counter, "I was just about to take my lunch break, and I hate to eat alone. Why don`t you join me?"

"Thanks, I`d like that."

Once seated in the café booth Diane reached over and gave Helen`s hand a reassuring squeeze, don`t worry, you`ll hear from your man."

A short laugh escaped Helen`s lips. "You`re very kind, but he`s not my man." Diane`s look of surprise prompted Helen to continue. "He`s married, Diane. He`s gone home to divorce his wife…or not." Helen found herself sharing their story, his illness, his fantasy, and his hopes. "His illness was messing up his life, taking away his life`s dream, and robbing him of his place in his family. His solution was to leave it all behind, and run away from home."

Helen paused as the waitress stopped at their table. Diane ordered a double cheeseburger with fries, Helen settled for a simple salad. "No wonder you stay trim," Diane scolded. "I feel obligated to my wardrobe to keep working at this plump figure of mine."

Once the waitress left, Diane turned to Helen, her blue eyes serious, "I`m curious about something, though it may be none of my business."

Helen`s steady gaze met her companion`s inquisitive one, "I have no secrets."

"What made you volunteer to set off on a trip halfway around the world with a dying man?"

Helen sat silent and slowly stirred the dark liquid in her coffee cup. Finally she spoke, "I was lonesome after my husband died, and I couldn`t get my life back together again. There were no children who needed me, there was no career as I`d retired, and there seemed to be no purpose to my existance."

"I know the feeling, Helen. I felt the same way after my divorce, though I`m sure it`s worse with a death. I sometimes wish we`d had children."

"Everything reminded me of Clyde, our house, and everything about the boat. I lived in the memories of places we`d been, things we`d done. It took a year for me to bring myself to put the Sea Witch up for sale. Even then, I wasn`t sure I could do it, we`d had such a good time aboard her. So when Rodger shared his plans for a trip to Tahiti…well, it just seemed like a good idea. I could leave my problems behind and still enjoy the Sea Witch."

Diane ran her fingers through her shoulder length, graying hair, "Sounds like you`re running away too."

"Yes, I guess I am." Helen replied slumping back in her seat. "I just didn`t think I`d be attracted to him."

"Imagine sailing off into the sunset with a dying man who suddenly has an attack of conscience and needs to resolve the problem by either dumping his wife or maybe aborting the trip and his new friend and Skipper."

"Diane! You make him sound heartless. I don`t see Rodg that way at all. He`s a nice guy, a nice guy with a dream and a serious health problem. He finally realized he couldn`t leave his family that way, so he returned to talk it out. Give him a break, Diane, he`s trying to do the right thing by all the people concerned."

Diane sat pensive for a while as she pushed her food around on her plate. "I just want this to be right for you, Helen. You`re too nice a person to be hurt by Rodger because of his problems."

"I appreciate your concern, but I`ve really enjoyed our voyage so far, and the future, if there is one, could be very fulfilling for both of us.

"Ah ha! Cupid has entered the picture."

"Let`s just say Rodger and I are compatible." Having finished their lunch, both rose to leave when Diane suddenly walked around the table and embraced her. "I want the best for you, girl."

When Diane and Helen returned to the office after lunch there was a phone message from Rodger. It said he would be arriving by seaplane tomorrow, and a decision had been made.

Helen turned to Diane, "Thank goodness, I still don`t have an answer, but I will tomorrow."

* * *

The next day the daily seaplane made its spectacular, noisy approach to Port Angeles shooting a landing three hundred yards off shore and taxiing in. Coasting to a stop alongside the floating dock, Helen stood waiting. Rodger, smilimg, scrambled across the plane`s pontoon and gingerly stepped aboard the floating dock. Taking Helen`s hands in his he said, "Irene has set me free, but doesn`t want a divorce. She wants a legal separation, and I have agreed. When we make it to Tahiti, if I want a divorce she won`t fight me on it. He put his arms around Helen and hugged her tightly, as if he was embracing a new beginning for them. "Yes, we`re going to Tahiti."

Helen allowed herself to sink deeper into his embrace murmuring, "Thank God!"

Still hand-in-hand they walked to the finger pier where the Sea Witch rode easily at her moorings. The sun was warm as it passed its zenith, the wrinkled skin of the water gave hint of a slight summer breeze from the north, and it looked ideal for an afternoon sail to their next landfall, Neah Bay.

Rodger led Helen aboard the Sea Witch and they embraced. He then held her at arms length, "You won`t believe how relieved I feel since I made the trip to Seattle. Irene and I have mutually filed for legal separation using the family lawyer. Irene came up with the idea. After some serious talk we realized neither of us needed this marriage any longer."

Rodger and Helen sat down on the cabin roof as Rodger brought her up to date. "We were staying together out of convenience and habit, neither of us living our lives as we wanted. We still care for each other and nothing changes as far as our estate is concerned. Irene will continue to live in our house, and I`ll live aboard the Sea Witch. We`re both free to continue the rest of our life`s journey as we individually choose."

"The big surprise to me is that Irene doesn`t want to run the business. She wants our son, Junior, to run the business for us while she pursues a career in painting. Isn`t it amazing that we both had fantasies, but she didn`t talk about hers."

"Our sons say they will support our decision, even though it certainly wouldn`t be their choice for us. I think they now realize I`ve stifled my dreams in order to be a good father and husband, but that`s no longer necessary; Irene did the same. Incidentally, she`s never looked better, and is looking forward to doing what she would have done after I died."

Helen turned and looked deep into Rodger`s eyes, "I`m speechless but happy. I told you I`d abide by your decision, but you know I so wanted us to be together in pursuit of your dream. You see, your dream has become my dream. Now, let`s go ashore, have lunch and settle with the harbormaster. I`d like to say goodbye to Diane as she`s been a real friend these past days. Helen glanced across the bay, if we can leave by one o`clock, we should make Neah Bay by six o`clock tonight. That`s if that breeze out of the north continues to hold."

Rodger stood at attention and half-shouted, "Aye, Aye Skipper."

* * *

After lunch they settled with the Harbormaster, and Helen and Diane embraced as they said their goodbyes. Diane, with tears in her eyes, watched Helen and Rodger board the Sea Witch, start the engine, caste off the lines, and slowly back out of the transient slip.

The breeze had stiffened, enabling them to hoist the sails as they traversed the long run of Edez Hook. The Sea Witch, once again, was on its way to Tahiti.

Chapter Seven

"With the wind and tide in our favor, the Sea Witch seems to be performing well," Rodger stated as they moved northward to their next port-of -call, Neah Bay.

"Right you are, Mate. At this rate we`ll make Neah Bay about dinnertime, which makes me wonder why I use eating as a yardstick for travel? I guess this fresh air and good company makes for a robust appetite." Helen sat beside Rodger with the tiller between them.

"I wonder how the family is tonight?" Rodger said. "I wonder if they have gotten used to the idea that Irene and I will no longer be living together. It takes a little getting used to on my part too, as I`ve forgotten how it is to be single."

"Are you having second thoughts, Rodg?"

"Don`t we always have second thoughts about the big decisions in life? I guess I just have to let the hand play out, at least for awhile."

"Well Rodg, anytime you think you`ve made a mistake, we can turn around. However, I suggest you do what you just said, let the hand play out for awhile."

"I guess you`re right," replied Rodger. "Now I can relax and just be here with you. I feel more comfortable about our trip each day, and I`m feeling more comfortable with us. In fact, I`m not sure comfortable is a strong enough word for how I feel."

"Easy Rodg, I suggest we let that hand play out, too. Right now you are vulnerable and I am too. This past year has been a roller coaster of emotion for me trying to learn to live without Clyde. I`m more comfortable with you, too, Rodg, so for now let`s concentrate on sailing this ship to the other side of the world and enjoy each day for what it is."

"Okay Helen, I hear you loud and clear; so what`s the new compass setting, as here`s the entrance to Neah Bay."

"That sneaked up on me. According to the chart it should be 240 degrees and about a mile to our night`s moorage at the municipal marina."

Rodger stood in the bow as the area opened up with the usual evergreen trees of Douglas fir, Western Red Cedar, and Northern Hemlock, mixed with deciduous Madrona and Alder crowding down to the shore. A portion of the bay`s perimeter on the south side housed the Indian village of Neah Bay. Masts of commercial trollers dominated the waterfront scene, and large drums on the stern of other boats indicated gill netting also shared in a part of the fishing activity here. Smaller fishing boats, some commercial, some pleasure, occupy the rest of the slips in the marina.

The village, being the heart of the Makah Indian reservation, is a mixture of old and new buildings. A single road ran through the center of town and serviced the waterfront, then disappeared into the forest at the far end of the bay leading to Tatoosh Peninsula. This being the very tip of the state of Washington and is flanked on one side by the Pacific Ocean, and is stopped by the Straits of Juan de Fuca. Just off the tip of the peninsula, a distance of a few hundred yards lays Tatoosh Island, its only inhabitant a lighthouse keeper. It is apparent Tatoosh Island was once a part of the peninsula. Time, with its erosion, has been at work here.

As the Sea Witch entered the bay, Rodger turned his attention to the marina and its surroundings. "They must have some pretty heavy weather here if they need a breakwater for a marina inside a bay this small."

"I think they do because we`re less than a mile from the Pacific Ocean. Also, there`s a swale up ahead in those hills and I can imagine the wind really rips through there when there are storm conditions on the ocean."

Rodger stood at the tiller looking at the surrounding hills, "I`m assuming that a swale is a valley or low spot. That`s what I`m seeing in that line of tree-covered hills between us and the ocean."

"Right you are, Rodg. I keep forgetting you`re learning a new vocabulary." They motored into the marina with Rodger at the helm. After a successful approach, they were soon berthed for the night. Helen finished tying the lines to the mooring cleats as Rodger flaked the sails. "Do you want to eat ashore or aboard?" she asked.

"Based on what you told me earlier, I opt for eating aboard. We have some lean hamburger for gourmet patties, a canned vegetable, and I`ll make a salad; how does that sound?"

"Heavenly! While you cook I`ll go ashore and buy charts for the West Coast and a Pacific Coast Pilot book. I `ve put this off until I knew for sure we were actually going."

"Very conservative of you. That surprises me."

"Well, we almost didn`t go, remember? I guess it`s just a part of my upbringing."

"Speaking of upbringing, where were you brought up?" inquired Rodger as he sat jotting down their arrival time in the daily log.

"That`s a long story; let`s save it for dinner conversation. I want to get to the chandlery before they close. I hope they have the charts we need, at least for the first leg of this journey; we can buy charts later for the crossing."

Going below deck, Rodger gathered the makings for their dinner and placed them on the counter near the stove. While the stove was heating, he formed the hamburger into two large, thick patties after lacing them with chopped onions, garlic salt, pepper, and Worcestershire Sauce. As the meat cooked in a cast iron skillet, he sautéed onions to put on top of the patties. Contemplating their larder of canned goods, he chose canned corn as the vegetable, then turned his attention to the salad.

Deciding on a simple one of lettuce with sliced tomato, he spread them lightly with mayonnaise and paprika. After setting the table, he opened a bottle of Cabernet Sauvignon. Surveying his handiwork, it pleased him everything was coming together nicely when he heard Helen step aboard. "Good timing, Skipper, dinner is just about ready. Did you find the charts we need?"

"I did. We now have charts to take us from here to San Diego. That smells wonderful and am I ever hungry."

"Put the salads on the table, and I`ll open the wine. I apologize for not having a Riesling for the salads, but this is the economy class cruise. Only one bottle of wine per dinner and the meat demands a Cabernet Sauvignon."

"I say it again. You are a find, Rodger, a real keeper."

"You just keep thinking like that, Helen, and we`ll get along fine. Now, tell me about your family and your life growing up, that is, if I`m not being too personal."

"No, Rodg, you aren`t being too personal. After all, we are roommates, or should I say cabin mates. I was born in a little wheat-growing community in eastern Washington State called Jericho. It had a thriving population of about four hundred people, but the community was actually spread over an area ten miles wide and twenty miles long. You see, the ranchers had to have about 3000 acres to make a living, as it was high plateau country with no extra water for irrigation. The soil and natural water supply only allowed them to plant wheat every other year. On the alternate year the ground lay fallow, or they ran beef cattle on it."

"Did your family have a ranch?"

"No, my Dad was the superintendent of schools; he was a teacher before he became the elementary, junior high, and high school principal. Spending his entire career in Calico; he`s a pillar in the community."

"What about your mother and siblings, do you have brother`s and sisters?"

"Mother was a stay-at-home Mom, for which I`m very thankful. I have two older brothers who treated me like a brother in my younger years; I fit into the tomboy role easily." Helen`s green eyes twinkle as she warmed up to the subject, "When I turned sixteen, they miraculously realized I was a girl. From then on they were overly protective. So much so that I wasn`t asked out on dates often. It was like having three fathers waiting at the door. It took a very self-assured young man to run their gauntlet of questions and instructions."

Rodger exploded into laughter that unfortunately ended in a coughing, wheezing fit. "Sorry about that, but you do paint a vivid picture. No wonder you waited to marry."

Helen sipped at her second glass of wine. "I decided to be a teacher like my father, and before I knew it I was so wrapped up in my teaching and my students that the years got away from me. For some reason I never met Mr. Right until I was nearly fifty years old. Clyde and I had ten great years together, then he had a heart attack, and I was a widow. It was a year before I could bring myself to sell the Sea Witch. Reluctently I put an ad in the paper, and that`s where you came in."

Rodger stood and started clearing the table, "You know Helen, I`m sure I `d like your family. Are both of your parents still alive? They sound like salt-of-the-earth type people."

"Yes, Dad and Mom are enjoying retirement, still living in Jericho eight months of the year. They have a trailer they keep in a remote area in Baja, Mexico. It`s a little place called Punta Chivata, where they spend December through March."

"Thanks for the run down, I can see why you`re such a down-to-earth type of person." Rodger, feeling very relaxed from the food and wine, sat on the divan as he watched Helen wash the dishes.

"Sometimes I wish I wasn`t so down-to-earth," she blurted out angrily. "Sometimes I want to kick over the traces and do crazy things: dress like a gypsy; sing, dance, maybe drink too much wine, find a man to run away with."

Rodger paused for a long moment. "Well, in a way, isn`t that what you`re doing?"

Helen`s eyes widened in astonishment as she pondered Rodger`s remark. "Do you suppose that`s what I`m doing, being here alone with you on this adventure? If it is, I didn`t know it when I offered to skipper the Sea Witch to Tahiti."

"Think about it, Gypsy." Rodger had an urge to grab her in an embrace and smother her with kisses, but thought *it might be too much too soon*. "I`m going topside and have my pipe while you finish the dishes."

Sitting on the cabin roof with his legs stretched out and feet on the gunnels, Rodger lit his pipe of tobacco with a kitchen match, and watched the flame temporarily light up a small portion of the night sky. The simple act of blowing out the flame brought a series of coughing and wheezing, bringing him back to the reality of his health problem. *If only I wasn`t staring death in the face, Helen and I could be Gypsies* *together. Come to think of it, what I`m doing isn`t too far from what a Gypsy might do: throwing caution to the wind; giving up all of the responsibilities I`ve assumed over the years; and running off with a fair maiden to an enchanted island. Sure sounds Gypsy-like to me.*

He gazed out across the bow where waves lapped against the hull. With a sigh of regret over a possible opportunity missed, Rodger knocked out the tobacco residue in his pipe against the gunnels and watches the still-live coals cascade into the inky black liquid of the bay. *The calm water, the soft gently warm wind, the night sky spilling over with stars, this is a night for lovers, or should I say Gypsies*, thought Rodger.

Rising to his feet, he descended down the stairs leading into the salon where Helen lay snuggled up on the divan, with a book in her hand. "I see you`re settled in for he night, I was hoping we could play a game of cribbage or have a night cap or something."

"Well, I`m not sure what `or something` is, but I would enjoy a night cap. What are you offering for a nightcap?"

"I have a bottle of Drambui I've been saving for special occasions," ventured Rodger. "How about slipping on your jacket and we`ll go topside to toast the stars. They`re putting on quite a show tonight."

"Is this a special occasion, Rodger?"

"It could be," his voice reflected his warm emotions.

"Rather than my jacket, I`ll just slip this table cloth over my shoulders. Don`t you think it has a Gypsy-shawl look to it?"

"Now that you mention it, yes it does," he replied as he stepped back to survey Helen from head to toe. "However the stripped, flannel pajamas under the shawl doesn`t quite fit the gypsy picture, even though you do look fetching in them."

"Oops! I guess I have some shopping to do at our next port-of call." Helen giggled as she sprang lightly up the steps to the deck. "Oh how beautiful," she gasped, gazing at the star-studded sky above them.

Rodger`s gaze fastened on Helen and the stars in her eyes, "Maybe it`s time we picked up where we left off in Port Angeles," he whispered huskily.

"Where was that?" She said clutching the tablecloth shawl to her shoulders as she stood looking at him provocatively.

"You know… where we embraced when I returned from Seattle?"

"Oh, that!"

"Yes, that!"

"Well, I guess we could embrace and see what happens."

They kissed and a wave of passion swept over both of them, blending their bodies into one as they clung to one another, both feeling the warmth and pleasure of being wrapped in each other`s arms. Suddenly, Helen pushed her palms against Rodger`s chest stepping back one-step. "Rodg, I think that`s as far as I want to go tonight. This new relationship takes a little getting used to and I want it to be right for both of us."

"We both have some hurdles to get over," said Rodger, "but it`s exciting to be more than friends." The tablecloth dropped to the deck as Helen slipped her arm around Rodger`s neck; his arms slid about her waist, he lowered his face to hers and they kissed again.

"I agree, Rodg, we both have some hurdles to get over. Would you mind going below first? I want to stay up here by myself for awhile."

"I can do that, Gypsy."

Chapter Eight

Rodger was the first to awaken the next morning. Quietly dressing before pulling back the drape dividing his forward berth from the salon, he paused watching Helen sleep. *She looks so childlike curled up in her sleeping bag.* Rodger slipped into the bathroom, then made his way to the galley, and quietly put on the coffee pot.

As the coffee started to perk, the aroma permeates the salon, and Helen slowly came to life. She lay there for a moment looking at the ceiling trying to determine where she was. As recognition registers, she rolled over and smiled whimsically at Rodger.

"Good morning; I tried not to disturb you."

"I like to awaken to the smell of fresh coffee brewing. That means someone else is already up, and I get to start the day with a cup of my favorite beverage."

"I must confess I was as much concerned about my needs as yours."

"Okay, spoil my princess illusion. While you fix breakfast, I`ll go ashore, shower and continue my fantasy as best I can."

"Yep, I`m definitely creating a monster; however, a nice monster. What do you want for breakfast?"

"How about oatmeal and toast?"

"I can do that. I`ll go topside while you put yourself together."

"Sounds like a plan."

Rodger checked the mooring lines, and finding everything shipshape, took a sponge to wipe the morning dew off the flat surfaces of the boat. Hearing Helen moving about the galley area, he took that as a signal to return to the cabin.

Helen met him as she ascended the stairs. "Okay mate, it`s all yours; I`m off to the showers."

"Take your time. I`ll put the oatmeal on and join you there."

"The tide change is in an hour and a half, and I think we should try to cast off in an hour."

* * *

After breakfast Helen checked the chart and the weather report, and it looked like another good sailing day ahead. As they motored out of the bay, Rodger was busy preparing the sails for raising. Suddenly Helen shouted, "Hold up on the sails, Rodg."

"Why… there`s enough wind!"

"Instead of sailing around Tatoosh Island we can take a short cut between the mainland and the island. We need a full-slack tide to do that, and we have it. We`ll need to stay under power so we can follow a changing route that hugs close to the island`s hundred-foot high granite face. Your job will be to stand at the bow and watch for rock pinnacles that rise from the bottom. Tell me where they`re located using the clock-face technique I taught you, and we`ll be just fine as long as the calm weather holds. Right now we have just three knots of wind from the northwest, which is workable."

"I`m glad you know what you`re doing," called out Rodger looking ahead at their intended path. "It looks pretty dangerous to me with pinnacles showing all over the place between Tatoosh and the mainland. What caused them?"

"Tatoosh Island used to be a part of the Peninsula, but ocean waves and wind eroded the rock and soil over eons of time. The pinnacles are the parts of land and rock not yet eroded. The water close to the island is deep enough to get through with a sailboat even with a four-foot draft, if you`re careful and have a high, slack tide. However, if you`re not careful, be prepared to swim."

"I see pinnacles barely below the surface of the water causing plumes of spray, like little geysers."

"Those are not the problem. It`s the ones deep enough not to cause little geysers, but less than four feet from the surface that can tear the bottom out of your boat… but we save at least two hours by running this water-gap."

"I can see this is going to be an interesting trip," said Rodger grimacing.

"You wanted adventure… you`ve got it. Now go forward and be the lookout."

"Aye, aye, Skipper. How far below the surface should these pinnacles be?"

"If you can see them under the water, they`re too close."

Rodger scrambled forward and stood leaning over the bow sprite while holding on to the forestay behind him with one hand. "There`s a pinnacle at eleven o`clock."

"Rodger!" acknowledged Helen.

"Pinnacle at twelve o`clock,"

"Rodger," replied Helen as she expertly guided the Sea Witch on its serpentine course. "Darn! The wind is picking up; that`s not good."

"Do we turn around?"

"That`s more dangerous than going straight ahead; just keep looking for pinnacles. We`re through the worst of it, I think, however, it`s harder to see the pinnacles with a chop on the water."

"Pinnacle at two o`clock."

"Rodger!"

"Should we be this close to Tatoosh Island, Skipper? I can almost touch its granite face with my hand."

"That`s the way it`s got to be, as that`s where the deep water is. The granite face goes up a hundred feet and down twenty fathoms according to the Pacific Coast Pilot Book."

"Great! Now, how far did you say a fathom was?"

"Six feet, so we`re O.K."

"Pinnacle at eleven o`clock."

"Rodger, dodger, over and out!"

"What`s this Rodger, dodger over and out jazz?"

"That means the mission is over, we`re home free. We`re now in the Pacific Ocean."

"Phwee! This calls for a celebration. How about splitting an Old English 800 beer, even if it`s still morning?"

"Sounds good to me, but first let`s hoist the sails."

Helen pointed the Sea Witch into the wind, as Rodger hoisted the main and mizzen sails. They begin luffing violently until Helen let the Sea Witch fall off the wind fifteen degrees. Once the sails filled, Rodger hoisted the jib and they`re on their way. The wind, being out of the northwest, came across their aft quarter as they headed south along the Washington coast. Rodger went below and returned with two glasses half-full of the robust, amber-colored beer.

"I propose a toast," as he handed Helen one of the glasses. "To the three of us. May our voyage be successful and we see Tahiti."

"The three of us?" asked Helen as she stood beside the tiller guiding the Sea Witch southward.

"Yep, the three of us: you, the Sea Witch, and me; she has to be successful too."

"Agreed! Helen held her glass up to Rodger`s, "To you, me and baby makes three."

For a long time they sit side-by-side silently sipping their drinks, savoring the actual beginning of their ocean voyage. The wind increased to fifteen knots and the Sea Witch picked up the rhythm of the rise and fall of the ground swells. The air temperature remained in the high sixties, common for the Washington coast this time of the year. The sky clear except for a bank of white clouds on the far horizon. Helen broke the silence, "It`s the kind of day that makes mariners wonder why everyone doesn`t follow the sailor`s life."

"This is one big ocean," remarked Rodger as he stretch out on the bench seat.

"Did you know seventy percent of the earth`s surface is covered by water, Rodg."

"Really?"

"Jacques Cousteau has a lot to say about the ocean, he`s that French scientist who spent a lifetime studying it. According to him, it`s a shocking paradox that at the precise moment in history when we arrived at an understanding of the sea, we should have to face the question, `What if the oceans should die?`

"Really!"

"We`ve been ignorant and superstitious about the oceans and we`re just beginning to learn how to manage and exploit this vast resource."

"This sounds like one of your lectures coming on, teacher."

"Yes, I guess it is. But think about it, if the oceans should die… it would be the final catastrophe in the story of man and the other animals and plants with whom we share this planet."

"That gets my attention. As I sit here and look out at the ocean, it looks so big and full of life. It`s hard to imagine that it could become lifeless."

"It could happen according to Cousteau. If it did, the ocean would foul and become such a stench of decaying organic matter, it would drive people back from all the coastal regions in the world. That`s just for openers. The ocean happens to be the earth`s principal buffer, keeping balances intact between the different salts and gases our lives are composed of and of which we depend."

"I get the picture, Skipper. I have more respect for the ocean already and I`m sure there is more to this lecture, but you`ll have to give it to me in small doses or my eyes glaze over."

"Okay Rodg, in the meantime, here`s something else to think about. I think we need to add an autopilot to Sea Witch to make the trip more comfortable. Otherwise we`ll have to stand four hour watches around the clock and be constantly in control of the tiller."

"Around the clock watches sounds like a lot of work, and I`m for reducing work. Where`ll we buy such a device along this primitive stretch of coastline?"

"I think Westport would be a logical place to have one installed. There should be a marina there with a ship`s chandler near by and a mechanic to install it. Clyde was planning to have an autopilot installed when we took our trip to Tahiti. It certainly would make an easier trip for both of us. We`ll be relieving each other at the helm and sleeping in shifts, as it is. But there would be a lot less strain on us while we tend the helm."

"By all means, let`s stop at Westport and have one installed."

"Good. I calculate Westport is thirty hours south, so we`ll get a taste of standing watch four hours on and four hours off during that run. If the wind holds we should get into Westport tomorrow in the late afternoon. I`ll stand the first watch, starting now, so you are elected to fix lunch."

"What would you like, soup or sandwich?" Rodger stood in preparation for going below.

"Both. Sailing always gives me a ferocious appetite."

"You could lose that schoolgirl figure, Helen."

"That hasn`t been a problem in the past; just being aboard a moving, sometimes rolling vessel is a physical workout."

"I don`t have any weight I can afford to lose. In fact, I hope to gain some weight and strength."

"I can already see that happening, Rodg. The physical workout of sailing, the three hearty meals we`ve been eating, plus all of the exposure to sun and wind, has been doing wonders on your appearance. In fact, I don`t think you`re coughing and wheezing like you were when we started this journey two weeks ago. Maybe this is just what the doctor ordered."

"Thanks for the kind words, Skipper. I hope you`re right. On that happy note I`ll head for the galley and fix lunch."

The wind remained constant as the Sea Witch took on the characteristics of a colt set free from the corral turned out on an endless prairie to run to its heart`s content. The constant rise and fall of the waves that start as a water disturbance along the coast of China, causes the Sea Witch to take on a rhythm of movement that dips the bow into the nearest roller and the stern to lift on the last one.

The spray created by the bow moving through the water provides a rhythm of sound, adding to the ongoing symphony of the wind in the rigging. Because the rigging is held taught like a violin string, a unique sound not unlike the G-string on a viola is created by this same constant wind. The percussion section of this nautical orchestra is provided by the sounds emanating from the stern section of the hull as it is constantly rising and receding smacking into the waves. The reed and horn sections are the sails themselves; beat out a dramatic melody as the pulsing wind plays upon them vicariously. The conductor, standing tall with tiller in hand, which can be likened to a baton, conducts this beautiful orchestra with all the skill they possess into the rendering of a dramatic symphony of the sea.

After some time of contemplating the phenomena going on about her, Helen breaks the spell by shouting, "Ahoy mate! Where`s that food? I`m starved!"

"It`s coming right up, Skipper," replied Rodger as he sticks his head out of the hatchway. Expertly balancing a tray of food as he worked his way aft, "Do you think this will do?"

Eagerly eyeing the bulging tray of soup, sandwiches, and coffee she replies, "Yes, Rodg, you are good; it will do."

Rodger and Helen settled on the stern seat with the tiller between them, as Helen controled the tiller with her left hand and held her sandwich with her right hand. After Rodger finished his cup of soup he took the tiller so Helen could enjoy her bowl of clam chowder.

The wind held steady and the sun kept the temperature in the high sixties. The tell-tales on the upper part of the mainsail told Rodger they were trimmed just right for a broad reach. He slowly sipped his coffee, aware of the rhythm of the Sea Witch; which reminded him of a carousel horse with its steady forward movement lunging into the unknown.

"How long can we hold this tack?"

"Indefinitely, if the wind stays the same and our destination doesn`t change."

"This is the life; is the trip living up to your expectations, Helen?"

"Yes, definitely!" Helen settled back into the cockpit, "You asked and I told you about my beginnings, how about yours? Where did you grow up and how did you get where you were when we met?"

Rodger sat across from Helen in the cockpit, "I grew up in a small town in western Washington called Silverdale; my dad worked in the nearby Puget Sound Naval Shipyard. He plied his trade there for 33 years as a coppersmith."

"A coppersmith," repeated Helen. "What on earth does a coppersmith do in a shipyard?"

"A coppersmith is a plumber for ships and submarines. Navy ship`s plumbing has been copper for a long time. It resists corrosion and bends easily to the many angles of a ship."

"Oh, I had him making jewelry or artistic things in copper."

"He did some of that, but only as a hobby. My mother was a stay-at-home mom, like yours and most other moms at that time. I have two sisters who have married and have children of their own. In fact, I am an uncle eight times over. Irene and I married after college where we met in our junior year. Both being business majors, we went to work in the banking business in Seattle. After five years I had learned the ropes in the mortgage portion of banking and, with the help of a venture-capital group, started my own mortgage company. Irene joined me a year later after I determined we were probably going to be successful."

"That`s pretty impressive. I know you have three sons and some grandchildren; how many?"

"Seven by last count: five boys, and two girls."

"It appears that you and Irene have done well and have had a full and successful life."

"Yes but Irene and I have had our share of bumps along the way. I thought after I retired I would finally learn to sail and take my voyage to Tahiti. With this unexpected health problem, suddenly time was running out. That`s where you and the Sea Witch came in."

"I`m glad we did, Rodg."

Chapter Nine

A combination of the late afternoon sun and steady wind provided a comfortable path for the journey southward. Helen sat at the tiller while Rodger stretched out on the cabin roof attempting a nap. At 3:00 o`clock Rodger took his turn at the helm as the Sea Witch continued pushing through the gentle rollers. Small offshore islands dotting the coastline showed no signs of habitation. Like tall wooden soldiers, the fir, alder and madrona trees marched down to the rocky beach that separates them from the ever present, crashing surf. Strewn on the upward edge of the rocky beach, twisted, bleached driftwood formed interesting and sometimes grotesque configurations.

Outcroppings of 200 feet high cliffs, backed by tall Douglas fir trees, interrupted long stretches of low-forested areas. Small islands, looking as if they had at one time been a part of the mainland, huddle off the rugged coastline. Again, there were no signs of habitation, only the never-ending ocean stretching to the South, North, and West.

"Helen, do you have the feeling we are the only ones on planet earth?"

"It does seem that way right now, doesn`t it? We should be seeing some water traffic before too long since we`re in the shipping lanes. I`m having second thoughts about making Westport as our next port of call as La Push is only a few nautical miles ahead; we should make it there by late afternoon. I guess I`m not ready to sail at night along this coast with reefs, the possibility of uncharted islands, boat traffic, and not to mention the possibility of fog. We could go out beyond the shipping lanes, but I`m not ready for that either."

"Why Skipper, do I sense apprehension?"

"We`ll soon be in unfamiliar water, and all of a sudden I`m thinking, wouldn`t it be nice to have radar plus a navigational system, along with our soon to be acquired auto pilot."

"If that`s what we need, that`s what we`ll get. I want this journey to be a success. Would La Push have what we need?"

"No, it`s just a fishing resort and Indian village at the mouth of the Quillayute river. La Push is the tribal village of the Quillayute Indian nation. That`s why there has been no developments or roads for the past fifty miles of coastline, it`s the Quillayute Indian reservation. I was here once with Clyde, but this is as far south as we ever sailed. As I remember it, there`s a large haystack-shaped island called James Island, just off shore. The main river channel snakes around the south side of the island, and the other side is non-navigable. Though there`s water there, it`s never been dredged."

"I hope you remember which side is which," said Rodger as he stood and scanned the coastline. Up ahead he spotted the haystack-shaped island.

"We have to go beyond the island, then do a buttonhook turn to pick up the channel entrance," exclaimed Helen as she stood at the tiller. "A man-made jetty forms one side of the channel, and James Island`s wash rocks forms the other side. The opening is about 40 yards wide, and if we stay in the middle of the channel with the engine at full throttle and the sails close-hauled, we should be able to overcome the current of the river. We`ll also have the incoming surf to help push us shoreward at the most critical time."

"Really?" exclaimed Rodger. "This sounds almost too exciting."

"You said you wanted adventure, Rodg." Helen became silent as she looked over the indomitable entrance to be made by a sailboat into a river mouth coming from the ocean. This would be a test of her nautical skills.

"Just tell me what you want me to do, and when you want me to do it."

"Just before we get to the buttonhook turn, start the engine; then trim the sails so we`re close-hauled. After you finish those two maneuvers, come back with me at the tiller and be ready for whatever I tell you to do. If everything goes right, there will be nothing to do except enjoy the ride."

"What could go wrong, Skipper?"

"Well, we could have the engine quit and lose some of our ability to go forward. If that happens, slack off on the main and force the boom out by leaning on it with your bottom and walk it out with your legs right over the top of the cabin. We want it out as far as it can go in order to pick up as much wind in the sail as we can. If it will ease your mind, I`ll go below and call the Coast Guard to be aware of us. There is a Coast Guard station right here within 300 yards of the jetty."

"I`d like that."

"Okay, I`ll do it now." Helen moved across the cockpit to the companionway leading to the salon as Rodger took the tiller. A few minutes later she returned to the cockpit, disappointment written on her face.

"What`s wrong?"

"According to my radio contact, the Coast Guard station vacated La Push last year due to a lack of funds. The nearest station is either at West Port or Port Angeles."

"So much for that backup plan," quipt Rodger. "Why don`t we just sail south and be in Westport in the morning."

"I`m uncomfortable sailing at night without the equipment we need."

"Okay, then it`s in we go; the engine hasn`t been a problem so far."

"I suggest you get two life jackets out of the locker; we might as well be prepared. It`s standard procedure for situations like this. In fact, some sailors wear their life jackets all the time."

"I wouldn`t like that; I`d just as soon keep it close at hand, if we need it."

"Our turning point is a hundred yards ahead, so start the engine now. As soon as we make the turn, trim the sails… I`ll start our turn in three minutes."

"Aye, aye, Skipper." Rodger quickly went below to start the engine and returned immediately to trim the sails.

"The engine sounds fine, sit with me and enjoy the ride," Helen called out excitedly.

"Hmm, I see what you mean about a narrow channel. With a four-foot keel, the middle of the channel has to be the only route we want. I hope those engineers did a good job of dredging when they created this entrance."

"Sea Witch has been in here once before; I`m hoping the river bottom hasn`t changed since then."

"Those rocks in the jetty and the wash rocks are the size of Volkswagens; I`m guessing they wouldn`t make for a soft landing."

"We`re doing just fine," soothed Helen. "The Sea Witch is making about three knots against this current. See how the incoming surf lifts and pushes us through the entrance of the river? There`s smoother water ahead and just around that dolphin ahead we`ll hang a hard turn to starboard to the dock where the Coast Guard boats used to be moored. I`m assuming they didn`t remove the dock, or gangplank."

"Whoa, I don`t see a dolphin. A dolphin is a fish, right? And we`re going to use it as a bearing point to turn on?"

"Wrong! A dolphin is a cluster of three or more pilings driven into the ocean bottom by a pile driver, they`re bound near the top with a steel cable to keep them together and strong."

"For what purpose?"

"They serve as a guide post for boats or an emergency bumper for boats who can`t make a sharp turn without being bumped partly around. All ferryboat docks have them. They also are used to display navigational markers."

Suddenly Helen`s lesson was interrupted by a sputtering sound rising from below deck; then silence…"Damn… the engine died! Is this a self- fulfilling prophecy, or what?" shouted Helen. "Go forward Rodg, slack off the main sheet… now! Do as I told you earlier.

Jumping to his feet, Rodger released the main sheet, placed his bottom-side against the boom, and walked the boom out using the strength of his legs. Once they began to pick up more wind in the mainsail, they maintained their speed against the river current, Rodger dashed below deck in an attempt to restart the engine ---and it caught.

Between the engine, the wind in the sails, and the incoming surf, the Sea Witch continued to overcome the power of the river current and move forward upstream.

"Hurrah!" shouted Rodger. "We`re in smooth water, we`re beyond the river mouth and in the river itself."

"Right you are," a smile replaced the anxiety in Helen`s face. "Now we can relax as the current isn`t so strong. There`s our starboard turn up ahead at the dolphin and voila, there`s the deserted Coast Guard dock. I`m relieved that it`s still there as it assures us safe moorage for the night. The only thing we`ll have to contend with is the sound of the booming surf a hundred yards away."

"I don`t know about you," Rodger confessed, "but that was a heart-stopper back there when the engine quit."

"It was for me, too. But at least we had a back-up plan and it worked. Maybe it was good training for us. Who knows, we may have more tight spots in the future."

Rodger dropped the jib, mizzen, and mainsail as Helen made the turn into the wind. "I see a lot of boat moorage space up-river, but mostly it`s empty. Where have all the boats gone? It`s still the salmon season, isn`t it?"

"The boats left when the salmon left. There`s only a few thousand fish caught around here during a fishing season now. Once several hundred thousand salmon were caught in the nearby ocean and brought to the fish buyer`s barges that lined the bank over there between the empty boat slips and us. It was a great set-up as the commercial fishing boats had safe moorage up the river out of the turbulent ocean, and a place not only to sell their fish, but to also get the supplies needed to catch fish like fuel, ice, bait, and gear."

"How come you know so much about salmon fishing, Helen?"

"Clyde tried his hand at it several summers right here in La Push. That was before I knew him, but he told me about it when we brought the Sea Witch here. The dock`s coming up so I`ll slow down while you go forward and put out the bumpers on the starboard side, then tie on a bow and stern line.

"Aye, Aye Skipper."

"I`ll shift the engine to neutral now, so be ready to jump onto the dock and secure us."

"Aye, aye Skipper."

The Sea Witch settled nicely next to the dock and Rodger quickly tied the bow and stern line to the appropriate dock cleats. He then established a spring line to limit the boat`s motion fore and aft. After flaking the sails on the main and mizzen booms, he secured the jib with a bungee cord that now lie in a neat heap at the bottom of the bow`s forestay. Helen cut the engine and now only the rhythmic booming of the surf permeated the air.

The village of La Push was strangely silent. Only an occasional bark of a dog gave any indication of habitation. The late afternoon sun was well on its way to disappearing behind the evergreen trees surrounding La Push on three sides. The Quillayute Needles, a line of jagged rocks extending a hundred feet high and an eighth of a mile out into the ocean south of James Island, dominated the rugged ocean beach scene.

"Where is everybody?" asked Rodger. "This is eerie."

Helen replied matter-of-factly, "The commercial boats are nearly all gone. The marina is a quarter mile upstream where the sport fisherman put their boats in the water. There`s a store, cafe, and sleeping accommodations, if you`re not too choosy. The tribe has relocated up the hill a mile in new manufactured houses nestled in the surrounding forest, which are far better than what they had down here near the beach. Those empty shacks are all that is left of the original village. There`s only a general store, a trailer park, and motel on the beach road out to the main highway, which is twenty miles away.

"I guess we really are at a jumping-off place."

"Let`s take a walk before dinner and get the kinks out," suggested Helen. I`d like to walk the ocean beach once again. It`s been awhile since I`ve done that. There is something mesmerizing about the rhythm of the waves, and some believe it induces a state of meditation."

"After that close call at the entrance to the river, I could use a little meditation. Is there someone here that could look at the engine to determine the problem?"

"I think I know what the problem is based on the symptoms we experienced. Let me check the gas filter first. If it`s clean, then we`ll look for a mechanic. If it`s dirty, that`s probably the problem."

"Helen, you never cease to amaze me."

"Well, it all comes with the territory of being a skipper. We`ll check it out in the morning; right now let`s walk. I remember a path through the drift logs over there."

Sun bleached logs piled helter-skelter atop one another lined the pebble beach. With the tide out, a hundred feet of beach was exposed. The waves came in straight, curled, and broke a hundred feet out beyond the beach, then feathered to make smaller breaking waves a half-dozen times before dissipating on the rocks. The rocks shone as if dipped in lacquer. Muffled by distance, the first breaking wave created a soothing melody of its own.

"This is a beautiful spot, Helen. Let`s walk down to the water`s edge, I`d like to get a closer look at those ominous, needle-like rocks."

"Those are the Quillayute Needles named after this Indian Reservation of which, geographically, La Push is only a small part. They once were a part of the mainland, like Tatoosh Island where we ran the gap this morning. Wind and water formed them too. They`re a danger to boats, especially if you`re adrift. If you lose your power off the Needles, you'd better pray for an outgoing tide."

"You know, Helen, maybe the safest part of this trip will be when we`re crossing the open ocean away from the coastline."

"Time will tell, Rodg, time will tell. Let`s head back to the Sea Witch as I`m getting hungry; what`s for dinner?"

"I was waiting for that question. How does boiled bratwurst sausage, sauerkraut, potatoes, sourdough bread, and a salad sound?"

"Sounds like heaven, Mate, lead the way."

* * *

After dinner Rodger retreated to his favorite spot topside. There he could smoke his pipe and reflect on the day while Helen did the dishes. This day had two exciting moments: the running of- the-gap off Tatoosh Island, and sailing against the river current in the narrow opening to La Push when the engine faltered. He made a mental note to check the fuel line filter in the morning. If it just had residue in it, they`d have no need to seek the services of a marine mechanic, according to Helen. The easiest and best part of the day he concluded had been the six hours of sailing. The Sea Witch had become a living, breathing thing sending his senses soaring.

Rodger patted the bowl of his pipe into his open palm and let the ashes trickle into the dark water below. Helen had just finished the dishes when he returned to the salon, "Did you enjoy your evening, alone-time?"

"Yes, although I never thought of it in those terms. I guess we do spend most of our time together, don`t we? Don`t get me wrong, I like being with you, but we do need to get off by our self daily to collect our thoughts."

"Do you do that when I`m cooking?" Rodger asked as he settled on the divan.

"Yes, in fact I get three time-outs a day while you get only one, poor dear. I save all the dishes until after dinner to cut down on heating water. Besides, washing dishes is a chore I`m only willing to face once a day."

"Spoken like a true, dyed-in-the-wool pragmatist."

"A pragmatist? Yes, I guess I am. I`ve always felt that one should do whatever seems to work best."

"What do you say we turn in early tonight? I`m worn out after that exciting day."

"I`m with you, Mate!" exclaimed Helen, then breaking into a lusty laugh, "That is to say, I agree. I didn`t mean I`m with you... like in bed."

"I know what you meant...although the idea has a certain allure to it."

"Good night Rodger."

"Good night Helen."

Chapter Ten

The next morning Rodger checked the fuel filter and was overjoyed to find it had enough sediment in it to foul a carburetor. After carefully cleaning the glass bowl of the carburetor filter, he reinstalled it.

Since Helen was still sleep, he decided to take a brisk walk along the beach instead of testing the engine, which would awaken her. Inhaling deeply, he enjoying the pungent, heady, iodine aroma of kelp that lies off shore in shallow submerged beds. Spindrift, caused by the constant wind blowing across the exposed tops of breaking waves gave the air an `in-your-face` salty smell.

On his return to the Sea Witch, Helen was sitting topside, brushing her short, auburn hair. A pail sat beside her with socks and underwear soaking in warm water that had been laced with salt-water soap. "Ahoy Mate," she called as she spotted Rodger climbing through the tangle of beach logs nearby.

"Ahoy, Skipper; did you sleep well?"

"Like a baby; how about you?"

"My sleep was more like a 60 year-old man with the croup."

"I`m surprised, I didn`t hear you."

"You`re a sound sleeper, Helen. It would have taken quite a bit to awaken you last night. The German`s have a saying; *a clear conscience makes a good pillow*. You must have led a virtuous life."

"Yes," Helen replied smiling, "up until now."

"Oh, ho!" chuckled Rodger, "Now that`s a subject worth discussing ...later. For now, I checked the fuel filter and it was fouled as you suspected. I cleaned it, so it`s time to run the engine for awhile to determine if the problem is solved."

"The tide change is in an hour," said Helen. "I`d like for us to be on our way by then, if we don`t need a mechanic."

"I`ll start the engine, then put on the oatmeal; you can finish your laundry after I heat more water for you. In the meantime I recommend the beach walk; it is smashing, as we English are prone to say."

"Sounds like a plan, Rodg. I`ll dump the water out of my washing bucket, and if you`ll pour a teakettle of hot water in for rinsing, I`ll be eternally grateful. You do understand, you do your own laundry."

"I wouldn`t have it any other way," replied Rodger as he moved to the cockpit area to test the engine.

The engine caught immediately and Rodger set the throttle at idle speed, which ran smoothly. As the cooking oatmeal rose and fell in a rhythm of its own in the double boiler, Rodger put on the coffee. Brushing off the stovetop with a potholder, he placed two slices of sourdough bread on the stovetop to toast; then set the table.

Putting the oatmeal aside to thicken and cool, Rodger turned the toasting bread over. The coffee pot spewed its moist smell filling the salon with the pleasant and inviting aroma. When he heard Helen striding the length of the dock, he served up the oatmeal, toast, and coffee. Stepping back from the table, he draped a dishtowel carefully over his raised arm, waiter style. Descending into the salon backwards, Helen turned around to take in the scene before her. "Where have you been all my life?" she demanded.

"Eat your breakfast while it`s hot; I`ll shut off the engine and join you. Good news, by the way. The engine didn`t sputter once, so we`re home-free to head out after breakfast."

"Great! Mmmm, this is good oatmeal. I do like stove top toast, and the coffee is skookum."

"Skookum, is that good or bad?"

"That means it`s strong, or good. Or it could mean it`s good and strong. The word comes from Chinook Jargon, the former universal language of the west coast Indian tribes. It was developed so they could trade with the Hudson Bay traders a couple of hundred years ago."

"Well then, eat up and we`ll pray for a skookum wind for the day," replied Rodger, "but not too skookum."

* * *

Rodger cast off the lines and jumped aboard as Helen proceeded to slowly back the Sea Witch away from the dock in a 180-degree turn in order to face the river. She then shifted from reverse to forward and the ketch moved out of the back-eddy letting the current move the boat in a sideward motion until they were far enough into the river to turn to port; they now faced the ocean. Adeptly maneuvering the Sea Witch to starboard, Helen avoided the jetty rocks on the port side of the boat. The river current, with the help of the engine, moved them rapidly through the opening of the river into the open ocean.

A hundred yards off shore, the churning, choppy water of the entrance and surf dissippated into low rollers. Holding this westerly course for fifteen minutes, Helen took a new compass heading of one hundred and seventy degrees in order to stay a mile off shore. The wind held steady from the northwest so they maintained a starboard reach with the sails trimmed taut, the tell-tells parallel, and the hull speed reached a brisk six knots.

"Mate, would you take the tiller? I need to go below and dress a little warmer as there`s a touch of fall in the air."

"Aye, aye, Skipper. Would you get my windbreaker while you`re there?"

Rodger settled in beside the tiller feeling very much at home now with the Sea Witch. The wind buffeted his tanned face. Taking off his Greek fishermen's cap, he let the breeze play with his hair as he inspected the sweat line now staining his cap. Even his blue, turtle- neck shirt came close to fitting after a couple of washings and his dungarees didn`t have that new look any more. The new beard was grayer than brown, which surprised him.

"Here`s your windbreaker and a cup of hot coffee. Did I interrupt something?"

"As a matter of fact, you did; I`m getting older."

"Welcome to the club. I`d say we`re both well into the second half of our life`s journey"

"I think you are being generous. For you perhaps, not me."

"Well, I may be too, as life is full of surprises."

"As long as we`re having this discussion, did you have a mid-life crisis, Helen? You know that period that marks the transition between the first half of life's journey and the second half."

"As a matter of fact, I did. Mine came when I awoke in the middle of the night and asked myself, is this all there is? That`s when my radar went to work and I met and married Clyde."

"You have radar? Tell me about that."

"I`ve discovered, when I really know what I want… information… opportunities… people somehow show up on my radar screen to make it happen. It`s like they were always there waiting to give me what I wanted or help me get it. However, because I didn`t really know what I wanted they didn`t get through to me, they didn`t get on my screen. We seem to have a filter system which blocks out unneeded information or stimuli. We really need this blocking device or we would probably go crazy as we`re constantly being bombarded with stimuli or information. When we really know what we`re looking for, the filter opens up allowing what we need to get in."

"Interesting! Is that why, when I really knew that I wanted a sailboat to sail to Tahiti, everything fell into place? You had a boat to sell and then offered to skipper it for me because the need was there."

"Yes." Helen sat back on the bench seat obviously enjoying her role as teacher as Rodger continued to monitor the sea ahead of them as he asked questions.

"That`s amazing!"

"It is, isn`t it? That`s why you have to be careful what you ask for, Rodg, because you`ll probably get it."

"So you asked for a husband and you got Clyde."

"Yep, that`s it in a nutshell. At a subconscious level, I always thought I would get married, but hadn`t really pursued it. I let circumstance dictate my life up until my mid-life crisis, and then I knew I had to try to fulfill my unmet needs. I think that is what the mid-life crisis is all about."

"So you had an unmet need, put up your radar antenna, and in walked Clyde?"

"That`s about the size of it."

"That`s mind boggling." Rodger stood to get out the stiffness he was feeling in his legs from prolonged sitting.

"You know Rodg, probably a lot of things that happen in life can be explained this way."

"You sound like a psychology professor."

"Now that you mention it, I do have a minor in psychology and once thought about going back for more training if I burned out teaching physical education. Fortunately, in teaching you get to use everything you ever learned at one time or another, so I didn`t get burned out or bored."

"On that happy note," injected Rodger, "would you like fresh coffee?"

"Yes, please. I`ll take the helm."

"You`ve got it, Skipper."

* * *

The wind held steady from the northwest at ten knots as the Sea Witch moved rhythmically through the three-foot waves toward Westport, the next port-of-call. Seagulls followed hoping for a handout. With nothing forthcoming they soared off to other potential feeding grounds. The cloudbank on the far horizon promised a pleasant late summer day with temperatures in the high sixties. Occasionally a seal popped its head out of the water with round staring eyes and mottled gray-black coats shining brightly in the morning sun. They, too, were looking for a meal and soon tired of the present company when nothing was offered.

Rodger sat on the foredeck with his back to the mainmast drawing in deep breaths of tangy sea air. Unbuttoning his fading denim shirt to expose his lightly tanned skin to the morning sun brought on an unexpected siege of coughing. Gaining control, he once again sat back to view all that was going on about him. Occasionally, saltwater spray peeked above the gunnels, only to fall back to the sea. Seabirds soared overhead checking out the Sea Witch and its occupants. Satisfied the Sea Witch belonged there; they fell off in a sweeping chandelle turn disappearing in the distance.

"Helen," called Rodger over his shoulder, "does it ever get any better than this?'

"No, Rodg. This is about as good as it gets."

"If it did, I couldn`t stand it. Would you like me to take the helm again?"

"Oh… you want to conduct the orchestra?"

"Yes. It is like conducting an orchestra, isn`t it?"

"Take the tiller while I go below and call the Coast Guard at Westport. I`d like to find out the best time to cross the bar." Helen stood releasing the tiller to Rodger.

"Cross the bar? What are you talking about?"

"The bar, landlubber, is a submerged sandbank built up by the outflow of silt and sand at the mouth of any river, bay or harbor. In this case we`re talking about Gray`s Harbor into which five rivers flow: the Elk, John`s, Chehalis, Hoquiam, and the Humptulips River."

"Wow! That`s a mouthful, Humptulips."

"Yes, the native Indian names are a mouthful, but all a part of the beauty of the Northwest. It`s important we cross the bar at slack tide in order to get the smallest wave action. Waves break when their height match the depth of the water beneath them, so they start breaking when passing over the bar. They have been known to cause big and small boats to roll over in heavy weather when navigated at the wrong time of the tide."

"By all means, call the Coast Guard."

Helen turned the tiller over to Rodger and disappeared below. After spending a few minutes on the two-way radio, Helen returned with a wry smile. "Guess what?"

"I`m afraid to ask," replied Rodger as he stood scanning the travel path before them.

"The Coast Guard informed me the best time would be between one-thirty and two-thirty this afternoon. We can`t possibly make that tide change because Westport is fifty miles ahead. The next tide change is six hours later, but it will be close to sunset when we would go over the bar and dark by the time we find moorage."

Rodger looked at Helen questioningly, "What are our choices?"

"We could stand-by out beyond the harbor, but it would be twelve hours before we have both daylight and slack tide. We would also have to stand four hour watches."

"I vote to go in at sunset and dock in the dark. At least we would be in a safe harbor for anchoring, even if we don`t find moorage."

"I`m with you, Rodg. Besides, there will be a fair amount of illumination from the town of Westport, and we`ll have lighted channel buoys all the way. Once we find Westport, the marina should be well marked with lights. Just remember red, right, returning."

"You`ve mentioned that before; what`s that about?"

"When you`re returning to a port or harbor or marina the entrance will be marked with a red marker or a red light on your starboard side, and a green light or marker on your port side. If that isn`t what you see, you`ve missed the correct entrance. Stop immediately, or you could end up on the beach. Then, back up or turn around until you can see both markers, and be sure that the red marker is on your right as you are returning to a port. Thus the saying, red, right, returning."

"I`m glad you know what we`re doing."

"Evidently you never did any of your power boating at night, Rodg."

"Nope, I was strictly a day sailor. I always planned to take a course in navigation, but never got around to it."

"You were fortunate not to run into trouble when navigating around Puget Sound."

"I`ll drink to that, which reminds me it`s time I fixed lunch, and I could sure use an Old English 800 about now."

"Do that Mate, and I`ll take the tiller."

Roger went below and surveyed the cupboard and icebox. *We`re going to have to fill the larder before we leave Westport, plus drinking water and fuel for the stove and boat engine. With radar, G.P.I., and autopilot in our future, we`ll be making port less often for supplies.*

Finishing his preparation of lunch, Rodger returned topside. "I thought we`d have a Mickey Mouse Special, chips, and our beer of choice."

"What`s a Mickey Mouse Special? I know what our beer of choice is," replied Helen grinning.

"Your culinary knowledge is really lacking, Skipper. A Mickey Mouse Special is a peanut butter and jam or jelly sandwich."

"Well, I do admit my shortcoming in the culinary field, but I am a very experienced eater and the sandwich sounds delicious. Don`t forget, red, right, returning."

"I`ll probably never forget red, right, returning."

* * *

The hours sped by as the Sea Witch surged forward like a playful porpoise diving into the wind and waves. The wind remained constant, as the sun passed its zenith on its journey to the far horizon. Afternoon sailing conditions were ideal for a heavy-built sailboat like the Sea Witch. When Rodger took over the helm, Helen started looking for a comfortable place to nap. Rodger, seeing what she was about, suggested "Why don`t you stretch out in the cockpit, my lap makes a good pillow."

"Well, that`s nice of you, Rodg, I do feel like a nap. It must be all this fresh air and warm sun." Helen stretched out on the cockpit bench-type seat, and after adjusting her position a few times to get comfortable, drifted off to sleep.

Twenty minutes later, upon opening her eyes, she discovered Rodger smiling down at her. "Oh, that was a nice nap," making no signs of moving. "I hope I didn`t snore."

"Like a buzz saw."

"Really?"

"No, but you did have a low, rhythmic purr, and I did wipe the drool from your mouth on several occasions. Other than that, you were quite charming in your slumber."

"Rodg, you are despicable," still making no move to sit up. "It`s nice to lie here and watch the clouds drift by; I hope you don`t mind."

"You don`t get it, Helen. I love the closeness I feel to you at this moment. Now, if my legs hadn`t gone to sleep, I would suggest you stay there longer."

Helen sat up slowly and murmured, "You really are despicable."

Rodger stood up straightening his legs, massaging them with his free hand. "You thought I was kidding. I would love to have you stay there forever."

"Forever, Rodg?"

"Well, at least until supper time. Speaking of supper, what do you want for supper?"

"We just had lunch, Mate. When the time comes, you can surprise me. In the meantime, if you`d like to change positions, you can take a nap."

"I can`t think of anything I`d rather do."

Rodger curled up on the bench-seat and lay his head gently on Helen`s lap. Lying there watching the waves trying to climb over the gunnels, he drifted off into a light sleep.

Helen smiled as she looked down at Rodger. *His gaunt look has disappeared with the daily exposure to sun and wind, and he`s putting on weight, so he must be thriving on his own cooking. He still has that terrible cough, but doesn`t cough so often now.*

After a few minutes Rodger opened his eyes, "Have I been asleep?"

"Yes, Rodg, but only for five minutes; go back to sleep."

"That`s easy for you to say," he mumbled, but immediately fell into a deeper sleep. When he awakened he was still looking at the top of the waves at the nearby gunnels. "You know, Helen, I had the strangest dream about waves; I mean big waves."

"Well, they have them here on rare occasions; they call them Tsunami waves."

"Oh, I`ve heard of them; how big do they get?" Rodger sat up to make eye contact with Helen.

"Bigger than you`ll ever want to see. I`ve heard of them being seventy to a hundred feet high." Helen continued to scan forward in search of potential obstacles in their path.

"Wow! That is bigger than I want to see; what causes them?"

"Underwater movement of the earth`s crust or volcanic eruptions," replied Helen as she moved to a standing position with the tiller encased under her arm.

"No kidding? I do know they have earthquakes up and down the Pacific Coast, but I hadn`t thought about the resulting wave action." Rodger sat back wih his hands entwined behind his head giving Helen all of his attention.

"There are two earth crust plates that come together about fifty miles off shore from where we are now called the Pacific Plate and the San Juan de Fuca Plate. When they move, they disturb the water action and can cause a Tsunami wave. Also an earthquake as far away as Alaska or Japan can cause a Tsunami right here on this coast."

"Really? Are they just one big wave or are they a series of waves?" Rodger asked, now fully ingrossed in the subject.

"Usually there are a series of waves and they move rapidly, but run out of water soon. Even people on land head for high ground when they get word of a Tsunami heading their way."

"I`d hate to be in a boat and have one coming at me. What would you do?"

"Put the boat`s bow to the wave, if there`s time and pray. There are rogue waves occasionally, but they`re not as dangerous as a Tsunami. Waves have a pattern of seven; the seventh being larger than the preceding six waves. Sometimes that seventh wave can be twice as big as the preceding waves, for whatever reason. It`s called a rogue wave and can be dangerous."

"On that happy note, I`m going to retreat to the safety of the galley and start dinner."

"Just stay where you are, Rodg. It`s too early to start dinner; lie back down. I like the feel of your head in my lap."

"Well, we can get even closer, if you are a mind to."

"No… Rodg, but after being alone for a year it`s nice just to touch, to be near, just to talk. Do you know what I mean?" Helen`s voice resonated softly, but with emotion.

"Yes, Helen, I do. Even though Irene and I were married, there was a distance between us for years. I felt lonely a lot of the time, which probably was as much my fault as hers."

"You know, Rodg; I think you and Clyde would have liked each other; I know he would have liked you for your openness and honesty."

"That`s a nice compliment, Helen, and there`s one thing he and I have in common."

"Oh, what`s that?"

"You."

Chapter Eleven

The sun hung momentarily on the far horizon as the Sea Witch approached the mouth of Gray`s Harbor, and lights were coming on around the perimeter of the bay. Up ahead the water was lumping up with a wave line apparent. The beach scene had changed from rugged cliffs to long sandy stretches interrupted by an occasional Indian village like Taholah or a seaside town like Moclips. For over fifty miles it had been virgin timber, being a part of the Olympic National Park and the Quinault Indian reservation, but now it was low sandy beaches backed up by berms, marshes and tanglewood.

"That`s the bar up ahead, Rodg; it`ll be choppy for a short while, but nothing we can`t handle. We`ll be going with the waves so it should feel like a surfboard ride. Ever ride a surfboard?"

"Yes, I have… I`m going to like this."

"Good! If I thought this was dangerous I`d have us put on our life jackets. On second thought, that might not be such a bad idea."

"Somehow I`m getting a mixed message, Skipper."

"Just hand me my life jacket without the analysis and keep your eye out for drift logs and dead heads; you never know what to expect in these harbor areas."

"I see the red marker, Skipper, it`s on our starboard side and the wave line is coming up fast."

"Hold on, Rodg…here we go."

"You`re right," Rodger whooped. "This is like riding a surf board. I can feel the waves grab us amidships just like they used to grab me at the waist when I was a body surfer in southern California." Rodger stood to better watch the line of the waves about them.

"I didn`t know you were a body surfer, Rodg. I`ll bet that was fun."

"It was more fun than board surfing." Rodger continued to look out to the wave line, "You became the surfboard, just like the Sea Witch is the surfboard on this wave at this moment"

"I see what you mean," said Helen letting her eyes travel the wave line as Rodger had. "I do feel like we`re the surfboard and look at that bow wake. The wave action ahead is petering out, so I guess our ride is over."

"That was fun, now we need to find Westport." Rodger scanned the coastline of the large bay before them. It was in that moment of time between daylight and night called twilight when images become distorted and waiting shadows tend to dominate.

"With these long, northwest twilights, finding the marina shouldn`t be too much of a problem." Joining Rodger in the coastal search for their destination, she let her eyes scan mostly to starboard. "See how the bay has opened up to become many times wider than its entrance. The lights to starboard belong to Westport, and when we get closer we should be able to pick out the marina and its entrance," she continued. "If our approach is correct, the red marker will be on our starboard side; red, right, returning."

"I get the picture, Skipper, but shouldn`t we have our running lights on?"

"Yipes! I was so hung up on surfing and navigating I forgot them. Thanks for the reminder. Go forward and check the bow lights? It`s hard to tell from here in this twilight whether they`re on or not."

"The green and red bow lights are on," called out Rodger as he moved forward to the bow. "The white running light on the top of the mast is also on; we`re in good shape. "

"There aren`t many boats out this time of night," stated Helen, "as most people seek a snug harbor long before nightfall. Keep your eye out for the marina entrance and we`ll find our snug harbor, too."

Rodger moved back to the cockpit beside Helen. "There it is directly ahead, good navigating Skipper. Rodger now stood on the gunnels to starboard as he scanned ahead while holding on to the mainmast shroud. "I can see the red light; if you`ll veer a little to port, that`ll put it on our right side. Red, right, returning; I haven`t been there, but I am returning, right?"

"Let`s not overdo it Mate," cautioned Helen as she stood letting her gaze join Rodger`s. "It`s time to go in on the engine. As I turn into the wind, go forward and drop the sails. Then flake and tie them so they`ll be out of the way, and get three bumpers and three mooring lines ready for docking."

"Aye, Aye, Skipper."

"Also keep an eye out for the harbormaster`s office; the transient dock should be near it. I hope they have a transient slip for us, as I`d prefer not to anchor out."

"There it is to starboard, Skipper; over by the gas dock." Rodger stood pointing to port with three bumpers dangling from their lines he held in his hand.

"I see it! Tie the bumpers on the port side and tie a bow and stern line for us. I`ll shift to neutral and we can glide in. Grab the boat hook and be ready to snag a deck cleat on that dock coming up." Helen strained to see as the docking distance shortened. "I`ll give the engine a little reverse power to slow our glide. Be ready!"

Rodger leaned over the rail with the boat hook in hand, snagged the upcoming deck cleat and brought the Sea Witch to a complete stop. Jumping onto the dock, he tied the stern line loosely, then the bow line. Readjusting both lines, he tied a spring line. They were now able to leave the boat to register for the night with the harbormaster.

A tall, angular man looking as if he had just stepped off the label of an `Old Spice After Shave` bottle assigned them to a slip for the night and collected the mooring fee of fifteen dollars. This also included a simple map of the facilities, with their appointed slip circled in red, and a handout pertaining to the marina rules.

Returning to the Sea Witch, they made their way to the assigned slip. After securing the boat for the night, they grabbed their towels and toilet kits and headed for the marina showers.

"Two days without a shower takes some getting used to," said Rodger as they walked along the floating walkway. "There seems to be a fair number of pleasure boats here, but not the commercial fleet it once had."

"How do you know that?"

"I was here once for sport fishing, that`s when salmon were plentiful. These slips were mostly full of charter boats, and this was a very busy place. Today it looks like it`s operating at half capacity. Here`s the shower area; I`ll meet you at the Sea Witch afterwards."

"O.K., but take your time. I plan to have a long, hot, shower."

"Sounds like heaven," replied Rodger as he turned and walked into the men`s part of the facility.

* * *

Rodger was in the galley fixing dinner when Helen stepped aboard; her hair wrapped in a towel. She now had on clean denims and a long sleeve polo shirt. Rodger had changed too, but he`d changed something else that brought a gasp from Helen. "Rodger, you`ve shaved off your beard."

"What do you think?" He stood back for her to get the full effect of his new appearance.

"Why, I think it makes you look ten years younger. I wish I could erase ten years that easily."

"I`ll take that as a compliment. I`ve tried to grow a beard before, but I`ve come to the conclusion that some men are just born to shave, and I`m one of them. I couldn`t stand that scruffy looking, itchy beard any longer."

"I do like the mustache, Rodg; I`m glad you saved that."

Rodger`s eyes twinkled as an impish smile tugged at his lips, "George Bernard Shaw, the playwright and author, said `kissing a man without a mustache is like eating your food without salt and pepper.` Come here and see if you agree."

Helen didn`t move, but her face lit up with pleasure. "What brought this on?"

"I guess a woman fresh out of a shower and her hair tied up in a towel turns me on."

"How could a woman resist an invitation like that?" Helen moved over to the galley side of the salon and stood beside Rodger. He turned, smiled, took her in one arm, and kissed her tenderly.

"George Bernard Shaw was right," replied Helen. "There is something special about a kiss from a gentleman with a mustache. By all means Rodger, don`t shave it off."

"Why don`t we celebrate tonight. Let`s have supper at one of those restaurants I saw across from the marina."

"What are we celebrating, Rodger?" Helen asked coquettishly.

"Maybe we can figure that out later," he replied.

Rodger put away the start of his dinner preparation while Helen dried and brushed her hair. Grabbing a light jacket, they walked up the steep gangplank to the street level of Westport. The main street looked to be four blocks long with all of the businesses on one side of the street; the water and marina on the other side was at a much lower level. This gave every business a view, as Westport sat high above the bay so the businesses looked right over the top of the marina.

Neon signs lit up the night sky and the sidewalks were crowded with happy vacationers. Businesses seemed to have struck a deal as to their locations along the street. There would be a restaurant; a gift shop, a charter boat office, and a dress shop featuring nautical wear. This sequence was repeated over and over again. The jovial crowd carried Helen and Rodger along until they came to a restaurant sign that stopped them in their tracks. The sign read "Sea Witch."

"How could we not eat here?" asked Rodger.

"I agree,"said Helen taking his arm and pulling him through the door. "Oh good, it looks like they have room for us."

The proprietor, a short man with a happy smile greeted them and led them to a table by the window. The furniture had a patina from many years of use, as did the floor and walls. The décor was definitely nautical and a sultry looking woman`s face and upper torso had been painted on the main wall of the dining room, and draped fishing nets provided a border. Her long, tousled, sea-weed-like hair hung over bare shoulders and bust, finally ending at her waist. She had an inviting, but sinister half-smile on her pale, brooding face. Her arms stretched out, as if to embrace or perhaps strangle a man who might approach her.

"There`s the Sea Witch, Helen, but I prefer our Sea Witch."

"I do too, but enough small talk. Let`s eat; I`m starved."

"One thing about you, Helen, you are consistent."

"First things first, Rodg. First I satisfy the beast within and then I can concentrate on other things." Helen then hid her face in the menue.

"Like what?" asked Rodger not willing to drop the subject?

"Like whatever it is we are celebrating. What is it we are celebrating, Rodg?" She put the menue down, sat back and waited for an answer.

"Well, we can be celebrating the fact that we`re not eating my cooking. Or we could be celebrating our safe arrival at Westport, or we could be celebrating that kiss. Take your pick."

"I like your cooking, the fact that we arrived safely today is no big deal, because we had no major obstacles to overcome. I guess that leaves the kiss. Her face grew serious as her eyes fastened on Rodg`s face. It was a very nice kiss; what does it mean?"

"It means I want to be more than friends, Helen. It means I want what you want, whatever that is."

"Well, let`s leave it there for the time being as this takes some serious thinking. She looked away breaking their gaze. In the meantime let`s enjoy each day on our trip to Tahiti. Tomorrow we`ll find a chandler and see about buying the accessories we need."

The waiter interrupted them so they stopped their conversation to peruse the menue. When he returned they ordered steaks and a bottle of Cabernet Sauvignon.

"A chandlery is one type of store I didn`t see on main street, but there has to be at least one in a oceanside town like Westport," replied Rodger. "I noticed sailboats like ours with the rudder connected outside the transom used a weathervane type of apparatus for auto-steering. Is that what you had in mind, Helen?

"It could be. I want to talk to a boat mechanic first. Buying these things is one thing, we have to hire someone to install them, unless you are a mechanic."

"If I knew how to install radar, a radio, and autopilot, you`d be the first to know. As it is, I am not a handy man, I`m in the mortgage business, or at least I was. Ahhh, here`s the wine."

The steaks were excellent as was the rest of the meal. They finished the bottle of wine and lingered over coffee. Deciding to have a nightcap aboard instead of dessert, they walked back to the Sea Witch arm-in-arm enjoying the night air. As they made the step over the gunnels to the deck, Rodger extended his hand to lead Helen aboard. He then preceeded her down the companionway and stood at the bottom with arms outstretched. Helen immediately walked into his arms and they kissed long and passionately.

"What do you have in mind, Rodger?" Helen asked, knowing the answer.

"I think it`s time for us to be lovers. Do you want to be lovers, Helen?"

"Yes… Rodger, I do."

Again they embrace. Then stepping apart Rodger reached down and began to unbutton his shirt, but stopped as Helen`s hand closed over his. "Let me do that for you." Rodger`s eyes widened in surprise. Helen continued, "You like to unwrap presents at Christmas time, don`t you?" Then without waiting for his answer, she said, "So do I."

Rodger stood silently while she unbuttoned his shirt, never taking his eyes from hers. Then she slipped his shirt from his body. Smiling at each other as they played the game, he reached across to release the buttons on her polo shirt. Helping her lift the garment over her head, she now stood before him with only her breasts covered by her brassiere.

Again they embraced, thrilling to the touch of each other`s skin. Their kisses became longer and more passionate. Now relaxing, Rodger stepped back as Helen knelt to unbutton his trousers. As they dropped to his ankles, he stepped out of them, kicking off his deck shoes. Dressed only in his boxer shorts, Helen stood to embrace him.

Reaching around her as they embraced, Rodger unfastened her brassiere, pulling it from her and exposing white, ample breasts. Placing his hands beneath each one, he caressed them, watching his mounting passion reflected in her smiling, welcoming eyes. He unbuttoned her jeans, bringing them down to her ankles where she stepped out of them; then reached down and removed her sandals.

They stood facing each other for a moment, then without further hesitation, Helen slipped beneath the covers of the bed-divan, followed by Rodger. Quickly removing their own last garment, they lay wrapped in each other's arms, exalting in the total nudity of the other. As their passion continued to rise, Rodger, supporting his own weight above her on his forearms and knees, looked down at her face thinking *passion and gravity has transformed her face like that of a very young woman waiting to* receive her very first lover. Then in a husky voice he said, "Give up?"

Barely audibly she whispered, "I give up."

United as one, they shared a passion beyond their expectations, one only deep love can bring. All was right with their world, and they remained wrapped in their embrace for a long, long time.

Chapter Twelve

The sun streaming through the salon window awakened Helen. She snuggled into the sleeping bag reluctant to release the warm memories of the night before. Closing her eyes, she listened to the morning sounds: the lapping of the waves against the hull; the roar of a boat`s engine coming to life at the far side of the marina; and the sound of high-heeled shoes clicking down the dock disrupting the morning wakeup serenade of the marina. Helen thought, b*oat people don`t wear high-heeled shoes. They wear soft-soled shoes to protect their boats and to avoid a possible fall overboard.*

The hard-soled shoes stopped outside the Sea Witch, and then a knocking sound on the side of the hull. "Anyone home?" asked a feminine voice.

"Yes," Helen answered. "Just a minute." Pulling on her clothes, she worked her way up to the deck. A young, well-dressed woman in a business suit complete with briefcase stood alongside the Sea Witch.

"What can I do for you?" Helen inquired openly scanning the woman up and down.

"Is there a Rodger McCauley aboard this vessel?"

"Yes, but he`s sleeping; we were up pretty late last night."

"May I see him? It`s important I do." The young woman stood resolute.

"I`d ask you aboard, but he`ll not be ready for company. Helen cast a meaningful glance toward the woman`s feet. Besides, high-heeled shoes don`t belong on a boat. Wait here and I`ll get him."

Helen disappeared down into the salon and made her way to the forward v-berth area.

"Rodg, you`ve got company."

Rodger rolled up on one elbow and stared sleepily at Helen. "What? Who wants to see me? Who would know I`m here?

"I have no idea, but she`s pretty and she asked for you by name. Have you not been telling me everything, Rodg?"

Rodger quickly pulled on his clothes, patted his rumpled hair a couple of times as he crossed the salon to the stairway. He stumbled up the stairs, his mind still groggy with sleeps. *Who knows I am on the Sea Witch, in Westport, and has business with me?* "I`m Rodger McCauly. You want to see me?"

The young woman stepped closer and reaching across the gunnels handed Rodger a sealed envelope.

Opening it Rodger stared at the sheet of paper now in his hand. "What`s this? A subpoena? Is this about the legal separation?"

"I`m a process server and your wife wants to see you in court. I`ve done my job, so goodbye Mr. McCauly." She turned to walk away.

"Wait! How did you know we`d be here in Westport and at this time?"

"Simple. I asked the marina to notify me when you hit port. This was the only logical place for you to stop along the Washington coast. Does that answer your question?"

"I guess so. What happens now?"

"Read your subpoena, Mr. McCauley." She turned, her high heels clicking on the wooden dock, as she retraced her steps.

"Well!" said Helen, "this is a surprise. What does the subpoena say?"

Rodger sat down on the cabin roof of the Sea Witch and slowly worked his way down the page. "I have a court date for September 15th in Seattle at the courthouse at nine o`clock with a Judge Long. Today is the twelfth of September, so I have two days to get back to Seattle. What could she want that we haven`t already talked about and settled?"

"There`s just one way to find out. If you don`t show up, she gets it, what ever it is."

"I guess you`re right. Do you want to go with me?"

"No, this is your affair Rodg; I couldn`t be of any help to you. I`ll stay here and get the new accessories we want installed on the Sea Witch. I`ll have plenty to do while you`re gone."

"Damn, this is a nuisance. Rodger slapped the paper against his palm. I can`t imagine what this is about. Maybe I should call Irene and find out what the problem is."

"Suit yourself, but it probably won`t effect the court date."

"If I call, at least I`ll have an idea of what I`m walking into."

"Let`s start the rest of the day off right. Go shower, put on your traveling clothes, and I`ll cook us some breakfast."

"Okay. I`ll check the bus schedule while I`m at the harbormaster`s office and make my call to Irene. Maybe the trip can be avoided."

"O.K. Rodg, but just know you have power; don`t let her run over you."

"I hear you! I`ll be gone a half hour at least, so don`t rush breakfast."

Rodger collected his clean clothes, towel, toilet kit, and walked to the harbormaster`s office. The marina had started coming to life; seamen and vacationers were beginning to fill the sidewalks and dock area of Westport. Rodger found a bus schedule posted on the bulletin board near the shower area. *A bus departs at 10.00 o`clock a.m. and arrives in Seattle at 3:00 o`clock p.m. after a transfer in Olympia. That`ll give me a day in Seattle before the court date.*

Showering and completing his morning ritual, Rodger dressed in kaki pants, polo shirt, loafers and windbreaker-type jacket. Studying himself in the mirror, he was surprised at his reflection. Looking back at him was a man, tan from the sun and fuller in the face than he remembered. *This is the new me. The dark shadows are gone from under my eyes and I look more alive. I`m not coughing as much, and even when I do, it`s less painful. Life on the Sea Witch and life with Helen is definitely agreeing with me.*

Rodger located a phone outside the shower area and dialed the familiar number. He listened, picturing the room as the phone rang. *Is this still my home? Is this still a part of my life?*

"Hello," a woman`s voice replied.

"Hello, Irene; this is Rodger."

Hesitantly the voice on the other end of the line asked, "Where are you?"

"I`m in Westport. I was served a subpoena this morning by your process server, and I want to know what`s going on?"

"Our attorney wants us to go to court before you leave the continental United States and get our property settlement legalized. He also wants the judge to be able to ask you the traditional questions before he can grant us a legal separation. He has reason to believe you won`t be available at the end of the ninety day waiting period for this part of the process. This won`t change the time-line on the legal separation, if that`s what we still want."

"Are you having second thoughts, Irene?"

"Let`s hear what the judge has to say."

"I`ll arrive at the bus station this afternoon at three o`clock, if you want to pick me up. Otherwise, I`ll take a taxi home. It is still half my house, so I guess I can call it home."

"Yes, it`s still your home and mine. Either Junior or I will pick you up at the bus station at three."

Rodger`s voice softened, "It`ll be good to see you and the family." He hung up and walked back to the Sea Witch as he reviewed the phone conversation and wondered, *did Irene tell me everything that was on her mind. It seemed straight forward enough and logical, but on the other hand she went to a lot of trouble to stop me on my journey. Well, I`ll know soon enough.*

After breakfast Helen walked him to the bus stop. Taking in the sights and sounds of Westport, they made their way through the vacation crowd and those that served them. As the bus pulled up, Helen kissed Rodger lightly on the mouth, then stepped back to watch his departure.

"I should be back in four days," called out Rodger. "I`ll leave a message for you at the Harbor Master`s office if there is a change in plan."

* * *

Helen slowly made her way back through the crowd of people. As her mind sorted through the arrangements she needed to tend to before Rodger`s return, she noticed a group of four Hispanic seamen working with stacks of crab pots. Placing the pots one on the other in long rows, they had about a hundred pots ready to be used in the nearby bay and ocean.

Helen approached the oldest member of the group, not knowing whether she should speak in English or her poorly spoken Spanish; she decided on English. “Excuse me, is there a ship`s chandler in Westport?” Much to her surprise, the oldest man wasn`t the one who answered. A younger man with a noticeably Spanish accent chose to be the spokesperson for this group.

“What is that, Senora?”

“Is there a ship`s chandler in Westport?”

“What is that, Senora? A ship`s chandler, I never heard of----”

“A place that sells parts and supplies for boats,” interrupted Helen.

“Oh, Yes, Senora. There is such a store, one block beyond Main Street that sells to us the things we need for our boats. It`s called Westport Marine Supply.”

“How do I get there?”

Pointing, he said, “Go one block beyond Main street, turn left, and it`s a couple of blocks down on the right side of the street. If you come to the Coast Guard Headquarters, you`ve gone too far.”

The four men paused in their work, entranced with this woman who wanted to do business where they did business. “What did you call that again, Senora?”

Helen laughed. “A chandler, and thanks for your help.” She crossed the street following his directions. She was amused at the names of restaurants, stores, motels, and hotels she passed. Whale was used more than any other nautical word. “The Hungry Whale” was a restaurant on her right, opposite it a charter business named “Whales Are Us,” which was beside a hotel called “Orca Inn.” It became apparent salmon is no longer king around here.

Arriving at a one story, flat-roofed building with a small sign that read “Westport Marine Supply Co.,” she opened the door. A young, male clerk turned, started toward her; then seemed to have second thoughts and abruptly turned and walked away. M*ale chauvinist*, she thought. The tall stacks of marine supplies overwhelmed Helen. There didn`t seem to be any order to things. She approached the only employee in sight, a middle-aged woman positioned at the cash register.

The woman`s haircut, and clothes were those of a man, but she wore jewelry and cosmetics. Taking a long drag on her cigarette, she slowly let the smoke roll out of her mouth before she spoke, "What are you looking for, Honey?"

The affrontry of the greeting lifted the hairs on the nape of Helen`s neck. Regaining her composure she forced herself to calmly reply, "I`m looking for a G.P.S. navigation system, a radar system, and a weather-vane type auto pilot to be installed on a thirty-one foot sailboat. Do you sell these?"

"Are you the skipper?"

"Yes! Do you have these things?"

"Well," drawled the cashier, "we have catalogues and we can order it for you; we`re just a branch store here. The main store is in Astoria, Oregon, but we can get it here by auto freight in two days."

"Is this the only chandlery in town?"

"We`re it, Honey."

Helen felt the hair moving again on the back of her neck. "Do you install what you sell?" she asked bruskly.

"No, but John Day does; he lives in South Bend."

"I hope that`s not the South Bend in Indiana," replied Helen trying to keep the sarcasm that she was feeling out of her voice.

"No, our South Bend is 45 miles from here and John`s on call. I`ll give you his phone number, if you`d like. You can find out what his workload is before you order your systems. He does good work and his per hour rate is reasonable."

*I`ll just go with the flow*, resolved Helen. "What`s his number?"

"It`s 360-465-8321. If you have a phone calling card you can use my phone."

"I don`t have a calling card, but I could ask the operator for charges and pay you. I`m going to be out of the country and won`t be receiving or paying any bills for a while. Why don`t you call your wholesaler first and see if they have what I want before I make arrangements for someone to install it?"

"Sounds like a plan, Honey." Helen struggled to control her impatience as the cashier placed her call…then chated amicably for several minutes with the person on the other end of the line. Replacing the phone the cashier turned back to Helen, "They`ve got what you need, Honey. It`ll be here in two days."

Helen placed her call to John Day. He promised to make himself available when the systems came in. "In fact," he added, "I`ll be in Westport tomorrow on a small job and I`ll stop by the Sea Witch to scope it out, as I`m not familiar with a Tahiti Ketch."

Helen gave him the dock and slip number, "I`ll try to be aboard when you arrive, if you can make it around noon. "Helen then turned her attention to the catalogue. With a sigh of relief, she handed the cashier the check Rodger had pre-signed and given her.

"I thought you said you were the skipper? This isn`t your check," the cashier stated flatly.

"I am the skipper, but not the owner of the boat. If this is a problem, call his bank and I`ll pay for the call."

"Sounds like a plan, Honey." Helen fought back the indignation threatening to capsize her self-control. The cashier placed the call, satisfied, she faced Helen, "Where`s your boat, Honey? We can have it delivered there, if you like."

"No, have it delivered here; I`ll call or stop back to see if it`s in. John will be here to install it in three days."

"See you later, Honey, or should I say, Skipper?"

"Do me a favor; since I`m not your honey, or ever will be, just call me Skipper." Helen, having made her point and resisting an urge to slam the door behind her, strode briskly out of the marine supply building to walk the two blocks back to the center of town.

* * *

As she walked, Helen noticed an observation tower at the end of the street raising above all the buildings and the sea wall. It was obvious the sea wall kept the Pacific Ocean out of the streets of Westport. She decided to go the extra two blocks to the tower in order to get a better look at the lay of the land. Upon reaching the bottom of the tower, her attention was drawn to a derilect old man seated by its base. In front of him was an array of dry clamshells split in half with various sailing ships outlined on their insides in India ink.

With a polite nod of her head toward the man, she proceeded up the four flights of stairs to the observation platform. Standing at the railing she looked westward to the ocean. The immensity of the trip that lay before her registered full force, causing her to feel very insignificant and vulnerable. Mentally shaking herself, she regained her composure. *One step at a time, Skipper, one step at a time.*

She then let her eyes sweep to the mouth of Gray`s Harbor where riprap jetties on both sides formed a perfect opening for incoming boats. The bay opened up and took on the shape of half an hourglass. As she turned east, she could make out Hoquiam and Aberdeen, which were mill and seafood towns. The bay, being about twenty miles in diameter, looked to be very shallow with the low tide exposing several square miles of mud flats. Channels had been dredged and marked with buoys so deep-keeled ships coming from foreign ports could get to these two small cities to take on loads of logs, agriculture products, and sea food.

The fishing resort of Westport lay on the south side of the harbor`s mouth: the fishing and vacation area of Ocean Shores to the north, and separating them the immense shallow bay housing the crab and oyster industry. All this gave Gray`s Harbor the badge of prosperity. The fishing resorts, once prosperous when salmon were plentiful, now added the new tourist attraction, whale watching. Helen suddenly realized they hadn`t seen a whale. She hoped the whales hadn`t become an endangered species like the salmon.

Intoxicated by all that lay before her, Helen reluctantly descended the four flights of stairs, and on a whim paused to inspect the derelict seaman`s wares. He sat quietly beside his pitifully small spread of shells. Helen determined to buy at least one shell to make for certain he would eat today.

The dirty Greek fisherman's cap matched his darkly soiled clothing. His creased face had seen many storms and much wind and weather; the deep lines were partially obscured by a four-day growth of whiskers. A roll-your-own cigarette never left his mouth as he sucked in the smoke as a regular part of his shallow breathing.

Helen looked at each shell carefully, lending an air of importance to her final selection. She settled on a three-inch shell with an 18th century English Bark drawn on it having two masts and schooner rigged. On the shell was listed the boats type, name, and the year it was commissioned printed in India ink. “I`ll take this one,” Helen announced. “How much is it?”

The old vender looked at the shell and then at Helen. “That one is three dollars.”

Hellen fished three one-dollar bills from her pocket. “Here you are; I like what you are doing. Is this what you do for a living?”

“Yes, I`m an artist,” he said off-hand holding up a book. “I bought this book with pictures of ancient sailing ships. I use it as a guide.”

“Have you always been an artist?”

“No, Ma`am, I used to be a sailor as I`ve sailed ships all over the world from 40 to 80 footers.”

“What put you on the beach?” asked Helen, using a nautical term to make the conversation more intimate.

“I just got too damn old for that life. This seemed to be as good a place as any to settle, so here I am.” Offering his weather-wrinkled hand he said, “I`m Arron Bradley.”

Helen extended her hand, “I`m Helen Davis, skipper of the Sea Witch.”

“Really? A woman skipper; you don`t see many of those. Where you headed?”

“Tahiti, by way of Peru.”

“I`d sure like to be making that voyage again; need a deck hand?”

Helen started to laugh, but thought better of it. “No Bradley, I have a deck hand, in fact he`s the owner. He`s never been a sailor, but he`s learning fast; we`re a small ship, only thirty-one feet.”

“Too bad. I`m getting tired of being on the beach. I think I could still carry my weight on a craft like yours. But, I like being an artist, though it`s not much of a living.”

“I`ll be here a few days, Bradley. Perhaps we`ll meet again, and I can look at more of your art.”

“I`d like that, Skipper; maybe I`ll see you on the docks. I`ll keep an eye out for you.”

Sauntering back to the marina, pausing now and then to peer into the windows of tourist shops, Helen let her mind drift back to last night and Rodger. *He`d said, "I told you I wanted to be more than a friend." He then asked, "Do you want to be lovers?"*

I replied without hesitation, "Yes, I do."

Chapter Thirteen

The bus moved easily along the freeway as traffic was light for a Friday morning. Rodger sat by a window, enjoying the day, watching the rural scene unfold. The few passengers on the bus seemed lost in thought. Rodger let his own mind wander back to the previous night. *I`d offered himself; she`d accepted. Our relationship is on a new plane now. It had been a little awkward in the beginning, but our passion soon took over. We flowed into each other`s world, each giving to the other until all we wanted to do was lie back and hold each other in the silence of the night.* A gentle smile crossed Rodger`s face as he relived those moments.

The agricultural scenery changed to forested foothills, and the road steepened considerably as they ascended the lower portion of the Olympic Mountain Range. On merging with I-5 in Olympia the traffic, though heavier, still moved steadily onward. After a short stop in downtown Olympia to change busses, Rodger was once more on his journey. Arriving in Seatle on schedule, he saw Irene standing at the passenger-loading ramp beside the bus station. Making his way to her, he was surprised to be greeted by a familiar, if perfunctuary, hug and kiss.

"You look great, Rodger. I haven`t seen you look this good in a long time. Life at sea must agree with you."

"Thanks for the compliment. You look good, too Irene. What is this court date about?" Without an immediate answer forthcoming, the two of them walked silently to the parking lot.

Irene fumbled nervously with her purse obviously searching for the right response. "As I told you on the phone, the judge wants to question us now before granting the legal separation since you won`t be available at the end of the usual 90 day waiting period."

"Well, I guess the court is calling the shots. We`ll see him tomorrow, right?"

"That`s the plan." Irene slipped behind the stearing wheel of the car automatically.

"These past weeks have made a big change in my life, Irene, and I`m learning to be a sailor."

"So this Helen actually knows how to sail, I thought perhaps that was just a part of the big lie; that she had been someone in the shadows."

"Believe me, what I told you is true. Without her I`d be on the beach somewhere or worse. I didn`t know how much skill was needed until we got underway. I don`t think most people know how complicated sailing is." Rodger sat back and surveyed the city scene as they proceeded through the Seattle traffic to Bellevue.

Irene gripped the wheel, her eyes fixed on the road ahead. "Are you sleeping with her?"

"If you had asked me that question two days ago, the answer would have been, no," Rodger replied reluctantly. "However, the situation has changed. I`m sure you didn`t want to hear that, but you asked, and I want to be truthful with you. If we hadn`t filed for legal separation, the answer would have been different."

"I`ve been having second thoughts about the legal separation," said Irene with determination. "This may complicate things for you and your lover, but I`ve decided I don`t want a legal separation."

"What made you change your mind?" Rodger asked.

"I think this is a fling with you and Helen. I think your fear of dying is affecting your power of reasoning. I`m your wife who has given you thirty years of my life, three sons, and helped you build a successful business. I don`t think this Helen-come-lately deserves any of the rewards."

"What about this court date?" Rodger looked directly at Irene as she looked straight ahead.

"We won`t need to keep it, unless you plan to fight me or want a divorce."

Rodger stared out the car windshield. After several moments of deep concentration, After picking his words carefully he replied, "No, I won`t fight you, at least not now. I have a voyage to complete. If I succeed, I`ll probably be asking for a divorce. If I don`t succeed, there`s no need for either a legal separation or divorce…is there? However, if I don`t make it, for whatever reason, I want Helen to have the Sea Witch, if it still exists. Is that understood?"

"Agreed." said Irene with a sigh of relief. "I`ll call our lawyer when we get home and have him cancel the court date."

"When did you come to this decision?" Rodger turned to study Irene`s face.

"Oh, I`ve been thinking about it for several days, but I made up my mind about five minutes ago. I`m angry and disappointed, but I`m more convinced then ever legal separation is not the answer. At the end of the voyage will be the time to settle our affairs."

"I can live with that, Irene. I understand your anger, but I have anger, too. I think we`ve disappointed each other. It`s never just one person, is it?"

* * *

After sleeping the night again in the guest bedroom, Rodger awakened early the next morning to the sounds of the neighborhood coming to life: children`s voices at play, a car starting its engine and backing out a long driveway, and the sound of someone moving about in the kitchen. After showering and dressing, he walked a familiar path ending up in the kitchen. "Good morning, Irene. The coffee smells wonderful; you Swedes do know how to make a good cup of coffee."

Irene was startled as she sat at the kitchen table reading the morning paper, "Thanks, it helps start the day. When do you plan to go back, Rodger?

"Tomorrow, today we can concentrate on our business. We need to get Junior in the driver`s seat." Pouring himself a cup of coffee, Rodger stradled the chair he`d pulled away from the kitchen table. "I`m not trying to justify my actions, but I would like you to know where I`m coming from. When Dr. Smith gave me a year or less to live, I came to believe that desperate times required desperate action. That`s when the trip to Tahiti that I`d planned in retirement became all-important. I knew you and the family would try to talk me out of it, that`s why I prepared for the voyage in secret. It became my obsession, helped me deal with the illness. Helen, or anyone like her, was not a part of the original plan. She was a total surprise, but she is an important part of it now."

"You certainly are living out your fantasy. If that`s made these last months better for you, I`ll try to understand, though I don`t like it. Maybe we can both live out our fantasies in our remaining time."

"How are you coming with your painting?"

"It`s on hold until Junior takes over the business. As you say, we need to get him in the driver`s seat."

"When do you want to turn it over to him?" asked Rodger.

"Immediately, why don`t we go to the office after breakfast and take care of it. You can say goodbye to our employees; I`m sure they`d love to see you, again."

"Good idea! Let`s eat, then make your phone call to our lawyer, and I`ll get ready to go to the office."

Irene called their lawyer bringing him up to date. He thought it a good idea, and he agreed to call the judge and cancel the hearing.

* * *

Downtown Bellevue was busy as usual. As Rodger pulled into his old reserve parking spot, he discovered he had mixed feelings about returning to the office. It was a familiar thing to do, but he was happy it was only a visit. He wouldn`t trade his old life at the mortgage company for his new life on the Sea Witch.

On seeing Rodger enter with Irene, Sylvia, the receptionist, exploded with a happy shriek that drew the attention of all four employees. They converged on Rodger mimicking Sylvia`s reception. It was a festive reunion for all as Rodger had always been more than a good employer, but a friend as well.

A phone call to a local bakery brought a box of pastries; someone put on the coffee pot, and the next half hour was filled with questions and answers about his trip. Rodger was careful to avoid any mention of the skipper of the Sea Witch.

Eventually Rodger, Irene, and Junior excused themselves and sought the privacy of Irene`s office; the employees took this as a signal to return to work. Irene did not sit at her desk, but invited Junior to take her chair. Now they were in private, Junior`s first question was, "I thought you had a court date; what happened?"

Irene replied, "We canceled it! It wasn`t necessary since we`ve decided to drop the legal separation proceedings."

Before Junior could register surprise or question them further, "We have a surprise for you." Rodger replied taking his place as the senior partner of the firm.

"I haven`t liked your surprises lately, but I like the one today about the separation." replied Junior.

"Your mother and I want to retire, but we don`t want to sell the business. We want to keep it and have you manage it for us."

"I am surprised. I guess I expected to manage this for you two in your old age, but not this soon. Of course I`ll do it, but why do you want to retire, Mother? You`re not old or ill, like Dad."

"Hey," replied Rodger. "I`m ill, not old. But then, I guess health is a better measurement of age then chronological years."

"Sorry Dad, a slip of the tongue."

"I`m delighted that you`re willing to manage the company and someday own it," said Rodger. "This business has been our baby, we`ve nurtured it for twenty-seven years. It`s prosperous, and we want to keep it in the family."

Irene joined in, "I`m pleased too, dear. You`ll have to hire another employee to take your place, as you will be replacing me. I suppose you could ask your brothers, but they both have other other chosen fields. I doubt they`d want to change their careers, but you`re the manager; do as you like."

"I don`t think either would be interested, Junior agreed, but I`ll ask. If you leave the business eventually to the three of us, and it needs to be sold to cash them out, I would want the first-right-of-refusal when the business goes up for sale. That way it would stay in the family."

Rodger looked relieved, "That`s settled then; we`ll have our lawyer do the paper work, and wrap this up."

"Great!" replied Junior, "and I am happy you`re not divorcing.

"Me too," said Irene as she walked over and put her arm around Junior. Rodger stood, walked over to his son and joined in a three-way hug.

* * *

The next morning Rodger said his goodbyes, and Junior drove him to the bus station. They arrived just as the Trailways transporter rounded the corner. Parking the car, they walked in silence to the loading zone where Rodger turned and embraced his son. "You`re the head of the family while I`m gone, son. Look after your mother, she`s not always as strong as she sounds." As the bus for Olympia pulled up, Rodger stepped aboard and gave a goodbye wave to his namesake, who returned his wave watching the bus pull out of the terminal amd into the busy street on its way to Westport.

Chapter Fourteen

Deciding to indulge in the luxury of sleeping in while Rodger was gone, Helen snuggled down into the warm, double-sized sleeping bag. Stretching her graceful, athletic body, like a house cat, she enjoyed the warmth and coziness of the bed. The slap-slap of the waves on the hull eventually lulled her back to sleep. Re-awakening at nine o`clock she continued to lie there, smiling to herself as she once again reviewed the quick turn of events in her and Rodger`s relationship. *He`s a passionate lover who has taken me to the mountaintop, but best of all, we really love each other.*

Rolling out of bed, she stretched again. W*ho would have thought after being alone for a year, I would find myself in love with another man…a man who`s dying.* The last thought quickly smothered Helen`s happy mood. Dressing in clean dungarees, polo shirt, and sneakers, she threw a sweatshirt around her shoulders, and the idea of breakfast ashore lifted her spirits.

Cowboy Bob`s looks like a place where I could get a hearty breakfast. Choosing a seat at the counter, she grabbed a menu as she passed the cash register. The waitress, carrying a coffee pot, paused in front of her and looked inquisitively, "Is this what you want?"

Helen nodded. After studying the menu for a moment, she decided on sausage and eggs. The robust coffee went down easily and she mussed, *there*`s n*othing like a good cup of coffee to start the day off right.*

After breakfast Helen walked up Main Street, amused as she read the hype that appeared in nearly every store window. It was all about whales and whale watching. At the end of the street she found herself drawn once again to the four-story observation tower. Sure enough, there were Bradley Arron sitting… eyes closed, with his wares spread out on one of the tower`s huge cement pedestals. It was apparent he faced the sun to inhale the heat and healing into his timeworn body.

Helen greeted him with a cheery, "Hello."

Bradley opened his eyes, his face wrinkling into a characature of a smile. "Hello, yourself. I knew you`d be back."

"How did you know?" Helen stood looking at his shells, picking them up and turning them over to study the back as well as the front of each shell.

Looking intently into her eyes, and in a croaking voice said, "We sailors have a way of knowing things, especially when it comes to women."

"Why, Bradley, you sound like a ladies man," Helen`s voice was warm with pleasure.

He grinned, still with a homemade cigarette hanging from his lips: "I`ve had my day in the sun. Had a girl in every port, but never married one. How you doing with your boat repairs?"

"Nothing is happening yet, the parts won`t be here until tomorrow. John Day is coming aboard about noon today for a look-see. He`s doing the installation of our radar, navigation system and auto pilot."

"John`s a real pro," Bradley said, slowly and with apparent effort stood to face Helen eye-to-eye.

"That`s good to know, as one never knows the quality of work you`re going to get when traveling. By the way, you said you had other art works to show me. Did you bring them?"

"No, but you can come to my place to see them, if you`d like."

"If you think I`d go home with a sailor who had a girl in every port, you`re sadly mistaken."

Bradley`s face shone with pleasure at the conversation. "Well, this old salt has been in dry dock for a long time, you`d be safe with me. But by your looks, kid, I think you can take care of yourself."

"I`ll take that as a compliment, Aaron; call me Helen."

"It was meant to be a compliment, Helen. How do you like the new shells I have today?"

"I like this one especially; the picture on it is similar to the Sea Witch."

"Well then, it`s yours." Aaron straightened, thrusting his shoulders back in pride.

"Oh, no. I couldn`t do that. How much is it?" Helen was taken back by this turn of events.

"I want to give it to you. I`m not so damn poor I can`t give a friend a gift."

"Well, okay. I`ll take it as a token of our friendship. I really do like it."

Helen took the shell and carefully put it in her shopping bag. "I`ve got to go now and get ready for John Day. I may see you tomorrow." Helen turned to leave. "Thanks for the gift, Aaron."

"Goodbye Helen; tomorrow I`ll bring some more of my shells."

She gave him a lighthearted hand salute, "See you later sailor."

Strolling back through the crowd of tourists, Helen let the sights and smells flood her senses. Always the tangy, sharp smell of iodine from the kelp beds that clung to the huge rocks forming the nearby jetty. The pungent smell of garlic, heavily used in some oriental and seafood restraraunts drifted out through open doors as she strolled along. The tantalizing odor of bakery goods fresh out of the oven, with the aroma pumped deliberately through an outside vent to entice passerbys, was impossible to ignore. Helen purchased coffee rolls for breakfast and a glazed doughnut to go.

* * *

John Day arrived shortly before noon, and Helen invited him aboard to eye-ball the job. "Do you want the radar installed, in the cockpit or below deck?" John asked, as he sat down on the bench seat to size up the configuration of the cockpit.

"In the cockpit." Helen said, after a moment`s thought.

"How about the Navigation system?" John looked up at Helen as she stood nearby.

"Let`s put it in the cockpit too." Helen had predetermined she wanted everything as handy as possible.

"I see you have an externally mounted tiller; it should be easy to install the auto-steering. I`ll pick up the parts at Westport Marine tomorrow and be here about ten o`clock, if the freight truck`s on time." John rose to leave.

"Sounds good."

After John left Helen sat down on the cockpit bench seat to take stock as she looked at nothing in particular. *If Rodg gets his court date on Monday, he should be here on Tuesday, and we can be on our way. That`s assuming John is able to install the new add-on`s without any problems, and Rodger resolves his marriage situation. In the meantime, I`ll think positive and fill the larder so we`ll be ready to sail.*

Chapter Fifteen

Rodger`s bus ride back to Westport was uneventful. He was eager to see Helen and his new home, the Sea Witch. Striding the length of the dock to the slip where he`d left the Sea Witch in its double slip beside the "Lone Star", he looked and stopped dead in his tracks. *The Sea Witch isn`t here! Have I mistaken the moorage? No, this is the right slip. There`s the Lone Star, but no Sea Witch. Perhaps the harbormaster moved us to another slip. Easy Rodg, there`s probably no problem."*

Rodger looked for a place to stash his overnight satchel. Knowing the owner wouldn`t mind, he tossed it on board the Lone Star. As he turned to leave, a spasm of deep, chest coughing convulsed him. Clinging to the gunnels of the Lone Star until the coughing subsided, he was still unsteady when he walked to the marina office building. As the harbormaster stood at his window surveying the marina below him from his second story, street-level office, it was a moment before he became aware someone had entered. "Oh," he said, regaining his composure, "what can I do for you?"

"I`m Rodger McCauley. Have you moved my boat from slip A-20 to another location?" asked Rodger, trying to be matter-of-fact.

"No, why do you ask?"

"My boat`s gone and it shouldn`t be," he blurted out. "I have a partner, but I don`t think she would take it out without me." Rodger showed nervousness now as he mentally tried to unravel the mystery.

"Is that the boat John Day is working on?"

"It could be, my partner was to have navigation, self-steering, and a radar system installed. Does John Day do that type of work?"

"Yes. Maybe he and your partner took it out for a shake-down cruise."

"That`s possible, I guess all I can do is wait for awhile to see if that`s what`s going on."

Rodger walked the length of the marina back to the slip, wanting to believe this was the solution to the mystery. He thought of other possibilities, but nothing else made sense, she wouldn`t desert him. Suddenly the smell of frying bacon from a nearby boat reminded him he hadn`t eaten since breakfast.

Stopping at the first restraunt he came to was Cowboy Bob`s. The waitress took his order, called it in over her shoulder to an invisible cook, and poured him a cup of coffee. "You look like you`ve lost your best friend."

"Well, I`m not so sure I haven`t, but I didn`t realize it showed. I came back from Seattle today expecting my Tahiti Ketch and my partner to be waiting for me. Both are gone, and I`m worried. The harbormaster thinks my partner and a local mechanic may have taken it for a shakedown cruise."

"What`s the name of you boat?" the waitress asked as she made a mental connection.

"Sea Witch. Why?" asked Rodger, as he leaned toward the counter and looked directly at the waitress.

"Well, I think I`ve met your partner, if it`s a woman."

"My partner is a woman."

"Well then, she`s been in for breakfast the past three mornings; her name is Helen, right?"

Rodger brightened, "You know Helen? Did she say anything about going out in the boat today?"

"No, but I think I saw a Tahiti Ketch go out about noon. I can see the Marina entrance from here and a ketch rounded the farther-most marker buoy heading north."

"Was the person at the helm alone or with someone?" Rodger asked, showing signs of relief.

"I only saw one person, but it wasn`t Helen." The waitress momentarily stepped to the kitchen to get Rodger`s order. Returning with the food she said, "Here, this should make you feel better. Do you want ketchup for those fries?"

"Yes, please. I guess all I can do is wait." Rodger`s mind raced. *Why wasn`t Helen on deck if it was the Sea Witch? Or at the tiller? Is something wrong? Am I letting my imagination run away with me? Could this John Day have been at the tiller, trying out the new auto-navigation system? Could Helen have stepped below deck? Could it be someone stealing my boat?*

Rodger ate his hamburger and drank his coffee in silence. When he finished he thanked the waitress for the information and walked quickly across the street to a vantage point where he could see if the Sea Witch had returned. His spirits sank when once again; he looked at the empty slip. *If I climb to the top of the observation tower by the breakwater, maybe I can spot them, if they`re still in the harbor.*

Upon approaching the tower, Rodger noticed an old shell peddler located at one of the four concrete pedestals of the tower with his wares spread out. Climbing the stairs, he reached the observation platform only to have his body racked with coughing and convulsion forcing him to his knees. After a few minutes, when he was finally able to stand, he slowly and carefully stood up and surveyed the entire expanse of the harbor. Being summer, there were a lot of boats out. Eight were sailboats, two of them were ketch-rigged, but too far away to determine if either was the Sea Witch. Turning ninety degrees, his eyes swept over the ocean view. A few larger commercial fishing boats and a few sailboats were plying the coastline north and south, but none resembled the Sea Witch.

He rested for a few moments allowing his breathing to return to normal. Scanning the waters of the bay to the north, he spotted a small boat near the middle of Gray`s Harbor. *There`s one that looks like the Sea Witch*! He took the steps down from the top of the observation tower with a surge of new energy and lifted spirits.

Buoyed up with new hope and anticipation, Aaron Bradley watched him hurry by as he returned to the marina. He contemplated going back to the slip to wait, *but there`s no view of the harbor from the slip. The ketch was definitely headed for the marina as it tacked starboard, then to port, making her way into the wind.*

His fears quieted some, allowing him to become aware of the beauty of the day. Chiding himself for being so upset when confronted with the possibility of losing Helen and his dream, he realized this had become his real purpose for living.

Standing beside him at a viewpoint off the sidewalk, a tourist scanned the ocean panarama through a pair of binoculars. "Quite a view," the man remarked.

"Yes it is magnificent," Rodger replied, then suddenly realized the solution to his problem was close at hand. "Would you mind letting me use your binoculars for a moment? I`m looking for my boat that`s out on a sea-trial, and I`m concerned about her whereabouts."

The tourist extended the glasses toward Rodger, "You`ll probably have to adjust them, as I am near-sighted."

Rodger carefully put the binoculars to his eyes, making a slight correction. The view that came into focus made him want to shout for joy. "It`s my Sea Witch; there she is!" Rodger instantly felt the tension draining from his body, and gratefully handed the binoculars back to the tourist. "This calls for a celebration, can I buy you a beer or something?"

"No thanks," the man replied, grateful to have his binoculars back from this excitable stranger. "I`m with my family, and they should be along any minute."

Rodger all but ran back to the dock entrance at street level, savoring the moment when he and Helen would embrace. *I guess it was Helen not being here that was the most upsetting to me, not the Sea Witch being gone. I haven`t felt this way about a woman since I was a young man. Perhaps some things don`t change after all.*

Rodger made his way down the gangplank to the floating dock. Retrieving his satchel from the deck of the Lone Star, he used it for a pillow as he stretched out on the finger pier to await the return of the Sea Witch. The sun felt so good he hadn`t known how tired he was. *Perhaps a little nap is what I need.*

Soon awakening, Rodger became aware of a face inches from his. Partially opening his eyes he saw Helen kneeling over him laughing, and about to kiss him. *Okay, have it your way.* When he felt her lips touch his, he reached out with his arms quickly encircling her, "I`m home," he whispered.

John Day stood watching the scene with amusement. “Everything checks out,” he interrupted, “and she`s ready to go whenever you are.”

“Great! How much do I owe you?” Rodger asked rising to his feet.

“Five hours labor at fifty dollars an hour adds up to two hundred seventy one dollars with tax. Also, I`ll accept a check, Westport Marine vouched for your credit.”

“I appreciate that.” Rodger wrote the check and handed it to John Day, “Thanks for giving us such good service.”

“You`re welcome; happy sailing to Tahiti.”

“Thanks again; this new equipment will help make it possible.” As John walked back down the dock, Rodger turned to Helen, “Are you ready to leave with the morning tide?”

“You bet! Evidently the court date worked out all right. The Sea Witch is ready to leave as I`ve filled the larder for a week`s sailing. That should get us as far as central California.”

“Sounds good to me, but let`s go below now, and I`ll bring you up-to-date on my trip to Bellevue, plus we have other things to talk about.”

Taking Rodger`s hand, Helen led him aboard the Sea Witch saying, “That`s kind of what I had in mind; the other things we have to talk about.”

Chapter Sixteen

It was early when Rodger awoke; the sun wouldn`t make its appearance for another thirty minutes. Glancing at Helen with her back to him now, she was still wrapped in sleep. Reluctant to awaken her, Rodger focused his attention on the cabin`s interior. *The warm patina of the mahogany comes only with care and age.* His gaze shifted to the kerosene lantern suspended above the table, swaying slightly as the boat rocked. *Gimbeled, isn`t that what Helen called it? Gimbeled, both the lantern and the cook stove, allowing them to swing with the roll of the Sea.*

The morning sun, now brightly illuminating the far wall of the cabin, awakened Helen. Feeling Rodger`s warm body beside her, she remained still allowing herself to enter slowly into the day and extend this moment. Memories, still lingering from the night before, reminded her of their conversation during dinner. Irene`s refusal to agree to a legal separation or divorce until the journey to Tahiti was completed. *Dear, sweet Rodger, had been so worried about my reaction to Irene and his decision. The truth is, I don`t have any energy on it. A legal separation hadn`t been an issue when we set out on this trip and it hadn`t been a factor when I fell in love with him. That`s really all that matters anyway, I`m in love with him.* Rolling over, she lay within reach Rodger`s outstretched arm.

His arm quickly encircled Helen, drawing her body close to his. Silently they both lay there savoring the moment. Then Rodger reached down with his free hand and gently turned Helen`s face toward his.

Gazing down tenderly into her eyes, he whispered softly… "Where`s my morning Coffee?"

"What a romantic you are, Mr. McCauley. I`ll put on the coffee, if you`ll make the breakfast."

"You`re the skipper." Helen rolled out of bed while Rodger indulged himself in the pleasure of watching her lithe, nude body gilded by the morning sun; move gracefully aft to the bathroom. Pulling on his shorts he said, "You go to the showers, while I do coffee and breakfast; I`ll shower later. We won`t get a shower for a couple of days while we`re at sea, so make the most of it. Incidently, where is our next port-of-call?"

"Newport, Oregon, it`s 150 nautical miles south; usually a two-day run depending on the wind. This will be our shake-down cruise for the new equipment."

Upon returning to the salon area, Helen planted a kiss on the back of his neck as he stood facing the galley. Then, "I`m off to the showers" she called out as she started for the stairs carrying her toiletries and fresh clothing.

* * *

After Helen`s return they ate a leisurely breakfast, even tarried over a second cup of coffee. With the tide change in two hours, Rodger had no choice but to bundle up his toiletries and head for the showers. While the water heated for the dishes, Helen made a quick check of the rigging, sails, and electronics. Returning to the cabin, she converted the bed back into a divan and once again the salon was their all purpose room.

Since Rodger had joined her in the salon for sleeping, the v-berth at the bow made a good place to store bulk food, foul weather gear, extra sails, and storage for their sleeping bags now permanently zipped together.

Rodger returned from his shower and immediately joined in the preparation for departure. "According to the Canadian weather report, we`re going to have a good sailing day for our journey south. The wind is out of the northwest from 5 to 15 knots, with morning clouds and a possible weather front from the south later in the afternoon."

"That sounds like a go; start the engine, Rodg. I`ll stow the loose things and meet you on deck." Quickly clearing the stove and table, she joined him. Taking the jib out of the sail bag, Rodger readied it to hoist, then removed the lines around the flaked main and mizzen sail. The engine idled smoothly, so Helen took command of the tiller and signaled Rodger to cast off the three mooring lines and bring in the bumpers. Pushing the throttle into reverse gear, they slowly backed out of the slip into the main waterway leading out of the marina.

Once clear of the marina entrance, Helen signaled Rodger to hoist the mainsail, jib, and mizzen. She then allowed the boat to fall off of the wind until the sails filled. Rodger cut the engine, and the Sea Witch, with the wind coming over her starboard side, was sailing on a broad reach. Rodger felt a warm surge of pride at how well he now performed his nautical duties. Glancing toward Helen, he saw her smile and nod approval. He grinned back; all was well in the world.

"I can see the breaker line dead ahead of us," shouted Rodger. "It`s slack tide."

"Good. Restart the engine in case we need it. Then come back here and join me in the cockpit. We`ll stay on a broad reach until we get clear of the harbor opening by a quarter-mile, then we`ll make our turn south." The wind held steady as the hull glided through the frothing bar line without a hitch. Relaxing at the tiller, Helen looked contented.

"That was nice sailing, Skipper; what do you want me to do now?"

"We`re out far enough for our turn, so cut the engine and be ready to trim the main, mizzen, and jib lines. According to our new navigation system we need to be running as close to 210 degrees as possible."

As Rodger trimmed the lines on the three sails, the Sea Witch picked up the wind`s rhythm. Scanning the water, Rodger could see the two-foot waves up until now were becoming three-foot waves. The Sea Witch was handling the waves well, so he went below to heat the leftover coffee from breakfast.

While the coffee was heating, Rodger sat down and turned the marine radio to the weather station. The voice coming from the radio sounded American not Canadian; that meant they had sailed into the range of the station in Oregon. The announcer proclaimed small craft warnings for the coastal area, with a front moving in from the southwest. According to the forcast, there would be waves to four feet with winds from 25 to 35 miles per hour.

Rodger filled two mugs and returned to the cockpit to find Helen intent upon the new weather development. When the Sea Witch broke through the waves now, spray came over the rails.

Calling out over the sound of the rising wind, Helen shouted, "Set the mugs in the holder and bring up the foul weather gear and storm jib. This is going to get sloppy."

Rodger stowed the cups and made a quick dash for the v-berth below deck where the gear was stored. Arms bulging with their yellow slickers, boots, hats, and life jackets, Rodger made his way back up the steps to the cockpit. With Rodger at the tiller, Helen pulled on her bib overalls, slipped into her jacket and eight-inch rubber boots. After adding a sou`wester hat, and life jacket to her ensemble, she returned to the helm while Rodger struggled into his own gear.

Braced at the tiller, Helen faced into the sharpening wind. "Douse the jib and mizzen, and bend on the storm jib," she shouted above the rigging noise. "That`ll give us steerage. Then lower the mainsail some and we`ll start tying reefing knots to reduce its size. Flake the mizzen and lash it securely to its boom. Stow the jib sail in the sail bag, and put it below so it`s off the foredeck. Then secure the forward hatch."

"Aye, Aye Skipper," replied Rodger with a look of admiration on his face for her command of what needed to be done. He went quickly about his assigned work and in twenty minutes had the Sea Witch prepared for rough weather. After Helen`s nod of approval, they sat with the tiller between them prepared to face the oncoming squall.

Salt spray peppered their faces as it came over the rails and bow. Sheets of rain drenched them, but they stayed dry inside their rain gear. The cockpit, although self-bailing, soon filled ankle deep with water. The squall enveloped them as wind ripped at their rubberized jackets, water swirled at their feet, and ran in torrents from their sou`westers down their back. Helen clung tightly to the tiller fighting to keep the Sea Witch on course, with defiance and laughter in her eyes…and then, it was over. The wind died down like someone had turned off a giant fan, the rain became a drizzle, then stopped altogether. Helen and Rodger stared at one another for a moment. Grinning, Rodger reached over and wiped away a drop of water dripping from Helen`s nose. Her eyes… so intense a moment before, now crinkled at the corners, then they burst into laughter.

Rodger stood to better survey the ocean about them. "What happened to our sunny day?"

"That`s the way the weather is on the ocean, Rodg. These squalls and fronts come up out of nowhere, giving a thrilling ride, a good soaking; pass on through, then `voila` everything is fine again."

Rodger added, "Wasn`t it Barkley, that seventeenth century philosopher, who said, `the sublime is experienced through terror; not through pleasant happenings and surrounding*s*.` For a brief moment I felt the sublime, I think you did too."

"You`ve got that right. Now, if you`ll take the helm, I`ll go below, get out of my gear, and put on some fresh coffee."

Rodger sat back at the helm and marveled at how the squall disappeared as quickly as it came. The self-bailing cockpit had only an inch of water in it now. Then without warning a spasm of coughing tore through his lungs robbing him of breath and doubling him over. Gripping the tiller until his coughing subsided, he layback exhausted, thankful Helen wasn`t there to witness it.

Helen returned to the cockpit with hot coffee and sat down next to Rodger. He tried to hide his exhaustion brought on by the coughing spasm; however, Helen saw the strain in his face and his lack of strength in his hand on the tiller. "You`ve had one of your spells, haven`t you?"

"Yes, but I`m O.K. now."

"Are they getting any better?"

"They don`t happen as often, but they seem as debilitating; it`s such a nuisance. If I get worse, I`ll let you know. I`m taking my medication faithfully, so all I need beyond that is fresh air, sunshine, and you."

"Maybe having me is part of your problem; we`ve been pretty intense."

"Our relationship is more important to me than anything else. I`m just fine most of the time. Let`s forget my health and enjoy the trip, okay?"

"I can do that, but I want you to be up front with me, Rodg. We`re in this together and I want to know what`s going on at all times. Have I made myself clear?"

"Crystal clear, Skipper. I`ll tell you if I have a turn for the worst... or for the better. I hate laying this health burden on you."

"I came into this with my eyes open, so put your guilt away. It has no place here."

"Aye, aye Skipper. By the way, does a sailor ever get to call his Skipper, `Sweetheart`?"

"Only when we`re below deck."

* * *

The waves receded to a one-foot chop; the wind lessened to 10 knots, the Sea Witch regained her former rhythm. Rodger replaced the storm jib with the Genoa jib, took the reefing knots out of the mainsail, and re-hoisted it; then added the mizzen sail.

The sky cleared as the sun reached its zenith; its warmth caused steam to rise from the wet deck and cabin roof. Occasionally a fish jumped and squawking sea birds swooped low looking for a handout; when none was offered, went on their way looking elsewhere for the next meal. Now and then a harbor seal poked its shiny black head above the waves to stare wide-eyed at the passing boat. Life forms appeared everywhere about them, and once again everything seemed right with their world.

At lunchtime Rodger came from belowdeck with a tray containing two generous sandwiches, chips, and beer. "I hope you like my specialty sandwich today."

"I`m sure I will, Mate. What is it? All I see is lettuce from here."

"I call it Rodger McCauley special, it`s one of my favorites and easy to fix. It`s peanut butter, mayonnaise, and lettuce."

"Well the proof is in the tasting; hand me a half and I`ll let my taste buds be the judge. Mmm, Good. You do have a way with food, Rodg."

After lunch Helen looked over at Rodger who stretch out on the benchseat. "Do you feel rested enough to take over the tiller? I need to go below for a nap, it`s going to be a long night, as I won`t be sleeping while our new steering device handles the boat at night."

"I`m fine, Rodger insisted; sweet dreams, Skipper." Helen hesitated momentarily, then disappeared into the cabin. Sitting beside the tiller, Rodger`s mind drifting back over the past few weeks. *I`ve learned a lot about sailing from Helen. But more important, I`m in love with her. In this short time we`ve changed from being strangers to lovers. I`ve returned home twice and I think Irene and I have finally come to an understanding regarding our relationship. She no longer considers me a runaway, nor does the family. I`m glad I returned home and straightened that out.*

My future health is still an unknown factor. I look healthier and feel stronger in most ways, but the tuberculosis hadn`t gone away. The voyage to Tahiti has exceeded my wildest expectations. I never thought there would be another woman in my life, and what a woman she is. She has strength I can draw on, if need be. I know I`m not a coward, but I`ve never dealt with death looking so closely over my shoulder before.

Rodger always loved the sea, and this journey intensified that feeling. He now realized Helen, too, was on a quest. She yearned for an escape from loneliness, boredom, and the loss of her husband. Helen hadn`t been looking for another man in her life after her beloved Clyde died, and he never expected another woman in his life. Yet here they were, two middle-aged people, head-over-heels in love, and acting and feeling like they were twenty-year-olds. Rodger tried to project his thinking to the end of the journey, but his mind refused. He had today.

Chapter Seventeen

Helen lay awake on the divan; the sleep she sought eluded her. The magnitude of her responsibility on this voyage regarding their safety was a challenge she had never experienced before. Even though she rationalized they were expendable, her survival instinct and her desire to succeed remained paramount. In addition, she and Rodger hoped having some time together after they arrived in Tahiti.

She was thankful she had admitted to Rodger her need for assistance: help with navigation, the G.P.S.; help at the tiller, the autopilot system; and a ship-to shore radio, the means of communicating with the outside world. These additions would help keep them from ending up a statistic in the coast guard`s category, "lost at sea." Rodger never hesitated when he needed to put up money for the add-ons.

In all kinds of weather the GPS system would give accurate worldwide fixes 24 hours a day, and having it interface with the autopilot practically added a new crew member aboard who took over the helm much of the time. This phantom crewmember possessed a genius mind for navigation by receiving signals sent by high altitude satellite, determining their location within 6 meters, 95% of the time.

Helen felt their chances to succeed on the Sea Witch were now greatly improved. *Rodger has such faith in me. I hope I`m worthy of his trust* she fretted before sleep finally eased her burden.

* * *

"Helen, can you come up here?"

She awoke with a start, "What`s wrong?"

"You`ll want to see this. Nothing is wrong, but this is something unusual. I think I`m looking at the topside of a whale."

Helen bolted up the stairway. Fifty yards off to starboard lay a mottled, gray hulk apparently with no beginning, and no end.

"It just emerged out of the ocean and now it`s sinking back into the ocean. There is a gaping hole on the top of the hulk spouting a spray of water."

"Yep, that`s what it is, a great gray whale basking in the sun. The blow hole enables it to stay like that for long periods of time." Helen held on to a shroud while she balanced on the gunnels for the best observation point.

"It must be eighty feet long. I can`t see its head or tail; nor do I want to." Rodger stood close to Helen while the new instruments ran the ship.

"Good thinking, Rodg, let it sleep. It`s luckier than some people I know."

"Oh…Okay, I get the message… go back to sleep. I promise I will awaken you only if we have a major emergency."

Helen went below and lay back on the divan. H*ow like a little boy he is in some ways. Of course that could be said about most men. Rodg is such a dear, but he can be strong when the situation requires it.* She drifted back into sleep.

Rodger watched the weathervane device attached to the tiller react to the navigation display on the GPS dial. *Makes me feel more like a passenger on the Sea Witch rather than being in command,* he mused. *The instruction booklet on the GPS did list a few things that it couldn`t do, like yell, "Man overboard." Well, I guess we just must avoid falling overboard.*

That got Rodger to thinking about what he would do if Helen fell overboard, or vice versa. *I would keep an eye on her, jibe the boat, and come back on a beat. Then I would have to fish her out, but how? If she`s wearing a life jacket it will be easier, Helen could remain buoyant. If the water`s kicking up, and it probably would be, I would need a pole with a hook on the end to get her to the side of the boat. With her help, I could* *get her aboard, but what if she were injured or knocked out by being hit by a jibing boom? How would I get her aboard? I`ll have to run this by Helen when she awakens. Come to think of it, she would have a harder time getting me aboard than I would have with her. I must outweigh her by forty pounds.*

I`ve seen other sailboats at the marina, and they have a lifeline type of railing around the gunnels of the boat. The crewmembers wear a harness with a line attached to it and tied to a bolt secured to the main structure of the boat. Maybe when we reach Newport, Oregon we`ll need to do a little more fitting out for this trans-ocean trip. Right now we only have life jackets and a coast guard approved emergency kit. What if we need to abandon ship? Would the dingy be sufficient for the open ocean?

Helen`s appearance at the cabin opening interrupted Rodger`s pondering. "Well, whale watcher, I had a good nap; and I should be able to take the first and third watch tonight."

"Tell me about that?" Rodger slid over on the bench seat to make room for her.

"We`ll both be up until dark, then I`ll take the tiller, or I should say I`ll sit by the tiller and watch it steer itself with the aid of the autopilot and the GPS navigation system until twelve o`clock. Then I`ll awaken you, so you`ll do the same from twelve o`clock until four o`clock. You then awaken me, and I`ll take the third watch from four o`clock until eight o`clock. By then you`ll be awake and have fixed breakfast. Then it`s all yours until I finish the rest of my night`s sleep."

"Sounds like a plan, Skipper. I`ll go below and fix dinner to fortify us for our first night at sea. Remind me to talk to you about a man overboard procedure."

Rodger retreated to the galley and opened the icebox hoping to get an inspiration for dinner. A pound of hamburger sat on the top shelf. *It`s been awhile since we`ve had gourmet hamburger patties.* Grabbing the makings for a salad, he closed the lid on the icebox, noting the need to take on more ice at the next port-of-call, Newport, Oregon. Once they were making their crossing to Tahiti there probably wouldn`t be opportunity for the gourmet meals he`d been serving. He planned to wine and dine Helen for as long as he could.

Spreading the dinner ingredients on the small counter, he hummed to himself as he put the dinner together. Starting with a salad of lettuce, tomatoes, and green chopped onions and bellpepper, he added a salad dressing of crumbled blue cheese, soybean oil, apple cider vinegar, sugar, and salt spices.

The salad called for white wine, like a Chardonnay, the beef called for a Pinot Noir. With the table set and dinner nearly ready, Rodger called out through the hatch and in his best head waiter`s voice announcing, "Dinner is served."

"Give me a minute to make sure everything is shipshape, topside." Helen checked the trim of the sails, the GPS screen, and the autopilot. The weather is stable; the wind is steady out of the northwest at ten knots, and the temperature is moderate. Satisfied, Helen descended the steps into the salon. Rodger stood at the bottom step with open arms, Helen walked easily into his embrace. After a long, tender kiss she turned her attention to dinner. "Let the festivities begin. With a spread like this we`ll have to take it to the cockpit so we can linger over it and watch the helm and the sunset."

Rodger put the salad, bread and wine glasses on a tray and carried it topside. Helen followed carrying the wine bottle. "It all looks so inviting," she called out as she ascended the steps. "The evening air is comfortable, the sun`s near the horizon, the seabirds are on their way home; oh, it`s an ideal setting for our floating restraunt."

Rodger placed the tray between them on the bench seat. "This is a meal to celebrate the third member of this crew; we`ll have to give it a name."

"You`re talking about the autopilot and the GPS combination?"

"Right."

"That will take some thought. In the meantime this salad looks inviting, I`m eating."

"This is a salad dressing I copied from a French cheese store. Ironically, we are near the Oregon coast where it was originated, Tillamook, Oregon. We`re off the Columbia River right now, so we`ll pass Tillamook during the night."

"After tasting this dressing, Rodg, I`d say you did a good job, and the wine is a perfect match for the bleu cheese taste." Rodger smiled in appreciation. "What can you tell me about this part of the world?" Helen continued, "geography was never my thing."

Rodger finished his salad, took a sip of wine before replying, "I looked up some history on it in the U.S. Coast Pilot book I found on the shelf of books in the salon."

"Those were Clyde`s books; I left them there as I felt they belonged on the Sea Witch. What did it say about the Columbia River?"

"Let me serve the rest of the dinner, and I`ll give you a narration while we eat." Putting the empty salad plates on the tray, Rodger disappeared below deck. Reappearing with the gourmet hamburger patties, peas, and bread on two plates plus two glasses of Pinot Noir, he continued his narrative.

"The Pilot book says the Columbia River rises in British Columbia and flows for 360 miles before it enters the United States. It then flows southerly to the mouth of the Snake River; then westerly between Washington and Oregon where it empties into the Pacific Ocean."

"I`m impressed. How long is it in total if it`s over 370 miles long before it leaves British Columbia?"

"It`s over a thousand nautical miles long, and up to a mile wide as it winds through the Columbia River Gorge on its way to the Pacific Ocean. At the mouth of the river it`s about five miles wide, if you include the marsh lands and low islands."

"Wow! That`s some river. It must wind around a lot if it covers almost seven hundred hundred miles going through the state of Washington. If I remember correctly, Washington is only three hundred miles across."

"Some say the Columbia River is like a woman who keeps changing her mind, deciding on one direction and then another. According to the Pilot, it`s navigable upstream for deep-draft ocean steamers as far as Portland and the Dalles. Light-draft steamers go farther, to Lewiston, Idaho."

"I had no idea it was that navigable. That would be an interesting boat trip in itself, wouldn`t it?"

"Helen, you`re not diverting our trip to Tahiti, are you?"

"Of course not! By the way, the gourmet patty is delicious. I hate to break up this little interlude, but I suggest you close the dining room before it gets dark. I`ll even have to sneak out on the dishes, as I need to continue tending the helm."

"I`ll do your dishes tonight, but first I`ll bring you coffee to keep you awake on the first watch, and we can continue sharing this glorious sunset."

"Sounds great, Mate." Helen stood scanning their water path forward as she waited for Rodger to return.

"Here`s your coffee, Skipper; it`s robust and should help keep you awake. The sun has a ways to go before final sunset, so explain how the auto-pilot works?" Rodger seated himself beside Helen enjoying the subtley difused light and shadow of the approaching twilight evening.

"It`s not that complex, Rodg. Just pick your desired heading, hold the course for a few seconds, press the auto button, and release the helm. The autopilot takes over and becomes the helmsman; you are merely an observer. But, I might add, an important observer. You just don`t have to have your hand on the tiller."

"That`s all there is to it?"

"Yep, the autopilot will lock the course heading in memory, and will respond with helm corrections to keep that course."

"Amazing. It`s probably more accurate than when we`re holding a course."

"That`s true; it doesn`t get tired and it has an infinite attention span, which saves time and fuel, if you`re under power."

"So what are the draw backs, besides not being able to shout *man overboard?*"

Helen, sipping her coffee and letting her mind skim back over the manual replied, "When it`s difficult for us to steer manually, it`s difficult for the auto pilot also. For example, when the helm is not balanced because of the wrong trim to the sails, or when the boat is yawing in a following sea, it`s difficult steering for us and the auto pilot."

"Yawing in a following sea? That`s a mouthful. What does that mean?"

"Remember a few days back when the wind came over our stern, and we seemed to be surfboarding when we sailed into Gray`s Harbor? Do you also remember how the bow kept swinging off our heading, first one way, then the other? That's yawing in a following sea."

"I`ve got the picture. Anything else about the autopilot I should know?"

"Well, autopilots can`t see, so they can`t avoid obstacles or other vessels. That`s why we must always maintain a watch."

"Darn, I was hoping this genie in a bottle would allow us to stay in bed while it tended the Sea Witch without our help."

Helen smiled. "You said you thought we should give our third crewmember a name. How about Genie? She is almost magic."

"Sounds good to me, but I didn`t know a genie was a woman. I always thought of genie as a man." Rodger sat on the gunnels and faced Helen even though her gaze was fixed forward.

"I guess it all depends on your point of view. Genie, for you, can be a man, for me it`s a woman. Or we could compromise and declare that it is non-sexual and Genie is an it."

"I don`t like that idea, but Genie does sound like a good name." Rodger replied shifting his gaze to the far horizon.

"So be it, Genie is bi-sexual. For you it`s a man, for me it`s a woman. How about a coffee refill with a jigger of Drambuie? After all, this is a celebration."

"What are we celebrating?" asked Rodger hopefully.

Helen smiled, but chose to ignore the inference. "The arrival and the naming of our third crew member, Genie, of course."

Taking her coffee mug, Rodger disappeared below. Helen sat at the tiller smiling as she relived their recent conversation and scanning the ocean waters ahead. The water relatively flat except for the gentle rise and fall of rollers that reminds her of a children`s roller coaster ride. She closes her eyes going inward. *This is turning out to be a wonderful trip, and Rodg is a great companion; he gets more attractive every day. Is it that I see him in a different light, or is it because his health is returning? He looks more like a sailor now with tanned skin, a sparkle in his eyes, and sun-faded clothes. Even his Greek fisherman`s hat has a sweatline in the band. Yep, I believe my first mate is a man with whom I could spend the rest of my life.*

Helen was snapped out of her reverie by Rodger`s reappearance on deck. "This ought to put starch in your legs Skipper, and I propose a toast."

"O.K. Mate, have at it."

"To Genie, welcome aboard the good ship Sea Witch. May you always be true to your task, and with fair winds we three shall see Tahiti."

"I`ll drink to that, now let`s sit here at the helm and watch Genie do her job."

"Move over here Helen; we don`t have to have the tiller between us now as long as Genie is doing his job."

They laughed at their word play and snuggling together as they watched the sun set over the Pacific Ocean. Dramatic brilliant shades of red steadily pulled the blue of the sky over the far horizon. The radiant colors emphasized the layers of clouds, as the great fireball dropped off the edge of the ocean. It`s fiery rays continued to slash upward at the encroaching dusk. The sky darkened steadily, its hues changing from light blue to deep purple until finally giving way to night. In the distance, a lighthouse penetrated the darkness casting spears of light toward them at one-minute intervals.

"Magnificent," exclaimed Rodger at the beauty of the scene as they stood together locked in each other`s arms.

"Wasn`t that sunset amazing? And it`s all an illusion," Helen murmured softly.

"What do you mean an illusion? What illusion? Rodger asked, surprised at Helen`s remark.

"The sunset." Helen turned to face Rodger, a smile wrinkling the corners of her mouth.

"The sunset? The sun did set," countered Rodger. "What`s an illusion about that?"

"No, it didn`t," replied Helen with a `gotcha` tone to her voice.

"What do you mean it didn`t? We just sat here and watched it set. Where`s the illusion?"

"Rodger, Sweetie… I mean Mate. The earth is rotating on its axis and the sun is stationary. We are turning on our axis away from the sun, not vice versa."

"I`ll be darned… that`s right; I guess it is an illusion. However, most of the people of the world would say they saw the sun set; not that they saw the earth rotate on its axis away from the sun."

"No Rodg, you can join the rest of the world and say, `let`s watch the sunset`"

"You`re always a teacher, Skipper. I guess it`s time for me to get some bunk time, so I`ll say goodnight, and expect you to awaken me at midnight. Do I get a good night kiss, or is that against the rules?"

"The Captain doesn`t usually kiss the First Mate good night . . . but let`s bend a rule." They stood wrapped in each other's arms and kissed long and passionately. "Goodnight love." They said in unison.

* * *

Helen turned her attention to the sails and the instrumentation mounted in front of her as Rodger makes his way forward to the salon. Opening the divan he spread out the double sleeping bag, and after going through his nightly ritual, slipped into bed. Sleep didn`t come immediately as he lets his mind wander back over the events of the day. We *ran the bar out of Gray`s` Harbor, saw a basking whale, had a wonderful day of sailing, a gormet meal, and watched a brilliant sunset. It seems strange going to bed alone after sharing this bed with Helen these past few days. Too bad you can`t park a sailboat like you do a car for the night. On the other hand, it`s nice to have the journey continue twenty-four hours a day. Perhaps we`ll be able to average a hundred miles a day with good wind and favorable currents. At that rate we could be in San Diego in two weeks, counting an occasional day in port.* Rodger finally succumbed to sleep as the steady, rhythmic splashing of waves on the hull created a lullaby known only to sailors.

* * *

Helen sat by the tiller for a long time watching the moon. *What a friendly companion the moon is.* The only other lights assuring her she was not alone were the shore lights, and the on-again, off-again beams of light from a lighthouse. The beacon light was coming from behind now so she pulled out the U.S. Coast Pilot to determine their position. *We spotted hundred-foot high Tillamook Rock just before sunset; a lighthouse standing off the mainland by a strand of wash rocks. Since it`s far behind us now, we`re probably about fifteen miles south of it. Haystack Rock is coming up next, and should be easy to identify being* two *hundred and thirty five feet high. I guess we`re about three miles off shore, the wind is holding steady at nine knots from the southwest, and no known obstructions lay ahead of us.* She listened to the autopilot making occasional corrections to the tiller. *Good old Genie,* she smiled. *How I love her.*

It was time for Rodger`s watch so Helen scanned the sea for obstacles such as floating logs or other boats one last time. Satisfied all was clear, she went below and lit the oil stove to brew a fresh pot of coffee. When it started to perk, she awakened Rodger. "Rise and shine, Mate. There`s hot coffee to awaken you and hopefully keep you awake for the next four hours."

"Is it really my watch already? I just closed my eyes." Rodger slowly sat up in bed more asleep than awake.

"That was four hours ago, Mate." Helen gave him a friendly push causing him to fall back to his pillow. Leaning over him she plantd a kiss on his mouth, then withdrew before he could grab her.

Helen returned topside, while Rodger slid out of bed and dressed. After splashing cold water on his face, he filled two coffee mugs, grabbed his jacket, and ascended the stairs to the deck level. When he entered the cockpit, Helen was leaning back staring at the top of the mast. Rodger following her gaze asked, "What do you see up there, Skipper?"

"Just checking the wind direction by the weather vane on top of the mast. We`re sailing about 30 degrees off the wind, on a broad reach, and the knot meter says we`re making six knots. At this rate we should be in Newport by lunchtime tomorrow."

"I`m all for that; maybe then I can catch up on my sleep. Here`s your cup of coffee, would you sit here beside me while you drink it?"

"Yes, I can do that." Rodger put his arm around her shoulders, pulling her close to him to share their body warmth.

"Where are we, approximately?" asked Rodger as he looked into the night sky.

"Do you see that foothill over there? The one that`s about a thousand feet high, heavily wooded, and pitches abruptly to the sea ending in that rocky broken cliff."

"Yes, I see it."

"That`s called Double Peak, and it puts us half way between Cape Falcon and Tillamook Head. The GPS tells us we have 68 nautical miles to go before we get to Newport."

Rodger tapped the GPS dial face gently. "The autopilot interfacing with the GPS sure relieves the tediousness of a long sail. Having it mounted out here on the cabin bulkhead is handy, but what about water damage in heavy weather?"

"I was going to talk to you about that when we make Newport. I think we should buy a dodger to protect it and us from heavy weather."

"A dodger? What`s a dodger?"

"It`s like a wrap around windshield with an arched canvas roof to fend off rain, wind, and bow spray. It`ll protect Genie, and we can get under it too, since Genie has control of the the tiller."

"I`m liking Genie more all the time," Rodger said with wonder and amusement in his voice.

"It`s your watch, Mate. If you see an obstacle, override the tiller and steer around it. If there`s a drastic change in the weather, wake me so we can trim the sails, or do whatever has to be done. If it`s only a moderate change, watch your tell-tales and trim the sails yourself. If you have a problem of any kind, awaken me. Now that my watch is over, I`ll note in the ship`s log the latitude and longitude, and our course. You do the same after your watch, and I`m off to bed."

"Goodnight, Skipper." Rodger zipped his down jacket against the night air and settled beside the tiller. *The GPS tells me the heading is one hundred eighty-five degrees, with a nine-knot breeze out of the northwest, so it should be a comfortable sail.*

The night sky appeared dark, but not foreboding, and some stars were visible through the low-level clouds. Phosphorus in the water made the edges of the bow wake sparkle in the night. Occasionally a fish darting away from the hull became apparent as it left a trail of phosphorus similar to an airplane`s vapor trail in the sky.

Rodger threw the remains of his coffee over the side, and carefully checked the water path ahead for dead heads or other obstacles, before he went below for a coffee refill. Helen laid facing away from him on the divan, but still he could hear the gentle rhythm of her breathing. Fighting his urge to slip into bed beside her, he only smiled at the thought of holding her close, as she looked so vulnerable. He poured a mug of coffee and threw in a shot of Drambui as a compensation for his unfulfilled desire. Returning to the cockpit, he stood beside the tiller sipping coffee, watching the night sky, and watching the water path ahead. They were maintaining six knots and all was well.

It was four o`clock when Helen stuck her head out of the companionway calling, "Good morning."

Rodger, lost in his reverie, came to with a start. "Well, I was just about to go below and awaken you, but all these stars got in my eyes."

"I would like to think that you weren`t asleep, Mate," she said testily. "That would be a Captain's Mast offense."

"That sounds pretty bad, whatever it is. No, I wasn`t asleep, just day dreaming."

"What were you dreaming about, Rodg?"

"I`ll tell you after you tell me what a Captain's Mast is."

"A Captain`s Mast is a trial before the Captain for the breach of a rule. Falling asleep on watch is very serious, especially in wartime."

"Believe me Helen, I wasn`t asleep...are we at war?"

"If you say you were day dreaming, I believe you; that`s the end of it."

"I`ll take my day dream with me and go below, Captain. See you in the morning."

Helen scolded herself for being upset over the possibility that Rodger might be asleep. *I have to realize he`s not used to being awake for four hours in the middle of the night. On the other hand, he has to realize how important it is that he stays alert for obstacles and wind change. Perhaps we should split the mid-watch.*

Chapter Eighteen

Seated at the Sea Witch`s tiller, Helen watched the sunrise as it splashed the scattered clouds in vibrant shades of pink. *Red in the morning, sailor takes warning,* the old marine`s omen came to her. *And that`s exactly what I`m going to do, take warning, even though the weather conditions appear to be stable. The GPS tells me we`re still fourteen miles from Newport, Oregon.*

In the far distance Helen could see the large concrete bridge arching the ocean entrance to Depot Bay. According to the Pilot Book, the bridge has a vertical clearance of forty-eight feet, but boats are cautioned against entering the bay at night, although floodlights illuminate the bridge. Even so, Depot Bay is considered the best all-weather shelter for small boats on this stretch of the coast.

She momentarily wondered why she hadn`t chosen that as their port-of call. Then remembered she`d chosen Newport instead of Depot Bay because Newport is a customs port of entry, thus giving it a high priority as a good place to stop on their journey south. Helen studied the coastal chart carefully; she knew the Yaquina Reef had to be carefully navigated. Located a half-mile off the entrance to Newport, it was a ridge of hard rock and sand with water depths of only five to thirteen feet. Running parallel to the shore for one and one half miles, the only opening to get to Newport is in the middle of the reef. This opening divides the reef making it two reefs; the north half is called

Yaquina Reef, and the south half is called South Reef. A bell buoy marks the southern end of Yaquina Reef, so it`s relativly easy to find.

As the wind picked up, the smooth rollers changed to a two-foot chop crowned with whitecaps. Helen adjusted the sails, and ratcheted down the jib, main, and mizzen lines. The stronger winds, with the sails close-hauled, made the Sea Witch heel over 25-degrees, and the hull speed increased to six knots. Helen put on her life jacket and banged on the cabin roof with her coffee cup.

A couple of minutes later Rodger stuck his head out of the companionway and instinctivly surveyed the sky. "Do we have a problem, Skipper?"

"No, but I think you should be on deck as there`s a small craft warning on the weather report. We`ll be approaching Newport within an hour, and we have to find a buoy-marked channel. I`ve never been this far south, so it`s all new to me. Put on your life jacket as things could get exciting."

Rodger appeared on deck fully dressed including his life jacket. "Do you want a cup of coffee and breakfast?"

"Sounds good to me, Mate, but let me fix it; you take the helm. I`m stiff from sitting with Genie."

Rodger came aft and wrapped his arms around her. "You look like you need a little tender loving care."

"You`re right, Rodg, I do; I`m not used to four-hour watches either. However, we`ll get used to it, I`m told."

"Go below and lie down for awhile; I`ll call you if I need a hand. It`ll be an hour before we have to be on the lookout for the marker buoy according to Genie."

"You`re thoughtful, Rodg, I didn`t realize how tired I was," Helen said leaning into Rodger`s outstretched arm. "I apologize for being short with you last night. I thought you weren`t completely awake and in control of the helm."

"Apology accepted, Skipper. Sometimes my medication makes me look a little spacey."

"Is the cold night air giving your lungs trouble?" Helen asked as she drew away and started for the companionway leading to the cabin`s inviting warm interior.

"Only when I breathe," said Rodger expecting a reply to his attempted humor; none came.

Going below, Helen slipped off her deck shoes and stretched out on the bed Rodger had just vacated. Rolling over in a state of exhaustion, she buried her face into his pillow who`s scent still permeated it causing her to smile and soon drift off into sleep.

Rodger studied the GPS confirming they were still nearly an hour north of the bell buoy they sought. *The sky`s clear, so I shouldn`t have trouble finding it. The change in the weather might make our journey more exciting. I`m feeling more comfortable sailing the Sea Witch now, I guess I`m learning to be a seaman, and I could probably handle the Sea Witch alone, if need be. However, it would be a lonely trip without Helen. She`s wonderful! I got lucky when I chose to buy her boat.*

Rodger snuggled down inside his jacket to get out of the weather when a sudden fit of coughing doubled him over. He tried desperately to control it, because he knew it enflamed his throat lining to the point of closing it. Forcing himself to take a series of shallow breaths, he regained control. Wiping the tears from his eyes, he sank back exhausted. *I`d better get myself to a doctor in Newport for a check up.* He slipped a pill into his mouth and quickly washed it down with a swallow of luke-warm coffee.

Even though the waves were building, he was able to make out the marker buoy he was looking for when it was still a quarter-mile away. Pulling out the coastal chart, he studied it carefully. *I know I have to make a ninety-degree turn after I reach the buoy. I need to slacken the sails to spill some of the air before I make my turn, as I`ll have both wind and sea on my beam. This could be courting* a *knock down, but I think I can do it with Genie at the helm. Good old genie… I`ll let Helen sleep.*

Once he`d slackened the mizzen and mainsheet; Rodger moved aside to slacken the jib sheet, in order to spill a third of the air from the sails. The hull slowly righted itself from twenty-five to ten degrees. After passing the South Reef buoy he momentarily overrode Genie and slowly brought the bow around to port. Quickly determining the new compass setting for the GPS, he adjusted the jib, main, and mizzen sheets until the tell-tells were parallel. The hull speed dropped to four knots. They were now a half-mile from the entrance to Newport harbor.

Rodger sat back and smiled to himself, *I`ll bet Helen will be proud of my seamanship.*

As the Sea Witch came within three hundred yards of the bridge, Rodger made a fist and rapped his knuckles on the cabin roof. Helen thrust her head out of the hatch opening and quickly took account of their position. "You made that turn in these winds without calling me?"

"Yes," surprised at her obvious agitation. "I thought I`d do it and let you sleep."

"Not smart, Rodger. We could easily have had a knockdown. One rogue wave or wind gust would do it."

"Okay, I guess I wanted to show you, and myself, I could handle the Sea Witch even under heavy weather conditions. You didn`t say you wanted me to awaken you before we made the turn."

"You`re right, I didn`t. I just assumed you`d call me and we`d do it together with me at the helm. Obviously, you knew what to do and you did it. Congratulations are in order, I guess, but next time I`d like to be awakened."

"You bet, Skipper, as I've said before, I`have a good teacher." Rodger was relieved at the Helen`s return to a more pleasant attitude as she took over the helm.

"Drop the sails and flake the mizzen and main on their booms, stow the jib in its sail bag, and leave it connected to the forestay. Then, crank up the engine and we`ll come in under power. We probably won`t be in Newport more than a day, unless we decide to have a dodger installed." Helen`s orders were delivered in the once again crisp, authoritative voice of a ship`s captain.

After starting the engine, Rodger returned to the cockpit to watch their entrance into Newport harbor. "I like the idea of a dodger," he said. "It would be good to have a windshield for the cockpit with a roof for protection from the elements. It`s a long way to Tahiti, any protection we can get sounds like money well spent."

Helen stood at the helm scanning the approach. "I`m sure we`ll find a shop near the marina that does canvas work. I traveled by car through Newport once and it has a well-protected harbor. Actually, it`s a typical seaport town where life is dictated by the tides and weather. The depletion of native salmon forced the town to cater more to tourists. It has an ocean setting to attract travelers, and people still like to go out on the ocean, even if they don`t have fishing as an excuse."

Rodger settled into the cockpit opposite Helen. "If it isn`t a working port, is tourism driving the local economy?"

"It`s both. There still are some salmon and other kinds of fish and sea life. You`ll see trollers, crabbers, long-liners, shrimpers, draggers, charterboats, and pleasure craft." Helen pointed the bow to be in line with the tall bridge archway they would go under and on into the large, protective bay of Newport.

"I know about charterboats and pleasure craft, but what is a troller, a long-liner, a shrimper, and a dragger?" asked Rodger as he stood at the gunnels surveying the approaching entrance.

"A troller is a commercial fishing boat with two tall trolling poles. The poles drop down to a thirty-degree angle off the water when they are fishing and two steel lines go down from each pole. Each line has six lures or spreads attached at one fathom intervals starting from the bottom. Therefore, they pull twenty-four lures through the water at one time.

A long-liner fishes for halibut by putting hooks on a long line that lies on or close to the bottom where the halibut congregate. Some lines are a mile long with a thousand hooks. A shrimper drags a sock-like net behind searching out schools of shrimp in order to scoop them up in the sock. A dragger is used to harvest salmon, sea bass, or mackerel and has a drag net also like a shrimper only the net has a much larger mesh. That`s about as much as I know about commercial fishing."

"I`m surprised you know that much," said Rodger as he stood in the cockpit watching the scene before them. The bridge, that was a part of the coast highway, loomed high above them, and other boats were coming and going under it. A festive tourist crowd lined the railing of the bridge above them to get a better view of all the water activity.

"Clyde used to point out the different work boats and tell me how they fished. He had a wealth of information about the sea and those who made a living from it."

"Has this trip helped you in your transition back to life without Clyde?"

"Yes, however I will always cherish the ten years Clyde and I had together."

"That`s the way it should be. We are capable of loving more than one person in our lifetime; each partner will always be an important part of our past."

Helen responded, "I agree as we are the sum total of all our life experiences. How about you? Do you miss Irene and your sons?"

"I think of them daily, and I know they will always be a part of my life." Rodger said as he paused to watch Newport Bridge loom overhead. "Incidentally, that bridge we are about to go under is spectacular. It seems strange to be going on the other side of the coast highway by boat, but it certainly will give us a safe, sheltered moorage. Look up there at people that are waving to us, they probably wish they were down here."

"Yes," said Helen. "I`m sure we make an enviable picture sailing in from the ocean on the Sea Witch. Look to port along the left bank of the bay beyond the bridge where those women are working at those two fish cleaning tables."

"They really are skillfull at cleaning those salmon for the sport fishermen. I see there are still some salmon left and men don`t always like to clean their own fish, do they?"

"You got it, "said Helen, "and those sea birds are loving the scraps being thrown to them. Did you ever hear such a cacophony of sound?"

A yawn interrupted Rodger`s observations, "I've never heard a sound like that, but right now I could sure use some sleep."

"An hour from now we can go to bed; in the meantime we have docking and registering to do."

"Aye aye, Skipper. I can hardly wait."

Chapter Nineteen

The Sea Witch rocked gently at her moorings as the mid-September sun cast rays directly overhead filling the salon with light. The first thing Rodger saw as he opened his eyes was the gimbaled lamp directly above him swinging gently back and forth to the rhythm of wavelets that rocked the hull. Rolling out of bed Rodger glanced toward the clock fitted into the bulkhead across from him. "Good Grief, it`s 12:15. We`ve slept half of the day away."

Helen stirred. "So?" she yawned. "We obviously needed sleep after our two-day sail from Westport. Do you have something more important to do today?" she questioned as she propped herself up on one elbow.

"Yes, I do," replied Rodger as he swung his legs out on his side of the bed. "We need to find someone to make a dodger, but first I vote for locating a good restaurant for breakfast."

"Now you`re talking. I`ll grab my things and head for the shower while you make the coffee. Helen slowly swung her legs over the edge of the divan, her feet resting on the floor beside Rodger`s. Leaning her body against his, she teasingly tangled her fingers in his hair. "By the way," she murmured, "last night was a wonderful stroll to the mountain top and a nice stroll back down."

"For me too, love. Now, go shower before you start something. I`ll make the coffee, but you`d better make that a cold shower."

Helen gave his hair a playful tug. Pulling on her jeans and a tee shirt, she grabbed her toiletries and bound up the steps pausing at the top. "Spoilsport," she taunted over her shoulder before disappearing out of the passageway.

Falling backwards on the bed, Rodger closed his eyes savoring a moment longer its heady memories of the preceding night. Reluctant to leave this haven where they had satisfied their love for one another, he thought, *Wow! She`s something*. Finally, with a sigh he slipped into his cloths, and lit the oil cook stove for the coffee making.

While it perked, Rodger stepped on deck to survey their surroundings. The harbor was well protected from the ocean. In fact, he couldn`t see the ocean. The raised highway that formed the bay ran between the harbor and the ocean. The picturesque arched bridge, under which they had sailed yesterday, was the only access to or from it, except the Yaquina River that flowed into it. The bay had extensive mud flats visible now with the tide being out.

A voice interrupted his sightseeing, "Hi there Mate, where are you headed?"

Rodger turned in the direction of the voice. The inquirer, a middle-aged man whose darkly tanned skin, sun bleached hair, and wearing apparel gave him the look of a mariner.

"We`re bound for Tahiti." Rodger replied turning to face his inquirer.

"No kidding!" Rodger`s visitor rested one foot on the gunnels of the Sea Witch. "That`s a far piece; I was in Tahiti back in `83. You look like you have a boat that`s up to the job, a Tahiti ketch, haven`t seen one in years. He leaned forward extending his hand, "I`m Dorm Stillwell."

Rodger gripped the proffered hand, "I`m Rodger McCauley. "he responded. "We left Des Moines, Washington three weeks ago," he went on to explain, "but we`ve had several delays enroute; we`re not really on a tight schedule."

Dorm laughed, "If it`s taken three weeks to go four hundred miles, I guess you aren`t on a tight schedule." Dorm was a tall, handome man in his forties, pleasant to talk to.

"I think we`ve resolved our problems," said Rodger warming up to the stranger. "The boat`s nearly ready for the rest of the trip."

"What do you have left to do?" he asked, as his eyes swept the Sea Witch from stem to stern.

"We thought we`d find a sailmaker and have a dodger made. We have equipment we`d like to protect, besides ourselves."

"There are several canvas shops in Newport and they`re all good, but the closest one is in that large van-like truck over there in the parking lot." Dorm had stepped back on the dock and pointed to the far side of the marina parking lot. "Charlie can usually finish and install a dodger in one day."

"That sounds like what I`m looking for. We`re anxious to get farther south before the weather turns on us."

"You said we… you have a shipmate?"

"My skipper is in the showers, she should be along any minute," Rodger replied matter-of-factly.

Dorm`s eyes widened. "You have a woman skipper?"

Rodger laughed at Dorm`s surprise, "She`s the former owner and she`s teaching me how to sail."

"You`re not a sailor and your going to sail to Tahiti with a woman in command?" Dorm`s smile turned to a look of disbelief.

"Yep," Rodger`s voice took on a hint of defensiveness. "She knows enough for both of us, and I`m a fast learner."

"Well, good luck, Rodger, you`re probably going to need it." Dorm turned and walked away slowly shaking his head from side-to-side.

* * *

Rodger was sitting on the cabin roof enjoying his first cup of coffee when Helen arrived fresh from the showers. Her face shone with delight as she returned to the Sea Witch. "I recommend the showers; I`ll hold down the fort while you take yours."

"Okay. I just talked to a guy who said the closest sailmaker was doing business out of a van in the parking lot. I`ll stop on my way to the showers and see if he can do it today. If he can, I`ll send him over."

"Good! I`ll spruce up the cabin while you`re gone, then I`m up for going to breakfast."

Rodger grabbed his toilet articles and headed across the parking lot looking for some sign of activity from the van. As he approached he said, "Ahoy, any one here?"

"What can I do for you?" a voice boomed from the far depth of the van.

Rodger peered in to the van`s interior. At the far end a hulk of a man sat at a sewing machine, his attire consisted of tan shorts and black tank top exposing muscular tanned arms and legs, both generously adorned with tattoos. A salt-and-pepper ponytail hung to the middle of his back and held in place by a tooled, dark leather band. "Do you make dodgers for sailboats?" Rodger inquired.

"You bet I do," replied the sailmaker as he rose and walked to the opening of the van. "How soon do you need one?"

"Today, if possible." Rodger stood on the tarmac looking up at the man.

Stepping down from the van, he still towered over Rodger. "Tell me where you`re moored, if I see your layout I can tell if I can get it done today. It depends on the metal framework; the canvas and Plexiglas are the easy part."

"We`re in slip A-15. I`m on my way to the showers, but my skipper is aboard; she`s expecting you." The sailmaker`s eyes widened as he realized the man`s skipper was a woman, but said nothing.

Rodger showered and returned to the Sea Witch just as the sailmaker was finishing up measuring. Helen sat near the tiller watching the procedure as Rodger called out to the sailmaker, "I see you found us. What do you think? Can you do it today?"

"Yep, it`s do-able. What color do you want: Red, blue, tan, or white?"

"What do you think?" said Rodger looking at Helen.

"White will match the rest of our canvas."

"Then white it is; how much to do the job?" Rodger looked directly at the sailmaker, knowing it was a done deal regardless of price. Rodger wasn`t in a shopping or bargaining mood, he was ready for breakfast.

"Two-hundred-seventy-five dollars should cover it."

"Sounds like a deal. We need to find a restaurant, any suggestions?"

"Well, I like Mo`s up on Bay Street. The sailmaker jerked his head toward his brawny left shoulder. Tell them Charlie sent you, and they`ll treat you right."

"Thanks, Charlie, by the way this is Helen, I`m Rodger."

"Pleased to meet you." He dipped his chin in acknowlegement, the long ponytail bobbing with the nod of his head. "I should have your job done by the end of the day."

Following Charlie`s direction, they headed toward Mo`s restaurant. "Wow! Helen exclaimed squeezing Rodger`s hand. "What a hunk, and I don`t mean handsome."

"He`s big all right, and if the tattoos are any indication, he`s probably a sailor. It shouldn`t surprise us if most of the people we run into in a marina are sailors…or ustabes…or wannabes."

Mo`s restaurant was a good choice. Strolling the main street of Newport after breakfast they paused beside a large bronze-plated monument inscribed with the names of locals who had gone out into the Pacific Ocean and never returned. Rodger sensed a slight quickening in Helen`s breathing, taking her hand in his, he turned to face her. "Look, if you`re having second thoughts about this trip, now is the time to say so. We don`t have to do it, you know. All fantasies aren`t fulfilled."

"I know, Rodg. Sometimes, I do have second thoughts, but then I quote Helen Keller to myself, `all life should be an adventure, ` and I believe that. She smiled up into Rodger`s face, then impulsively flung her arms around his neck and planted a hard and passionate kiss on his lips.

Taken by surprise, it took Rodger a moment to catch his breath. He wrapped his arms around Helen drawing her close. "I agree about all life being an adventure. All life should be an adventure, and with you in my life, it definitely is."

I've decided to see a doctor and have an x-ray while we`re here." Stepping back from Helen with his hands resting on her shoulders he continued, "I`d like to know if I`m holding my own."

"How do you think you`re doing?" a frown of concern creased Helen`s forehead.

"Most of the time I feel like I`m doing better, but once in awhile after a coughing bout I wonder."

"I saw a clinic near the restaurant," Helen remembered. "Let`s see if we can get a doctor to look at you."

"Do you want to go with me or do you want to be a tourist and shop for that gypsy negligee?" he added with a chuckle.

"Of course, I want to go with you. The negligee can wait... can`t it? We`re in this together, remember? And I don`t mean the negligee."

Rodger laughed at the remark and hand-in-hand Rodger and Helen entered the clinic. Dr. Barklay, a middle-aged man with a Scottish look about him and a slight burr in his speech pattern, greeted them. He listened carefully while Rodger described his illness and the reason for his visit to the clinic. After hearing their state of transientness, Dr. Barklay agreed to work Rodger into his today`s schedule. Partly to accommodate Rodger, he admitted to himself, and partly because it wasn`t everyday he ran into a diagnosed case of Tuberculosis.

After examining Rodger, he ordered x-rays to be taken. Once the technician took and delivered the x-rays, Doctor Barklay invited Helen to join them in his office. "Your`s is an interesting case, Rodger. I don`t have your last x-rays to compare these with, but I see scarring on your lung walls, which is a sign of healing. Unless I miss my guess, I would say you`re doing better than just holding your own. However, I think we should also have Helen x-rayed. This is communicable and you are living in close quarters."

Rodger quickly responded,"I was told I wasn`t contagious. If I`ve infected you, Helen, I`ll never forgive myself."

"Easy, Rodg," Helen soothed, pulling Rodger back down beside her. "He only wants to x-ray me. If I am infected, I`ve always known being with you was a risk. I factored that risk in right from the beginning."

Rodger clung to Helen`s hand, his face contorted with dispair. "My doctor told me I wasn`t contagious once I started taking my medication,"he insisted.

Dr Barklay rose from his chair, "If you`ll come with me, Helen, I`ll take you to x-ray. Helen followed Dr. Barklay from the room, the door closed behind them leaving Rodger alone. He dropped his head into his hands. "Oh, dear God," he moaned. "Not Helen?"

It was only a matter of moments before Doctor Barklay re-entered his office, seating himself across from Rodger. "I guess you know having Tuberculosis is a serious condition, and you tell me you`re sailing to Tahiti? I wonder if that is the best thing to be doing in your condition?"

"Look Doctor, that`s the whole point," repied Rodger, his voice trembling with emotion. "I was given less than a year to live and this trip is something I`ve always wanted to do. In other words, time is of the essence."

"I get the impression you two haven't known each other long. Are you married, or is that any of my business?" Dr Barklay sat back in his chair inviting conversation.

"No, we are not married, but we live like we are, as I trusted my doctor`s diagagnosis."

"If she tests positive, Helen wouldn`t necessarily have gotten this from you."

"What do you mean, she might not have gotten it from me?" Rodger stared in disbelieve at the doctor.

"One third of the world has been expose to this disease. Some authorities feel each of us have a spot of something in us just waiting to become active when the time is right."

"That`s a very disturbing thought, doctor." Rodger squirmed in his chair uncomfortably.

Helen and the technician re-entered the office interrupting their conversation. Accepting the x-rays from the tchnician, Dr Barklay stood and placed them onto the light window, studying them intently. "Helen, you have the early stages of tuberculosis, but let me explain what that means."

"Oh God," Rodger interrupted grabbing Helen into his arms. "How could I have done this to you?"

Helen shuddered, surrendering for a moment, to the warmth and support of Rodger`s body as she tried to assimilate what the doctor had said, what Rodger was saying. Slipping out of Rodger`s embrace, she sank into a nearby chair. Glancing first towards the doctor and then at Rodger, a sad smile replaced her look of bewilderment. "We really are in this together aren`t we love?"

"I never should have trusted my doctor`s diagnosis," he fumed. "What can be done for Helen, Doctor?"

Moving to her side, Dr. Barklay took Helen`s hand gently in to his own. "This isn`t the end of the world. We`ve detected this early on, and with today`s advanced medicines, your chances of a full recovery are excellent." He turned to Rodger, "However, you`ll need to hold up on the trip a little while. I need to prescribe medicine for Helen and have her around for at least three days to see how she responds; we can start treatment today."

The room was silent as the three exchanged glances, each trying to read one another`s thoughts. Rodger was the first to speak. "We`ll do whatever is best for Helen; the trip can wait."

Helen rose from her chair and crossing over to Rodger, took his hand; her eyes searching deeply into his. "We`ll do what the doctor says Rodg, but the trip doesn`t have to be put off for very long. I have a healthy constitution. I`m sure I can beat this thing."

"You`re so brave, Helen. You know what T.B. can do to a person by looking at me."

"I`ve been looking at you for a month, and I`m in love with what I see." She turned back to Dr. Barklay. "Give me the prescriptions doctor; I want to go back to the Sea Witch and lie down. This has turned out to be a fatiguing day after all."

"Keep in mind that you will be contagious until the medication takes effect." Dr. Barklay advised. "That is another reason I want you here. Stay away from people until you come back to see me in three days. I could have you hospitalized, but, if you`ll quarantine yourself on your boat, that will be sufficient. Just stay away from everyone, except Rodger," he cautioned.

The doctor left the room and soon returned with two prescription bottles. Helen fought to regain and maintain her composure; Rodger held her hand. The doctor stated, "This is Isoniazid and Pyrazinamide. Take it according to the directions on the bottles. Here are some up-to-date brochures concerning tuberculosis and an explanation of the medicines I have perscribed."

Helen exclaimed, "I had no idea tuberculosis was so prevalent in the world, nor so easily cured, if caught in time. Did you know that, Rodger?"

"I knew there are a lot of us with tuberculosis," Rodger replied, "but I had no idea it was so common. It used to be called consumption, I`m told. I just wish I`d been diagnosed sooner." He dropped his handhold and put his arm around Helen`s waist, "We`ll get back to the Sea Witch now and follow your directions, Doctor. Is it okay to walk to the marina or should we take a taxi cab?"

"It`s only three blocks," replied the doctor. "Walk, just avoid close contact with people, even cab drivers. They won`t get infected by touching you or things that you have touched. It`s enough if you stay away from people."

Helen held out her hand to the doctor, "Thanks for picking up on this; I`ll try to be a good patient," she added brightly as she looked up at Rodger. "Rodg, and I will see this through."

"Right, Helen, we`ll see it through. From now on or at least for awhile, I`ll not only be your deck hand, but your nurse."

"O.K. nurse, let`s get back to the Sea Witch. I need some T.L.C."

"Really?" replied Rodger smiling.

"Not that kind, Rodg."

Chapter Twenty

Awaking early the next morning Rodger lay silently beside Helen listening to her rhythmic breathing. Careful not to disturb her, he slid one leg over the edge of the bed. Helen stirred, "Good morning love," she murmured. "Don`t get up, I want to talk to you."

"What about, Sweetie?"

"I want to know about tuberculosis. I know what the doctor said, but you have the disease, so what didn`t he tell me?"

Rodger rolled up on one elbow to face Helen, "I`ve learned there are ten to fifteen million Americans infected, but only ten percent will get sick from it. Unfortunately, you and I are in the ten percent group. Being detected early, you`ll get well as long as you take your medicine. On the other hand, I may, or may not, beat this thing, according to what Dr. Barclay said yesterday. That`s better news than what I've been living with the past few months."

Helen rolled on her side facing Rodger, "How come we don`t hear about tuberculosis? I thought it was a thing of the past, like polio."

"Unfortunately, after thirty years of decline, T.B. is on the increase in the United States and around the world. In 1993 the World Health Organization declared tuberculosis as a global emergency because it claims more lives than any other infectious disease."

"Just our luck," sighed Helen. "How come Dr.Barclay said I might not have gotten it from you?"

"According to what I've read, a healthy adult, being exposed for twenty-four hours a day to a contagious carrier has a 50% chance of getting it. The contagious carrier didn`t have to be me, but it probably was. I hate the thought that I could have been the one who infected you. It just so happens, I had an advanced case before I knew what was wrong with me. I`ve always hated going to doctors and I kept putting it off. I couldn`t get rid of my cough, and it wasn`t until I started spitting up blood that I went to see Doctor Smith in Bellevue."

Helen pushed Rodger back on the bed and rolled over on him. Gently placing a kiss on each eyelid, the tip of his nose, and his mouth, "Don`t be too hard on yourself, Rodg; I have it, and I`ll do what ever is necessary to get rid of it."

Rodger wrapped his arms around her pulling her body down firmly on his. "The doctor said he wants to see you in three days, if the medicine does its job, you`ll not be contagious to anyone. I`ll get up now, if you`ll let me, and fix breakfast so you can take your medicine."

"Did I ever tell you you're a spoilsport?"

Rodger laughed, "Under different circumstances, believe me, I wouldn`t be." Rodger kissed her softly and extracting himself from their embrace saying, "It`s amazing that Dr. Barclay`s pharmacist said thirty dollars worth of medicine will not only control tuberculosis, but will usually cure it. Unfortunately, not everyone in the world who has been infected with T.B. has thirty dollars for the medicine."

"That is sad isn`t it? I have thirty dollars, so let`s get on with our lives. I`ll have eggs, bacon, hash-browns, and toast, if you please."

"That`s my skipper. In the meantime, lie there and enjoy your forced convalescence."

"Ugh! I just realized I can`t leave the boat to even take a shower. This isn`t going to be much fun."

"It beats being in isolation in a hospital room, and I`ll serve you better food. I`ll put on the coffee and head for the showers via the sailmaker`s van. He`ll be wondering why we didn`t show up yesterday for the dodger. Then, I`ll fix breakfast."

"Okay Mate, I`ll just lie here like a slug and read until breakfast is ready."

Rodger gathered fresh clothing, his shaving kit, and headed for the van. Boaters, taking advantage of the unusually warm days for

September, crowded the marina. At full tide, with some boaters going out to cruise on the ocean and others going up the Yaquina for a day on the river, the bay bustled with activity.

The van sat in its usual place on the far side of the parking lot with a large sign painted on its side that read, *Charlie`s Sails and Accessories*. Rodger walked around to the back of the van and called, "Ahoy there."

An angry voice boomed from the van`s interior. "What happened to your need for a rush order on the dodger? It was ready for you yesterday afternoon."

"We had an unexpected change of plans," Rodger explained. "Helen was told by a doctor to go to bed for three days."

Charie`s head appeared through the van`s rear opening. "Nothing serious, I hope," the anger now dissipating from his voice.

Avoiding the truth, Rodger replied, "No, she just needs to rest for a few days before we continue our trip to Tahiti."

"Tahiti is it? I spent a week in jail there once, back in my misspent younger days. Nothing serious, just a typical bar fight."

"Were you a sailor in the Navy, or a civilian sailor?" Rodger asked, relieved at Charlies change of attitude.

"I`ve been both, but at that time I was a civilian crewing out on a sixty- three footer out of New York. If I`d been in the Navy, the shore patrol would have sprung me out of the local jail in no time. Of course, they would have put me in the brig aboard ship. It`s still confinement, but the food is a hell of a lot better, and the company is more selective."

Rodger turned to leave, "I`m on my way to the showers; I can pay you now and pick up the dodger on the way back to the Sea Witch."

Charlie stepped down and out of his van.onto the asphalt of the parking lot. "I`ll carry it to your boat while you shower. I can just hang around there until you get back, and you can pay me then."

"Well, O.K, but don`t disturb Helen, she`s sleeping."

"No problem." Charlie chuckled at the apprehension he heard in Rodger`s voice.

Rodger quickened his stride as he walked to the shower area. He liked Charlie, but he didn`t totally trust a guy with all those tattoos, a ponytail, and for sure one who had been in jail in Tahiti. Rodger showered, but didn`t linger. Dressing quickly, he finished with his toiletries in record time. As he neared the Sea Witch, he saw Charlie sitting on the rail near the cockpit smoking a cigarette and apparently enjoying the beauty of the day.

"Hi Skipper," he called out as Rodger approached.

"You beat me here; I appreciate your delivery of the dodger, but I didn`t mean to interrupt your work this long."

"I needed a break from my van, especially on such a beautiful day. I haven`t heard anything from below, so I guess your lady is still sleeping. Charlie slipped from the railing and stooped to pick up a box and the dodger lying at his feet. I brought along tools needed to install the dodger in case you want me to do it. I work cheap on a day like this, if it were raining, the price would be higher."

Rodger laughed. "How much is cheap, Charlie?"

"Twenty five dollars would bring your tab up to an even three hundred dollars."

"You`re hired. What about tax?"

"Not in Oregon, we pay a state income tax, but no sales tax." Charlie moved the dodger parts aboard as he spoke.

"That sounds good for the out-of-state tourists. How do you feel about it, Charlie?"

"I don`t have a big income, so it`s better for me," he said moving his toolbox closer to the job.

Helen stuck her head out of the hatch opening and surveyed the scene before her. "How can a lady sleep when there is all this talk going on outside her bedroom?"

"Sorry Skipper. Charlie`s here with the dodger, he`ll install it while I fix brunch."

"All right, I`ll go back and lie down."

"You called her Skipper?"

"Do I have to go through this with you, too? Dorm Stillwell had the same question yesterday. What`s with you guys? Haven`t you ever heard of a woman skipper before?"

Charlie stopped working and faced Rodger. "Well, for sure it would be a problem for Dorm, he hates women. Now me… I love women. I only have trouble with it because skippering a sailboat requires a lot of knowledge and some strength."

Rodger grinned, "Helen has both, believe me."

"Okay, you ought to know," replied Charlie returning to his work. "It`s just that we haven`t had many women skippers around here. I might go back to sea myself, if I could find a woman like that."

Rodger went below to fix breakfast while Charlie continued installing the dodger. He expected to see Helen lying not sitting on the divan. "You`re supposed to be in bed."

"I`m tired of the bed and it feels good to be up and clean after my sponge bath. Now, what do I do for the rest of the day?"

"Stay quiet and after breakfast go back to your reading. Dr. Barclay says rest is very important at this stage of the illness."

Helen busied herself setting the table while Rodger made breakfast of oatmeal, toast, and coffee. "I wonder what he meant when he said some authorities think each of us has a spot, or flaw, in us that could do us in, if conditions were right?"

"We`ll ask him when we see him day after tomorrow. By the way, I didn`t see you take your pills?"

"Okay nurse, I`ll take my pills if you`ll give me a hug. I feel a need for more tender loving care."

Rodger wrapped his arms around Helen and held her tight, thrilling as her body pulsated against his. Gently pushing her head back, he kissed her firmly, but lovingly, on the mouth.

"Hey you two," Charlie yelled down the open hatch. "I`m outta here."

Rodger helped Helen settle back on the divan and then went topside to pay Charlie. After a quick inspection, he turned to the sailmaker, "The dodger looks good. I`m sure there`ll be times when we`ll really appreciate the protection it`ll give us. Here`s your money and thanks for the rush job, even though, as it worked out, we didn`t need a rush job."

"Okay Skipper, …er, I mean Mate." Charlie shook his head and grinned. "No sir, I never did see a skipper like her."

Chapter Twenty-One

Rodger called a taxi to take them to their appointment with Dr. Barclay. The receptionist, who hadn`t been there on the first visit, greeted Helen and Rodger and then escorted them to the doctor`s private office. Dr. Barclay rose as they entered. "It`s good to see you looking so well, Helen. Rodger must be a good nurse."

"He is a good nurse."

Dr. Barclay continued, "I`ll need to have some blood work done and an x-ray before we can say for sure the treatment is effective. He paged his nurse on the intercom, "Mary, would you take care of Helen`s testing and x-ray? Helen, come back here as soon as Mary is through with you. He turned to Rodger, "You and I will have to wait here for the results."

Once Mary escorted Helen from the office, Dr. Barclay sat back in his chair interweaving his hands behind his head. He signaled Rodger with a nod to have a seat opposite him. "So, you two are headed for Tahiti, sounds like a wonderful adventure. Have you made any other trips like this?"

"This will be a first," replied Rodger not sure where the conversation was going. "Helen is the skipper, and I`m the mate. She and her deceased husband sailed for ten years around the Northwest before I bought the boat from her, as I wanted to satisfy a long held fantasy of sailing to Tahiti. When Helen discovered I wasn`t much of a sailor, she offered to skipper the boat for me." Rodger was beginning to feel more comfortable as the doctor continued his questioning.

"Really! How big is this sailboat?"

"It`s a thirty-one foot Tahiti Ketch, but it has the latest instrumentation."

"Thirty-one feet, that`s not very big for such a long, ocean-crossing. However, smaller boats have done it. I just hope Helen is going to be strong enough for the trip. Her cure requires not only medication, but also moderate activity."

"We`re both going to be disappointed if we have to postpone this trip, however, you`re the doctor. We`ll let you tell us what is possible. Incidently, the other day you made a statement that puzzled us. You said some authorities think that within each of us is a spot or a flaw that could bring about our demise."

"That`s the theory," replied Dr. Barklay, mentally shifting to this new subject. "I believe that within every person there is a weak spot or flaw, which could be his or her undoing. I probably shouldn`t have mentioned it, as it`s only a theory. However, it doesn`t just pertain to physical health, but can include mental health as well," he continued warming up to the subject.

I first read about this in the writings of the Scottish New Testament Interpreter, William Barclay," he smiled. "I would like to think he`s a relative of mine, but who knows? Anyway, he was talking about temptation, which, is usually a mental thing, but tied to the physical. He says temptation, such as is common to man, comes not only from outside us, and it also comes from within us. He says if there were nothing in us to which temptation could appeal, it would be helpless to defeat us." The doctor continued his relaxed sitting position in his chair. "Barkley concludes by saying that in every one of us there is a weak spot or flaw; and at that spot, temptation launches its attack."

"Really! Are you saying that we all have a predisposition to some flaw of character or a physical flaw, or both."

"Yes, but can I prove it? No."

"Well, it`s something to think about." *Where is he going with this?* Rodger wondered.

"Yes, it is...isn`t it." Dr. Barklay stood as he heard footsteps approaching from the hallway.

Helen and Mary entered the room bringing an end to this unusual conversation. Mary handed the doctor two documents and left the room. Glancing over the page, he turned to Helen, "Good news! The medication is effective. You should be able to continue your adventure, as long as Rodger does the heavy work for awhile."

Rodger gave Helen a hug, both breathing an audible sigh of relief. Rodger grinned at Helen, "We`ll leave tomorrow, if that`s okay with you Skipper?"

"Based on what Dr. Barclay said, I guess I should turn the command over to you, Rodg. You`ve been a good student, and I think you can sail the Sea Witch, even without me if you have to."

Stepping back, Rodger took Helen`s hand in his, "Probably so," he said softly, "but I don`t want to ever sail without you. As far as I`m concerned, you will always be my skipper."

"Then your skipper says, we sail at morning slack-tide, weather permitting."

"Aye, Aye Skipper," replied Rodger smiling.

Chapter Twenty-Two

Rodger opened his eyes to find Helen smiling down at him. "Okay sleepy head, it`s time to hit the deck."

"What time is it?" Rodger muttered as he rolled over.

"Six-thirty and slack tide is at eight o`clock." Helen ignored Rodger`s groan. "We`ll have to scramble to catch it as it only lasts an hour."

"What`s so critical about slack tide?" Rodger yawned, still groggy from sleep.

"Did you notice the water conditions under the bridge when we came in four days ago?"

"Yes, I remember it was turbulent, and the tide pushed us in at quite a clip."

"That`s what we don`t want going out. If we can`t have it going our direction, we want slack water for an easy exit."

"Okay, have it your way, Skipper. I`ll start breakfast while you shower. Rodger rolled out of bed, and in one motion he was on his feet and wrapped Helen in his arms. "I`m pleased we can return to the ocean today and be real sailors again. But most of all, I`m happy you`re on the mend, and back to your normal, sweet, loving, fascinating self."

"Hold it! Let`s not get carried away, Mate," Helen countered. "Remember, I`m the skipper first, and your bunk-mate second."

"Not in my book," Rodger grinned. "Go get your shower and we`ll finish this discussion later."

Helen grabbed her toiletries and disappeared up the companionway to the deck. While Rodger dressed, he mentally put together the ingredients for breakfast. *Let`s see: eggs, bacon, hash browns, toast, juice and coffee. That ought to take the wrinkles out of our stomach.* Returning to the galley area, he lit the oil cook stove and set the coffee pot on to perk. Sticking his head out of the hatch, he studied the sky. Cloud formations to the west, and the feel of a cool breeze on his face told him it should be a good day on the water. Returning to the salon, he switched on the radio for the weather report.

The coffee had finished perking, and Rodger immediately filled his mug. Putting two frying pans on the stovetop, he laced one with bacon, the other with hash browns. Placing the sour dough bread slices on a clean area of the stovetop for toasting, he decided to hold up on the eggs. Everything was nearly done when he heard Helen`s footsteps on the dock`s floating walkway. Pushing the bacon aside he broke two eggs and dropped them into the same pan.

Helen paused on the steps of the companionway, "Oh my, that smells wonderful!" Continuing into the salon, she rose on tiptoe to kiss Rodger`s cheek, "I`ve said it before and I`ll say it again, you are a keeper, Rodg."

"I`d like to think that my attributes go beyond my culinary skills."

"Take it from me, Mate, they do. When God made you, she threw away the mold."

"She? Uh-huh, for right now I`ll settle for the compliment intended."

After they finished breakfast, Rodger headed for the shower. While Helen did the cleanup she listened to the weather report on the radio. The forcast was mixed: winds from the south at ten to twenty miles per hour and with possible squalls. *We`ll have the winds to move us even if they are hitting us on* the nose, however *we just may get wet in the process. Two-days should put us in Eureka where there`s a well-equipped marina the book says. It`s two hundred nautical miles, but that should be within our ability. If all goes well, we`ll be there in forty-eight hours.*

The Sea Witch rolled gently as Rodger stepped aboard returning from the showers.

"My, don`t you look nice in your clean blue denims, and matching ironed shirt. You`ll have to give me the name of your launderess."

"I sent our things to the local laundry while you were convalescing. If you`ll look in the forward hanging locker you`ll find your laundry, clean and pressed."

Helen flung her arms around his neck, "How thoughtful of you, love," she sighed. Their long embrace ended only after she playfully pushed him away. "Go topside and get the deck ready for departure, while I change into my freshly laundered clothes."

On deck, Rodger took the jib sail out of the sail bag, fastened it to the forestay, and then took the cover off the mainsail and the mizzen sail. Once the lines were in their proper places, all was ready for sailing. Starting the engine, he returned to the empty salon, "Ready when you are Skipper."

Helen emerged from the salon dressed now in crisp, pressed, blue denims and shirt, then Pirouetting like a model, she showed off her fresh wardrobe. "Thanks for your thoughtfulness, Mate."

Rodger, running an appreciative eye over her trim figure, said "My pleasure, Skipper, I guess it`s time we shoved off, if you say slack tide starts in fifteen minutes. It`ll take that long to get to the bridge."

Taking her place at the helm, Helen eased the gearshift into reverse. The Sea Witch slowly backed out of the berth and into the waterway leading out of the marina and into Yaquina Bay. Most of the fishing fleet had gone out several hours earlier and were either on their way to the fishing grounds, already fishing, hauling in crab pots, or reeling out long lines. The commercial boats were spread out across the water as far as the eye could see.

The arched bridge loomed high overhead, and a few tourists could be seen standing at the railing watching boats go out to the ocean or to return. The outgoing river current, although countered by the incoming ocean waves, still helped move the Sea Witch several knots faster. Rodger stood on the deck ready to raise the mainsail on command, as the breeze gave a promise of good sailing conditions. Helen, standing with the tiller directly behind her, determined when the wind would be strong enough to let it take over. When satisfied, she called out, "Hoist the sails."

With Helen holding the bow directly into the wind Rodger grabbed the mainsail halyard and, hand-over-hand, raised the sail until it reached the top of the mast. Cleating it off, he then raised the mizzen sail and jib. Caught by the head-on force of the wind, the sails luffed vigorously, like a dog shaking a rag. When Helen let the Sea Witch fall off the wind, it caused the sails to billow out to port side. Taking the slack out of the mainsail with the winch, she checked the tell-tails. They were now parallel to each other. Completing the task by tightening the boomvang, which gave added downward pressure on the mainsail, thus tightening it further. Helen was now satisfied it was drawing well.

Rodger tended the jib and the mizzen sails in a similar manner. Turning off the engine, it was possible to hear the soothing hum of the wind in the sails and the rhythmic lapping of the waves against the hull, which replaced the chugga-chugga-chugga sound of the small diesel engine.

They smiled at one another sharing the satisfaction of a job well done. "Hurrah!" shouted Helen to Rodger, "we`re sailing again."

Rodger stood and raised his arms skyward in a sign of victory.

"You know, Rodg, I think we have a good thing going here. High adventure, good companionship, good food, good weather, and a good ship beneath our feet."

"You`re right, Skipper." He then settled back on the high side of the cockpit bench seat to be near Helen, but out of the way. "What`s the name of that mountain off to port, Skipper?"

"That`s Mary`s Peak, and according to the U.S. Coast Pilot book, it`s about 4,100 feet high and although the sides are covered with trees, the top isn`t. I guess the timber line in this part of the world must peter out around 4000 ft."

The coastline became more rugged as they progressed farther south. Jagged promentaries and isolated offshore rock islands became the norm. Beaches were limited to coves and inlets. Only near the occasional seaside town were houses evident.

"It`s good to be on our journey again, and it won`t be long until we`ll be looking at palm trees instead of fir, pine and cedar trees."

"Rodg, would you take the tiller?" Helen`s voice suddenly seemed weak, "I need to go below and lie down awhile, as I don`t have my sea legs yet and I`m feeling woozy."

"You bet, Skipper. Rodger was on his feet and at her side. I want you to always tell me when you need to rest, and I`ll take the watch. After you feel better, you can sail up until dark, and then relieve me at daybreak. During the day we can spell each other," said Rodger, his eyes showing concern, "and don`t forget to take your medicine."

Once in the comfort of the salon, Helen took her midday pills and then stretched out on the divan. Watching the overhead lamp`s hypnotic swaying, she slowly drifted into sleep.

Her dreams were helter-skelter at first, but soon included Rodger, the Sea Witch, and the adventure that they were on. Except the adventure wasn`t the sea voyage to Tahiti, but the adventure of their love affair. She saw herself standing, on a high rise of land bordering the sea, beside a stone cottage trimmed in white. Dressed in a frilly dress, not dungarees; she was running diwn a path towards Rodger, who appeared to be returning home at the end of a workday. Suddenly, above and behind him threatening storm clouds appeared to be bearing down on him. As they were about to consume him, she cried out a warning that awakened her to the sound of her own voice.

While on deck, Rodger heard her cry out. "Are you all right?" he called down the companionway.

Sitting in a huddled position on the edge of the bed with her head in her hands, she fought to regain her composure. *The dream that had started out so beautiful, ended so frighteningly. What could it mean?* she puzzled.

Rodger scrambled down the steps to the salon. "What`s wrong? My God, you look as if you`ve seen a ghost."

"Oh, Rodg, my dream was so beautiful in the beginning, but became so frightening." Rodger sat down holding her in an embrace as she explained; "We lived in a cottage on a high bluff, overlooking the sea. I was running down a path to meet you, that`s the good part, then I saw this ominous black cloud forming behind you and moving like it would envelope you. That`s when I cried out…to warn you. It was scary."

"Well, love, I appreciate your concern for me," Rodger soothed, "but all dream's don`t come true. It probably just reflects your fear that the beautiful life we`re experiencing now could come to an end somehow."

"Yes, I suppose you're right, but it could be a forewarning of something?"

"Why don`t you lie down again and see if you can continue your nap."

"Absolutely not! I`ve had enough of that dream. What`s for lunch?" she demanded; determined to change the subject.

"How about a tuna fish sandwich, chips and coffee?" Rodger said as he rose from the bed and moved toward the galley.

"Sounds good; has the wind held while I slept?"

"Yes, we`ve been averaging 5 knots. A cloud layer has moved in overhead, but nothing to be concerned about."

"Good; if you`ll fix lunch, I`ll take the watch. The autp pilot and the GPS can only sail her successfully if there`s nothing in the way."

"You and I know Genie really needs us: she can`t chart her course, set her sails, or run the engine," replied Rodger trying to be light-hearted to help Helen`s mood.

"Okay Rodg," she laughed, "I`m coninced we`re still in control, but how about that lunch, I`m starved, and Genie can`t do anything about that either."

Chapter Twenty-Three

After lunch Rodger slept while Helen scanned the water ahead watching for dead heads and other obstacles, and at the same time monitor Genie`s readings. The weather remained overcast and the breeze held steady at fifteen knots out of the southwest. *This is a great day,* thought Helen. *It doesn`t get any better than this. Rodger`s tuberculosis is in remission, our relationship is wonderful, and the Sea Witch is handling beautifully.*

I`m able to function at about eighty percent of my former strength and endurance, so with the aide of our new electronics, we should be able reach Tahiti. Even if we have to buck heavy weather on the open ocean, working together, we should be able to handle it. Even a knockdown, as the hull is self-righting. While I appreciate Rodger`s offer to stand a long night watch without a break, it`s not necessary; Rodger has a health problem of his own.

The seduction of the continuous lapping of the waves against the hull drew Helen into a deeper state of euphoria. *How I love that man and what a future we can have together, if only his tuberculosis remains in remission.*

Suddenly a strong surge of wind in the sails brought Helen to full-attention. She gasped as the Sea Witch quickly heeled over an additional fifteen degrees, putting the rail in the water. *The sails need adjusting... now,* her mind shouted. Quickly and expertly she let out the lines spilling wind from the sails. Soon the tell-tales were parallel, and the list of the hull was less threatening. The sudden gust of wind had been violent enough to roll Rodger out of bed. He lay there momentarily bringing his thoughts into focus. *What`s going on?* he thought. Groggily he slipped into his deck shoes and struggled topside.

"What`s up Skipper?"

"We`ve got a problem! A weather front hit us right on the nose. I guess I was daydreaming and didn`t see it coming. Go below and get a weather report on the radio; we need to know what`s going on up ahead and what to expect."

"Aye, aye, Skipper," Rodger, yelled over his shoulder as he ducked below deck. *Helen looks worried; this must be serious.* Hastily he turned the radio to the weather station; the report was out of Eureka, California this time instead of Vancouver, Canada. An offshore low-pressure area is moving rapidly up the coast around Point Arena, the newscaster announced, bringing 30 to 40 knot winds from the southwest. Scrambling back up the steps to the deck, Rodger relayed the information to Helen.

"This will be a real blow," she shouted. "We`ll have to turn into the wind to douse the jib and mizzen sail, but first go below and get the storm jib out of the sail locker."

"Aye, aye, Skipper." Rodger returned shortly with a smaller sail to take the place of the larger Genoa jib. Dropping the jib, he quickly unhooked the metal hanks from the forestay and replaced it with the storm jib. Raising it, he watched it luff violently as the Sea Witch continued to plow head-on into the wind and waves. Releashing the boomvang, he lowered the mainsail to be able to double-reef it. When hoisted again, it was a quarter of its former size.

Rodger dropped the mizzen sail, flaking and tying it securely to the mizzen boom. Helen let the Sea Witch`s bow drop off to the wind allowing the storm jib and the reefed mainsail to fill with air; they now had forward motion and steerage.

"Good job, Mate! Take the tiller, I`ll go below and get our foul weather gear. There`ll be rain with this front coming at us." Changing places, Helen descended to the salon and then forward to the V-berth area. Taking out the yellow slickers, bib overalls, sou`wester hats, and boots from a hanging locker, she thought, *I`ve never experienced anything like this before; I hope I can handle it.* Donning her own gear quickly, she hurried topside.

Helen took over the tiller while Rodger hastily climbed into his foul weather gear and life jacket. "We`ve got to change course ten degrees to get more distance between us and the coastline. Be ready to tend the sails, as I swing the bow to starboard. The wind has been shifting from southwest to south, so we must be off Point Arena. After you trim the sails, Rodg, go below and dog down all the portholes. We`ll put the hatch boards in the cabin opening when you get back. I wish we had harnesses; we would put them on and clip ourselves to a lifeline. That`s something we`ll have to get in Eureka for the next storm."

"Aye, aye, Skipper, anything else?"

"Yes, secure things below as best you can, then come back to the cockpit, and we`ll ride this out together. It might be a wild dance, Rodg, but I think we`re ready for it."

Sounds of the wind in the rigging steadily increased, building into a crescendo known only to seamen under heavy weather conditions. The building waves, huge, turbulent, dark-green walls of water, rose above the Sea Witch. Like cruel sea monsters, they advanced upon the small craft and its occupants as if determined to swallow them up.

The bow of the Sea Witch climbed doggedly, steadily to the top of each wave, breaking through just before the peak; then starting its slide down the backside into the trough, only to face another oncoming mountainous wall of water. The strong winds blowing off the top edge of the waves produced a spray of white water and frothy foam; the spindrift, hurtling through the air like missiles, splatting against the dodger and anything else in its way.

At the tiller, Helen held the Sea Witch on its course. From the other side of the tiller, Rodger watched her as she commanded the boat to her bidding in defiance of the shrieking wind and the unrelenting waves; he knew his turn would come.

"Tell me when you want me to take over, Skipper."

"Not yet! Let`s hope it doesn`t get any worse." She fought to keep the bow between fifteen and twenty degrees off the wind for steerage and forward movement. The wind wanted to push the Sea Witch broadside into a knockdown, so it was important they keep steerage, which they had only if they kept moving forward. Rodger continued to tend the jib and reefed main sheet by use of the winches; ready to immediately let up on them to spill air from the sails, if need be. Failing to do this, the Sea Witch would heel over too far and take a knockdown.

"I`ve changed my mind," Helen suddenly shouted. "Take the tiller, while I go below. I`m going to send a May Day message to the Coast Guard. This is getting worse by the minute."

"Aye, aye, Skipper." Rodger quickly took Helen's place at the helm, standing now as he firmly gripped the tiller. Helen ducked down in the protection of the dodger for a moment, turned, facing Rodger, silently mouthed, "I love you."

Rodger smiled and shouted, "I love you, too."

Removing the hatch boards from the cabin opening, Helen disappeared below deck. The wind howled like a wild banshee in the rigging; the relentless, powerful waves continued to build. Rodger left the tiller momentarily as he put the hatch boards back in place, thus making the cabin watertight. To keep from being thrown overboard, he sat down on the cockpit bench seat firmly holding the tiller with both hands as his adrenaline pumped and his senses heightened. He`d never know such exhileration. Throwing back his head, and facing into the stinging spray, he shouted to the storm Gods, "Is this your best shot you sons-a- bitches?"

Holding the tiller, Rodger could feel the strength of the Sea Witch through his arms and shoulders as she valiantly dove time and again headlong into the monster waves. In his inner being, he had become an integral part of this gallant craft. Then, momentarily, he felt the ultimate power of being in total control… until he saw the huge, powerful wall of water coming at him, twice as high as the last, just as it crashed over him.

The Sea Witch shuddered from stem to stern. The bow, fighting its way out of the maelstrom, kept raising… too far… going over backwards. Turbulent, angry waters tore Rodger`s hands from the tiller; he felt the stern fall beneath his feet. As his arms thrashed desperately to keep his head above the sucking, swirling water, the bow came crashing down on him. Mast and rigging, torn loose from the deck, hit him broadside taking him away with them… where he sank slowly and lifelessly into the ocean depths.

Chapter Twenty-Four

Helen sat, staring into the flames of the granite stone fireplace in her parent`s living room. Her teenage niece and nephew, Joanie and Gregory, sat eagerly at her feet waiting for her to resume her story of the shipwreck she had endured two months earlier.

"Please, Aunt Helen, tell us what happened next? We know some of the story, but we want all of it," pleaded Gregory.

"You ask your questions, and I`ll answer the best I can," replied Helen, "as you know I had a concussion and was unconscious during the shipwreck." Helen sat back more relaxed now. "In fact, I was unconscious for several days."

"Yes, we know that," Joanie said, "but what caused the shipwreck?"

"A rogue wave hit us head on. The Sea Witch tried to climb the giant wall of water, but the wave was too tall, too powerful. I remember sitting at the ship`s radio one minute, in the next I was falling as the Sea Witch went over backwards. I slammed into the bulkhead across the salon; then all went black. When I awoke in the hospital, they told me I had been unconscious for two days."

Gregory, looking up into his aunt`s eyes, asked, "What happened to Rodger?"

Helen, fighting to control her emotions, replied, "Rodger was never found. The coast guard and others searched for days, but never located a trace of him. I`m told drowning is not such a bad way to leave this earth, but oh, how I miss him."

Joanie sat down in a chair beside Helen and extending her arm tenderly around her aunt. "What about the Sea Witch? What happened to it?"

"Actually, she was pitch-poled. That`s when a boat goes over backwards, then usually rights itself after a short time, if it`s a self-righting hull, and the Sea Witch was. The pitch-poling took away her masts and swept her deck clean. Rodger had put the hatch boards in after I went below deck; this sealed the cabin and saved my life. The rocking motion of the waves and the heavy keel caused her to right herself, and the coast Guard found us soon after the storm, even though I hadn`t had time to send a `May Day` message."

"Where is the Sea Witch now?" asked Gregory as he continued to sit looking up at his aunt.

"Rodger had willed the Sea Witch to me, and since I decided to give up sailing for good I soon discovered I couldn`t bring myself to sell her. The Sea Witch is the only part of Rodger I can hold on to. An old seaman I met in Westport lives aboard her now at Coos Bay, Oregon. Aaron Bradley admired the boat and was in need of a home, so I invited him to live aboard and be its caretaker. He collects shells and paints the likeness of ships on them, like that shell over there on the fireplace mantel. It was a gift from him when he and I first met."

"Did he know about the shipwreck?" Joanie asked.

"No, not until I recovered from my injuries and drove to Westport to find him. There he was at the base of the observation tower with his shells spread out for sale, just as I`d left him. He was delighted to move aboard a ship again, even without masts. The Sea Witch will probably never sail again, but she`ll be home to an old sailor who appreciates and loves her. When Aaron Bradley is gone, I may move aboard her myself. I thought about scuttling her, but changed my mind. She wouldn`t be joining Rodger at the bottom of the ocean, he`s not there. His spirit has gone on, and I pray that we`ll meet again."

"What about Rodger`s family?" continued Joanie.

"They grieve for Rodger, just as I do. They had a memorial service for him; I was invited, but chose not to attend.

"Why not, Aunt Helen? Why didn`t you attend; I thought you loved him?" Gregory questioned.

Helen stood to emphasize what she was about to say, "I did love him, and I do love him. Someday you may understand. I had my own private memorial service for him. Rodger never made it to Tahiti, but he told me a few days before the shipwreck of a revelation he had.

He said to me, "If we never see Tahiti, this voyage has been far more than I`d ever hoped for. It`s been a great adventure, but I've discovered that the greatest adventure of all is a love affair."

CHAPTER TWENTY-FIVE

Elbows on the bar, he studied the contents of his beer glass, then glanced again toward the woman sitting alone in the corner booth. He`d noticed her staring at him and wondered if she was someone he knew? He`d not gotten used to people staring at him, but at least he understood why. He was shocked anew each time he looked in the mirror and saw the angry red scar slashing upward from his cheekbone, across his temple, and disappearing beneath the protective helmet his doctor had ordered him to wear. That might be why the woman was staring, and yet there was something familiar about her. Was she someone he`d known before the amnesia. *Does she recognize me*? He had to find out.

Slidding from the barstool, he made his way across the room, pausing in front of the auburn-haired woman in the corner booth. His eyes searched the woman`s ruddy face, her grey-green eyes, then...the name slipped from his lips, "Helen?" It sounded almost like a plea. Startled, the woman, whose eyes widened like a frightened deer about to bolt to safety, sat riveted in her chair not answering.

Confused, disoriented, he turned on his heels and stumbled out the nearby door into the Monterey afternoon sunshine. Feeling suddenly ill, he leaned against the side of the building.

What made me do such a foolhardy thing? he agonized. *What seemed so familiar about that woman? Why did I call her Helen...Helen?* He lifted his head, pushing himself away from the building. *Wait! Helen.*

Helen and Rodger. I remember…me…I`m Rodger…Rodger McCauley. But what am I doing here…I remember…a storm…something striking me on the head…I remember. I need to sit down.

Stumbling to a nearby park bench, Rodger sank to its sitting surface. *That`s better… I have to remember… the storm…a sailboat…a wave, bigger than we could rise above… coming at us…Helen and me. Helen? Who`s Helen? … My Skipper… my lover. Oh my God…where is Helen? Is she alive? Below deck…I remember…she`d gone below deck… to radio an S.O.S..*

Rodger pressed his fingers against the throbbing in his temples, it`s all so hazy. I know I now live with other people at a place called Johnson House. I…I remember going there from the hospital. But how did I end up in the hospital? What was it they told me? Oh, yes. A fishing boat crew found me floating face up; picked me out of the water more dead than alive off the Oregon coast… cargo hold full of fish… had to continue on to their fish buyer…Monterey… lucky wearing a life jacket. Rodger`s hands dropped to his lap. *Monterey! That`s in California… hundreds of miles south of where the storm hit us.*

Rodger stared out across the waters of the bay trying to organize the rush of sudden memories exploding like fireworks in his brain. *Amnesia, the doctor says I have amnesia. Tuberculosis, he`d mentioned I have tuberculosis that seems to be in remission. I think I need to get back to the Johnson house, get my head together to find out about Helen.*

Rising stiffly to his feet, Rodger made his way along the familiar two blocks that had been his whole world until just a few minutes ago; Johnson House, the tavern, and the two-block walk between. Nearing the two story white frame house, suddenly he stopped short. *I remember another house. A woman…Irene… people there…my family.* His knees threatened to buckle again; he staggered to the edge of the walk, clutching the boards of the picket fence bordering the carefully tended yard. *Oh my God. My family. They must think I`m dead. And Helen---if she`s alive. She thinks I`m dead too.*

Bill Smith, Johnson House`s manager, sat at his desk sorting through the monthly bills when Rodger burst into the room. “Bill, Bill!” he shouted, “I know who I am.” Rodger leaned over the desk that separated him and Bill, “I know what happened to me. I remember the shipwreck. I need to find out about Helen. You’ve got to help me.”

"Hallellulia! Of course I`ll help you, but first calm down. Bill had risen from his seat and guided Rodger to a chair. "Okay, John, let`s start from the beginning, who are you?"

Rodger sank gratefully into the chair, "Why did you call me John?"

"You've been John Doe to us for the past two months. We`ve been waiting for you to regain your memory and now, you have."

"I`m Rodger McCauley," Rodger began slowly. "Helen and I were sailing to Tahiti. We ran head-on into a storm off the Oregon coast. Helen went below deck to radio for help. The waves were getting higher. I put the hatch boards in place after she went below to keep the water out of the cabin and keep her safe, if we rolled over. Then a gigantic wave, too high to climb ...water`s in my face...a terrible pain in my head. I awoke in the hospital." Rodger stood now looking down at Bill, "Do you know anything about Helen? Did she survive the storm?"

"First, I`m happy to meet you, Rodger McCauley," Bill said extending his hand in greeting. "Second, I know nothing about Helen. We would have known nothing of your shipwreck here. Shipwrecks are common off the Oregon coast, but seldom make our newspapers. Is there any way you can reach your Helen? Do you know her phone number?"

"No, I don`t." Then Rodger`s face brightened, "But, I know where she lives, if she`s still alive."

"Great! We`ll call information, they`ll find it for you."

Bill dialed directory assistance, then handed the phone to Rodger. After Rodger gave the operator the name of the city and state, it seemed an eternity before a crisp voice finally informed him, "Here`s your number."

His hand that held the phone grew moist, his fingers shook as he dialed the number he`d scratched onto the note pad on Bill`s desk. "I pray she`s alive and if she is I hope she doesn`t have a heart attack when she hears my voice," he said to the manager. *What if there`s no answer?* he agonized to himself.

"Want me to stick around?" Bill offered, then in response to Rodger`s negative nod he gave a "good luck" salute and left the room.

With the phone pressed to his ear, Rodger heard the click as the receiver was being lifted at the other end of the line.

"Hello…a woman`s voice…her voice.
Rodger swallowed the sudden lump in his throat. Hello, Helen?"
"Yes."
"This is Rodger."

Chapter Twenty-Six

Pacing the living room area of Monterrey's Johnson House, an outpatient facility, Rodger watched and listened for the arrival of a taxicab. Helen had insisted on flying to see him immediately after his unexpected phone call when she learned that he hadn`t died in the shipwreck as she and the world thought, but was very much alive. Receiving a blow to the head by the broken mainmast during the storm knocking him overboard resulted in a brain concussion and amnesia. After being picked up by a passing fishing boats, Rodger has been hospitalized in Monterrey, California, and only regained his memory yesterday afternoon. He immediately phoned her.

* * *

Helen fidgeted with her clutch bag as the taxi made its way along the ocean boulevard in Monterrey. Slowing down, the taxi driver turned into the circle driveway facing the large, white, three-story house. The sign beside the stairs leading to the front door read *Johnson House Rehabilitation Facility*. Quickly paying the driver, Helen grabbed her overnight bag, and ran up the stairs like a teenager. Rodger met her at the door where they fell into each other`s arms. Tears flowed freely as they shook with emotion, feeling the reality of being together again.

"Oh Rodg, this is a miracle and a prayer come true. How I've grieved for you these past two months." Stepping back, she held Rodger at arm`s length looking at him from head to toe. "I can see the results of your head injury, and you still look good to me."

"I can only imagine what you`ve gone through, Helen, but we`re together now, that`s all that matters." Taking Helen`s bag, Rodger led her into the living room. "Sit here on the couch, Sweetie, we have so much to talk about"

Helen snuggled close to Rodger, "I haven`t been called `Sweetie' for so long. It`s wonderful having you back … tell me what happened."

"For openers, I was lucky to have had a collared lifejacket on when I was swept overboard. It kept my head out of the water when I came to the surface, unconscious. The current carried me quite a distance from the Sea Witch, and I was picked up by a commercial fishing boat bound for here at Monterrey, California. At that point I was more dead than alive. Their radio had been knocked out by the storm, so they had no way of letting anyone know they`d picked me up. With a hold full of fresh-caught fish, time was of the essence for them, so they continued south non-stop.

Helen, turned to face Rodger, "The Coast Guard looked for you for days after the storm subsided. No wonder they didn`t find you, you were five hundred miles south in Monterrey, California."

Rodger, took Helen`s hands in his, "Not only did I have my head laid open, but with amnesia I didn`t know who I was or what happened."

"That must`ve been awful." Helen stood examining the red scar running from his upper cheek into his hairline and along the right side of his head. "You told me on the phone you had to wear a protective helmet. Where is it?"

"It`s not a thing of beauty, so I chose not to wear it at our meeting today. I wanted to look as much like my old charming self as possible."

"Well, Love, you haven`t lost your sense of humor."

"Now that we`re together, I feel totally alive for the first time since the shipwreck."

"Now that we`re together, I feel the same, totally alive."

"I love you Helen, and I want to return home to Bellevue with you as soon as the doctor will release me."

"How long will that be?"

"He said possibly in a few days."

"In the meantime we can pretend we`re on holiday; would you like to see my room?"

"You bet I would." Helen rose from the couch anticipating Rodger`s embrace.

* * *

Returning from the dead has been quite an experience, thought Rodger, as he maneuvered the pickup camper combination south through the Seattle traffic heading for Coos Bay, Oregon, home of their dismast ketch, Sea Witch. *It`s been six months now recuperating at Helen`s home, although returning to Bellevue with my former wife, Irene, had been an option. It was good to reunite with my family, if only as a visitor. Irene had I mutually agreed to move ahead with the divorce procedure and the divorce would be final soon.*

Helen, snuggling beside him on the wide pickup seat offered, "A penny for your thoughts; you look as if you're miles away, Rodg."

"I was thinking about my phone call to you after I came out of my amnesia four months ago."

"Oh, Wow! That was the shock of my life. I had just begun to accept the terrible fact you were gone, swept overboard, lost at sea, forever." Helen twisted around in her seat and planted a kiss on Rodger`s cheek.

"What`s that for? Not that I`m complaining."

"That`s for being alive and for being a hero."

"Really? I am alive, that`s for sure, and I`ll admit getting up at six a.m. this morning wasn`t easy, but I wouldn`t go so far as to say heroic."

"No, silly. I mean when you put the hatch boards in place in the cabin after I went below deck to send a Mayday message. That act saved my life as the Sea Witch didn`t fill with water and sink after being hit by the rogue wave that pitch-poled us."

"Yes, it did give you a chance to get out alive. As it turned out, we both made it."

Helen grew silent, staring at the highway ahead, lost in thought. Rodger glanced over at her and smiled pensively, choosing not to interrupt her reverie. The shipwreck brought back painful memories for both of them, but especially for Helen. *She had to live with the thought I was dead after the Coast Guard had given up the search for me after the storm.* Rodger suppressed a sigh. *Some things are better off not dwelt upon.*

Eventually Rodger ended the silence, "It`s decision time. We`ve talked about refitting the Sea Witch and continuing the voyage to Tahiti or selling her as is. What do you want to do, Skipper?"

Helen smiled. "You haven`t called me Skipper for awhile, Rodg. Does that mean you want to return to our Tahiti fantasy?"

"I asked you first."

Helen leaned back in the seat and stared down the freeway lost in thought. After awhile she broke the silence, "I said I`d never sail again, that`s when I thought you were dead, but I've had second thoughts. It was such a great adventure up until the storm".... She smiled up at Rodger, a sudden twinkle in her eye... "I really would love for us to continue our journey to Tahiti. "

"Hey! That`s what I wanted to hear," Rodger shouted visibly excited, but keeping his eyes on the road ahead .

Looking over at him Helen added, "How great it`ll be to be sailing to Tahiti again. I hope there`s a boatyard in Coos Bay that can do the refitting. If not, we`ll have to motor the Sea Witch to another port, and that`s always risky on the ocean with no sails as a backup."

"This is exciting just thinking about getting the Sea Witch recommissioned."

*   *   *

The early morning traffic was slow until they reached Olympia, with people going to work, truckers going about their business, and early vacationers heading both north and south filling the freeway. Once they were beyond the Puget Sound megalopolis, freeway travel became faster. Rural valley country dominated the immediate scene being bordered by the Cascade Mountains on the East and the Coastal Range to the West. An occasional town broke the pattern of evergreen trees that alternated with open farmland. The weather, pleasant for a day in early March, had buds showing on the deciduous trees contrasted by the evergreen`s deep, lush green.

"We should make Coos Bay by supper time," speculated Rodger.

"There you go using meals as navigation points. You're a good eater Rodg"

Helen and Rodger felt comfortable in their new role as single, independent people choosing to live together and share their intimate life. They talked of marriage in the future, when the time was right. It seemed easier for Rodger`s three adult sons to accept the divorce of Rodger and Irene when he hadn`t rushed out and remarried. Because Helen was a widow and had no children, it didn`t seem to matter to her parents and two adult brothers if they lived together without the legality of marriage. She had decided to let Rodger take the initiative as to when they would marry, if ever. The important thing is they love each other and enjoy sharing their lives.

Pulling in to an R.V. park they had discovered on an earlier trip to Coos Bay, they were greeted warmly by the owners. Rodger went about hooking up the camper to the utilities at a site while Helen held a flashlight to assist him in the fading light of day. After completing the task, Rodger walked to the office to register while Helen chose to stay behind to start the ritual of preparing it as their home away from home.

Entering the camper she looked about. The living space in the camper was comparable in size to the Sea Witch`s interior although entirely different in layout design. There was nothing nautical about the camper, only efficiency of arrangement for dining, cooking and sleeping. They had a few personal items about, adding to the homey feeling.

Rodger, pausing in the doorway on his return, surveyed the domestic scene before him. "Now that`s what I like to see, dinner being prepared by someone else."

"That part of our relationship has changed, hasn`t it? After six months of living together at home, I`m a more confident cook, but I like to think meal preparation is still a combined effort. Tonight I cook, you do the dishes, and for right now you can pour us a glass of wine. Oh yes, and you can give the cook a kiss to stimulate the creative juices needed for meal preparation."

Rodger put his arms around Helen pressing his lips to hers in a long, passionate kiss, then returned to pouring two glasses of Merlot.

"I feel more creative already; does chicken pot pie with a gourmet vegetable salad meet with your approval?"

After handing Helen her glass of wine, Rodger held his wine glass up as a salute, "To one of my favorite meals."

"Did you ask in the office about a shipyard in Coos Bay capable of refitting the Sea Witch?"

"Yes, they thought the Coos Bay Boatyard and Marina could do it; we`ll check it out tomorrow."

* * *

At 7 a.m. they awakened to the sound of fellow travelers breaking camp eager for another day on the road. Helen rolled over to face Rodger as they lay in the bed situated over the truck`s cab roof. "Good morning, Love. Are we going to look for a shipwright to refit the Sea Witch today?"

"That`s the plan. I`m anxious to see the Sea Witch again; it`s been a couple of months since we`ve been here and she`ll probably need a wash down, at least."

Rodger planted a light kiss on Helen`s forehead and started to roll out of bed. Helen grabbed him and kissed him hard on the mouth. "There… now you can start your day, Mr. McCauley."

* * *

A short drive to town put them at the private dock where the Sea Witch lay moored. "She sure looks forlorn with no masts or rigging," said Rodger, "and she does need a wash down. I`ll get the cleaning equipment from the storage locker and give the lady a bath."

"Now, that`s a pretty provocative statement. How many ladies have you bathed?"

"Only ladies like the Sea Witch…not counting you, of course."

"Sorry I asked…end of conversation." A blush appeared on Helen`s smiling face as she playfully gave Rodger a punch on the shoulder. "After the wash down we can have lunch and then check out the boatyard."

The day, growing warmer, burned off the morning coastal mist by noon. "I think we`re in for another beautiful spring day. These last days of March can be delightful along this part of the Pacific Coast."

After finishing the wash down and a quick wipe down of the porthole windows and brass fittings, they put away the equipment and strolled the two blocks to Joe`s café. Having discovered it on their trip to Coos Bay two months ago, it was no surprise when the owner greeted them and directed them to a booth near the front of the small café. "The special today is crab cakes with cole slaw or chowder," offered Joe as he extended two menus.

"Hmm," said Helen, "that sounds good."

Looking over at Helen and getting confirmation, Rodger stated, "Make that two of today`s special." He handed his menu back without opening it. "Also two cups of coffee while we wait."

* * *

After lunch they strolled hand-in-hand through the small coastal town to the shipyard just beyond the city center. As shipyards go, it was small, but appeared to be prosperous with the open boatyard nearly full of boats of a variety of sizes and styles. Its marine railway held several boats with heavy blocking beneath their hulls to keep them upright and secure in the process of being repaired. These were housed under a high shed-type roof with open sides.

Boats could also enter the shipyard from the water by way of a concrete ramp. Smaller boats were put on a customer`s trailer or forklifted out of the water and then given a parking space in the yard and blocked up for on-the-spot repairs. All in all, there was an air of activity everywhere.

Approaching the small building facing main street, Rodger and Helen entered an austere office. Seated beyond the counter at the only desk was an elderly, wiry-built man with thinning gray hair and a pleasant, business-like demeanor.

"Can I help you?" he asked looking up from his work.

Helen responded, "We have a dismast, ketch-rigged, sailboat needing to be re-commissioned. The deck was swept clean when it was pitch-poled north of here in a coastal storm last year. Do you do that kind of work?"

"Yes, we do. What`s the length of your boat?"

"Thirty one feet; it`s a Tahiti Ketch."

"I've seen the boat. It`s moored at Stimson`s dock, isn`t it?"

"Right, the Sea Witch. Can you handle the job?"

"Yes, if you're not in a big hurry. I can`t get to it for a couple of weeks, but we could order the masts, spars, sails and rigging in the meantime. I could probably have it done by the end of April."

Helen turned toward Rodger, "What do you think?"

Rodger was obviously pleased with this news, "What kind of money are we talking about?"

"I could work up an estimate this afternoon and have it for you tomorrow at this time, assuming my suppliers have what we need and prices for me."

"That sounds like a plan," replied Helen feeling comfortable in her former role as skipper. "We`ll be here tomorrow and look at your estimate."

The man behind the counter seemed amused at the reversal of traditional roles by this pair of strangers. "I`ll have the figures for you tomorrow. By the way, I`m John Davidson, owner."

"I`m Helen Davis and this is Rodger McCauley," Helen replied extending her hand to the boat yard owner. "I`m the skipper and he`s first mate when it comes to the boat. Does that answer your question?"

"Yep! Sure does. See you tomorrow Helen and Rodger."

* * *

The next day was mild for Pacific Coast country, ideal for being on or near the water. After unhooking the camper from the utility connections at the RV Park, Rodger and Helen drove to the boatyard. John Davidson, seated at his desk and deep into paper work, suddenly became aware of their presence. "Hello, Helen and Rodger, good timing. I`ve just finished your estimate." Sliding the estimate sheet across the counter toward them, he sat back in his chair to study their reaction to the price quoted.

Helen accepted it and she and Rodger quickly scanned the pages of figures and items listed. "If you don`t mind, we`ll take this with us and let you know tomorrow what we decide," replied Helen.

"That`s fine. I`ll look forward to seeing you tomorrow."

Once outside, Helen turned to Rodger, "Well Rodg, what do you think?"

"Eight thousand, eight hundred, and forty dollars is about what I expected. We have the money, so it`s do-able."

"I wish we could get a second bid just to compare prices."

"That could be time consuming, although a good idea. Instead, why don`t we ask him for references. That would be faster and would speak to workmanship as well as price," suggested Rodger

"Good idea, Rodg. You go back and ask him, and I`ll hit the grocery store over there and meet you at the truck. What do you want for dinner?"

"How about a couple of small steaks and a bottle of Cabernet Sauvignon for a celebration.."

"What a romantic you are, Rodg. However, returning to our voyage does call for a celebration. See you at the truck."

Rodger retraced his steps to John Davidson`s office. The tinkling bell over the door announced his arrival. John looked up from his paper work on his desk. "Yes Rodger, what can I do for you? Have you two made up your minds already?"

"No, but we do have a request. We`d like to have the names of two or three references who have done business of this type with you recently."

"I can do that." John went to his tall, metal filing cabinet and pulled out the bottom drawer. Rifling through folders, he pulled out three and laid them on the counter. "These should tell you what you want to know." He copied the names and phone numbers from each of the folders on a legal pad and handed the top page to Rodger.

"Thanks, John. We think this is just good business procedure."

"I do too, and following good business procedure, I`ll need to have a thirty percent deposit before I order several thousand dollars worth of masts, spars, rigging and sails."

Chapter Twenty-Seven

Rodger rolled out of bed and stepped down to the floor level of the camper. He then ran a sink of cold water to wash the sleep from his eyes and start his day. As he gathered fresh clothing for his trip to the nearby shower, Helen stirred.

Rising up on one elbow she moaned, "Morning all ready? I was having such a wonderful dream."

"Tell me about it, Sleepy Head."

"We were sailing on the Sea Witch en route to Tahiti."

"Well, that`s what we plan to do, so we`ll work at making that dream come true. After talking to John`s references yesterday, they had nothing but praise for his work and his prices."

"Good, so let`s do it."

"Agreed, we`ll tell John it's a go when we go to town for supplies."

"Back to the dream. Because it was happening right now, that`s what made it so wonderful. What on earth are we going to do while we wait for the refitting of the Sea Witch?"

"We could go home and wait or do what you`ve talked about several times this past winter; go to Baja, Mexico." Sitting down on one end of the dinette, Rodger watched for Helen`s reaction to his suggestion.

"Wouldn't that be great? I would just love it."

"It`s settled then." Rodger grabbed Helen about the waist from his sitting position and hugged her tight. "Tomorrow we`ll head for Baja, Mexico while the Sea Witch gets her new masts, rigging, and sails. Two good things will be happening; you`ll get your wish, and the Sea Witch will get hers. I`m sure she wants to go to sea again; that old girl isn`t ready to be scuttled yet."

Helen bent down, giving Rodger a kiss on the top of his head, and then pressed his head against her bosom. "Thanks Rodg. Now we`ve got to get the camper ready for travel, take aboard groceries, and hit the Laundromat. This is getting exciting, and I`m ready for an adventure. That`s not to say we haven`t had adventure at home. It`s been great just being together, living each day to the fullest, and being thankful for each day. After all, you have come back from the dead."

Rodger thought *how lucky I am to have this lady in my life. She brings such a lust for life into everything we do.*

Turning to survey the cupboards, Helen took pencil and pad and started making a list of things needed.

"Remember, it`s not like being at sea. There are stores and gas stations along the way. In the Baja, government-owned gas stations are strategically placed every forty miles in the desolate areas, so you have gasoline and other basic needs even when there is no town or village. There are mom-and-pop-type grocery stores in all the towns and villages, but few super markets. I was there years ago and able to get everything I needed."

Helen stopped her list making and turned to Rodger, "Okay, I get the message. I`ll only buy for a couple of days at a time, like we do now. You can be the skipper in the camper; I`ll be the skipper on the Sea Witch, agreed?"

"No, I don`t agree! Skipper is your title, so come over here Skipper and give the First Mate a hug, then we`ll go to the boatyard and tell John our plans for the next month."

"Whatever you say Rodg….er, I mean Mate."

* * *

Helen and Rodger arrived at the boatyard just as John Davidson was leaving for lunch. He surprised them by inviting them to join him for lunch. They quickly agreed. John seemed to enjoy their company and they, in turn, sensed he was a nice, but lonely man.

"I hope you like home cooking as Nelda`s fare is pretty much that," he said as they walked across the street and down the half-block to the restaurant. "I eat here often, as I get tired of my own cooking."

"You're a bachelor, John?" inquired Helen.

"Widower. My wife died two years ago; life hasn`t been the same since. We only had one child. My daughter, granddaughter, and son-in-law visit three or four times a year, but that still leaves a lot of alone time. I`d retire, but there is nothing to retire to. Actually, work at the boatyard is the easiest part of my life. It`s the nights that are difficult."

Entering the small cozy café, a dark-haired, middle-aged woman hailed them. "Hi, John, you've brought friends today?"

"Hi, Nelda. Yes, they`re customer friends from out-of-town. I've been bragging about your cooking."

Nelda glowed with pleasure at the compliment. "That`s nice of you John, I hope I can live up to your expectations. The special today is one of your favorites; I hoped you`d be in today. It`s meatloaf with mashed potatoes, gravy and corn."

"Marvelous," replied John beaming with pleasure. "Just bring two menus for my friends; you know my order. By the way Nelda, this is Helen Davis and Rodger McCauley. Helen and Rodger, this is Nelda… er…you know Nelda, I don`t know your last name."

Nelda blushed, but managed to sputter, "Brennon. Nelda Brennon. Pleased to meet you Helen and Rodger, are you boaters? Of course most of John`s clients are, I guess that figures, him owning a boatyard and all…listen to me run on! Here`s your menus; I`ll bring water."

Helen answered Nelda`s question when she returned. "Yes, we`re boaters, but we had a shipwreck a year ago up the coast off Point Arena. That`s a story John can tell you sometime." It was apparent Nelda had more than a friendly interest in John and would welcome any kind of social contact with him, even a story about two strangers.

"Our sailboat was swept clean of superstructure, so John has the job of putting it back together. You may have seen us moored at Stimson`s dock on the other end of town."

"Yes, I have. Coos Bay isn`t large and doesn`t often have dismast sailboats moored here." Nelda reconfirmed John`s order, "You want the blue plate special, John, how about you Helen and Rodger?"

Helen spoke up, "I`ll have a BLT and coffee."

"I`ll have a John`s special," replied Rodger chuckling as he handed Nelda his menu. Nelda smiled and disappeared in to the kitchen.

John`s eyes followed Nelda`s retreating figure, then turned back to his companions. "Nelda is also the cook and sometimes even the dishwasher. She works hard to support herself, I don`t think she has a husband. I've never seen or heard her speak of one, or children; she`s a very private person."

After they had finished eating lunch Helen turned toward John, "Rodger and I have talked by phone to the references you provided. They praised your work and we`ve decided to have you do the recommissioning of the Sea Witch."

"Great!" John extended his hand for a handshake from the two of them to seal the deal, "I`ll look forward to bringing the Sea Witch back to life for you."

"Rodger and I have decided to take our camper and head south to Baja, Mexico in the morning while we wait for the Sea Witch. Are there any loose ends that need to be taken care of other than giving you a check for three thousand dollars?"

"Going to the Baja… that sounds like a good way to spend the next month. No, I can`t think of anything other than the retainer, but give me your cell phone number just in case something comes up and a decision has to be made by you. Oh yes, you`ll need to motor the Sea Witch over to my boatyard this afternoon."

"Not a problem," replied Helen.

"I`ll wait for you at the dock in an hour," said John, "if that`s a good time for you?"

Helen, once again comfortable in her role as Skipper, said, "That`ll work, John."

* * *

Helen and Rodger drove to the Sea Witch`s dock and prepared for the short trip to the boatyard. Rodger went below to start the engine while Helen loosened the mooring lines. Once she heard the engine come to life, she cast off the bowline and spring line, then stepped to the helm. Rodger cast off the stern line as Helen shifted the transmission from neutral to forward. As the Sea Witch slowly pulled away from the dock, he took in the three bumpers leaving them tied to their cleats as they would soon be needed when the Sea Witch reached John`s boatyard. Also the three mooring lines were coiled neatly around their cleats on deck.

The afternoon weather was surprisingly pleasant for this time of year; early spring in Coos Bay often is rainy. Various types of boats plied the local waters and all took notice of the Sea Witch cruising through the bay devoid of masts, rigging and sails. Standing at the helm in her familiar roll, Helen thought, *how good it is to be standing here with the sun at my back and a gentle breeze in my face; I never thought this would happen again. It`s funny how things work out some times. Six months ago I was devastated by the loss of Rodger being lost at sea; today we`re back in our adventure … unbelievable.*

"Skipper, we`ve got to make our turn to port after we pass that channel buoy dead ahead."

Helen, startled, turned and replied, "Okay Mate, I guess I was lost in thought."

"We might have been having the same thought. It`s great to be back aboard isn`t it?"

"Yes, it is, and it`s great to have you back, too, Rodg. Now, put out the bumpers and go forward with the bowline to hand off to John."

"Aye, aye Skipper." Rodger flipped the three bumpers down, took the bowline in hand, and stood ready to cast it to John.

"Ready for mooring?" called out Helen.

"Ready, Skipper."

Helen shifted the transmission into neutral allowing the Sea Witch to glide to a near stop, settling easy alongside the floating dock. The approach was so smooth Rodger merely leaned over the gunnels and handed the bowline to John who immediately threw a double half hitch around the dock cleat, allowing some slack for maneuvering. After the stern and spring line was set, Helen called out, "Thanks John. Is there anything else we need to do before we head off for the Baja?"

"Not as far as I`m concerned. I`ll have the Sea Witch ready for you when you return; unless we run into some unforeseen circumstances. Oh yes, leave the keys in the ignition."

Helen stepped over the gunnels onto the dock, then turned and patted the Sea Witch as she would a pet. "See you in a month, girl." Turning to John, "We`ll call once a week to see how things are going."

"That`s good! I`ll be anxious to hear how your trip is going, too."

Rodger stepped forward and extended his hand, "You`re a good friend, John." He and Helen then walked hand-in-hand back to Stimson`s dock and their pickup truck.

"Well, that's done," Helen stated referring to the successful transfer of the Sea Witch to the boat yard. "Now we need to get ready for our departure tomorrow."

Chapter Twenty-Eight

Helen awakened to the sound of eager RV`ers breaking camp on their way to another day of adventure. Looking at the clock, she groaned, "Seven fifteen, gimme a break."

Rodger opened his eyes and stared at the ceiling which was just two feet from his face, "I wasn`t looking for an early start either."

Helen rolled over to face him, "Well, we`re awake so we might as well get up."

"There are other options," replied Rodger as he drew her close to him.

"There may be other options, but I`m a night person, remember?"

"Okay, killjoy, night will come you know."

"Yes, and I`ll look forward to it," teased Helen as she gave Rodger a kiss to show her intent. Rolling out of bed, Helen was startled as she put her bare feet on the cold linoleum floor. Quickly stepping into her slippers and slipping on her robe, she headed for the community bathroom calling over her shoulder, "Put on the coffee pot, Rodg."

Rodger slowly slide down from the bed, experiencing the same shock as his feet touched the cold linoleum. Grabbing the coffee pot, he filled it with coffee ingredients and placed it on a burner. Having completed his designated chore, he put on his robe and slippers, and followed Helen`s route to the community bathrooms.

The RV Park had many trees, mostly evergreens, providing privacy between the campsites. Even though the paths and roads were paved with asphalt, the park had a very natural look. The morning sky was overcast, but the local weatherman promised a day without rain.

*   *   *

Ten o`clock found them a hundred miles down the road and back on I-5 heading south. The Siskiu Mountains gave way here to high plateau country. Gradually losing altitude, the land became fertile flat stretches of grains alternating with orchards of fruit and olive trees. Fruit stands began to appear on side roads near and accessible to the freeway.

"Let`s stop at a stand and see what they have," suggested Helen. I`d like to lighten up our diet for the next few days with some fruit."

Rodger pulled in at the next fruit stand, which was located on a narrow dirt road running parallel to I-5. "You buy the fruit, and I`ll stretch my legs with a short walk along this dirt road."

Because it was too early for fresh fruit, what was for sale was canned fruit from the previous season, dried fruit, jars of olives, and fresh baked fruit pies. It didn`t take Helen long to fill their needs for several days. Returning to the camper to stow her purchases inside, she kept out a few pieces of dried fruit to nibble on as they drove.

Looking down the country road, she spotted Rodger coming toward her from a distance... but he wasn`t alone. A dog trotted at his heels and kept looking up at him. He evidently was talking to the dog as they walked along together. Helen decided to meet Rodger and get a little exercise herself. As they came together, Rodger hailed Helen. As if on cue, the dog also responded with a friendly bark, glancing up at Rodger as if looking for approval. Rodger announced, "I have a new friend."

"So I see," her tone being one of guarded caution. "You do have a way with women, Rodg; please tell me it`s going to be a short relationship."

"I do feel like the little boy telling his mother `the dog just followed me home, can I keep it, Mom? ` Somehow, this dog and I just click; she reminds me of a dog I had as a boy. If we determine she`s lost, or a runaway, or a deserted pooch, would you consider including her in our family?"

She could see how attracted Rodger and the dog were to each other and gave careful thought to her reply. "I've never had a pet, nor felt a need for one, but if it`s that important to you Rodg, and there is no apparent owner, I`m willing to give her a try. That`s with the understanding, if she doesn`t fit our life style we find another home for her."

A broad smile lit up Rodger`s face, "Agreed. Let`s go into the fruit stand and ask if they know anything about the dog." Rodger approached a man who seemed to be in charge. "Is the little terrier out there with my partner your dog?"

The owner replied, "No, I don`t keep my dog down here, but I've seen that dog around for the past three days. I've been giving her scraps from our lunch, however, I think she`s been abandoned, and she`s been sleeping in that olive grove over there at night."

"Really!" Rodger replied with growing enthusiasm. "She looks like a good breed, I`m surprised she`d be abandoned."

"It happens once in awhile. A customer drives off without a pet, either because they don`t know the pet got out of the car or they forgot they let the pet out. Sometimes they discover their loss soon enough to return for the dog. I've heard of some cases where the discovery wasn`t made until the end of the day, especially if the dog travels in the trailer or camper and there`s no contact until they stop. Occasionally they make the trek back, but that dog`s been here three days, that`s a long time for someone to still return."

"We like the dog and we`re willing to give her a home. Would it seem appropriate for us to take her?"

"Sure, why not? I`d say the pooch is lucky to get a home. She`s become a little scruffy looking since I first saw her, and I don`t think sleeping in an orchard living on handouts is much of a life, even for a dog." He then returned to his cash register, as if the decision was a done deal.

"We`ll leave our cell phone number and our home address in case someone comes looking for her," Rodger called after him.

"Okay, if you want to. I`ll post it on our cash register for a few days." He turned and handed Rodger paper and pencil, then left to wait on a customer. Rodger wrote down the information, laid the note and pencil beside the cash register, and then walked back to Helen who was still kneeling down beside the dog.

"I can see why you`re attracted to her. She`s such a gentle, sweet thing; what did you find out?"

"We`ve got a dog if we want one; last chance to change your mind." Rodger looked at her questioningly.

"I`m game if you are, as long as we both agree we find her a good home if she doesn`t fit in. She`s got`ta be a traveler and a sea dog, that`s for sure."

"Agreed… now we`re three." He bent down and scooped up the little dog holding her like one might a child. "Okay dog, you're one of the family now. First we feed you, then we bathe you, and then we name you. What do you think of that?"

The dog soaked up Rodger`s embrace looking at him adoringly. *Oh, if I could only talk*, she seemed to say.

* * *

Helen found several pieces of lunchmeat in the refrigerator, and this along with a bowl of milk was quickly devoured by what`s-her-name. Gently placing her between the two of them on the bench-type truck seat, Rodger said, "Here`s your new home."

She looked up at each of them in turn and seemed to understand that she had a new master and mistress. Then she looked straight ahead down the road, as if to say *we can go now.*

Rodger looked at Helen with an amused, but knowing smile, "We have been given permission to *leave.* The bath will have to wait until this evening, but we can work on a name; have any ideas?"

"Well, it should be feminine, and maybe something to do with boating."

"How about Gunnels?"

"Good grief, Rodg, give her a break," Helen laughed.

"Okay, your turn."

"Well, how about Jeanie?"

"We`ve already named the GPS system that," objected Rodger. "How about Salty?"

"That's not very feminine," she replied, trying hard to control her laughter. "How about Bilgee? Not bilge, but Bilgee."

"That's nautical, but the bilge is the inside bottom area of a boat, how feminine is that?" "I like the sound of it; it's cute, and I guess cute is feminine."

Rodger, half-turning, leaned toward the dog and said, "Bilgee," as if he expected an answer.

The terrier looked questioningly at Rodger, then turned her head forward and gave a sharp bark.

"That settles it, I guess. Bilgee, you're going to get a bath as soon as we make camp. Sleeping in the wild has given you a wild aroma."

"Where do you plan to give Bilgee a bath oh-fastidious-one?"

"If they have a sanitary tub in the laundry area, the problem is solved. If they don't, we either find a dog groomer or she and I take a shower together."

* * *

As the afternoon wore on, the Interstate continually lost altitude and the land lay flat and fertile on both sides of the highway. Several rest stops later brought them to Corning, California and time to start looking for RV parks. Turning off the Interstate they soon found a suitable place and settled in for the night. Stopping at a Mom-and-Pop grocery store, they picked up a few things for dinner and breakfast, plus dry dog food and biscuits, which Bilgee quickly approved by gobbling them up.

"I think this dog is really hungry. We probably should have stopped earlier and taken care of that," offered Rodger.

Helen countered, "We'll have her on a routine in a few days and she'll be just fine. Are you up for a couple of microwave Lean Cuisines and a walk after dinner?"

"That sounds good after a day in the camper. I'll take Bilgee for a short stroll, but I'll be back in time to fix our before-dinner cocktail, if you're up to being cook. If not, we can switch roles."

Without answering Helen opened the door to the camper and stepped inside to begin the evening meal. Rodger took Bilgee on her new leash and headed for the nearest watering hole for pets. The sunset was beautiful over the Coastal Range, and the weather, now warmer and drier, actually feeling balmy compared to their Seattle or Coos Bay weather. Rodger walked slowly as Bilgee sniffed her way toward the nearest shrubbery. Although apparently she was used to walking on a lease, she looked up often to be sure everything was okay.

Soon Rodger turned around and led Bilgee back to the camper. As he opened the door, pleasant dinner smells enveloped them. Helen, busy at the counter making a vegetable salad, exclaimed, “Welcome you two, dinner is in 15 minutes and the Scotch is in the cupboard.”

* * *

The next morning they got an early start after a hearty breakfast and a necessary walk for Bilgee. Entering the pickup, Helen put the dog on the window-side of the bench seat in order to sit next to Rodger. “I can`t have this dog coming between us, especially since she`s cute.”

“I’ve finally arrived, I have two women fighting over me.”

“Enjoy it while you can, Rodg. For all we know, Bilgee may have a master or mistress grieving over her and will want her back.”

“It is a mystery, isn`t it...her living in a fruit orchard? I can`t imagine anyone dumping her out. I wonder if we`ll ever know what really happened?” Bilgee looked over at Helen and then Rodger. She seemed to know she was the topic of conversation.

“I think we need to get her a bunky seat,” stated Rodger as he looked over at Bilgee sitting below window level on the car seat. “I`m sure she`d like to look out at the passing scenery”

“What`s a bunky seat?”

“It`s a small seat for children that is placed on an adult-size seat or chair to bring the child up to window or table height.”

Helen smiled, stifling a laugh, “Whatever you say Rodg. Maybe Bilgee can go along on the shopping trip and pick out the color and texture. That`s an item I never thought I`d be shopping for, but it does make sense. My folks used to put their Pekinese, Maggi, on the dashboard of their motor home as they traveled, so she could see out.”

“There`s a thought.”

“Not a good idea Rodg; their dashboard was three time the size of ours. Ours is too narrow and with Bilgee there, I couldn`t see the road.”

"We`ll be around Sacramento at lunch time, perhaps we can find a store that sells children`s bunky seats. I wonder what kind of a store that would be?"

Helen looked puzzled, "I wonder if an automotive parts store would have them; after all it is something to be used in a vehicle."

"That makes sense. If not, they may know where we can go to buy one. We need to gas up soon, maybe I can ask the cashier at the gas station."

"Sounds like a plan, Rodg. There`s an exit ahead and the freeway signs advertise gas stations and retaurants."

Pulling off the freeway, they picked a gas station and Rodger filled both of the truck`s tanks while Helen took Bilgee for a potty break; then went inside to talk to the cashier about a bunky seat.

The cashier, a young college-age girl responded to Helen`s question with a smile. "There`s an auto-parts store across the street; I think they have them."

Helen thanked her and carried Bilgee to the camper. "The cashier told me to go across the street, Rodg. I`ll walk over and see what they have; just stay here with Bilgee, and I`ll only be a minute."

Helen soon returned with a bunky seat in hand and a broad smile on her face. "I told them this was for my granddaughter."

"This isn`t a clandestine affair, Helen!"

"I know, but I`d feel foolish telling them it was for our dog."

Bilgee looked at the bunky seat with some apprehension, but didn`t resist Helen`s effort to put her in it. Sitting there she could see out and seemed to understand what it was all about. Rodger and Helen watched her as she looked down the road ahead.

Rodger spoke first. "I think this is a good idea, even if you did buy it under false pretenses."

"She seems fascinated by all that she sees; enjoy the view, Bilgee."

The flat land was partioned with canals big enough to accommodate good-sized grain ships. This area seemed to be the breadbasket of California. Stopping at a rest stop, they had a leisurely lunch in the camper. As they lingered over their coffee, Rodger's face darkened with a puzzled look. "I just thought of a possible problem at the Mexican border. Can we take Bilgee across the border and if so, can we bring her back into the United States?"

"That`s a topic I know nothing about; how would we find out?"

"I would think any veterinarian would know. We`ll keep our eye out for a vet before we settle in for the night. Of course driving the freeway doesn`t give us much of an opportunity to see a veterinarian`s clinic. We can stop a little early today and seek one out where we plan to spend the night."

"Where do you see us spending the night, Rodg?"

"I thought we`d continue traveling on I-5 through the San Jaoquin Valley all the way to Los Angeles. It`s the easiest and most direct route, but there are few towns and no cities until you get almost to Los Angeles. It`s a full half-days drive from Sacramento and would put us in about suppertime. My vote is we see a vet tomorrow morning. If we do that, our stopping destination would be San Fernando."

"That sounds good to me. I've been told the drive down I-5 offers a great view of the irrigation system turning the San Joaquin Valley into an agricultural marvel. I`d like to see that."

"With air-conditioning it`s a wonderful drive; without it you`d better pick the winter months or early spring, like now."

The scenery changed markedly as they moved south changing from natural growing agricultural crops to a drier landscape interrupted by huge acreage of planted grains and fruit trees surrounded by natural grasses. Irrigation canals acting as borders to the various crops, and running with water helped along by strategically placed pumping stations filled the landscape on the driver`s side as far as they could see.

On the passenger`s side they saw grasses dotted by oak trees and an occasional Torre pine. The hills, gently rolling, made delicate creases and small arroyos in the immediate landscape. The sky, brilliant blue interspersed with wispy clouds that rolled over the rounded ridges from the Pacific Ocean that lay seventy miles to the west.

"Beautiful," exclaimed Helen. "And what a contrast of landscapes. It`s a bountiful cornucopia on your side and a near-arid grassland on mine."

"I thought you`d be impressed. That`s the Diablo Range on your side, which will segway into the Temblor Range in about a hundred miles. There are a lot of oil wells in the Temblor range which we won`t see from the highway."

"How do know so much about this part of the world?"

"I lived in southern California some years back, and visited friends in those hills occasionally. It was always a trip of contrasts from Southern California," replied Rodger.

"I think we need to find a rest stop soon for all three of us. I know I need to stretch and Bilgee is becoming restless. That has to mean something."

"There`s a sign offering gas and food ahead, hold on Bilgee."

"How about hold on, Helen?"

"Okay, I get the picture."

* * *

Soon the irrigation crops showed on both sides of the freeway. Highway 99, which had paralleled to the east, merged with the freeway, I-5. Another fifty miles and the Los Padres and Angeles National Forests loomed ahead. The climb over them was steep. This stretch of the freeway had been named the Grapevine many years before it ever became a freeway. Gaining elevation quickly and steadily, they soon reached the summit and were on their way down into the San Fernando Valley.

"Keep you eye out for an R.V. Park, Helen. I`m getting tired and it can`t come too soon."

"There`s the amusement park Six Flags Magic Mountain on my side, so there has to be places for tourists to stay."

"Ah, there`s one advertised just ahead," said Rodger. "I`ll move over in the outside lane and it will be our home for tonight."

* * *

The next morning Rodger headed for a veterinarian`s clinic recommended by the RV manager. It was a couple of miles down the freeway on the outskirts of San Fernando and easy to find. Rodger pulled into the parking lot and headed for the office door while Helen and Bilgee toured the parking area. Entering the smartly decorated office Rodger walked to the receptionist's desk.

Overstuffed chairs lined the perimeter of the large room, chairs occupied by well-groomed women holding well-groomed dogs and cats. They were obvious in their scrutiny of this ruggedly handsome, middle-aged man as he approached the desk empty-handed. Rodger stood at ease waiting to be recognized by the young, female receptionist.

Looking up from her appointment book, she exclaimed, "Good morning. Do you have an appointment?"

"No, but I have a question. Is there anything I need to know or do if I want to take a dog across the Mexican border?"

"Let me ask one of our veterinarians." She disappeared through the door leading to the clinic area. Returning in a few moments she said there were four shots required to get back into the United States with a dog. The veterinarian suggests that they not all be given in one day as some dogs, especially small ones, often become ill. He suggests two today and two tomorrow; does that work for you?"

"Yes, but this dog is a stray we picked up on our journey south. We have no health history on her, can we give her two shots now and a physical examination tomorrow plus the remaining shots, if you have an opening.

The receptionist perused her appointment book briefly. "We could have a technician give her the first two shots now, and Dr. Baker does have an opening at 9:30 tomorrow. Do you want that appointment?"

"Yes, we can make it work."

"What`s the dog`s name and what`s your name, sir?"

"I`m Rodger McCauley and the dog`s name is Bilgee. I`ll get her from the camper and be right back for her shots."

Rodger walked across the parking lot to the camper. Helen and Bilgee sat in the truck watching for him. Bilgee showed recognition of Rodger by standing and putting her front paws on the dashboard, shaking in anticipation of his arrival.

"You sure have made a hit with this dog, Rodg," said Helen. "What did you find out?"

Rodger filled Helen in on the information. He then fastened the leash to the Bilgee`s collar and the two of them walked back into the veterinarian's clinic. As Bilgee walked through the door, she froze in her tracks as she saw the conglomeration of pets and owners. Looking up at

Rodger with a worried look, she accepted being scooped up by Rodger as he walked to the receptionist's desk.

The receptionist silently pointed to the door leading to the interior of the clinic. A young Asian man dressed in a white lab coat was waiting for them. He produced a hypodermic needle and two vials of serum, and in the matter of a minute he had administered the two shots and carefully massaged the area. "She is a nice patient," he volunteered. "I`ll look forward to seeing her tomorrow."

Rodger paid the cashier and headed for the truck. Once he put Bilgee down, she walked ahead on the leash and seemed to take this experience all in stride. Helen stepped out of the camper and hurried to meet them.

"Well, how is the patient?'

"Not a problem; evidently she`s been to a veterinarian before."

"Well, good for you, Bilgee. Let me hold her while we drive back to the RV Park. It has good facilities, a swimming pool and getting a space this early in the day shouldn`t be a problem. I could use a day of rest and some physical exercise."

Bilgee snuggled into Helen`s arms enjoying being held on the short trip back to the RV Park. After hooking up to the utilities, Helen and Rodger slipped into their swimming suits, put Bilgee in her bed in the camper, and headed for the pool. The March weather was surprisingly warm, and a gentle breeze with the pungent smell of Eucalyptus trees rounded out the ingredients needed for a perfect southern California day.

* * *

The next morning the three of them headed for the veterinarian's clinic on the edge of the city of San Fernando. They soon were in the waiting room with Bilgee sitting on Rodger`s lap. Being inquisitive, she studied the other pets waiting for their appointment. This time her fear disappeared, and it became apparent that Bilgee wasn`t an overly anxious dog as some small dogs are. She continued to survey the animals and the people with the demeanor of one who is curious, not frightened.

When the receptionist called her name, Rodger, Helen, and Bilgee were escorted to an office off the large central room of the clinic. Dr. Baker, a large, kindly looking Englishman, turned to face them saying, "Good morning." He reached up to scratch behind Bilgee`s ear, "I understand you picked her up as a stray on your journey south."

"Yes," replied Helen. "We know nothing about her; in fact we aren't even sure of her breed."

"If you`ll wait here, I`ll examine Bilgee in the other room and report back to you in a few minutes. As far as her breed is concerned, she looks to be a Cairn terrier; it`s a Scottish breed.

* * *

A few moments later Dr Baker returned with Bilgee on her leash gaily running beside him. The smile on the doctor`s face was a sign all was well with Bilgee. "She`s a fit little dog. I gave her the two additional shots, and she`s ready to travel, and here is the exam form with the shots listed for your border crossing."

"Thanks, we`re relieved to hear she`s healthy and now with the shots she should stay that way," replied Rodger.

As they walked back to the camper Helen said, "Well, that`s over, now we can be on our way with our healthy Cairn terrier. We`ll have to stop at a library and read up on Cairn Terriers."

"I've never heard of that breed before," replied Rodger. Bilgee walked briskly at the end of her leash, looking over her shoulder at Helen and Rodger as if to say *hurry up I want to get out of this place.*

* * *

Soon they were back on the freeway headed south through the suburbs of Los Angeles. The further south they traveled the heavier the traffic became. Helen sat with eyes glued to the passing scene of a well-landscaped freeway and the backs of houses and small buildings, while Rodger concentrated on the road ahead. Bilgee lay on her bunkee seat, asleep.

Road signs told of suburban cities located on each side of the freeway, but everything seemed the same… houses, houses, and more houses. Large buildings loomed in the distance, but the freeway skirted them continuing south until Los Angeles was soon behind them.

"Let`s leave the freeway and head west to the Pacific Coast highway," said Rodger taking an exit. "It will be slower, but the view of the ocean and the scenic beach towns will be worth it. Speed is not why we`re taking this trip, right?

"Right you are, Mate; we`re here to see and experience. The sign ahead says Newport Beach, so, we should be seeing the ocean soon. Right?"

"Right."

The secondary road off the freeway was a four-lane road filled with cars headed to the beaches and the beach communities. The flat country that once was agricultural was filled with tract homes and strip malls. Suddenly the road started down an arroyo quickly putting them in the Oceanside town of Newport Beach. The crossroad before them, Pacific Coast Highway, hugged the base of the two-hundred foot cliff, but the town of Newport Beach lay on a large sand spit that bent to the South forming a mile-long back-bay that appeared to be home for hundreds of pleasure craft, mostly sailboats. The South end of the bay opened to the ocean with a protective jetty on each side of the opening that allowed a half-dozen boats to enter or leave the bay area at the same time, if need be.

"We`ll be sailing by this coastal town on our way to Tahiti," said Rodger. "Let`s make it a stopping place, as it looks like an interesting port."

"Agreed! It`s well protected from the ocean, and it apparently caters to sailors. You know, Rodg, those buoys spread out the length of the bay look like they`re there marking out a racecourse. In fact, I think I see a race forming before us. There`s a pair of powerboats near that yacht club on the far shore which could represent a starting line.

"Oh yeah, and there must be a dozen sailboats heading toward that point and another three or four-dozen farther down the bay just milling around. We could stop and watch for awhile, if you`d like."

"Let`s do it," exclaimed Helen enthusiastically. "Park in that turnout ahead and we can have lunch while we watch."

Rodger pulled the camper into the parking lot accommodating a short pier protruding into the bay. “Before we eat, let`s walk out to the end of the pier for a better look. They`ll have to go right by us.”

At the sound of screeching brakes behind them they turned to see a man leap from his parked car and run to the end of the pier.

“I wonder what`s that all about?” said Rodger as he held Bilgee tightly on her leash.

“He seems to be excited about something. Let`s walk to the end of the pier and ask him what`s happening.”

Helen, Rodger, and Bilgee hurried to the end of the pier and stood beside the man. He looked young and strong; dressed like a sailor. A bandage on his forehead covered what appeared to be a fresh wound. Leaning forward, he stood at the very end of the pier straining to see to the far side and down the bay.

“Is this a race and are you a part of it?” Rodger ventured.

“You bet it is,” the man quickly replied. “I`m the Skipper of that PCC 217 that just crossed the starting line and we`re in third place.”

“If you're the Skipper,” asked Helen perplexed. “What are you doing here?”

“We were doing some preliminary sailing before the race to acquaint a new crew member with his job tending the starboard winch that controls the jib sheet. I accidentally jibbed the boat causing the boom to swing across the cockpit hitting me on the forehead making this gash, he replied. “The crew put me ashore so I could get to a doctor for stitches. They could pick me up here as they sail by, if I can get their attention. I`m ready for a run-and-jump boarding, if they see me.”

“Really!” gasped Helen. “This I've got to see.”

“Me too,” exclaimed Rodger. “Would they slow down for you?”

“I hope not, as they`ll have to swing a little wide to pick me up as it is.” The young man leaned forward again straining to see his boat as it rounded the turning buoy at the end of the bay. Because it was now heading back towards him, he started waving frantically to get their attention. The sailor at the tiller stood and waved back in recognition. It was a desperate plan, but he was young, fearless, and looked upon it as great sport. “In the worst-case scenario,” the Skipper continued, “I take a dunking, they pick me up, and we`d be on our way. We`d lose our third place position in the race, but it`s a twenty mile race to Long Beach, so maybe we could out-sail them and catch up."

"Wow!" interjected Helen. "This is exciting. Why are all those other boats milling about on the other side of the race course?"

"They`re waiting for their turn to approach the starting line. Being a race against the clock, there are five groups of a dozen boats each started in ten-minute intervals. This spreads the boats out for safety sake here in the turning basin. Once they get in the ocean, there usually is no problem with collisions."

"Tell us about your boat," Rodger asked. "What kind is it?"

"She`s a thirty-two foot Pacific Coast class racing sloop. Being a class boat race, every boat in the race is exactly the same, and the boat with the shortest sailing time from here to Long Beach is the boat with the most skillful crew and the winner."

"Here comes your boat and they`re swinging out of line to pick you up," said Helen.

"Well folks, another minute and I`m outta here."

"Good Luck," replied Helen and Rodger in unison.

The Skipper stepped back a half-dozen paces and as his boat approached he yelled, "Keep going!"

The three sailors in the boat were transfixed as they saw what he was about to do. Just as the bow passed by close to the end of the pier, the Skipper started his run and leaped into the middle of the open cockpit into the waiting arms of two of the crewmembers. Whoops of joy and merriment filled the air as the crew and Rodger and Helen cheered the successful boarding. The Skipper immediately took the tiller and swung the boat back into the racing lane.

"Wow!" said Helen. "I think I've seen it all now."

"Wasn`t that great? Oh, to be young and crazy."

"I've seen you do some things on the Sea Witch that came close to that run-and jump boarding. Don`t sell yourself short, Rodg. You may not be young, but you can be crazy."

"Is that so?" countered Rodger as he grabbed her in a bear hug.

Taken by surprise, Helen tried unsuccessfully to squirm out of Rodger`s arms. Finally crying out, "I give up." Standing eye-to-eye with Rodger, she gave him his expected kiss. "Enough of this love making," she playfully pushed Rodger away, "Let`s drive further south and watch the race at the end of bay where the boats enter the ocean. Maybe we can find another place to park."

Rodger released Helen from his bear hug and the two of them with Bilgee trotting along side walked quickly back to the camper. The highway south brought them to the end of the bay where the twin jettys enabled boats to enter or leave the ocean. Pulling in to the parking area, they were lucky enough to find a place to park and walked out on the jetty to get a better view of the race. The jetty, comprised of Volkswagen-sized rocks, made their progress slow; more like rock climbing than walking. Sea life clung to the rocks up to the high water mark and the strong wind from the south sent unwelcome spray occasionally their way. The air was pungent with the strong odor of iodine from the kelp nearby.

The day was sunny and only a few white clouds dotted the blue sky. The air was mild due to the strong south wind that paralleled the coastline toward Long Beach, California, twenty miles to the north. Rodger said, "This will make for exciting sailing when they leave the turning basin and enter the ocean."

"The lead boat is just entering the channel to the ocean and our boat, #217, is still in third place." Helen waved excitedly to the skipper, but he was too busy with the race to notice her greeting. Suddenly, as the boats approached the middle of the channel entrance, a loud crack, like a pistol shot, sounded above the noise of the wind. Helen and Rodger stared in disbelief. The force of the strong crosswind on the cinched-down rigging of #217 sheared off the top dozen feet of the wooden mast. All eyes of the four-man crew stared upward at the sound just as mast, rigging, and sails came hurtling down on their heads. Members instinctly raised their arms to protect themselves from the onslaught of rigging, sails, and broken mast coming down on them. No movement was seen, as the boat coasted to a stop.

"I can`t believe what I`m seeing," Rodger shouted over the wind.

"I can`t either. The poor guys... the race is over for them, that`s for sure."

As they watched, the crew finally scrambled to get out from under the pile of canvas and gain control of the boat. One of the crewmembers unhooked the jib from the top of the broken mast and reconnected it to a piece of hardware near the middle of the remaining mast. The makeshift jib billowed out giving them steerage and forward motion. The skipper, now had the ability to turn the boat around, and head back to the shelter of the bay. Other boats in the race quickly and expertly dodged them as #217 limped back the way it had come.

Helen leaned dejectedly against a boulder and took Bilgee in her arms. Rodger stood transfixed by the drama before them. "Darn!" said Rodger finally. "They tried so hard to compete in this race after their skipper was injured; I guess this just wasn`t their day."

"I`ll bet this is a race that crew will never forget," added Helen, snuggling Bilgee in the protection of her arms from the wind.

"Let`s go back to the camper and eat the lunch that got interrupted an hour ago. Nothing like a disaster at sea to sharpen your appetite."

"I really don`t think that`s necessary with you and your appetite, Rodg."

* * *

After lunch they set out for a brisk walk on the beach. The pleasant weather, with the strong scent of salt adding to the iodine smell, was an early spring bonus. The surf, breaking sharply at their side, created a symphony of sound. Sea birds making sport with each other dove and soared with the strong wind. "Oh, how good it is to be near the ocean again; I feel at home," said Helen.

"You're a sailor for sure, and I think it`s catching."

Bilgee walked at the end of her leash sniffing at all the treasures of scent lying at her feet. Rodger unsnapped her leash, as the beach was nearly deserted, allowing her to run free at a faster pace and giving her a bigger world to explore. Helen hooked her arm through Rodger`s and they, quickened their pace. "What a glorious interlude this is, Rodg. I`m glad we decided to use this month while the Sea Witch gets recommissioned to explore California and the Baja."

Chapter Twenty-Nine

The camper joined the steady line of traffic moving south on the Pacific Coast Highway. The ocean became a constant companion while meadows, interrupted by forty-acre man-made plots of flowers, spread out like huge colorful blankets on each side of the highway. An occasional road sign spoke of places like Crystal Cove and Emerald Bay, but Rodger paid no attention as he seemed to be lost in thought.

"I know it`s premature," said Rodger, "but I`d like to call John and hear how the recommissioning of the Sea Witch is going."

"Good idea, I`ll get your cell phone out of the glove compartment. By the way, where are we staying for the night?"

"I was thinking Laguna Beach might be a good place; they have a good walking beach. Years ago I used to do some body surfing there, but it was just a day trip for me then."

"You told me you used to live in southern California back in your youth. Where did you live?"

"About fifty miles north in a town called Fullerton. Trips to the beach happened often, as I love the outdoors. My friends and I would find any excuse to pool our money for gas and spend a day in the ocean surf."

"Sounds like fun, Rodg. Why don`t you pull up at that turn-out ahead and you can make your phone call."

Helen handed Rodger the phone as she opened the door and slipped to the ground from the high pickup running board and set

Bilgee down. Helen stayed close, however, in order to hear the one-sided conversation between Rodger and John.

"Hello John, this is Rodger McCauley. I just called to find out what was happening to the Sea Witch." Rodger repeated the conversation so Helen could follow.

"I`m pleased to hear the new masts and rigging have arrived and you're about to re-rig. How about the sails?"

"You haven`t heared from them yet? Is there anything else we need to know or any decisions to make?"

"O.K., John. By the way and maybe I`m being too personal but is anything happening between you and Nelda?"

"Really. You're having a date once a week. That`s great! We think you two are a good match, John, for whatever that`s worth. Tell Nelda hello for us and we`ll be calling you in a few days; you know how to get in touch with us. Good-bye, John."

"Well, that`s good news," replied Helen. "The recommissioning has started and John and Nelda are dating. Now, how about a short walk to get the kinks out?"

"Sounds good to me."

* * *

Driving into the Laguna Beach city center, a bronze sculpture of an older man leaning out to wave at passing motorists caught their attention. He had a big smile on his face and seemed to almost say the words "howdy friend, welcome."

"I`ll be darned," said Rodger. "Forty years ago when my friends and I came here to surf there was this man who took it as his life`s work to do exactly what that statue is doing. He stood for hours, day after day, waving to all who passed him. We always looked for him and he never disappointed us."

"What a great thing to do."

"He`s probably dead now and the city of Laguna Beach is saying `thank you.` It`s amazing how accurate that bronze statue portrays him. It`s almost as if he`s still doing his life`s work. I've often wondered what his story was."

"It would be fun to find out while we`re here."

"Let`s settle in for the night at an R.V. Park and tomorrow we can drive back for a little investigative work and a walk on the beach."

Helen waved to the statue as they drove by as they saw passengers in other cars do the same. Driving a mile south they came to an RV Park and went through the ritual of registering, being assigned to a pad, and hooking up to the utilities for the night. After a short walk for Bilgee, Rodger took his turn at cooking and Helen mixed their pre dinner cocktail.

"You know Rodg, I think we`ve got a good thing going here." Helen extended a cocktail glass to Rodger as he stood at the stove preparing dinner.

"You mean the cooking arrangement?"

"I mean everything, Sweetie."

"I agree." Rodger turned and accepted the kiss that Helen offered. They touched their glasses together and each said their daily toast, "Blatant Seduction."

* * *

Helen finished cleaning up breakfast dishes while Rodg unhooked the utilities and prepared the camper for another day on the road. Taking Bilgee for a short walk to the pet area, on her return she watched Roger check the truck`s engine oil level; clean the windshield, and then the door windows. "No sense taking a sightseeing trip if you have dirty windows to look through," philosophized Rodger.

"Right you are Mate. I was thinking, let`s not go back to Laguna Beach now. I`m anxious to get to the Baja and we can stop on our return trip to Coos Bay."

"O.K., I`m ready to move on. We should be in Mexico by this afternoon and I`m looking forward to less road traffic after we get beyond Ensenada, Mexico."

"How far is Ensenada?"

"About one hundred and seventy-five miles. We can pick up the freeway and skirt the city traffic. Ensenata is about seventy miles south of the border and the end of four lane roads. It`s two lane asphalt from then on and there`s a road sign that says,`This is the last stop light for twenty-two hundred miles`."

"Really! That will be a change of pace and scenery. Is it as desolate as some say, and with bandits?"

"That wasn`t my experience. It`s cactus country for the inland part of the peninsula, but there is a beauty in that type of country. It`s tropical near the Pacific Ocean on the west side of the peninsula and also on the east Sea of Cortez side. I only went six hundred miles south of the border, but I found it to be a hospitable country. No bandits, unless you call one happening an act of robbery."

"Tell me about that."

Pat Lettenmaier, a traveling buddy of mine, and I were in a State campsite on a beautiful sandy cove near a point of land called Punta Chivata. Being backed up to within thirty feet of the Sea of Cortez, we shared the cove with twenty other campsites. We were sitting playing our nightly game of cards when suddenly there was a loud knock on the door. I jumped up, being nearest to the door, and asked, "Who`s there?"

I looked at Pat, who was just as surprised as I, and again I demanded, who`s there?"

As there was no answer I cautiously opened the door and looked out into the dark night at many pairs of eyes looking back at me at me. I was speechless. Then with the piercing shout of many high-pitched voices I heard the words, "Trick or Treat!"

We then realized it was October 31st and even in the Baja the children and adults celebrate Halloween. Pat had joined me, looking over my shoulder as I turned on the camper`s porch light. There before and below us stood a dozen small children dressed in simple, homemade Halloween costumes smiling up expectantly at us. Four young mothers stood behind them smiling at the two gringos with the surprised look on their face. Our shocked expressions changed to happy relief as I responded, "Welcome, we have treats for you."

Pat looked at me questioningly?

"We have a five pound box of cookies that is nearly full."

"Good thinking; that should keep the Halloween bandits at bay."

"Oh Rodg, what a delightful story. "I thought the bandit stories I've heard were figments of fertile imaginations."

"Actually I felt safer traveling in Mexico than I did in the United States. Life was simpler there with time to be a part of loving family and to have good friends. No one seemed to be in a hurry, and I sensed a satisfaction with Mexican life wherever I went."

"I`m anxious to experience the Baja even more after your story. I`ll take Bilgee for a quick walk and we can be on our way.

* * *

As Rodger headed back to the freeway, and upon approaching San Diego, traffic became heavier. The weather continued to be pleasant and grew warmer as they approached the Mexican border. Road signs directing drivers off the freeway advertised towns like National City, Chula Visa, and Imperial Beach, when suddenly Rodger`s cell phone gave a merry jingle.

Surprised, Helen quickly took it from the glove compartment and said, "Hello?"

"Is this the party that picked up a dog at a fruit stand in northern California?"

Helen looked over at Rodger with shock replacing surprise. Rodger, momentarily taking his eyes off the road asked, "What?"

Helen continued, "Yes, we did. Why do you ask?"

The male voice on the other end of the line spoke hesitantly, "We lost our dog there five days ago, and for our children`s sake we called the stand in a final effort to find her."

"Can you describe the dog you lost?" asked Helen. Rodger gave Helen a worried look as he listened to the one-sided conversation.

"She`s a Cairn terrier, in a wheaten color and should answer to the name of Misty."

Helen looked at Bilgee and repeated the name, Misty. Bilgee quickly turned toward Helen with a questioning look in her eyes as if to say, "*What*?"

"What`s going on?" interrupted Rodger.

"Just a minute," Helen said to the phone caller. Turning to Rodger she replied, "It sounds like Bilgee`s former owner has called and wants his dog back." Rodger frowned, but said nothing.

"How did you lose your dog?" asked Helen.

The male voice on the other end of the line replied, "I took her for a walk down a dirt road while my family shopped at a fruit stand.

Misty and I left the road to walk near the river. This took us under a wooden bridge just as a car drove ovehead; the noise was deafening and she panicked. Unfortunately, I`d taken her off the leash and she bolted, running pell-mell she disappeared in a nearby olive grove. My family and I spent several hours trying to find her with no luck. Eventually we had to continue on to Roseburg, Oregon, as I had to return to work the next day. My wife and the kids have been grieving over the loss of Misty ever since. Do you have her?"

"I hate to say it, but I think so."

Rodger pulled in to a rest stop and demanded, "Will you tell me what`s going on?"

After taking down the caller`s phone number and promising to call right back, Helen repeated all that had been told her as she held Bilgee tightly in her arms. Rodger sat without speaking for a long moment. "Well, Bilgee or Misty, old girl," said Rodger, "I guess you do have a loving family after all." Turning to Helen he said, "We have to do the right thing for all concerned, so call them back and get an address; we can postpone the Baja trip until after our Tahiti trip."

"I suppose," replied Helen. "I`m disappointed, but as long as I know a trip to the Baja is in the future I guess I can live with the postponement of not going now."

Rodger took Bilgee in his arms while Helen called the party back, wrote down the address, and told them of their changed travel plans with a promise to return their dog in a couple of days.

"This is heart-breaking girl," he cooed to Bilgee as they both sat stunned by the turn of events. Bilgee looked from on to the other as Rodger snapped on her leash. Bilgee, oblivious to all that had transpired, walked gaily before Rodger and Helen staking out territory as they proceeded to the pet area.

* * *

Rodger did a turn around at the next opportunity provided by the freeway and they drove in silence for a long time. Finally Helen asked, "What `s our destination for tonight?"

“If we can make Sacramento today, we can be in Roseburg, Oregon tomorrow afternoon, return Bilgee or I should say Misty to her owners, and be back in Coos Bay before nightfall.”

“Our arrival will be a big surprise for John and Nelda.”

“Yes, but we can see first-hand how the recommisioning is going on the Sea Witch,” replied Rodger. “I`m disappointed in our aborted trip to the Baja, but the upside is that we can watch the Sea Witch come back to life, and we can return home and visit our families before we continue our journey to Tahiti.”

Helen put the dog between them on the truck seat, and with the aid of the bunky seat, Bilgee looked far down the road ahead. She then looked at Helen and Rodger, curled up and went to sleep.

“I`m sure going to miss our new friend, but her family must love her as much as we do,” said Helen.

“I`m going to miss her, too. She quickly became a part of our family and already we`re missing her…we could get a dog of our own.”

“I don`t know,” said Helen. “Maybe we should also postpone that until we get back from Tahiti. A dog might be a problem on board and they sure wouldn`t be of any help, unless you consider companionship and adoration like only a dog can give.”

“Isn`t that the truth,” said Rodger. “A dog seems to be totally devoted to their master or their mistress. In our case, I think she looked upon us as rescuers after her ordeal of being lost and/or abandoned.”

“Rodger, you’re calling her Bilgee when we know her name is really Misty.”

“Your right, but I guess she`ll always be Bilgee to me.”

“Me too,” sighed Helen.

* * *

Leaving Sacramento the next morning Rodger and Helen continued northward on Interstate 5 after arranging a meeting with Misty`s owners for one o`clock at their home in Roseburg, Oregon. The overcast weather lent support to the mood that prevailed in the cab of the camper. Light traffic, even in the areas around larger towns, made progress easy, but not enjoyable due to the nature of their mission.

"I hope these people appreciate the sacrifice we`re making," blurted out Rodger. "We would be in the Baja now enjoying a warmer, sunny climate and a totally different environment."

"I think they`ll be overjoyed to get their family pet back. I`m guessing Bilgee...I mean Misty will be beside herself with joy when she sees them; especially the children."

"Bilgee doesn`t have a clue what`s going on. She just seems content to be with us and stake out territory at every stop we make; I`m sure going to miss her."

"Me too. She`s always so eager to please and be a part of what we`re doing. I hope the pleasure we get in returning her to her rightful owners will be some comfort in having to say goodbye to her."

Rodger looked far down the highway lost in his thoughts about the drama that was about to take place. "I`m having some second thoughts about our decision to abort our Baja trip to bring her home at this time, but they`re expecting us so we`ll just make this meeting and the goodbye as brief as possible. Dammit... I wish she`d never come into our lives."

Helen picked up the sleeping dog and held her in a loving embrace. Bilgee looked questioningly at her and then at Rodger. Her eyes seemed to say, *what`s wrong?*

Rodger reached over and caressed her head as he continued to look far down the road. "We`ll be on time according to my calculations. Another hour and we`ll have this all behind us."

Helen`s voice cracked as she fought tears, "I guess we`re a couple of softies getting so attached to a dog and in such a short time. Imagine what it would be like if we had her for a while. No... the sooner we give her back; the easier it will be for all of us. Our happiness will have to come from knowing Bilgee...I mean Misty is with her loved ones giving them happiness."

"You're right! We can stop for a late lunch after we drop her off, although I don`t have much of an appetite."

The road sign said Roseburg three miles; the countryside had changed to timber country, and Roseburg appeared to be a lumber town. A large sawmill appeared reinforcing this conclusion as they entered the town from the south. Rodger looked closely at the map he had drawn based on the instructions from Misty`s owner. *Following it should be easy as they don`t live far off the freeway.*

"I wonder if Bilgee will recognize the scent of the neighborhood as we get close," said Rodger.

"She knows something is going on, but I see no signs from her yet and that`s their driveway."

Rodger pulled up to the curb in front of the house. As he did, two young children, a boy and a girl in their sub-teens, came spilling out of the house. Helen opened the door of the truck and stepped down to the sidewalk with Misty in her arms. The two children converged on her in great expectation.

Then they stopped in their tracks both saying in unison, "That`s not Misty."

Rodger had walked around the camper to be a part of this joyful meeting. "What!" he exclaimed. "This isn`t your dog!"

Helen stood speechless, still holding Misty.... or Bilgee?

The children`s parents came quickly out to the camper with big smiles on their faces until they looked at the dog in Helen`s arms.

"My God," stammered the father, "that`s not Misty. She looks a lot like her, but it`s not her."

Helen finally found her voice, tears gathering in the corners of her eyes, "I`m so sorry for your disappointment, but you don`t know how happy this makes us. We love this dog." Helen held Bilgee tightly while Bilgee looked from person to person questioningly.

Rodger put his arm around Helen`s shoulders giving her a squeeze as if to say, yes we do. "Well folks, we`re sorry for your loss, but as Helen said, we love this dog and now we`ll be on our way."

Looking through the rear view mirror Rodger watched the family standing at the curb, silent, but still a family. A disappointed family to be sure, but one that would probably get another dog and call her Misty.

"Can you believe this?" exclaimed Rodger. "We have our dog back and soon we`ll be on our way to Tahiti."

"This is one of the happiest days of my life," replied Helen. "I guess this shows how important our third crew member, Bilgee, is."

* * *

They arrived at the RV Park before dinnertime and chose their favorite campsite with a view of the bay. After separating the camper from the truck and connecting their utilities to the campsites utilities, they decided to have dinner at Nelda`s café. With any luck they might catch John before he closed for the day and invite him to join them.

As they approached John`s boat yard, they saw that it was still open and much activity was visible. Once parked, they headed for the dry-dock area in order to view the Sea Witch. John was giving orders to the boom equipment operator that was in the process of setting the new mainmast in place. "Hold it there, Tim" John shouted. "I `ll help guide it through the hole in the deck to the backbone of the keel while you hold it upright in place."

When John was satisfied with the position of the mast, he and his helper bolted the mast in place. They secured temporary halyards fore, aft, and to each gunnel. "There, that should hold it for now. We can put up the mizzen mast tomorrow; it`s time to call it a day." As he turned to walk to the office he noticed Rodger and Helen standing off to one side watching the procedure.

"Hi there. I thought you two were in the Baja."

"We changed our plans," replied Helen, "but that`s a long story. We can tell it to you over dinner tonight at Nelda`s café, if you`ll join us."

"I`d like to," replied John. "If you want to go aboard the Sea Witch while I close up, I could meet you in the office in about fifteen minutes."

"Sounds good," replied Rodger as he took Helen by the hand and led her toward the Sea Witch. Once aboard they opened the cabin door and stepped below into the salon. The air was dank, unpleasantly moist, brought about by being closed up. "Everything looks the same but let`s open some portholes and get some air circulation in here."

"It sure needs a good cleaning," said Helen. "Maybe we can do that intermittently when the workers aren`t working on her tomorrow."

* * *

Helen, John, and Rodger walked across the street and down the half-block to Nelda`s café. The lights of the small town had come on and evening had settled in like a comfortable lap robe. Nelda stood at the counter talking to the only customer when they opened the door. "Hi there!" she blurted in surprise. "I didn`t expect to see you two for another month."

"We changed our plans and we`ll tell you about it over dinner, if you can join us," said Rodger.

"I can, as this is an unusually slow night. Of course it can change in an instant. Hi John, how`s my favorite customer?"

"Hi Nelda, how`s my favorite person?"

"Say now," injected Helen. "What have we here?"

"John and I are, as the high school kids say, going steady."

"I guess John alluded to as much on the phone last week," replied Rodger, "I think it`s just great. "Love is for all ages; look at us. A year ago we were two lonely people and now we`re a couple in love and on a great adventure sailing to Tahiti. Come to think of it, it`s all a great adventure, even like this moment having dinner with each other and two friends."

Nelda clapped her hands, "How wonderful! I couldn`t agree more."

John sat quietly listening. "Now it`s my turn to speak. I know my feelings of loneliness has turned into anticipation for each new day, and Nelda has made all the difference. Now, having spoken my feelings, may we have three menus, please?"

* * *

The next day Helen and Rodger arrived in the middle of the morning armed with cleaning supplies ready to give the Sea Witch an internal cleaning. John and Tim had just finished "stepping" the aft mast up into position giving the boat a familiar look. The Sea Witch now began to look like a sailboat again even though she was still minus the sails, rigging, and booms.

The day was pleasant, even for early spring, and activity in the boatyard had picked up from the usual winter doldrums. Being Saturday, boaters were looking for an excuse to be with their boats even if it was only to scrape barnacles and add a new coat of bottom paint to the hull.

John hailed them as they approached the Sea Witch. "We`ll add the booms after lunch so you have a couple of hours to do what you want to do on board."

"Great! exclaimed Rodger. "That will give us a start on our cleaning project."

Helen waved to John and Tim, but said nothing as the Sea Witch had her full attention. Quickly climbing the ladder to the gunnel, she carefully stepped over and onto the deck. "Oh, it feels good to be aboard her again. I can hardly wait to get under way for the voyage South."

"I agree," said Rodger as he followed Helen`s example of boarding the Sea Witch that was propped up and totally out of the water. After the bottom had been pressure washed, scraped and repainted with a copper-based paint nicknamed red hand, it was soon to be returned to its natural environment, the sea.

Rodger looked closely at the hull before boarding and asked, "Why do they call the bottom paint Red Hand?"

Helen laughed. "Its name comes from the fact that you can`t apply it without getting some on your hands and it is difficult to get off. Consequently, a boater sports red hands for days after applying the paint."

"I guess we can be glad John`s crew did it for us."

"You can say that again. It`s a job I don`t relish, but enough of this chitchat. We need to use this next two hours to the max if we`re going to get our living quarters back in shape. After a good cleaning, we might consider touching up the varnish work and recover the counter with new vinyl."

"That sounds like a good idea."

Rodger and Helen had been cleaning the Sea Witch`s interior for two hours when John and his crew arrived to continue their work of setting the booms to the two standing masts and adding rigging. Making a quick exit, Rodger and Helen headed for Nelda`s café for lunch.

"I`m starved," said Helen. "I`m up for one of Nelda`s hamburgers with all the trimmings. I left food for Bilgee in the camper, so she`s okay.

"That sounds good. I think we`ve accomplished a lot in two hours. John said they will finish rigging the halyards and the fore and aft stays by three o`clock. We should be able to get another couple of hours of cleaning in after that."

When they arrived at the café, Nelda was a whirling dervish pouring coffee, making out receipts, collecting money at the cash register and bussing tables. Her new part-time cook was busy cleaning the kitchen from the onslaught of lunch orders. Helen waved to Nelda as they walked in calling out "Hi Nelda. Could we have two deluxe hamburgers and a couple of cups of coffee?" Nelda immediately passed this on to the cook and Helen and Rodger settled in a comfortably booth by the front window.

"You`re late for lunch," Nelda scolded, "but that`s not a problem, just glad to have you here." Nelda continued attending to her last customers at the cash register, as most needed to hurry back to their jobs. A few retirees, reluctant to leave the companionship of others, lingered over their coffee.

As Nelda brought the coffee pot to their booth, the cook brought out their order and disappeared into the kitchen for a final cleanup. "He`s a lifesaver for me," confided Nelda. "Most of my business is at breakfast or lunch time and he comes in for two hours each of those times. He had his own restaurant once and was a well-known chef. Actually, he works for me as a retirement hobby. Lord knows I couldn`t pay him what he`s worth."

"He sounds like a real find," Rodger said taking a first bite of his hamburger." His eyes rolled up and he reared back in the booth as a sign of approval shaking his head up and down. "You have a great cook here, Nelda, have you expanded your menu to show off his ability with food?"

"No, but that`s an idea. Although he says he`s satisfied with the hours he works. He stays pretty much to himself and lives in a cottage on the oceanfront south of town. I guess he`s married, as he claims someone on his W-4 tax form. He`s about to leave for the day, so I`ll introduce you. `Wolfgang, I`d like you to meet Helen and Rodger, they`re friends of mine.`"

The stocky-built, sandy-haired, older man walked over to the booth at Nelda`s beckoning. His German accent voice filled the small cafe as he extended his thick-fingered, strong hand accompanied by a friendly smile. "I`m pleased to meet you. Yah, a friend of Nelda is a friend of mine."

"I`m pleased to meet you, Wolfgang," replied Helen. "This hamburger is delicious. I understand you are a retired chef, which is good news for us as we plan to eat here a lot during the next three weeks."

"I don`t cook my specialties here," said Wolfgang, "just plain, good food, but before you leave maybe I can cook for you a duck."

"You`d have to make that dinner for four," injected Nelda. "John and I would want to be a part of that dinner party."

"I`d like to do that just for the fun of It," Wolfgang agreed laughing. "Maybe I could bring a friend and make it a dinner to remember."

"It`s settled then," said Nelda. "In three weeks we`ll have a Bon Voyage party for Helen and Rodger. Wolfgang will cook the duck and I`ll furnish the ducks."

"Yah, we would need two, five-pound ducks, for sure. I must go now, my friend is waiting." With a wave of the hand and a broad smile, he turned and walked briskly out of the café and into the Coos Bay world.

"Such fun," said Helen, "I can hardly wait for that Bon Voyage party.

Rodger agreed, then thoughtfully added, "I don`t think I've ever eaten roast duck."

Nelda finished pouring them a second cup of coffee and one for herself, and then added, "If Wolfgang cooks it, count on a real eating experience."

* * *

After lunch Rodger and Helen did cleaning on the boat until the shipyard closed at five o`clock. Returning to their camper, they found Bilgee waiting at the camper door. The anxious look on her face told them she had to go to the pet area… now! Rodger took her on the lease while Helen fixed their afternoon Scotch and Water drinks. When they returned Rodger took his drink and offered a toast, "To Kindness." Helen nodded in agreement as they sat in the dinette to talk over the day.

"Imagine, a Bon Voyage party for us," she beamed, "and cooked by a professional chef."

"Great, isn`t it? Oh, by the way, John told me the sails should be here any day. In the meantime they will install a lifeline around the perimeter of the boat and install hardware at a secure and convenient point to tether to so neither of us can be washed overboard again. We can wear a harness in addition to our life jacket when we have storm conditions, and we can hook up to this tether."

Moving closer to Rodger, Helen put her arms around him and said, "Oh, how I wished we had that from the start of this trip; some lessons come hard."

"Yes, but we don`t have to repeat our mistakes, do we?"

* * *

The next day Rodger, Helen, and Bilgee arrived at the boatyard to watch the progress on the boat. They were prepared to step in and do minor repairs and cleanup when the work crew wasn't working on the Sea Witch.

Being a small boat repair business, the work crew had to move about from job to job as various needs of the boatyard demanded. The weather, now cool and overcast, didn`t daunt their spirits, and Bilgee wore her black, fleece-lined doggie coat acquired for just such a day.

The crew was busy measuring the gunnels` perimeter and installing hardware for stainless steel stanchions two feet high, three feet apart to support the two plastic-coated, stainless steel cables that formed a lifeline around the Sea Witch. She took on a more finished look as each part of the new superstructure was added.

John walked over to Helen and Rodger as they stood watching the scene before them. "What do you think about the looks of the lifeline around the gunnels?"

"It looks good to me," said Helen. "It dresses up the old girl in addition to a safety factor it is designed for."

"I wish it had been there before. Maybe it would have kept me from going overboard," added Rodger.

"Maybe yes, maybe no," drawled John, "but the tether arrangement would have kept you attached to the boat even if you were in the water."

Rodger moved over beside Helen drawing her close to him. "This conversation stirs up unpleasant memories; probably for both of us. Let`s go to Nelda`s for an early lunch and come back aboard the Sea Witch while the crew is having their lunch break."

"Sounds like a plan. Do you want to join us, John?"

"No, I need to be here for this and several other jobs. I`ll see you later this afternoon." John walked them to the center of the boatyard and waved goodbye as he headed for another boat being placed in a crib for bottom repairs.

Rodger and Helen put Bilgee in the truck cab consoling her with a dog treat, then continued on to Nelda`s Café. The place was getting ready for the noon crowd that would appear in less than an hour. Nelda quickly arranged place settings at the tables and booths while Wolfgang prepared food in the kitchen. Looking out through the pass-through to the dining area he waved enthusiastically to Helen and Rodger as they came through the door. "Guta Morgan," he offered. "You two are early today. Is your stomach telling you it`s time to eat?" he asked as he walked through the swinging kitchen doors to greet them.

"Rodger can always eat," said Helen, "but we`re working around the crew at John`s boat works, so we`re taking lunch early."

"It`s good to hear Rodger enjoys a good appetite; he`s my kind of guy. I've added liver and onions to the noon menu today if you're interested, Rodger."

"Boy, am I`m interested. I haven`t had liver and onions since I can`t remember. I don`t fix it myself because I don`t like the feel of raw liver in my hands."

"Oh, you cook?" exclaimed Wolfgang.

"That`s a matter of opinion, but I guess I can give you a qualified yes."

Helen turned and faced Rodger. "I`d say you`re a darned good cook. You're the number one chef in our house."

Rodger and Helen sat down in a front booth as Wolfgang and Nelda stood looking down at them. Nelda had heard the conversation and turned to Wolfgang, "If you fix liver and onions for Rodger, fix me a half order. I haven`t tasted your liver and onions and I`m up for lunch before the crowd arrives."

"Count me in too," said Helen. Liver and onions have never been big in my life, but maybe you can change that, Wolfgang."

"What a salesman I am, and I haven`t opened my mouth yet," quipped Wolfgang. "When I cook for you the aroma of liver and onions will fill this place and Nelda will have a run on it; I guess I`d better get started." Wolfgang gestured goodbye with a friendly wave of his hand and returned to the kitchen. Soon the chopping of onions could be heard through the pass-through opening accompanied by a low whistling sound as the stimulated chef met this challenge with enthusiasm.

Nelda brought coffee and the three chatted until interrupted by a smiling Wolfgang setting three plates of well-presented, liver and onions, garlic-mashed potatoes and petite-sized peas before them garnished with a sprig of parsley. Sitting down beside them in the booth, he watched eagerly and waited for their response to his culinary presentation. Rodger was first to fairly explode with, "This is absolutely delicious. This is what I call good eating, and I've never tasted liver and onions that compared to this."

"Vunderbar," exclaimed a smiling Wolfgang as he stood with arms raised forming a `V' for victory to emphasize his joy at its being pronounced a culinary success.

Nelda and Helen added their praise, and a happy, proud Wolfgang returned to his kitchen. The three ate with little conversation. Nelda finished her half-order, was soon busy greeting noon customers. With the delicious odor of liver and onions permeating the small café, they soon sold out of the new menu item as Wolfgang had predicted. Rodger and Helen saved a little liver for Bilge and returned to rescue her from the truck cab.

* * *

The three of them walked back into the boatyard arriving just as John and his work crew stopped work to take their lunch break. "It`s all yours," he shouted as they neared the Sea Witch. "I was just thinking," he continued. "When we finish the life line around the perimeter of the Sea Witch you may want to take this a step farther to keep Bilgee from going overboard in rough seas. I sailed a lot when I was younger and with a dog. I put netting between the stanchions of the life line and other openings to keep Buster from going overboard and drowning in rough weather."

"That sounds like a good idea, John," said Helen. "We`ll do that before we continue our voyage to Tahiti. I`m concerned about Bilgee`s ability to move about on deck while we`re underway." Bilgee, recognizing her name being spoken, looked up questioningly at her mistress.

"There are a couple of things you can do for everyday sailing to help her," continued John. "Keep her toenails cut short to give her more gripping ability and paint the decks with an abrasive-type, non-skid finish. I used homogenized sand stirring it into good quality deck paint. Some sailors use a special, non-skid, manufactured paint with various abrasive items already added. Incidentally, it helps your ability to walk around in rough seas too."

"That sounds like something we should be doing anyway," added Helen as she bent down to pat a concerned Bilgee, reassuring her everything was all right.

"I guess we`d better start thinking more about out four-legged crewmember`s special needs," said Rodger as he knelt down beside Bilgee patting her side. "This brings up the delicate subject of Bilgee going potty at sea. Tell us how you handled that with your dog."

"He wouldn`t relieve himself on board at first no matter what I tried; sprays, a piece of turf, actually showing him what I wanted him to do. Consequently, I had to put him ashore once a day. This limited my sailing options; finally I just didn`t put him ashore. After forty-eight hours he found a spot on deck and relieved himself. I praised him, gave him a treat, and from then on that was his spot."

"I hope it works that way with Bilgee," replied Helen. "Are there any other things we should be prepared for when cruising with a dog?"

John thought for a minute and then added, "She should have a PFD on when she`s on deck."

"What`s that?" asked Rodger picking up Bilgee and holding her in the crook of his right arm continuing to stroke her back.

"That`s a Personal Floatation Device," continued John. "If she goes overboard you have a chance of rescuing her. As you know it`s possible to lose sight of a human in fewer than five minutes...even in a moderate sea."

"Somehow this conversation is making me feel uneasy," said Rodger.

"I understand, Sweetie," replied Helen, "but we need to avoid what happened before, for us and for Bilgee. Is there anything else we can do to help her become a safe, happy sailor?"

"I've seen some sea dogs with booties on," replied John with a faint smile showing at the corners of his mouth.

"Really?" gasped Rodger. "Booties like babies wear?" Bilgee became concerned with his master`s raised voice and looked up questioningly.

Helen continued, "Tell us about that, John."

"They are the equivalent of deck shoes for dogs. I investigated them in order to avoid repainting my deck with an abrasive paint. I was told there are three basic reasons for outfitting your dog with booties: to help provide traction on slippery decks, to protect your dog`s paws on long hikes over rough terrain or hot sand, and to protect the limp paws of injured or older dogs. They look like mittens without thumbs and can be snapped, buckled, or wrapped on with Velcro. Buster and I decided he wasn`t the type to make a fashion statement, so I painted my deck."

"Rodger and I will have to give that some consideration. Oh, if Bilgee could only talk."

Bilgee looked first at Helen and then at Rodger. Her expression seemed to say, "*I think I make myself understood.*"

Chapter Thirty

Rodger, Helen, and Bilgee arrived back at the RV Park in the early afternoon stopping by the office for their mail before traveling on to their camper site. They were in high spirits after two hours of work on the interior of the Sea Witch and their enjoyable lunch at Nelda`s. While Helen went into the office Rodger and Bilgee waited in the truck. She returned with a concerned look on her face as she held out a letter from a Seattle lawyer addressed to Rodger.

Rodger opened the letter without re-starting the truck`s engine and quickly read the letter from his law firm, Lasher, Holzapfel, Sperry, and Ebberson. After finishing the letter he sat back in the truck seat and slumping forward muttered, "I can`t believe this."

"What can`t you believe?" asked Helen.

"Irene has changed her mind and wants to go to court to reconsider the present property settlement agreement before the divorce is finalized."

"That doesn`t sound good; what`s she after?"

"My guess is she wants to punish me for making her the `scorned` woman by her asking for the lion`s share of the estate."

"Oh boy! This can get messy, and just when everything seemed to be going so right.

What does the letter ask you to do?"

"They want me to show up at a court date on April fourteenth; that`s ten days from now."

"You`d better give your lawyer a call and prepare yourself for that court date."

"Should we return home to deal with this?"

"Talk to your lawyer first; then we can decide." Helen put her arm over Rodger`s slumped shoulders and gave him a one-armed supportive hug. "We`ve had greater problems to face together than this… after all, Sweetie, it`s only money. Let`s go to the camper and I`ll fix you a double scotch and water. That`ll put a stiffener in your back."

"You're right. I can decide later how I want to react to this. I guess any feelings of love Irene may have had for me are gone. I understand the opposite of love is not hate, but fear. I wonder what she`s afraid of?" Rodger sighed as he dragged a hand across his face. "I think I`ll take you up on that drink"

* * *

Setting his drink aside, Rodger removed his cell phone from its case to call his lawyer in Seattle. "James, this is Rodger. I received your letter today with the court order stating I`m to appear in court on April fourteenth to reconsider a property settlement. What should I do?"

"You should be here to go to court. I received this court order through her lawyer the day before yesterday. My guess is she wants a bigger slice of the community property pie."

"That was my thought too. Can the judge arbitrarily give her more than half of the community property in the State of Washington?"

"Yes, if there are extenuating circumstances."

"Tell me about that," questioned Rodger with a tone of anger creeping into his voice.

"Usually it`s because one of the two principals is handicapped in some way. Washington is a no`fault-divorce' state, so why you're getting divorced isn`t the issue."

"That`s a relief, but Irene isn`t handicapped."

The voice on the other end of the phone stated matter-of-factly, "I`ll call her lawyer and ask specifically what she`s after; maybe we can avoid the court appearance."

"Okay, James, that`d be good. Call me when you find out something."

"I should be back to you in a few days, Rodg."

"I`ll wait for your call. Goodbye Jason."

"Goodbye, Rodg."

Helen, sitting in the dinette across from Rodger, looked at him expectantly. "Well?"

"Jason doesn`t know what she`s after, but he`ll attempt to find out, and perhaps we can avoid the court hearing if Irene and I come to an agreement on whatever it is."

"So what do we do until you hear from your lawyer?"

"Just keep on doing what we`ve been doing," replied Rodger, a smile lifting the corners of his mouth.

"Okay, I`ll take Bilgee for a walk; it`s your turn to fix dinner."

Standing, Rodger offered Helen his hand to help her rise to her feet. Then holding her at arms length he said, "It`ll be alright, we`ll get to Tahiti yet."

"Your darn right we will," countered Helen. "This legal storm is nothing compared to what we`ve seen so far on this trip, weather wise. We`ve got a good vessel and a good crew. What more could you ask for?"

* * *

The next day Rodger, Helen and Bilgee drove from the RV Park to the boatyard in time to talk to John before his lunch break. He was in his office dealing with a customer. Rodger and Helen waited until the customer had departed before approaching John. He beamed his shy smile and extended his hand in welcome to each of them. "You`re here to work on the Sea Witch during the lunch hour, I see. We`re still waiting on the sails, as sail makers have their own timeline. You can have the boat the rest of the day, if you`d like."

Helen quickly replied, "We`d like that as varnish work goes slow and it`s a good day temperature-wise to do that. We`ve just received some news that may take us out of town in about a week for a few days, so any extra work time we can get now is helpful."

"Good," replied John. "This works for both of us. I`m on my way to Nelda`s for lunch if you`d like to join me."

"No," replied Helen. "We ate a late breakfast; we`ll take a break about three o`clock."

"I`ll tell Nelda to expect you." John rose from his desk and escorted them to the gate leading to the boatyard. "The weatherman predicts a 55 degrees plus for today, so you should be able to varnish," John offered before continuing to the Café. Helen, Rodger, and Bilgee walked to the drydock area to begin their day`s work.

* * *

After sanding, masking, wiping the sanded areas down with a tack rag, and varnishing for three hours they stood back taking satisfaction on what they accomplished. "My knees and back say it`s time for a break," said Rodger.

"Agreed, I`m up for lunch and some strong coffee."

Bilgee, asleep on the foredeck, came to life and joined them as Rodger lifted her over the gunnels into Helen`s outstretched arms where she stood on the middle rung of the boarding ladder. Carefully backing down the ladder to the tarmac below, Helen put Bilgee down and moved away for Rodger`s descent. The three of them walked to Nelda`s Café with Bilgee in the lead.

Nelda greeted them at the door, "John told me to expect you about now. Wolfgang left some of his clam chowder out of the cooler in case you wanted his today`s specialty. He usually leaves for home about two thirty, and I don`t stay open for supper anymore as this is a working man`s town and it doesn`t pay to do so. Besides, "she continued, "I like my evenings off."

Rodger was the first to respond. "If it`s Wolfgang's specialty for the day, that`s good enough for me."

"Make that two," said Helen. "Clam chowder is one of my favorite soups and I`m anxious to try Wolfgang`s recipe. Is it all right for Bilgee to be in here? We can take her to the truck if it isn`t."

"You're the only customers here, so it`s okay. Normally I don`t encourage pets, but I can make an exception for Bilgee as long as she stays out of the way. Most of my customers are the `big dog' type, and you can see the potential problem."

"On behalf of Bilgee," cooed Rodger smiling, "she thanks you."

Nelda filled their coffee cups and disappeared in to the kitchen. A few minutes later she appeared with two steaming bowls of clam chowder and a small tray of soda crackers. "Do you want anything else?" she asked.

"No," said Rodger, "this`ll do it."

"Do you mind if I join you, I`m tired and I need to sit down. Besides, I have a question to ask."

"Please do," said Helen. "You don`t have to get permission, Nelda; we`re almost family."

Nelda poured herself a cup of coffee and joined them. "John and I are going to the dance Saturday night at the Community Center and wondered if you`d like to join us. Wolfgang and his wife, Silvia, will be joining us there, so we`ll have our own private party."

"Well," said Helen, "the mysterious person living with Wolfgang is his wife. It sounds like a fun evening to me. What do you think, Rodg?"

"Hey, count me in; I`m up for some fun and I`d like to meet Silvia and get to know Wolfgang on a social level."

"Great!" exclaimed Nelda, "I`ll tell John tonight when he comes over for dinner."

"John`s coming over for dinner? Hmmm. You two appear to be getting serious with your relationship," quipped Rodger," or am I just imagining that?" Rodger looked over at Helen giving her a wink.

"Let`s just say our friendship is growing and I've never been happier. John is such a dear person."

"Listening to John talk about you, I think it`s mutual," replied Helen smiling. "Tell us what you know about Wolfgang and Silvia. Have they been married long and do they have children?"

Nelda blushed at the compliment. "Actually, they`re newly weds. They married less than a month ago and this is their first home together. They`re both German nationality, but he was born and raised during World War Two in Germany; while she was born and grew up in Switzerland. Although she has been previously married and is a grandmother, she`s twenty years younger than Wolfgang."

"Really!" replied Helen. "Of course Wolfgang doesn`t seem to be a man in his seventies. He has a delightful sense of humor and acts much younger. How did they meet if they were from two different parts of Europe?"

"They met on the beach here in Coos Bay. Wolfgang was walking his dog and Silvia was here from Switzerland visiting her daughter and granddaughter who live here. Wolfgang said it was love at first sight for him, but Silvia returned to Switzerland three weeks later as planned only to find out she wanted to spend the rest of her life with Wolfgang. She told him so and returned immediately to be married."

"Wow! replied Helen, "that`s quite a love story. It just goes to show us that love doesn`t have age boundaries. Have you met her?"

"Yes, he brought her to the cafe last Saturday afternoon and we had a nice visit. John was here and that`s when we put this dance idea together for this Saturday night. John and I have been going to the dance regularly this past month."

"John seems so much happier now then when we first met him," injected Rodger. "Of course he was still grieving over the death of his wife." Rodger got up from the booth, walked over to the counter to get the coffee pot, and return to fill the three cups.

"He still is," added Nelda nodding approval to Rodger. "He says the future looks more promising now."

"Not to change the subject," said Helen, "but what do you wear to a community dance?"

"John wears slacks and a sport shirt; I wear a casual-type cotton dress. However, anything goes in this day-and-age. You do have to wear shoes and no swimming suits. "

"That`s kinda what I thought," replied Helen laughing. "It`ll be fun to go to a dance again; it`s been years since I've danced. In fact, Rodg and I have never danced together." Turning to Rodger she asked, "You do dance, don`t you?"

"I never gave Fred Astaire any concern, but, yes, I dance," replied Rodger.

"Maybe we should practice tonight at the RVPark, just in case we have some differences of opinion on the subject."

"Okay, ye of little faith. I`ll meet you under the street light in the parking lot at eight o`clock sharp."

"Gee," teased Helen, "we have a date."

* * *

At the community club dance the band was a local, five-piece group that seemed to be on a first-name basis with most of the dancers. As the evening wore on, Helen and Rodger became more comfortable with each other as dance partners and ultimately changed partners with John and Nelda, and Wolfgang and Sylvia.

Sylvia, an outgoing, attractive brunette with a happy countenance, fit in easily with the group even though Wolfgang had to help her with an English word or expression occasionally. It was apparent she and Wolfgang were very much in love, enjoying a second lease on life, and felt comfortable publicly showing their affection for one another. They were the most accomplished dancers of the group and enjoyed the South American dances while Helen, Rodger, Nelda, and John chose to sit those out and enjoy the show put on by Wolfgang and Sylvia.

"How come you're so adept at the Rumba, Tango, and Cha cha cha? " asked Rodger as the two dancers walked off the floor.

"I used to live in Argentina," replied Wolfgang, "as I've cooked many places in the world. Silvia is a good dancer, follows easily, and these dances are popular in Europe."

Just then a Latin appearing, middle-aged man walked over to Silvia and asked her to dance. Obviously flustered and surprised, she turned to Wolfgang for help.

Wolfgang laughed, "Don`t look at me, I don`t own you, and he didn`t ask me to dance."

"Thank you for asking, but I am new to your country and I don`t feel comfortable dancing with people I don`t know," replied Silvia.

"I`m new to this country too, and you dance the dance of my country, Spain, quite well." The man turned to go, disappointed, but understanding.

"On second thought," said Silvia, "I will dance with you as long as my husband doesn`t object."

Wolfgang stood taking Silvia by the hand and offered it to the stranger. "No more than one dance or she will turn into a scullery maid."

"Thank you, senior. I`m honored, and we wouldn`t want that to happen." The band, fortunately, played a Latin number, they danced beautifully, and the man escorted Silvia off the floor, thanking her profusely, and disappeared into the crowd.

"Well," injected Helen, "you have a mystery man in your life, Silvia."

"I hope not," quipped Wolfgang. "I really don`t want to share Silvia with anyone."

The dance came to a close at eleven o`clock and after an exchange of hugs and handshakes, they went their separate ways.

* * *

The following Monday morning Helen, Rodger, and Bilgee arrived at the boat yard to watch the fitting of the new sails that had arrived on Saturday. John and his crew were busy laying them out for the inspection of possible flaws. Being convinced the sails were made to specification and had no apparent flaws, he ordered the crew to attach and raise the mainsail, the mizzen sail and the genoa jib. Helen and Rodger stood off to the side watching intently, their enthusiasm growing as the Sea Witch returned to her former glory. Standing majestically, but high and dry on her cribbing in the dry dock, her three sails luffing gently back and forth in the soft breeze was a welcome sight to Helen and Rodger..

"She looks so good," exclaimed Helen as she slipped her arm over Rodger`s shoulder.

"She surely does," agreed Rodger. Then looking over at John, "When can we take her out for a shakedown cruise?" he asked.

"We have the bottom paint and zincs to put on and a little more work tuning the rigging. I`d say by the end of the week," he replied. It`s best to put the bottom paint on just a couple hours before we launch her. Being a copper-based paint to prevent sea growth, it never dries hard and slowly sluffs off," he explained. "That`s why you get to paint the bottom every two years."

"What day do expect to launch?" asked Helen dropping her hold on Rodger and facing John directly.

John pulled out his pocket memo book to determine when crew and equipment would be available. "If all goes well, we should launch Friday afternoon."

"Wouldn`t it be great to have a launching ceremony just like she`s a new ship, and in a way she is," Helen enthused.

"Hey, good idea," agreed Rodger. "There wouldn`t be much of a crowd, but who cares. We could invite Nelda, Wolfgang and Silvia and of course John and his crew will be here. A bottle of champagne to break across the bow, a couple bottles for us and I promise not to make a speech."

"As Skipper of this vessel, I`ll take care of that part of it," Helen grinned. "I`ll bet Wolfgang would make some hor`douervs and we`d have a real celebration for the re-commissioned Sea Witch."

"I've got some bunting I keep on hand for launching new vessels that we can use and really dress her up for her second life," offered John, "and I`ll bet Nelda will want a part in this celebration too."

The three of them walked over to Nelda`s café to eat lunch and share their idea of the re-commissioning party. They left Bilgee in the truck, as it was the lunch hour and they didn`t want to impose on Nelda`s friendship. The noon crowd was just forming, and as usual, Nelda was everywhere at once greeting customers, taking orders, and setting place settings where needed.

Wolfgang, busy in the kitchen, saw them enter and waved. He left the kitchen to ask Nelda a question and then walked over to the booth where the three sat perusing the menu. "Hello my friends, so good to see you." First wiping his hand on his apron, he shook hands around the table.

"What`s your specialty today, Wolfgang?" asked John.

"Clam Linguine, it`s pretty good, if I do say so myself."

"I`m sold," replied John.

"Me too," replied Rodger.

"I`m up for something lighter," injected Helen. "How about a BLT without the bacon?"

"Comin` up. I`ll tell Nelda I have your order." He smiled his big, happy smile accompanied by a half-laugh and returned to the kitchen eager to prepare food for his new friends.

"He`s such a happy fellow and appears to be very satisfied with his new life here in Coos Bay and with his new bride, Silvia," said Rodger smiling. "She too is such a delightful, happy person; Wolfgang keeps her laughing a good part of the time."

“”I wonder what Wolfgang’s story is,” added Helen. “He told me he grew up during World War Two in a war-torn Germany. That couldn`t have been easy. I wonder how he ended up here in America?”

“I`m sure he`ll tell us if he wants us to know,” replied Rodger. “He seems like a very open person.”

Helen leaned over to Rodger and touched him on the cheek, “That`s one of the things I like about you Rodg, you always see the best in people.”

Nelda worked her way to their booth and gave John a loving pat on the head. John responded with a smile that would light up all outdoors. “Nelda,” he said, “Helen and Rodger are planning a recommissioning party for the Sea Witch. They`re providing champagne for the christening and those in attendance, I`m providing the buntings and we were going to ask Wolfgang to make some hors d`oeuvres. What do you think of the idea?”

“It sounds like a real celebration. I`ll pay for the hors d`oeuvres ingredients and ask Wolfgang to make them on my time.”

John smiled and exclaimed, “I told you she would want to be a part of the party.”

“I`m going to wear my new dress,” said Nelda.

“The one you wore at the dance Saturday night?” asked Helen looking directly at her.

“No… my new, new dress.”

“You`re getting to be a regular clothes horse. What`s the motivation?”

“If you think that`s out-of–character, wait `til you see my trousseau.” Nelda put her hand to her mouth blushing. “Oh John, I`m so sorry, dear. We were going to keep it a secret for a while.”

“What?” exploded Rodger and Helen at the same instant. Sliding out of the booth and maneuvering to put her arms around Nelda, Helen held her tight. “This is so great! When is the happy event?”

“It`s April now... we thought June would be a nice time of year and it gives us time to know each other better. See how practical love becomes when you`re older?” Nelda, though usually shy, seemed absolutely glowing as she answered their questions.

John sat back soaking in her happiness, and said nothing. *This is her show*, he thought. *Let her have the spotlight.*

"You sly old dog; never gave us a hint," said Rodger looking over at John. "Well, that`s not exactly true. We`ve watched you and Nelda change before our eyes. As the song says, *Love changes everything.*"

"I didn`t know you were into love songs, Rodg," replied Helen. "Maybe I`d better pay closer attention."

"My life isn`t a total open book," grinned Rodger. "Almost, but not quite."

The playful bantering went on back and forth until lunch arrived. Nelda gave John a hug in her first open show of affection and returned happily to her work. John appeared content with the world also and then lost himself in his plate of clam linguine.

Shouting over to Wolfgang as he appeared behind the counter, "You did it again, absolutely delicious."

Helen and Rodger smiled at each other as they silently acknowledged the change from two quiet, introverted people to two senior citizens intent on getting the most out of the rest of their lives.

* * *

Returning to the RV Park that afternoon, there was a letter from Irene`s attorney confirming Irene would be at court in Bellevue on the fourteenth of April at 2:00.

"I guess I`d better call my lawyer as five days have passed and I've heard nothing from him," said Rodger.

Helen slid out of the truck taking Bilgee with her. "We`ll take a walk while you make your phone call. This isn`t the end of the world, this is only a hearing to reconsider the division of the property."

Helen, with Bilgee on a leash, headed for the pet area. Rodger sat on a picnic bench outside of the camper and dialed his lawyer on the cell phone. "James, this is Rodger. Have you found out anything about the hearing?"

"Hi Rodg, I've found out nothing except Irene would like to meet with you in private before the hearing. According to protocol, you aren`t supposed to do that. Once you both have a lawyer, everything is supposed to go through your lawyers."

"To hell with protocol, if she wants to talk to me I`ll call her on the phone. She is still my wife."

"As your lawyer, I advise against it. I can`t give you advice if I`m not there. Nor can her lawyer give her advice."

"Maybe we`ll live without our lawyers` advice. We`ve lived most of our lives without it so far."

"I know that, but you weren`t in the middle of a divorce either. It could end up costing you more money in the long run."

"I`ll take that chance. After all it`s only money and you're not exactly cheap."

"If you want me out of the case, just say so. I have a sworn duty to uphold the law, therefore I can`t advise you to circumvent it."

"I`ll see you in court on the fourteenth, unless I tell you otherwise."

"Okay Rodg, see you in court at one-thirty. We need to talk before we enter the court room."

"I`ll be there, James."

* * *

"Irene? This is Rodger. How are you?"

"Rodger! This is a surprise. I`m fine health wise, if that`s what your asking?"

"I've been notified by my lawyer that we have a court date on the fourteenth. What`s that about?"

"I`m not happy about the divorce. In fact, I've had some second thoughts."

"Really! What are you saying?"

"I`m saying, if you can give up Helen, I want us back together as we were before."

"This is a surprise! Aren`t you happy with your new life being retired, pursuing your art work, and being the matriarch of the family?"

"Not without you, Rodger. I guess one doesn`t know how you're going to react to a situation until you get there and try it on for size. Are you happy where you are?"

"Yes I am, Irene. Helen and I compliment each other. I know you don`t like to hear that, but it`s the truth."

"You're right! I don`t like to hear that."

"What is the court date about?"

"In part it was a way to get you back in town so we could have the talk we`re having right now."

"Damn it, Irene, I`ll always love you as the mother of our children, and the good years we had together. Circumstances took me to death`s door with my tuberculosis and the shipwreck, and I made some profound decisions."

"I know, Rodger; I`m not happy with myself for the way I gave up on you. I just thought if you weren't completely happy where you are right now, you might want to give our marriage another try."

"The bottom line is I am happy and Helen and I are doing what I always wanted to do, sail to Tahiti. We`re in the process of recommissioning the Sea Witch and we plan to be on our way in a matter of days."

"Unfortunately I understand… I hate being rejected again, but I had to try."

"I`m flattered by your proposal, and if I weren`t happy where I am, I`d give it a try."

"I`m going to hang up now, Rodger. Our sons and their families are all well, I`ll tell them you and I talked, and you send your love."

"Thanks, what about our court date?"

"I`ll see you in court on the fourteenth."

"Oh…for what purpose?"

"I want a bigger share of the estate"

"Really?"

"Really! I was not only your wife, but also your business partner. We`ll see what the court has to say about the business partnership and the community property."

"You really are angry, aren`t you. I think you're wasting the court`s time and mine, but we`ll let the court decide, now that we have a contested property settlement on our hands. I`m surprised you didn`t contest the divorce."

"I would have, but my lawyer said I didn`t have a case; this being a no-fault divorce state."

"I`ll see you in court, Irene."

"Yes, Good bye, Rodger."

* * *

"Well, did you make contact with Irene?" Helen had walked up to the picnic table where Rodger sat staring up at the sky.

"I sure did, and it wasn`t pleasant. I talked to James first; he didn`t want me to talk to Irene at all. According to the rules, I`m not suppose to."

"Really? That doesn`t seem right." Helen sat down beside him and took his hand in her`s sensing Rodg was upset.

"I called anyway and she really surprised me." Rodger turned to face Helen as the two sat side by side on the bench. "She suggested we give our marriage another try."

"Oh Rodg… what did you say?"

"I said no! I`m not willing to give up what you and I have, Helen. We`re soul mates and that just didn`t happen in my relationship with Irene, although we were compatible."

"I`m relieved we`re both on the same wave length," Helen sighed. "I`d hate to lose you again, Rodg. Are you still going to court on the fourteenth?"

"Yes. She`s really angry and now wants a bigger share of the pie."

"She`s not satisfied with the community property laws?"

"She says because she was my business partner, the business and the estate should be handled separately. I don`t understand her reasoning, but as I say, she`s angry."

"Is she angry or afraid?" ventured Helen.

* * *

The next morning Helen and Rodger with Bilgee sitting between them drove to the ship yard to finish up some final varnish work and prepare the cupboard and closet spaces for refilling of all the things necessary for extended ocean sailing. The day had the promise of being pleasant after the sun burns off the morning overcast. Coos Bay was alive with activity as the fishing fleet prepared for the upcoming season. Charter boats were being unwrapped from their winter`s inactivity and captain and crew were busy cleaning, painting and doing mechanical work on the diesel and gas engines. Everyone appeared to be in an optimistic mood looking forward to the new season of gambling on fish, weather, and tourists.

"I hope John`s crew can join us tomorrow for our launching party," said Rodger. "Otherwise, there will only be six of us, seven counting Bilgee."

"While you varnish," replied Helen, "I`ll run over to the liquor store and get the champagne after we get a confirmation from John. On the way back I`ll stop at Nelda`s and give her the head count for the hors d`ourves. I guess Wolfgang will come in early with Silvia to prepare them, or maybe the night before."

"Yesterday John told me 11:00 o`clock would be the target time for the launching," added Rodger. "Actually, he seemed as excited about this as we are."

Rodger, Helen, and Bilgee entered the shipyard, then stopped dead in their tracks. There, majestically, colorfully draped in red, white, and blue bunting loomed the Sea Witch towering over them even though she had been lowered to sit on the marine railway that would carry her down into the water.

"Oh, what a glorious sight," exclaimed Helen.

"I agree," added Rodger. "She is ready to be on her way to Tahiti."

"This is exciting! I wish I`d brought the camera."

Even Bilgee sensed the excitement of the moment and gave three sharp barks, then looked from Helen to Rodger for approval.

As Rodger and Bilgee went aboard the Sea Witch, Helen walked back to John`s office for a final confirmation on the time, and whether the work crew could be there long enough for the launching and refreshments or not. As she approached the office John walked out to intercept her. By the smile on his face Helen knew everything was on time, the boat work would be finished.

"Hi, Helen, I was expecting you. Eleven o`clock is still a good time for the launch."

"Great! How about the work crew? Can they have a half hour off to celebrate with us?"

"You bet they can, but only one glass of champagne. After all, we have a half day`s work ahead of us after the launching."

"How many will be there?"

"Four worked on the boat and they are proud of the work they did. It`s good for them to be included in this celebration."

"You can charge their time to us, John."

"No, that`s my contribution to the party."

"You're a real friend, and we won`t ever forget you and Nelda."

"That goes for us too. In a way you brought Nelda and me together by showing us that life goes on and new relationships can be as meaningful as the original ones. In some cases, even more so."

"Thank you, John. I`ll tell Rodger what you said. I`m on my way to Nelda`s; do you want to come along?"

"No, I have a full schedule, but maybe the three of us can have a late lunch together."

"We`d like that and we can talk over what to expect tomorrow. I've never been to a launching before."

They parted as John walked into the work area of the boat yard and Helen crossed the street to Nelda`s café. It was still early in the day and Nelda and Wolfgang were busy preparing for their lunch trade. Helen entered and walked up to Nelda to give her a friendly embrace. Wolfgang, seeing this yelled out, "What am I chopped liver?"

Helen laughed as she walked over and gave him a hug. "No, Wolfgang, you're not chopped liver. You are my friend who just happens to be a great cook. Which brings me to the question of hors d` oeuvres for the party tomorrow. There will be ten of us including you and Silvia."

"In that case," replied Wolfgang, "I`d better buy ingredients on the way home this afternoon and prepare them before I come to work tomorrow, I want them fresh."

"What do you plan to fix?" asked Nelda. "And remember, I`m paying for the ingredients."

"That`s my secret," laughed Wolfgang. "I promise you`ll like them."

"Great," replied Helen, "I like surprises. I`m on my way to the liquor store to get a bottle of champagne for the christening and a couple of bottles for the guests."

Wolfgang looked at Helen and smiled, "You`d better pick up a bottle of sparking cider as I`m an alcoholic and haven`t had a drink of alcohol for 23 years."

"Really! I had no idea, Wolfgang," replied Helen. "Of course I`ll have cider for you and perhaps others that may choose not to drink alcohol."

Nelda walked over to Wolfgang and put a friendly arm on his shoulder. "You're a good man, Wolfgang, and I`m lucky to have you working for me."

"I know," laughed Wolfgang, as if he had a private joke. "I know." Turning, he walked into the kitchen whistling.

Helen looked at Nelda questioningly and said, "I wonder what that`s all about?"

"I have no idea." Helen said goodbye and headed for the liquor store. After completing her shopping and locking the bottles in the truck, she headed back to the boat yard to join Rodger in the preparation work on the Sea Witch. Helen was elated with the way things had worked out on the recommissioning of the Sea Witch and looked forward to the shakedown cruise after Rodger returned from his court date next week. She had decided to stay in Coos Bay while Rodger drove back to Bellevue to hear what the court would decide about the final settlement terms of the divorce.

As the Sea Witch came into view the bunting of red, white, and blue that draped the bow section of the boat again momentarily startled her. *Oh what fun,* she thought as she focused on tomorrow`s christening party. Then the thought sprang into her mind, *I have a speech to prepare.*

* * *

That afternoon on the way to the RV Park after a productive day`s work on the Sea Witch, Rodger and Helen sat quietly each lost in their own thoughts. Bilgee slept between them perhaps lost in her own thoughts too.

Helen stared ahead watching the road but not watching the road. *What will I say tomorrow at the Christening,* she thought*? I guess I`ll give a rundown of the Sea Witch`s history as much as I know about it and express our hope for it for the immediate future. Perhaps other`s will have something to add. It doesn`t have to be earth shattering, after all I`m not running for an office.*

Rodger broke the silence. "I wonder what I`ll fix for dinner tonight? It`s my turn to cook, and there`s left over roast chicken. Maybe I`ll make chicken and dumplings. Bisquick for the dumplings and left over peas and a can of chicken broth should do it. That`s an easy meal and you can make a fresh veggie salad."

"Agreed."

"Here we are back at the homestead. I`ll take Bilgee for a walk if you`ll fix us our afternoon cocktail. I`m up for a Scotch and Water, how about you?"

"Sounds great."

Rodger, with Bilgee on her leash, walked the hundred yards to the pet area. The evening marine air was cool and the day`s shadows grew long. Several other dog owners were there and friendly conversation usually ensued, but not tonight. The pet owners were anxious to get back to the warmth of their traveling homes. *We won`t have the opportunity to go to a pet area when we return to sailing*, thought Rodger. *I wonder how that`ll turn out?"*

Helen had just finished making the drinks, and as Rodger came through the camper door, she handed him a Scotch and Water.

"That`s my girl, now let`s take a minute to talk about tomorrow. What do you see happening at the christening?"

"I think we`ll have toasts of champagne with hors d`oeuvres in front of the Sea Witch. Then I`ll give my yet-to-be prepared speech, take the ribbon decked champagne bottle and break it over the bow as John and his crew release the braking system on the railway crib and the Sea Witch will slide majestically down to the bay where she belongs."

"Wow! That`s quite a picture. Have you ever been to a christening?"

"No, but I saw several on news reels at the movies."

"Sounds good to me. I`m hungry, would you make the salad while I do the honors on the left over chicken?"

"Of course I will; aren`t I your right-hand kitchen helper?"

* * *

The boatyard was teeming with people as Helen and Rodger arrived at nine o`clock on the day of the christening. The morning air still had a tinge of coolness and the smell of the nearby ocean. The weatherman had predicted a pleasant 68 degrees by afternoon, which is warm for early spring on the Oregon Coast. Boat owners, whose boats stood on blocks in the boatyard were taking advantage of the weather to prepare their boat`s hull for bottom paint, zinc replacement, and sometimes shaft, propeller, and rudder repair or replacement.

After Rodger parked the truck in the parking lot, the three of them proceeded to the office to talk with John about the upcoming christening. John waved to them as they walked in to his austere but tidy office. "Everything is on schedule and I`ll have the crew there at eleven o`clock."

Helen replied, "That`s great John. I guess we should go to Nelda`s and see how the refreshments are coming along. Do we have a table to put the refreshments on?"

"I've already taken care of that," replied John. "It`s set up by the bow of the Sea Witch. You certainly picked a good day for the christening. I hope you don`t mind that I called the local newspaper to see if they wanted to send a photographer. It`s good for business and they`re always on the lookout for local news."

"That`s a surprise," laughed Rodger. "Maybe they`d like a copy of Helen`s speech."

"Oh, come now, Rodg. They might like a picture for the paper with a line or two about the event, nothing more."

John interrupted, "I hope I haven`t created a problem."

"No problem," replied Helen. "I`m not the shy type, and if they want my notes, they can have them."

John smiled in relief, "See you at eleven o`clock."

The bell above the café door tinkled as Rodger, Helen, and Bilgee entered the empty café; Nelda and Wolfgang could be heard working in the kitchen.

"Hello you two," called out Helen. "Can we join you?"

"Come on back," called out Nelda. Wolfgang is just putting the finishing touches on the hors d` oeuvres."

"Oh my," exclaimed Helen as she proceeded into the kitchen. "Those look delicious; do they have a name?"

Wolfgang replied, "These before me are cucumber rounds with smoked oysters. Those over there on the table are smoked salmon with cream cheese on toast."

"You have pulled out all the stops, Wolfgang," said Helen. "This exceeds anything I could have imagined."

"Good! I`m glad you like my choices; try one."

"I was hoping you`d say that," added Rodger as he quickly raised a small square of toast with a mixture of smoked salmon and cream cheese on it. "Hmmm! That`s good eating, Wolfgang."

Wolfgang replied, "I had a hard time deciding between six recipes I have for hors d` ouevers. But this being a fisherman`s town, I decided on a seafood taste that fisherman would probably enjoy."

Helen held a cucumber round to her lips with a small smoked Olympia oyster adorning the top and consumed it in one bite. Pleasure spread across her face like a morning sun coming up over the ocean. "Oh Wolfy, the guests are going to love these."

"Wolfy, you called me Wolfy? That`s what the girls used to call me in my younger days." Wolfgang beamed with pleasure and laughed heartily at the sudden turn in the conversation.

"I can`t imagine why they would call you that," chuckled Rodger.

"It`s ten o`clock," interrupted Nelda. "Let`s get this show on the road. "Wolfgang and Rodger, carry the two trays of hors d` oeuvres; Helen and I will bring the rest of the things."

* * *

Helen stood at the bow of the Sea Witch smiling broadly with a three by five note card in her hand. The bottle of Champagne in her other hand was attached to long braided multicolored ribbons that reached up and were tied to the ship`s railing above. She looked out at the group of people that included the four shipyard workers, John and Nelda, Wolfgang and Sylvia, a reporter and photographer from the Coos Bay`s daily newspaper, a few curious passersby's, and Rodger and Bilgee.

"On behalf of Rodger and myself," she began, "we want to thank you for helping us celebrate the return of the Sea Witch to her rightful place in the boating world. Eli Jacobsen built her fifty years ago at his boatyard in Tracyton, Washington. Being a master boat builder, he built her to the plans for a Tahiti Ketch. She`s 31 feet long from stem to stern post, weights in at nine tons, draws four feet of water, and built of solid oak ribs, stem and keel. She`s fir planked, spars are of solid spruce, and carries four hundred seventy square feet of sail.

The Tahiti Ketch has a reputation as a solid ocean-going boat. The moment you step aboard the Sea Witch the thought occurs to you 'this is not a boat, it`s a ship.' Everything about her confirms that descision: the wide decks, the high bulwarks, the snug cockpit, and the husky masts and booms.

She`s had a half-dozen owners, sailed mostly in the Northwest as far north as Alaska. I owned her for ten years and sailed mostly among the American and Canadian San Juan Islands. I sold her to Rodger in June of last year, a year after my former sailing partner and husband, Clyde, died. She started her journey south eight months ago to Tahiti, but was dismast in a storm off Point Arena on the Oregon Coast in September. Being towed here to Coos Bay, she`s been lived aboard by an old friend, Bradley Arnold, until two months ago. Bradley passed on and at that time Rodger and I decided to have her refitted for sailing and continue our interrupted voyage to Tahiti.

"That brings us up to this moment and with this bottle of champagne I rechristen thee Sea Witch." As Helen spoke these final words she raised the champagne bottle above her head and with a mighty swing, smashed it across the middle of the bow. Two of the boatyard crewmembers standing by simultaneously swung sledgehammers at the safety blocks holding the wheels of the marine railway, and knocked them away. John engaged the donkey engine of the marine railway system to brake the crib`s decent down the gentle slope to the bay. The rails creaked and groaned as the Sea Witch started its journey slowly downward. Everyone broke in to applause; hoots and hollers were soon added to fill the morning air with happy sounds.

Occupants of several cars parked along side the yard fence, who had been watching the ceremony from afar, honked their horns repeatedly to add to the cacophony of sound. Rodger stepped forward to lock Helen in a strong embrace and planted a firm kiss on her lips; much to the pleasure of the small crowd. Bilgee gave three joyful barks of approval and the christening was complete.

Soon the crowd dispersed, bunting was removed, tables put away, empty bottles dispensed with, and the Sea Witch bobbed majestically in the water alongside the dock bordering the marine railway. A colorful entwinement of ribbons held the top half of a broken champagne bottle dangling from the railing near the bow. The Sea Witch was now ready for her shakedown cruise.

Chapter Thirty-One

The trip to Bellevue was lonely for Rodger being used to having Helen and Bilgee with him nearly all the time. His unhappy mission would put him in verbal combat with Irene and her lawyer. Of course his lawyer would be there as his advisor and voice.

A northwest early spring rain caused the windshield wipers to beat a steady rhythmic tempo as he progressed up the highway. Traffic was light except around Portland. He had taken the bypass east of the city through the suburbs, but Portland`s continued growth had eliminated any chance of comfortable driving.

It was a one day trip of steady driving from Coos Bay to Bellevue and Rodger really didn`t want to be there. *Why couldn`t Irene be satisfied with the State`s community property laws,* he thought. *If she had, everything would have been settled and he would be back in Coos Bay getting the Sea Witch prepared for her shakedown cruise up the coast to Reedsport, Oregon.*

Arriving in the early evening he got a motel room for the night and called his lawyer.

The next day he arrived at the courthouse and met with James for a half hour before the court hearing. They determined it would be best to wait until Irene`s lawyer presented their case before they could prepare a defense against it.

Walking into the courtroom at the appointed time they took a seat at the long oak table to the right of the judge`s elevated desk. Irene and her lawyer were not there.

The judge called the bailiff forward to have a short, whispered conversation. He looked at the clock on the wall and asked if Rodger McCauley was present. James replied for Rodger in the affirmative.

It was now ten minutes after the appointed hour. The judge rapped his gavel and stated, "Because neither the plaintiff, Irene McCauley, nor her lawyer are present, I find against the petition for an `unusual settlement for the distribution of community property.` The case is dismissed."

Rodger and James sat there quietly for a moment before they realized that it was over before it began. They were like a prizefighter and his attendant ready to do battle and the opponent failed to enter the ring.

"I wonder what happened," puzzled Rodger?

"Call Irene and ask her," suggested James. "It`s good to have it over with, but this has cost you time and money, Rodg; not to mention mental anguish."

"Let me use your cell phone, and we`ll find out."

Rodger hurriedly dialed the familiar number. "Irene?"

"Yes."

"This is Rodger? Why weren`t you in court today?"

"I changed my mind this morning, Rodg, and called my lawyer. He wasn`t happy with me, but it was my decision. Didn`t he call the court?"

"No, and the judge was angry. He found in my favor by dismissing the case."

"Well, now you can go back to your true love and continue your childish fantasy."

"You really are angry, aren't you?"

"Hell yes I`m angry, why wouldn`t I be? You take the best years of my life and then you dessert me in my old age. What am I supposed to do with the rest of my life?"

"The same thing you would do if I was around. Enjoy each day with your family and friends, your hobbies, and anything else that may come along. Who knows what tomorrow holds?"

"That`s easy for you to say, you've got a new love to share your life."

"You could have too, if you allow it to happen. You're an attractive woman, Irene. You have a devoted family and a good income to allow yourself to indulge in just about anything you want to…the choice is yours. You can sit back and do nothing or you can meet life head on, optimistically, and see what happens. If you choose the latter, you won`t be sorry."

"Well, thanks for the pep talk, Rodger. We`ll see what happens. I`m tired of goodbyes, so I`ll see you around."

"Probably… we still share a family."

* * *

Helen slept in after seeing Rodger off for his drive to Bellevue and awakened to find Bilgee close to her side in the bed. *I wonder how Rodg is doing? He should be nearly to Portland by now.* Moving past Bilgee, she slid out of bed onto the cold linoleum covered floor. *I think I`ll skip breakfast and go to Nelda`s for brunch. It will be good to have some company and focus on them now that the christening is over. I do need to move the Sea Witch back to Stimson`s dock today to accommodate John. He needs the dock space.*

Helen dressed and did a few necessary chores before driving the short distance to the boat yard. The weather was a repeat of yesterday and Helen hummed a familiar love song, *Fly Me To The Moon*, as she watched the town of Coos Bay busy itself in its place in the fishing industry of the Pacific Northwest.

The bell at the door of Nelda`s announced Helen`s arrival. John was sitting in a booth with Nelda having his mid-morning coffee, and they were deep in conversation about something obviously of a serious nature.

"Hi," greeted Helen. "Can I join you "

"Of course," replied Nelda. "Need you ask?"

"What`s up? You two seem to be upset about something."

"It`s Wolfgang, he hasn`t shown up for work. John is about to drive out to his place to see if there`s a problem."

"Want to come along, Helen?" asked John.

"Yes, if I can take a cup of coffee and a croissant with me. I haven`t had breakfast."

"Really? It`s ten o`clock," stated Nelda. "Oh, that`s right. Rodg was going out of town for a few days. The two ladies he left behind are sleeping in."

Bilgee stood quietly waiting for Helen to sit down in the booth. When she didn`t, Bilgee looked up at Helen questioningly. Helen walked to the counter instead and seated herself on a stool close to the coffee pot, Bilgee followed.

"I`ll heat a croissant and get your coffee if John will let me out of this booth," said Nelda in feigned exasperation. "I am concerned about Wolfgang; this isn`t like him. I've called and no one answers the phone."

John slid out of the booth to let Nelda out and then walked over to the counter. "I have my truck out front so whenever you're ready," he said addressing Helen.

* * *

The two mile trip to Wolfgang and Sylvia`s beach house gave John and Helen an opportunity to talk about John and Nelda`s upcoming marriage in June. John was eager to answer Helen`s questions finding obvious pleasure in the subject.

"Are you two still on target for your June date?"

John smiled as he stared ahead through the windshield exposing the twisting beach highway ahead. "If I had my way, we`d elope tomorrow."

"Really?" gasped Helen. "You don`t strike me as the impulsive type, John."

"Let`s just say, I know what I want."

"Good for you. Have you approached the subject with Nelda?"

"Yes; she`s thinking about it." John turned to face Helen briefly, "This is strictly private information. Of course you can share it with Rodger, but maybe by the time he returns Nelda will have made a decision and there will be no need for secrecy."

John slowed the pickup and brought it to a stop in front of a small shingled bungalow that hugged the beach. "I wonder what`s going on with Wolfgang; I don`t see his car so maybe this trip is in vain."

Helen opened the door of the pickup and turned to John, "I`ll knock on the door and see if Silvia is home."

After knocking on the door and getting no response, she attempted to look in the window. Soon she returned with a questioning look on her face. "The place is deserted, John. I think they`ve moved out, and in a big hurry too by the look of things."

"Why on earth would they do that? It just isn`t like either of them to leave without at least saying goodbye to their friends, and especially to leave Nelda stranded with a noon crowd on it`s way."

"Let`s go back so I can help Nelda today. She can cook and I`ll wait tables. I did that once when I was going to college."

"That`s good of you, Helen, she`ll appreciate your help, and it doesn`t look like Wolfgang will show. I can`t imagine what`s going on. I know the owner of that rental bungalow; I`ll call him when we get back. Maybe he can tell us what`s happening."

* * *

John and Helen entered the cafe and went directly to the kitchen where Nelda was busy preparing food for her noon customers; it was now eleven o`clock. No one was in the café fortunately, and most of the tables had been set in preparation for the luncheon trade.

"Well! Did you find Wolfgang?" she demanded angrily.

"He and Silvia have moved out for what-ever reason," replied John.

"What? I can`t believe it. How am I going to get along without Wolfgang?"

"With the increase in trade," replied John, "you`ll have to hire a new cook, that`s for sure. Maybe one full-time so we can have more time together."

"I guess you're right, John, but in the meantime I need help now, like this morning."

Helen saw the smile on John`s face as she stepped forward. "Would I do as a waitress for a few days until you get a new cook?"

Nelda`s jaw dropped, "Really? Would you do that? Oh, that would be great."

"Then show me what you want me to do?"

* * *

The day was cool, but clear, as Rodger drove I-5 south to Coos Bay. The farther south he drove the warmer the day became. Spring was beginning to show in the form of opening buds on the deciduous trees. The rolling hills of Oregon were green with grass and freshly shorn sheep dotted the near and far view. They looked so forlorn as they stooped to eat the new grass with no long coat of wool to fill out their bony forms. Seldom was a sheep without a nick or two from the shears. These cuts were dabbed with a yellow-colored medicine that made the wounds stand out all the more.

As he drove, Rodger reflected on the past day in court and his telephone conversation with Irene. *I feel relieved I can return to my life with Helen aboard the Sea Witch, yet a little sad to have parted with my former life once and for all. I still have my sons and grandchildren that I`ll see occasionally, but even that part of my life will never be the same. Nothing ever stays forever. Change is really the only thing you can count on.*

It was dark by the time Rodger pulled into the RV Park. The camper was dark, which surprised him. *Surely Helen is home*, he thought. *It`s only nine o`clock which isn`t her bedtime*. Turning his key in the door he was greeted by the barking of Bilgee.

Helen sat upright in bed and frantically called out, "Whose there?"

Turning on the overhead light Rodger replied, "It`s me, Helen. I`m surprised you're in bed.

"I`m surprised your back, Rodg. I expected you tomorrow or the next day. Are you okay?"

"I`m tired from the day in court yesterday and the long drive back. How about you?"

"I`m tired from being a waitress at Nelda`s."

"What are you talking about?"

"It`s a long story, are you sure you want to hear it?"

"Make it a short story. Why are you working as a waitress at Nelda`s?"

"Wolfgang has left town, Nelda is cooking, and I`m taking Nelda`s place while she looks for a new cook."

"Really? That wasn`t such a long story."

"Your right, Rodg. Come to bed, we`re both tired."

* * *

After bringing each other up-to-date over a leisurely breakfast, Helen, Rodger, and Bilgee headed for Nelda`s. "I`ll drop you off and then move the boat to our moorage at Stimson`s dock."

"I would have moved it yesterday if I hadn`t volunteered to help Nelda out. John said he`d move it, if he needed the dock space."

Rodger dropped Helen off at the café and headed to the boatyard. John was in his office and moved to the counter as he saw Rodger walk through the door.

"Hi John, I`m here to move the Sea Witch. What`s this I hear about Wolfgang leaving?"

"You won`t believe what I've found out. I called Wolfgang and Silvia`s landlord, Fred, who`s a friend of mine, to find out what`s going on. He said Wolfgang called him saying he had an emergency, he was leaving immediately, and they were forfeiting their cleaning deposit."

"What was the emergency?"

"Wolfgang hung up without telling him. However, a Spanish looking man was in the house when Fred went out to check the house. He asked the stranger what he was doing there and he got really surly. He said he was after Silvia, who is an illegal alien. It seems he`s a bounty hunter, and there`s a price on her head."

"Wow! That`s hard to believe. Our Silvia is an illegal alien? How did he know she was here?"

"He was on the trail of another person last month here in the Coos Bay area and he danced with Silvia at the Saturday night dance two weeks ago. It seems she said something that got him to wondering about her. He checked with the authorities and sure enough she was on a wanted list for being in the country illegally. Somehow Wolfgang got wind of this bounty hunter closing in on Silvia, and they left in the middle of the night."

Rodger stood at the counter physically shaken trying to take all of this information in and to make sense of it. "Poor Silvia and Wolfgang, what a heck of a way to live."

"There`s more," continued John. "Wolfgang has a classy restraunt back East and is a world-renowned chef. Silvia worked for him, they fell in love, and when the Feds came to arrest her, they escaped together and have been on the run for over a year. Wolfgang can`t touch his money as they can follow the money and catch them. That`s why he`s taking small jobs in out-of-the-way places. That`s why they chose Coos Bay and Nelda`s café."

"Unbelievable," stammered Rodger. "Is this bounty hunter still around?"

"Nobody knows. He`s a pretty slick guy. You remember him at the dance don`t you, Rodg?"

"Oh yeah, he and Silvia made quite an attractive pair on the dance floor and he sure could dance those fancy Latin dances."

"Does Nelda know all this?"

"Yes, I filled her in immediately. She`s like you, she just shakes her head and says, unbelievable."

"I`m going to miss those two and I`m going to miss Wolfgang`s great cooking. No wonder he was so good at it. Imagine, a world renowned chef right here in Coos Bay, and he cooked for us."

"I hope Silvia gets her problem resolved and they come back to us," said John.

"I do to. Before I move the boat I think I`ll check in with Helen at Nelda`s. I need to talk to her about this."

"I`m sure Nelda has filled her in by now. She is probably as upset about this as we are. Silvia and Wolfgang are good people and good friends. You just don`t like to see your friends in trouble."

"You're right. I`ll be talking to you later, John, as I plan to get the Sea Witch out of your boatyard this afternoon. If you're looking for a boat ride, I need a deck hand?

"I could use a little diversion after all that`s happening right now; you`re on."

*   *   *

"Be ready to cast off the bow and stern lines, John. I`ll let the engine idle a little longer to be sure it`s okay after sitting for so long during the refitting. I appreciate letting us use your battery charger yesterday, so we`d be ready for today`s move."

"Does Stimpson know you`re bringing the Sea Witch back today?"

"Yes, I called him this morning before I left the RV Park. He had sub-let our moorage space while we were gone for the two months, but he said he`d have the space vacant before we arrived. We didn`t have to pay moorage for those two months we were in dry dock, which helps the pocketbook."

"What does Stimpson charge now?"

"Eight dollars a foot."

"Wow! When I started in the boating business thirty years ago it was a dollar a foot."

"The engine is running smooth so caste off the lines, John. I`ll back out, and we`ll be on our way."

The afternoon was pleasant with a 10-knot wind blowing from the south. Rodger had John take the sail cover off the mainsail and raise it to see how it draws under light wind. The nylon sail responded easily and filled immediately.

"Boy," said Rodger, "this new sail works great; much better than canvas."

"I thought you`d be happy to have switched to Nylon as it`s easier in every way to work with. Should I bend on the jib?"

"No," replied Rodger, as he stood tall before the tiller holding it behind him with one hand. "It`s such a short distance and hardly worth the effort. I just wanted to feel the Sea Witch under sail again; it`s even better than before. I could skipper this boat myself, but I prefer Helen fill that role. She still knows a lot more about sailing than I, but I`m learning,"

"There`s Stimpson`s dock coming up and I can see my dock space is vacant. Drop the main," called out Rodger to John who had been sitting on the foredeck obviously enjoying the sun and the sensation of sailing once again. We`ll come in under power."

"It`s been a long time since I sailed," replied John. I might have to get me a little sloop for some day sailing; I think Nelda would enjoy it"

Rodger shifted the engine into neutral and let the Sea Witch glide toward its destination along the long floating dock. John had put out three bumpers along the gunnels of the Sea Witch. When they approached the dock to starboard Rodger shifted into reverse without adding throttle. The Sea Witch shuddered slightly; its forward motion slowed nearly to a standstill. Rodger shifted out of reverse into neutral and let the boat settle gently beside the dock like a baby duck might settle in close to its mother. John stepped off forward with the bowline in his right hand and threw a half hitch around the forward dock cleat. Simultaneously, Rodger stepped off aft with the stern line in his hand and threw temporary half hitches around the stern dock cleat.

John strode back to Rodger. "That was fun, thanks for inviting me to be your deckhand."

"My pleasure; John; you made my job easy. I`ll adjust the stern line and put a spring line in place while you can put the mainsail cover back on."

"I wonder if we can hitch a ride from Vern Stimpson back to Nelda`s," said John. "If push comes to shove, we can walk, I guess. It`s less than a mile."

* * *

Vern let John and Rodger out of his pickup truck in front of Nelda`s café and drove off with a wave of the hand. It was late in the afternoon and Nelda and Helen had finished clean up after the lunch crowd. Regular customers were shocked to hear Wolfgang and Silvia were on the run from the immigration authorities.

"Have you heard anything about our friends?" asked John as he preceded Rodger through the door.

"Nothing," replied Nelda as she and Helen sat in a booth enjoying a cup of coffee after the busy two hours lunch period.

"Maybe no news is good news," added Rodger. "At least we can assume they haven`t been caught.".

Nelda automatically got up and headed for the coffee pot as John and Rodger slid into the booth. Helen smiled at Rodger and asked, "Did you get the Sea Witch back to its berth?"

"I did with John`s help, and the new mainsail works like a dream in light air. You're going to love those new nylon sails."

"I can hardly wait for our shakedown cruise and for Nelda to replace me here at the café. I forgot how strenuous being a waitress is."

Nelda returned with a fresh pot of coffee and poured a cup for John and Rodger. Filling Helen`s cup and her own she said, "I have a lead on a new cook and I`ll know this afternoon if I have one. She`s stopping by after she gets off work at her present job."

"Why is she looking for a new job?" inquired John.

"She wants shorter hours, less stress, and a smaller kitchen. She works at the big hotel south of town on the beach and she`s not happy there."

"Assuming she can cook, she sounds ideal," said Helen. "When can she start?"

"Immediately, she says," replied Nelda. "I guess she really isn`t happy there."

John looked over at Rodger and Helen sitting side by side in the booth and said wistfully, "I suppose you two will be bailing out, too, as soon as you have your shakedown cruise and take on provisions for your trip to Tahiti."

"Yes," replied Helen. "Everything says it`s time to go."

"We`ll miss you two," said Rodger, "just as we miss Wolfgang and Silvia. You've been good friends and we`ll come back to see you after our journey is complete; you can count on that."

"It`s time to go back to the RV Park and Bilgee, Rodg," said Helen. Turning to Nelda she said, "Let me know if you need me tomorrow; you have our cell-phone number."

Rodger and Helen rose and started for the door. Nelda intercepted them taking Helen by two hands, "You've been a god-sent Helen; thanks so much. I`ll call tonight and let you know if I hired a new cook."

* * *

Bilgee was overjoyed to see her master and mistress as they let her out of her portable kennel outside the camper. After giving her a doggy treat, Helen escorted her to the pet area while Rodger mixed their afternoon Scotch and Water and started dinner. Returning, Helen collapsed on one side of the dinette settee, took a long swallow of her drink, and let it slide slowly and soothingly down her throat. "That`ll warm the cockles of my heart; what`s for dinner?"

"That`s my girl; always ready for a good meal and a good drink. Not necessarily in that order."

"Right you are, Rodg, and a kiss from my First-Mate."

Rodger turned, took the two strides necessary to lean over, and planted his lips firmly on Helen`s upturned, smiling face. "And," he added, "I`m never too busy for a little romance."

"Later, Sweetie, first I need sustenance."

"That is sustenance," teased Rodger as he retraced his steps to the camper`s small convenient, galley. "However, we`ll have it your way. How does a small steak cooked on our portable grill, a micro-waved baked potato, lettuce and tomato salad, and a glass of Pinot Noir sound?"

"Like heaven, Rodg…however, I've been giving your sustenance lecture some thought. Maybe Bilgee would like to go out to her kennel and we could see if your argument has any merit."

"Bilgee," said Rodger quickly scooping her up in his arms, "you are going to love it outside in your kennel."

* * *

The next morning as the sun neared its zenith, Rodger and Helen awakened refreshed and ready for a new day. Rodger took Bilgee for her morning walk while Helen fixed breakfast. On Rodger`s return they made plans for the day as they ate. Bilgee sat contentedly beside Rodger in the dinette settee and appeared to be interested in every word spoken.

"I think we need to stock the larder today for our shakedown cruise," said Helen. "I've been having some second thoughts about going north as we planned. If we head south and need to turn back, for whatever reason, we have prevailing winds from the south to bring us back to Coos Bay, easily. If everything checks out, we`re already on our way south so no time is lost."

"That sounds like a plan to me, Skipper. What`s the next leg of our journey?"

"Crescent City, California is an overnighter of about one hundred and twenty-five miles. That would be a good break-in for both the Sea Witch and us."

"It will be good to be at sea again, even though we`re leaving good friends behind."

"We`ve got about nine months into this trip so far," replied Helen. "It`s time to go. Today we shop, take on fuel and water, and day-after tomorrow we leave."

"I just remembered," said Rodger, "John and Nelda talked about a farewell party."

"I think our christening party was our farewell party; I`m anxious for us to be on our way. I think they`ll understand."

"Let`s stop by and tell them our plans on our way to the store," suggested Rodger. I think we can skip lunch today as its nearly noon and we just finished breakfast."

"Well, I don`t know," quipped Helen. "I hate to miss a meal. Maybe we could stop later for pie and coffee and tell them our plans."

"That`s my Skipper," laughed Rodger as he stood to plant a kiss on Helen`s forehead. "You're right, it`s time to be on our way."

* * *

Having been told the night before that Nelda had hired a cook, Helen was free to concentrate on getting the Sea Witch ready for their continued journey to Tahiti. Shopping and stocking the larder was a tedious task, but by mid-afternoon they had completed it and had stopped by Nelda`s for pie and coffee. The bell over the door announced their arrival and Nelda greeted them warmly. John, who was sitting in a booth by the front window of the café, hailed them as they walked in.

"Hi John," replied Rodger as he headed for the coffee pot. "Do you have any pie left after the lunch trade, Nelda?"

"Only rhubarb. It`s good, but the younger generation go for a sweeter taste."

"How about you, Helen? Do you want a slice of rhubarb pie?"

"If it`s a la mode. After all this is our lunch, Rodg."

Nelda brought the slices of pie with a generous dollop of ice cream on top and joined the three at the booth. The café was empty of customers and the only sounds came from the kitchen.

"Is that you new cook, Nelda?" asked Helen.

"Yes, and she`s going to be just fine. Not as fancy as Wolfgang, but good enough for our trade. She`ll be leaving in a few minutes; I`ll introduce her."

"Speaking of Wolfgang, have you heard anything?" asked Rodger.

"Nothing," replied Nelda. "I`m told the bounty hunter has left town, too."

John inquired, "Who told you that?"

"The sheriff was in this morning asking if we`d heard from Wolfgang and Silvia, and he told me."

Conversation came to a halt as a large Scandinavian-looking woman emerged from the kitchen. I`m finished now, Nelda; I`ll see you in the morning."

Nelda stood and beckoned the cook over. "Mary, I want you to meet two friends of ours."

Mary walked around the end of the counter and over to the booth. Smiling, she extended her hand first to Helen and then to Rodger. "I`m so pleased to meet you. I guess you two are the ones headed for Tahiti in your sailboat. Nelda was telling me about your adventure."

"Yes," replied Helen, "we`re the ones. In fact we`re here today to tell Nelda and John we`ll be leaving in two days."

"Two days?" exclaimed John and Nelda at the same instant. "What about your shake-down trip," asked John?

Nelda interrupted before either Helen or Rodger could answer, "What about the bon voyage party we talked about?"

Helen responded, "We thank you for the thought of the party, but we just had a party with the christening of the Sea Witch and it wouldn`t be the same without Wolfgang and Silvia. The shakedown cruise will be our first day at sea, but we`re heading south. If a problem shows up, we`ll use the prevailing south wind to bring us back to Coos Bay to fix whatever needs to be fixed."

Nelda leaned over and kissed Helen on the forehead. "We`ll miss you two so much. It won`t be the same around here without you."

John reached across the table and extended his hand to Rodger, then to Helen, "I guess your plan makes sense, but as Nelda says, we`re going to miss you."

Rodger cleared his throat suddenly gone dry from emotion, "Thanks for everything you've done for us."

"Is there anything we can do to help you get ready?" asked John.

"Yes," replied Rodger, "we have to do something with our truck and camper. Do you know of a place where I can store it, or maybe even sell it?"

"Let me ask around, Rodg. I`ll call you tomorrow morning."

"Thanks, John.

Mary stood back smiling as she listened to this friendly, but animated, conversation. "I hate to interrupt, but I must leave now. So nice to meet you two; have a good trip."

Rodger and Helen both stood as Helen said to Mary, "Thank you, and it`s been a pleasure meeting you and knowing you`ll be here to keep Nelda from working herself to death."

"I`ll do my best." With those words spoken, Mary left.

"Well gang," said Nelda, "Tomorrow night John and I will take you to dinner, agree?"

"Agreed," replied Helen and Rodger simultaneously.

"We`ll work out the details tomorrow when I call you," interjected John.

Rodger and Helen returned to their truck and were met by an anxious dog ready to take a walk.

* * *

The next morning Rodger was first out of bed and greeted by Bilgee who was always ready for a walk. On their way to the pet area they passed, Ron, the owner of the RV Park, as he started his morning chores.

"We`ll be leaving tomorrow, Ron. I haven`t figured out what to do with the truck and camper yet, but if I don`t come up with a solution, do you have a place here where I can park it that`s out of the way?"

"I have an overflow lot where you can park for fifty dollars a month."

Rodger brightened at the offer. "That sounds like the solution to my problem. I`d need to move over there tomorrow about this time of day."

"Let`s walk over now and I`ll show you where to park. I have a form in the office that needs to be filled out either today or tomorrow."

As they walked to the further end of the park, Bilgee made her way ahead of Rodger and Ron sniffing and claiming territorial rights. The park was coming alive as travelers began to leave for another day on the road. An open area ahead that bordered the park had several vehicles, a bus, and three boats of varying sizes parked along side one another.

"When you park here, Rodg, take the next spot in the line."

"This`ll work. What are the chances of getting a ride to Stimson`s dock after we park here. We`ll have most of our stuff aboard the Sea Witch, but we`ll have a few things to carry if we spend the night in the camper."

"Not a problem. I was going to offer to get you there." "That`ll be great," replied Rodger. "I`ll be by the office this afternoon and fill out the form you mentioned."

"I guess I`d better get back to my chores; I`ll walk with you back to your camper."

The three of them retraced their steps to the center of the park, and then parted. Rodger opened the camper door and discovered Helen still in bed asleep. Bilgee scrambled past Rodger and jumped up on the dinette seat to be out of the way and have a better view of Rodger`s activities.

Soon Rodger had breakfast cooking and a cup of coffee in hand. Sitting down beside Bilgee, he offered her a doggie snack, which she readily accepted. The noise and smell of bacon frying awakened Helen causing her to roll up on one elbow to focus on the homey scene below.

"Okay, you two, how about a little privacy while I dress."

Rodger and Bilgee, like two children sent out to play, evacuated the camper in favor of a nearby picnic table. The morning marine air of the coast chilled Rodger causing him to wish he`d taken time to put on his jacket. Picking up Bilgee, he held her tight against his body for warmth much to her surprise and pleasure.

Soon Helen appeared at the camper door, "Okay, you two lovebirds, I`m ready for the day and breakfast."

"Good," exclaimed Rodger. "I`ll put the eggs on while you make the toast. We need to get an early start as it`s going to be a busy day getting ready for our departure tomorrow."

Helen sat down in the dinette beside Bilgee sipping her first cup of coffee while monitoring the toaster. "What are we going to do about the camper and truck?"

"Ron has a place for us to park for fifty dollars a month, which I've agreed to. We could put it on a consignment used car sales lot, but we both like the camper and it can take us to the Baja after our trip to Tahiti."

"I agree, I`m looking forward to resuming our Baja trip, and life aboard a camper/truck combination isn`t too different from living aboard a sailboat. We`ll have to transfer nearly everything in the camper to the Sea Witch today. In fact, it makes sense to sleep aboard the boat tonight."

Rodger placed two plates with eggs and bacon on the dinette table and sat across from Helen. "This could be our last meal in the camper for awhile as we`ll catch a quick lunch at the café and we`re invited to dinner with Nelda and John tonight."

"This is going to be a busy day. A soon as we do the dishes, I`ll clean out the refrigerator and you pack your clothes and personal items."

"Aye aye, Skipper." This brought a spontaneous laugh as they both realized they were mentally, if not physically, aboard the Sea Witch with Helen in command.

*　　*　　*

John had called setting the time and place for them to meet for dinner with he and Nelda. The day was spent taking needed things for the voyage to the boat and setting up house keeping there. Helen did a final cleaning job on the camper while Rodger took care of the paper work and payment to Ron for the leased space in the overflow lot. Bilgee stuck close to Rodger all day as she sensed something different was happening, and she didn`t want to be left behind.

After a busy day, they showered and dressed to meet John and Nelda at a local steak house for dinner. They, already seated, were sipping a glass of wine when Helen and Rodger arrived. Being a weeknight, the restaurant was only half-full and the noise level was low, making conversation comfortable. Rodger and Helen ordered cocktails as soon as the waiter seated them.

"I need something stronger than wine after the day we put in," said Rodger. "Back and forth, back and forth, packing and unpacking all in the same day. Not my idea of a good time."

"Be nice, sweetie, this is a celebration," said Helen. "You two look like you're ready for a night on the town."

"This is a night on the town for us," replied Nelda, turning and tipped her glass toward John. "Being with dear friends and about to enjoy a good dinner cooked by someone else is my idea of a night on the town."

"I`ll drink to that," replied John, first smiling at Nelda and then at Rodger and Helen. "I`d like to propose a toast." Holding his glass high, "To our dear friends, Helen and Rodger, who have brightened our lives and given Nelda and me an example of true happiness. May your journey be successful; then return to us and continue to be our friends."

They each lifted their glass and drank of it. Nelda beamed with pleasure as she turned to face John. "I didn`t know you had it in you, John; that says it all. I can only say, amen."

After dinner they talked about their relationship up to now, which included the interlude with Wolfgang and Silvia. Eventually they hugged one another and parted silently.

* * *

After spending the night aboard the Sea Witch, Rodger drove the pickup to their site in the RV Park and backed the truck under the raised camper to be reconnected. A few minutes later while driving to the overflow parking site he thought, *well old girl, we won`t see you again until we arrive at and come back from Tahiti.* He parked, disconnected the batteries, checked the windows and doors for closure, and locked them. Patting the truck on the fender as he passed he walked on to the office as he needed to give Ron the keys in case the camper needed to be moved.

"Are you ready for your ride to town, Rodger?" asked Ron as he walked from behind the desk toward the front door of the office. "You said you had some luggage to take with you."

"No, we changed our mind and slept aboard the Sea Witch last night, so everything is there, except me."

"We`ll take care of that right now." They got in Ron`s pickup and drove the mile to Stimson`s dock where the Sea Witch stood out among the smaller boats.

Ron stopped in the parking lot and walked with Rodger out the long dock to the Sea Witch. Helen sat on deck with Bilgee awaiting Rodger`s return.

"Are you ready to shove off, Skipper?" called Rodger on nearing the boat.

"Yes, we are mate, jump aboard." Helen stood shading her eyes from the morning sun; Bilgee, at her feet with tail wagging, spied Rodger and barked a `welcome aboard.`

Rodger turned, extending his hand to Ron, "Thanks for everything, Ron. If all goes well, we should see you in a couple of months. However, the way this voyage has gone so far, don`t stand on one foot waiting for us. If our plans change, we`ll let you know."

"I envy you two your adventure, enjoy it." With that said, Ron turned and retraced his steps back to his truck.

After starting the engine Rodger asked, "Do we need to do anything else before we shove off, Skipper?"

Helen walked to the tiller and turned saying, "Cast off the mooring lines, Mate, and we`re on our way."

"Aye, aye Skipper." Rodger hurriedly untied the lines fore and aft and lifted the bumpers aboard as soon as there was a little distance between the hull and the dock; he then moved to the cockpit beside Helen. Putting his arm around her, they stood side-by-side looking forward to the breakwater opening from Coos Bay to the Pacific Ocean.

"We`re on our way… we`re really on our way again. I had all but given up on this adventure, Helen, but thanks to you and circumstance, here we are."

"This has become our adventure, Rodg, not just yours, and with tenacity and luck, we`ll succeed. Helen stood tall at the tiller, Rodger continued to hold her with one arm, and Bilgee sat at their feet looking up adoringly at the two of them.

*   *   *

As they entered the open water of the Pacific Ocean outside Coos Bay the wind came steady from the south at 10 knots, the sky overcast, and the temperature a respectable 59 degrees. A two foot chop added to a day that had all the earmarks of being a good day on the water. The morning overcast burned off leaving mostly a clear sky. The seabirds, enjoying the air thermals, dove and swooped in a game of follow the leader. At the helm Rodger looked down on Helen sitting on the cockpit bench seat near the cabin bulkhead with her head thrown back as she deeply inhaled the salt-laden air.

"This is the life, Rodg. I`d forgotten how wonderful it can be out here on the ocean."

Rodger, momentarily lost in a daydream, heard Helen`s voice penetrate his reverie. Letting her words reverberate in his mind, he reclaimed the gist of what she`d said. "You're right, Skipper, this is the life. However, we know how unforgiving the ocean can be."

"We`re not likely to ever forget that, Rodg. Do you have some uneasiness now that we`re at sea?"

"No, just an expanded picture of what sailing is all about. I wouldn`t miss this for the world, and I`m just happy to be here with you."

"Good. We can hope to never repeat that storm and the shipwreck. However, we know we`ll have foul weather now and then, and once we start across the ocean to Tahiti we will run out of the options we have when we`re close to shore. There`s no place to hide out there."

"How`s the trim on the sails look, Skipper?"

"Drop off the wind a degree or two; I think we can fill the sails more."

"I could winch them down tighter if you want a straighter course."

"No, this is fine. Maybe this afternoon the wind will build and we can point up closer to the mark."

Helen smiled at Rodger standing tall above her and thought *how lucky can you get?*

Chapter Thirty-Two

Rodger watched the coastline as they journeyed from Coos Bay southward to Crescent City, California. Cape Blanco would be their first major point of interest enroute. The coastline was relatively straight bending in a south by west direction. The coastal mountains rose higher and the shoreline now consisted of high yellow sand dunes and cliffs broken by bold rocky headlands of moderate height, backed by low-covered hills.

Helen went below to take a nap in preparation for the night watch from eight o`clock to twelve o`clock. The easy roll and pitch of the Sea Witch as she made her way through the two-foot waves soon lulled Helen to sleep.

Rodger watched the GPS, or Genie; they had nicknamed the navigation device, which interfaced with the autopilot. With these two devices, a lot of the work of sailing had been reduced to watching ahead for obstacles in the water, avoiding them, and trimming the sails. The two devices couldn`t detect obstacles so the helmsman would need to take the tiller and steer around the obstacle. This could involve adjusting sails if a change of course was long-standing.

They were now passing Cape Blanco, and Rodger could see the Cape projected about one and a half miles out from the general trend of the coast. It appeared to be a small bare tableland, terminating seaward in a cliff over 200 feet high.

Rodger gazed shoreward at the lighthouse situated at the center or flat part of the cape. He`d read in the *United States Coast Pilot* book there were numerous sunken and visible rocks extending a half-mile into the ocean from the Cape. Double-checking his chart and the course Helen had lain out; he determined they were still nearly a half-mile off the coast at this point.

It takes a little getting used to…being in charge and alone on deck, he thought. *It`s comforting to know Helen is just a short distance away.* Checking the water ahead as far as he could see for obstacles, he determined there were none, so he quickly went below to heat up the coffee. Helen lay curled on her side facing the forward bulkhead with her back to Rodger. Lighting the oil cook stove and putting on the coffee pot, he returned topside to recheck the ocean for obstacles.

After five minutes he thought he`d given the coffee sufficient time to heat, so once again he ducked below deck to the galley.

"If you wake me up one more time, you could get seriously hurt," muttered Helen.

Rodger stiffened, "Sorry, Skipper, I thought I was being quiet."

Helen, still facing the bulkhead grumbled, "Think of a bull in a china closet and you`ll get the picture."

"I`m outta here," said Rodger filling his coffee cup quickly and retreating to the safety of the upper deck. Bilgee, lying on the bench seat in the cockpit, looked up from her interrupted late afternoon nap. Seeing a smile on Rodger`s face, she cocked her head as if to say *if the boss is smiling everything must be okay.*

Bilgee was proving to be a real sea dog. With her toenails clipped short, she moved about the Sea Witch easily, and content to be there.

At first the sea birds that swooped close to check out the boat and its occupants caused her alarm. She responded with barks as vicious as she could muster. However, she seemed to tire of this game and accept the seabirds as only friendly neighbors.

She`d picked out a favorite spot in the cockpit for her naps. Sitting up she could see over the combing board outlining the cockpit that kept renegade waves from splashing in. The spot she had chosen was out of the line of traffic, but close to the helmsman. Bilgee hadn`t figured out the toilet facilities totally, but she had been encouraged to use a spot on the foredeck in front of the cabin that had a piece of sod secured to the deck. When she relieved herself on the sod, Rodger had tied a line to a bucket, scooped water out of the ocean, and with a swish the sod was again clean, and its contents washed through the scuppers and over the side of the boat.

Rodger settled in by the tiller and studied the navigation chart for the journey ahead. The Rogue River mouth would be coming up to port soon if this late afternoon fifteen knot breeze held. The chart warned of "*staying out beyond the Rogue River Reef which ran northwesterly from the mouth of the Rogue for four miles. It was a half-mile off shore and because the bottom is very broken and inasmuch as the area has not been swept by a wire drag, vessels are advised to give this reef a berth of at least 1.5 miles.*"

Rodger immediately set the chart aside and took control of the tiller. Dropping off to starboard by 15 degrees for a half hour would enable him to gain the distance he sought from the shore to accommodate the reef. He trimmed the sails as dictated by the change of course and sat back satisfied with his seamanship. Bilgee looked over her shoulder at him and seemed to give an approving nod of her head.

Helen stuck her head out of the stairwell. "Hi Mate. Is everything okay?"

"Yes, Skipper, everything is now. I had to alter the course for awhile in order to get some distance from a reef coming up."

"Oh?"

"If you`ll check the chart, Skipper, that`s what they suggest."

"I should have checked it before I went below for my nap, but you've handled the situation well. You're learning the sailing game, Rodg."

Rodger stood a little taller, appreciating the compliment. "I`ll need to start dinner soon as I put out a couple of small steaks to thaw this morning. How does that sound?"

"Wonderful!" exclaimed Helen. "However, I `m up for a Scotch and Water for right now."

"Take the tiller and I`ll fix that right away." Rodger gave Helen a kiss and a smile as he turned to go down to the salon. Moments later he reappeared with a glass in each hand and made his way careful not to spill his cargo. He touched her glass with his in a toast. *To a successful night of cruising and no blatant seduction.*"

"Kill joy," replied Helen, "but we can enjoy each other`s company, and I should add Bilgee`s company. Her job, you know, is to be with whoever has the night watch to soften the vigil. Here`s a little pay beforehand, Bilgee." Helen found a doggie treat in her pocket and extended it. The three sat relaxed in the cockpit watching the friendly waters, the late afternoon clouds, and the seabirds flying southward.

Helen looked over at Rodger and asked, "If you don`t want to talk about this now, just say so, but I can`t help wondering how you feel about giving up your home, your marriage, and your extended family now that you've had some time to live with the decision?"

Rodger rolled on his side to look at her. "I`m comfortable with my decision. It has taken some getting used to, but that`s life. Just about the time you accept everything in your life, it changes. In my case I was accepting, but uncomfortable, with my marriage, my job, and then the health issue arose. When the doctor gave me less than a year to live because of tuberculosis, I ran away from all of it and did the one thing I had put on hold most of my adult life."

Helen studied Rodger`s face closely as she said, "Actually, that was a brave thing to do… to wring out of life all that you could, even when you were at death`s door."

"A lot of people wouldn`t agree with you; they`d think it was a selfish thing to do." Rodger rolled back and stared up at the top of the mast and the sky beyond. "I read an essay once by Ellen Key that spoke to this subject."

"Who is she?"

"She was a Swedish feminist who lived a hundred years ago, but what she has to say is right on target for me today."

"Well, what did she say that was right on target for you now?"

Rodger smiled enjoying the verbal game he`d initiated. "She said, `Great love, like great genius, can never be a duty. Both are life`s gracious gifts to the elect…"

Helen continued to study Rodger as he lay watching the afternoon sky. "Did you feel like you were being dutiful staying in a marriage and a job, when you wanted to be on an adventure?"

"Yes, when the doctor gave his prediction about the end of my life span, something snapped. I knew I had to do what I've always wanted to do, sail to Tahiti. That`s when I went looking for a boat and met you."

"Haven`t there been moments when you wished you could turn the clock back?"

"Nope, I lived that life, and now it`s over. Each day is an adventure when I`m with you and that`s the way I want it. You see, I happen to be in love with you lady, and I`m in love with our adventure. In fact, I`m even in love with Bilgee." Bilgee perked up at the sound of her name and looked questioningly at Rodger.

"Wow!" Laughed Helen, obviously pleased with what Rodger had said. "I hit the jackpot, three loves in a row."

Rodger rose, bent over, placed his lips gently on Helen`s, then taking her empty glass, went below to prepare dinner.

* * *

After dinner the three of them bundled up and sat watching the last streaks of light disappear into the dark velvet of night. The wind held steady at ten knots and they stayed out two miles off shore, which was still in the shipping lanes and required vigilance at the helm. Snuggled together, they shared each other`s warmth, but no conversation. Each had their thoughts to examine the day.

Helen broke the silence. "I`m curious, Rodg. When did you start reading feminist literature, and by a Swede who lived a hundred years ago?"

Rodger laughed, "It`s not my usual reading fare, but it was a quote from a book about the life of Frank Lloyd Wright, the architect, who lived about that time."

"That makes sense, not that I've pegged you as an anti-feminist, but I know you have an interest in architecture. Did Ellen Key have anything else to say about the subject?"

"Yes, she said *there can be no other standard of morality for him who loves more than once, than for him who only loves once, than the enhancement of life."*

Helen turned to face Rodger. "Really? A lot of people wouldn`t buy that. They think people should be like the swan who only mates once."

Rodger`s face was barely visible in the darkness, but Helen could sense by the tone of his voice that he was talking about himself. "She goes on to say that *he who is in love hears the singing of dried-up springs, feels the sap rising in dead boughs, and the renewal of life`s creative forces.*"

"Rodg, you've memorized what she said."

"Yes, I really relate to it, as Frank Lloyd Wright did."

"Okay, let`s hear the rest of it."

Rodger turned back to watching the Sea Witch`s path ahead as he mentally reached back inside his mind. "She goes on to say after the renewal to life`s creative forces, and I quote, *he is prompted anew to magnanimity and truth, to gentleness and generosity, he finds strength as well as intoxication in his new love. Nourishment as well as feast.... that man has a right to the experience.*"

"Wow! I`m impressed, Rodg. Is that what you experienced when we fell in love?"

"Yes."

"So did I, and to think that if we were swans we would never have what you and I have."

* * *

After a long night with Rodger standing watch from eight p.m. until twelve p.m. and again from four a.m. until eight a.m. they were due to arrive at Crescent City, California marina about four p.m.. Approaching Crescent City from the north the chart suggested staying off the coast eight-tenths of a mile to accommodate numerous pinnacle rocks. From Point St. George to Crescent City, a distance of about three miles, the coast is moderately low but rocky. The largest outcropping, Castle Rock, is 233 feet high, and lies 2.3 miles north of Crescent City. Rodger, again at the helm, noted it had a rather flat top with a small knob near the eastern edge.

Helen, sticking her head out of the companionway hatch, asked," Is everything okay, Rodg?"

"Yes, but I`m looking for some relief at the helm as I`m having trouble staying awake. I`m not use to only four hours sleep, and I couldn`t fall asleep after I got off watch at eight o`clock."

"No problem, Rodg. We`re not on four hour watches now; I`ll take her to Crescent City and call you as we enter the harbor."

Helen took the tiller from Rodger as he gave her a peck on the cheek and headed below for a quick nap. The bed was still warm from Helen`s body when he lie down on the divan bed. Looking up as he lay on his back he watched the gimbaled lamp swing gently back and forth with the motion of the Sea Witch as it worked its way southward to the Crescent City marina. Welcome sleep overtook Rodger in his attempt to restore the energy needed to do deck work when they entered the harbor.

* * *

Helen spread the chart out on the seat next to her, depending on Genie to follow the course she had punched into the navigation system. She could see Crescent City is on the northern side of a small rocky constricted bay about three miles southeast of Point St. George and midway between San Francisco Bay and the Columbia River. The harbor, formed by a 5700-foot breakwater from Whaler Island to the eastern shore, also had an inner breakwater from Whaler Island northwestward. *This certainly looks like well-protected moorage for tonight. Rodg and I could use a good night`s sleep. I hate to awaken him now, but I need him to lower the sails so we can power in on our auxiliary engine. I could probably do it myself, but it would be foolhardy to leave the tiller when we`re in close quarters with breakwaters and pinnacle rocks showing.* "Rodg, oh Rodg, I need you on deck."

Bilgee came out of her sleep and looked expectantly at Helen. "It`s okay, Bilgee, I just need your master on deck." Bilgee ran to the hatchway leading down to the salon barking excitedly as if she understood Helen explicitly.

Rodger soon appeared, eyes heavy with sleep, "What`s up?"

"We`ll soon be entering Crescent City`s harbor and I`d like to go in under power. Drop the mizzen, jib, and main in that order "

"Aye, aye Skipper." Rodger went about unloosening the halyards, dropping the sails and flaking the mizzen and main on their booms. He stowed the jib in its sail bag and left it on deck at the bow still connected to the forestay. Starting the auxiliary gas engine before he dropped the sails, they would always have steerage.

"Hey Skipper, would you look at those rafts, jetties, and small docks. They`re all covered with basking seals. I wonder if they will try to board us when we anchor out or tie up tonight."

"I hope this was a good idea coming here; I hadn`t expected anything like this."

"I see a sign ahead saying Transient Dock," shouted Rodger as he stood near the bow with one hand clutching the forestay for balance. "It only has a few boats there, but no seals, thank goodness."

"Put the bumpers out and bow and stern lines on the port side. We`ll talk with the harbor master and see if we have to be concerned with the seals."

As Helen put the transmission in neutral, the Sea Witch slowed in her approach and sidled up to the floating dock. Rodger stepped off and tied up fore and aft. Helen lifted Bilgee over to Rodger and the three of them quickly walked to the nearby harbormaster`s office.

They were greeted by a middle-aged, buxom, blond secretary who sat outside her boss`s closed office door. It was apparent that to speak to the harbormaster you`d have to get by his guard at the door.

Helen stepped forward with the aire of one who's in charge and asked to see the harbormaster. "What is it you wish to speak to him about?" the secretary asked.

"Seals," said Helen with feet firmly planted and not to be put off by an over zealous office worker. The secretary talked briefly to her boss on the office intercom. He apparently wanted to know if he would be talking to a boat owner or a do-gooder from the community. The secretary asked Helen if she was a boat owner.

"I`m the Skipper of the ketch you see tied up to your transient dock."

The secretary eyed Helen and with a noticeable change in attitude transferred the information to the harbormaster. Sitting back from the microphone, she signaled Helen with a nod of her head to go in to the harbormaster`s private office.

Rodger got up from his chair to join Helen and was immediately challenged by the secretary. "Only the boat Skipper has permission to talk to Captain Blazee, our harbormaster. Who are you?"

"I`m the owner of the Sea Witch."

"Oh,... well... go on in."

Behind the desk sat the epitome of what Hollywood would think a harbormaster should look like: middle aged, tall, handsome, gray streaks in his dark hair, a handsome mustache that curled at the ends, and cool gray eyes directed now at Helen. "What can I do for you?" he asked in a baratone, business-like voice.

Helen stood at his desk, not being offered a chair. Rodger stood beside her, eyes fixed on the Harbormaster. "We`re concerned about the seals that seem to be lying on any available flat surface, said Helen. "We want moorage for the night, but we don`t want to share our boatdeck with seals; is that liable to happen?"

"It`s a possibility, but we have a way to discourage that, which usually works."

"What do you do?" asked Helen.

The harbormaster smiled, "We throw M-80 firecrackers at them at night, and believe me, they don`t like the noise."

Helen laughed at the ridicules picture that flashed in her mind. "It must sound like World War Three around here at night; what do the neighbors say?"

"They aren`t happy about it, but they understand the problem." The harbormaster sat back in his chair and put his hands behind his head. "I know it`s an unusual procedure, but it is the only thing that has worked, so far."

Rodger said, "I see you don`t have many boats at your transient dock, is it because of the seals?"

"Partly, however, it`s still early in the year for boaters, and we`re not the only marina with this problem. It`s something boaters have learned to live with. The seals come and go, so it`s not a continual problem. They`ll be heading north soon, but in the meantime we control them with M-80`s."

Helen turned to leave, asking over her shoulder, "What time does the fireworks start?"

"Just before sundown, that usually moves them out for the night, at least as far as the outer breakwater. It`s almost become a game or nightly ritual," said the harbormaster. As I watch them I sense they are waiting for me to do my part."

Rodger stepped forward and extended his hand to conclude their business. "We`ll only be here tonight, but we appreciate the effort to keep the seals off our boat."

Helen and Rodger walked hand-in-hand out of the harbormaster`s office back to the Sea Witch, which was riding easily in her moorage at the transient dock. Bilgee laid spread out on the cabin roof tethered to the mast apparently enjoying the privacy of having the Sea Witch all to herself.

Rodger smiled at the thought, "I wander if she sees herself as Skipper of the Sea Witch right now?"

"Oh, Rodger, what an imagination you have."

"Don`t you ever wonder what goes on in her mind? Who knows what dog`s aspirations are."

Helen grabbed Rodgers arm with both of her hands and playfully tugged at him, "I suspect her highest aspiration is to make us happy, to be our companion, and to get enough to eat."

"I wonder in what order those aspirations might be? Speaking of food, let`s go out for lunch. I saw a café not too far from the harbormaster`s office."

"Okay, Rodg. We`ll let Bilgee play Skipper for a while longer."

* * *

A boisterous lunch crowd filled the café to overflowing. Most people seemed to know each other and conversation was rampant, loud, and pantomimed. The waitress made her way through the maze of chairs and tables to their table by the window, handing them a menu she asked, "Anything to drink while you decide?"

Helen looked at Rodger and asked, "Are you up for a glass of wine, Sweetie?"

"You read my mind. I`ll have a glass of Merlot."

"Make that two as I`m going to have a steak sandwich."

Quickly scanning the menu, he added, "I`ll have the French dip, but bring our wine first."

"Anything else?"

Rodger looked at Helen, and then the waitress and replied. "No, that`ll do it."

They sat back after their wine arrived and savored the mixed blend of the red wine. The noise of the crowd seemed to envelope them, reminding them of the warmth of Nelda`s café and the friends they had left behind. Helen was the first to speak. "I wonder how John and Nelda are doing in their budding romance?"

"It`s only been two days since we`ve seen them, although it seems longer, doesn`t it? I`m sure nothing has changed there. I wonder how Wolfgang and Silvia are, and where they are."

Helen scooted her chair closer to Rodger as they sat across from each other at the small table for two. Lowering her voice she ventured, "It must be terrible to be on the run."

"It`s not like they`ve committed a serious crime. Being an illegal alien is not that uncommon. I`m sure they`ll get it straightened out some day. Worse case scenario is they would have to return to her native Switzerland. Wolfgang grew up in Germany so Europe wouldn`t be foreign to them."

"Yes, but her only crime is wanting to live in this country," said Helen, "and she doesn`t have a green card. I wonder what they have to do for her to get one?"

"Wolfgang`s smart enough to figure a way out of their problem. Someday we`ll see them again, I`m sure,"

The waitress arrived with their lunch and they immediately went to work on their sandwiches.

* * *

Returning to the Sea Witch they found Bilgee just as they left her, sound asleep on the cabin roof. The craft rolled under their weight as they stepped onto the gunnels, bringing Bilgee to attention. Ever the obedient watch dog, she barked even though she hadn`t determined what caused the boat to roll. Seeing Helen and Rodger, she relaxed and showed her affection for them by wiggling all over and giving a series of happy barks to welcome them aboard.

"Good job, Bilgee," said Rodger in his soothing, most positive voice. "No one is going to steal this boat while you're in control."

Helen patted Bilgee on the head and stepped in the passageway to go below to study the chart for tomorrow`s destination. Spreading the chart on the drop leaf table, she took her protractor and dividers to lie out tomorrow's course. With Bilgee tucked under one arm, Rodger entered the salon and stood facing Helen. "What`s our destination tomorrow, Skipper?"

"If we get an early start, we should be able to make Eureka in twelve hours assuming the wind cooperates. It`s about 60 nautical miles according to my calculations and five to fifteen knot winds are predicted for tomorrow."

"I`m all for that. We wouldn`t have to stand four hour watches and we`d get an uninterrupted night`s sleep. Speaking of sleep, how about a nap? I could do up the bed in no time, and we could make up for last night at sea."

"Okay Rodg, maybe we should put Bilgee outside to be sure no seals board us while we sleep."

"Good idea, Skipper. We don`t want to be disturbed."

"Rodger, do I see a glint in your eye?"

"I hope so."

"You make up the bed, Rodg, and I`ll freshen up a bit. If I`m going to be your lover, I don`t want you to think of me as Skipper."

"That`s a transition I find very easy to make Helen. Right now, as far as I`m concerned, Bilgee is Skipper."

"God help us," laughed Helen as she turned to go into the forward compartment.

* * *

They awakened to the sound of an M-80 firecracker reverberating through the Sea Witch like a shock wave. Bilgee let out a howl and wildly tugged at her leash to escape the sound that took everyone on the Sea Witch by surprise. Rodger quickly rolled out of bed and lunged toward the hatch opening to rescue Bilgee. Untying the leash he held a trembling, wide-eyed and whimpering dog in his arms. Returning below he offered Bilgee to Helen who held out her arms to accept the shivering dog.

"I didn`t plan on falling asleep and what a terrible way to wake up. I don`t know which is worse," said Rodger, "the problem or the cure."

"I fell asleep too, Rodg, and I agree, what a way to wake up. We don`t have a choice regarding the M-80`s, but I wish there were some way to help Bilgee understand what`s going on. I guess it wasn`t a good idea putting her outside."

Rodger lay down on the bed beside Helen as Bilgee returned to normal due to Helen`s words and touches of affection. "I hope the harbormaster only does that M-80 treatment once, and I can only hope the seals were as shocked as we were by the loud firecracker."

Handing Bilgee off to Rodger, Helen arose from the bed and stuck her head out the open hatchway. "I don`t see anyone or any seals, so I guess it`s over. Let`s dress and take Bilgee for a walk; it may help all of us calm down."

"Good idea, Skipper."

Rodger put Bilgee on her leash and the three of them walked the length of the floating dock to the gangplank that took them up to the street level. The marina lay nearly deserted as the evening shadows turned into night. The day was over and the seals snuggled in for the night on the far jetty. The seals had reluctantly left the Inner Harbor Basin to the sailors and their boats for the night. Tomorrow they would return to take up temporary residence on any available flat surface.

* * *

The next day they got an early start and the weather proved to be what the weatherman had predicted, winds to 15 knots, and a temperature of 60 degrees with overcast sky. By 10 a.m. they could see False Klamath Rock. "We`re making 6 knots Skipper and we should have no trouble reaching Eureka by nightfall, assuming the wind holds. According to the Pacific Coast Guide we need to stay off shore to have at least 50 fathoms of water depth to avoid the rocks and reefs that are prominent on this part of the coast."

"If we stay out a nautical mile, we should be in good shape," replied Helen as she slipped her arm around Rodger. "It`s good to be at sea again, isn`t it Rodg?"

"You bet, Skipper. I noticed some seals heading north a few miles back; maybe the migration has begun."

"That will be good news for the local marinas," quipt Rodger as he sat down beside Helen on the cockpit bench seat. "There`s something I've had on my mind that I`d like to propose."

"What is it?"

"When we get to Tahiti, what do you think about getting married?"

"You really are proposing to me, aren`t you?"

"Yes, I am. I`d like to spend the rest of my life with you, and marriage seems to be the appropriate thing to do."

"Appropriate? I don`t give a snap for appropriate," replied Helen, a tinge of anger coloring her words.

"I`m surprised. I guess I thought you`d want to get married."

"Marriage, as I see it, is a way to protect children and property and that`s certainly not the case here. Somewhere along the line the legal system took over. It may have started as a sacrament of the church, and I know it`s often done in a religious setting by a minister or priest, but you need a state license to marry and it`s undone by divorce in a court of law, which makes it a complicated legal device."

"I`m surprised; I thought you`d be more receptive to my proposal."

"I love you, Rodg, and I want to share my life with you, like we`re doing, but you don`t have to marry me for that to happen."

"Is that a no?"

"It`s a maybe. If it`s important to you for us to marry, I would consider it. Why do you want to get married?"

"I guess I've always thought it was expected if a man and woman wanted to live together. I hadn`t thought about the church`s one-sided role or the children and property angle. You're right, of course, a justice of the peace or a judge can marry you as well as a minister, and so I guess it is a legal device or contract."

"Let`s put it on hold until we get to Tahiti and if we want a legal contract to love, honor, and cherish, we can consider it then. I know my position on marriage may seem unromantic, but it isn`t. Clyde and I never married."

"You didn`t?" Rodger looked directly at Helen. "I just assumed you were married; you called him your husband."

"Why not? Marriage... real marriage is in the mind. You love, honor, and cherish the other person because that`s what you want to do in response to their treating you the same way. We weren`t going to have children because of my age, so Clyde and I had a simple property agreement?"

"What you're saying is marriage is in the mind, not a piece of paper, or someone saying until death do you part." Rodger faced the ocean as he turned the thought over in his mind. "As I now have some distance from my former marriage with Irene, I can see where our marriage came apart."

"Oh," replied Helen studying Rodger who was looking beyond the gunnels to the waves coming at them. "Tell me about that."

"Irene was not a demonstrative type of person. She seldom praised people, including me, and tended to find fault."

"That doesn`t sound very loving to me. How about you? How did you handle that?"

"I didn`t respond in kind, but I can see why I became silent and drew unto myself."

"Did she talk about your faults only to you or to other people?"

"She made fun of my short-comings in a joking, humorous way in front of other people, but we both knew she wasn`t joking. It undermined me with the children, family, and friends. Her family began treating me differently, so I knew she was sharing our private life with them."

"Oh Rodg, I still hear the pain in your voice. What a terrible thing to do. If a person has a problem marriage, they should go to a professional, not family. They always give you a very biased opinion, which is the last thing you need."

"You know, I feel better having isolated the problem and looking at it from the distance of time. I can see now Irene and I are better off for our divorce. Yes... I guess it stopped being a marriage a long time ago; we just didn`t realize it. You can get used to almost anything, you know."

"Do you still want to marry me?"

"Let`s talk about it when we get to Tahiti. In the meantime, let`s enjoy what we have."

* * *

Finding their way to the transient dock at Eureka didn`t prove to be a problem as everything was well lit and adequately marked. After a long day at sea Helen and Rodger chose to go to bed without bothering about supper and soon put the day behind them after taking care of Bilgee.

The next morning Rodger awaken first and lay there looking at the gimbaled light overhead swaying gently back and forth. This told him that there was some movement to the water even inside the marina. Was it wind, current, or boat activity on the water near them? He decided instead of finding out, to snuggle close to Helen and enjoy their closeness and the warmth of the bed.

"Hmmm," muttered Helen deep in her voice, "are you awake?"

"Sorta. It`s cool this morning and the bed feels too good to leave, as you do."

"We don`t have a schedule to keep today, so let`s just be lazy. I could use more sleep if you`d back off a little."

"Okay killjoy, you sleep and I`ll lay here and think about what might have been."

"On second thought, I`ll need to go to take care of a thing or two first; I`ll be right back."

After setting Bilgee on deck with her food dish, Rodger stripped off his pajamas and lay under the covers expectantly. *What a great woman I have*, he thought.

When Helen returned she slipped into bed beside Rodger. Feeling his naked body next to her`s motivated her to move her fingers gently over his body, "If I told you I thought you have a great body, would you hold it against me?"

"That`s an old joke, Helen, but the answer is definitely YES!

* * *

After a hearty breakfast at a local eatery close to the marina, Helen, Rodger, and Bilge walked slowly back to the transient dock enjoying the early spring day, a fragile sun shone occasionally between the low overhead cloud layer and the open blue sky. The air was strong with the smell of the ocean, and seabirds sat on an adjoining field nearly covering it with their vast numbers.

"I`d better check the weather report," said Helen. "I`d expect the birds to be flying over the ocean searching for food or thermals to ride. If a storm is imminent they`ll know it and seek protected land to sit it out."

"Do you think so?" I hope they`re wrong. Eureka is okay, but I`d rather be sailing."

"Me too. I normally check the weather report long before this, but we were preoccupied."

He took her hand as they walked toward the marina; smiled at her and said, "Yes, we were. Life is exciting and full of surprises, isn`t it?"

"It sure is. When you were lost at sea and believed dead, I never thought I`d ever be happy again, and look at us now."

He squeezed her hand in silent answer and looked to the sky for signs of a weather front that might be coming in.

They reached the transient dock just as a forty-foot sloop sidled up to the floating dock near them. A middle-aged man stood at the helm and a middle-aged woman on the gunnels stood ready to step ashore with the bow line coiled in her hand.

"Throw me your line," shouted Rodger stepping forward to the edge of the dock.

The woman expertly threw the line to Rodger who caught it and secured the boat to a dock cleat. She then moved aft, grabbed a stern line, and stepped off the boat to secure it. Turning to face the skipper at the helm, he gave a `thumbs up` for a job well done. Stopping the engine, he secured a spring line to check the forward and backward movement of the boat. Satisfied with the security of the boat, he turned to her and said, "Thank goodness we`ve made it before the storm hit."

Helen and Rodger stood aside and watched the pair while this activity went on. The woman extending her hand toward Rodger, "Thanks for the help, Skipper."

"You're welcome, but I`m not the skipper of our craft, Helen here is." Helen laughed and stepped forward to extend her hand to the woman.

"That`s a mistake a lot of people make," said Helen. "His job is the same as yours, first Mate."

"I`m Gertrude Kaylor," offering her hand, "and this is my husband, Art."

Art extended his hand and after salutations said, "We`re thankful to have gotten to port ahead of the predicted weather front coming at us; it`s going to be real lumpy out there in short order." Art was about Rodger`s height and age, but heavier with a deep tan and blue eyes dancing mischievously out of a slightly pudgy, English-type face topped off with thinning, sun bleached, light brown hair. Gertrude, smaller and thinner by comparison, but not thin, also had a heavily tanned face set off by graying, straight hair pulled back into a ponytail. Both looked to be in their late fifties or early sixties.

Helen glanced at Rodger, "I guess we`re not going anywhere today." Turning to Art she inquired, "You say a storm is on its way. When is it supposed to pass through here?"

"In about an hour if the weather man is correct. We`re supposed to have winds to fifty knots and torrential rain. It`s nothing you`d want to be in, if you had a choice."

Helen said, "Gertrude, "I`ll bet you're relieved to be snug in port with a sturdy rip-rap breakwater between us and the pending storm?"

"You bet I am, Helen. Why don`t you and Rodger come aboard in half an hour? By that time I can have coffee brewed and we can really get acquainted."

"Sounds good; we`ll bring coffee cake," replied Helen looking to Rodger for reassurance. He nodded and smiled at the idea of a coffee klatch instantly set up by the two women. He thought, *women are the social organizers regardless of their rank on the boat.*

* * *

After walking, feeding, and securing Bilgee to the Sea Witch, Helen and Rodger arrived on schedule shouting out for permission to come on board. Art appeared at the entrance hatchway to welcoming them. Once inside Helen exclaimed, "Wow! Imagine having a spacious salon like this and still having another room to sleep in."

Rodger followed her down the five-step ladder to the cabin below. "Your right Helen, these are pretty spacious quarters." Extending a coffee cake he added, "Hi, Gertrude, if you could pop this in your microwave for a minute it will be ready to eat."

"Thanks Rodger," she replied, taking it from him. "Sit down over on the divan beside Art. Helen and I can pull up chairs and join you as soon as I pour the coffee."

Helen joined Gertrude in the galley and soon returned with a tray of hot coffee while Gertrude brought small plates of coffee cake with a pat of butter beside it and utensils. "There," she said, "That should do it."

The four made short order of the dessert and then slowly sipped the hot, robust coffee. "Tell me," asked Art, "Where are you from and where are you headed?"

Helen replied, "We`re from the Seattle area and we`re headed for Tahiti."

"Really?" responded Art. "We`re headed for Tahiti, too."

"No kidding?" said Rodger as he turned and leaned forward to eagerly face Art. "Where are you making your crossing?"

"We`re leaving from San Francisco, how about you?"

Helen answered, "We`re taking off from the coast of Peru following the Humbolt Currrent."

"I've heard of people doing that," said Art, "but it`s a long way to Peru and this is shorter though you could run into slow sailing at or near the doldrums."

"This time of year, we`re told, is better for crossing here at San Francisco," said Gertrude.

Helen and Rodger looked at each other with a questioning look. "Maybe this is something we should think about," said Helen to Rodger. "I`m getting anxious to start our crossing and it is a long way to Peru."

Art jumped into the conversation excitedly, "We could travel together and look out for each other."

"That`s an interesting offer," said Rodger, but it would be a big change of plans and something we need to think about; right Helen?"

Helen replied, "You're right, Rodg, but it`s certainly something to think about while we wait out the storm."

* * *

After their visit, Helen and Rodger returned to the Sea Witch and sat on the sofa bed with Bilgee between them contemplating the offer. Helen finally broke the silence, "It`s a tempting offer, I must admit. We would probably speed up the trip, and we would have experienced companions close at hand if anything goes wrong."

Rodger turned to face Helen, "We`d start our crossing earlier, but would the crossing be as fast?"

"Probably not, so it`s a matter of priorities. Time is not of the essence in either case, so it`s a matter of safety, a better chance of a successful voyage, and a different adventure."

"I guess the matter of safety and a successful voyage puts the decision towards the Kaylor`s offer," said Rodger. "I vote to start across as soon as possible, and if we need more adventure there`s one hundred and eighteen islands to visit in French Polynesia."

"How do you know that?"

"I've studied about Tahiti. I didn`t just want to sail to Tahiti because I liked the sound of the name."

"Well Rodg, I`m surprised you haven`t been giving me a lecture on the virtues of Tahiti this past year. What else do you know about it?"

"It`s half way between the United States and Australia, it`s divided into five geographically distinct archipelagos covering an area equivalent to the size of Western Europe and as different as the 50 United States."

"Really," said Helen as she sat back, obviously impressed with the information Rodger extolled on the subject.

"The Society Islands," continued Rodger, "encompass Tahiti, Bora Bora, Moorea, and a few other islands have the most world attention, but, as I said before, there are one hundred and eighteen islands to explore."

"You're right Rodg, we could get all the adventure we`d ever need without sailing to Peru. The next thing to consider is what do we know about the Kaylor`s, and how well will we get along?"

"Right, and we don`t have much time to find that out. However, we could hold off on our decision for a few days as we travel together from here to San Francisco."

"Good idea, Rodg. If they are the kind of people we want them to be, I`m sure they`ll understand our asking for more time on this decision."

"Let`s go over after dinner and get to know them better. By the way, speaking of dinner, what are you up for?"

"I like your poached salmon recipe, Rodg, and I can make a shrimp salad to accompany it."

"Sounds good, Helen."

Bilgee barked her approval as the serious conversation came to an end and the action now centered on the Galley.

* * *

After dinner and the dishes, after exercising and feeding Bilgee, they made their way to the Kaylor`s boat. Helen carried a bottle of Drambuie and Rodger carried four liqueur glasses to compliment the evening nightcap they were about to propose. Helen spied the transom of Art and Gertrude`s boat and was taken back by the name painted in bold black letters trimmed in gold paint, *Kitchen Pass.*

"Helen spoke first, "There`s got to be a story behind that name."

"I agree, but first things first."

Helen knocked on the gunnels near the entrance, an opening in the lifelines that surrounded the very nautical, trim, fiberglass boat. Rodger stood aside smiling as he thought about the name on the transom.

The hatch door opened and Art stuck his head out to see who was there.

Helen called out, "Permission to come aboard?"

"Granted," said Art as he came out to greet them. "What a pleasant surprise. Come below, Gertrude is just finishing the dishes and she`ll be pleased to have company; especially company bearing gifts," spying the bottle and glasses.

Helen led the way down into the salon, Gertrude saw them and squealed with delight, "Oh what fun, a party."

They soon gathered as before with the men sitting on the lounge and Helen and Gertrude sitting on folding deck chairs. Gertrude poured and served the drinks. Rodger, Helen, and Art sat back; content to be waited on. As they sat there with the small liqueur glass in hand,

Helen proposed a toast. “To our new friends, Gertrude and Art, who have come into our lives in this grand adventure of sailing to Tahiti.” Each raised their glass in a toast of mutual agreement.

“Does this mean you’ve accepted our offer to cross to Tahiti together?” asked Art.

“It`s a generous offer and one we are seriously considering,” said Rodger. “We would like to hold off on our decision until we reach San Francisco. We have many things to consider and perhaps we can travel together that far.”

“I think that would be a good thing to do,” injected Art. “We can see how compatible our boats are as to cruising speed.”

Helen responded, “Our`s is a six-knot hull. How about yours?”

“Even though our boat is larger, that`s about our hull speed too,” said Art.

“Oh, such a great idea,” said Gertrude. “I`ll look forward to company and especially with a woman who skippers; that`s got to be a first in my sailing experience.”

Helen`s eyes swept from Art to Gertrude and back to Art, “What`s your sailing experience, Art?”

“We`ve been on Kitchen Pass for six years,” said Art, whose eyes sparkled as he pronounced the name of their boat.

“Where did you get the name for your boat?” inquired Rodger.

Gertrude jumped into the conversation, “That was the name that came on the boat when we bought her. We asked the former owner the same question and he told us he owned a construction company, and when business was slow, he`d offer to take his employees for a day of sailing. Sometimes they returned late because the wind would die down. This often lead to anger on the part of the employee`s wives, so he made it a rule they had to inform their wives beforehand or get permission, if you will. That evolved into the name Kitchen Pass. We`d been told it was bad luck to change the name of a boat and we liked the name, so Kitchen Pass it stayed.”

Art took over the conversation. “We`d been invited to a weekend sailing trip with friends and fell in love with sailing, so we started looking for a boat of our own in anticipation of retiring. I retired a year ago and we`ve spent a lot of time on her since.”

After their drinks were finished Gertrude offered to make coffee.

"No thanks," replied Helen. "It would keep me awake and it`s our bedtime."

"I noticed when you introduced yourself you have different last names," said Gertrude.

"We`re not married," said Helen. "We`ve thought about it, but felt no need for a legal agreement. Maybe someday we`ll feel different. It`s not that we`re against marriage, Rodger`s been there, but we like our life just the way it is."

"Gertrude?" asked Art mischievously, "should we get a divorce so we can find out what they`re talking about?"

"Would you shut up, Silly? What would our grown children and friends say?"

"We`re out of here," teased Rodger, "Before the fight starts."

Rodger and Helen excused themselves and made their way back to the Sea Witch just as the anticipated wind and rain engulfed them. Scampering below deck, they quickly shut out the storm as they pulled the hatch door behind them. Bilgee stirred from her bed, greeted them, and demanded they take her for a walk regardless of the rain. "It`s my turn," said Rodger. Grabbing his slicker, he headed for the hatch door with Bilgee tucked under one arm.

Chapter Thirty-Three

The next morning the front of the storm passed through, but the rain still beat a tattoo on the cabin roof. Helen awakened first and lay there listening to Rodger`s rhythmic, innocent breathing. *What fun to be a part of this man`s life. We`re both fortunate to share these later exciting days in our life, a sort of bonus for lives we both thought were basically over. We both seem to be on the same page in nearly everything that pops up. I wonder what we`ll decide about the crossing. I like Art and Gertrude and I`d feel more comfortable sailing with another boat, especially one that has an experienced skipper. I know my limitations even if Rodger doesn`t. When we both thought he was going to die in a year and I was still grieving over the loss of Clyde, it didn`t seem so important that we succeed. But now we have the possibility of so much more ahead of us, success is far more important.*

Rodger stirred and became aware Helen was awake. Both lay there without saying a word for several minutes. "A penny for your thoughts?" muttered Rodger as he snuggled close to her.

"I was thinking of the decision to be made regarding the crossing. I hope Art and Gertrude prove to be good traveling companions during the next few days. I like the idea of traveling with another boat for a lot of reasons."

"I do too; it`s a long time to be at sea by yourself, and if an emergency arises, there`s someone to turn to for help. How long do you think the voyage will take, Skipper?"

"As far as I can calculate, I think we`re looking at fifty plus days."

"That long? I guess I was thinking more like a month."

Helen rolled over on one elbow facing Rodger, "It`s nearly forty-five hundred miles and if we make a hundred miles every twenty-four hours, it`ll take at least forty five days; and then there`s the doldrums."

"That makes Art and Gertrude`s offer more important all the time. I wonder when this storm is going to pass?"

"I`ll check the weather report on the radio while you let Bilgee out; then perform your magic act in the bathroom and get handsome," teased Helen.

"That act is getting more difficult as time goes on. Would you settle for just acceptable-looking instead of handsome?"

"Handsome is in the eye of the beholder, so just go do it."

Rodger rolled out of bed after planting a kiss on Helen`s pursed, waiting lips. "This sounds like a day for reading a good book, but let`s hear what the weatherman says."

Rodger returned to the salon having shaved, and hair in the process of drying. "The coffee`s ready, can I pour you a cup?"

"You bet." Helen sat in her bathrobe at the ship-to-shore radio listening to the weather report. As Rodger put a cup of hot coffee in front of her, she pushed back to share the report. "We`re not going anywhere today. This is supposed to last until late afternoon, so we can relax, have a leisurely breakfast, and maybe go visit Art and Gertrude this afternoon. Better yet, we could invite them for dinner if you feel up to the task."

"Let me think about that; I don`t see myself as a great cook."

"Don`t sell yourself short; your clam linguini is breathtaking."

"Breathtaking? Oh, come now, good maybe… but breathtaking?"

"Maybe you're the one that`s breathtaking, and I just happen to love clam linguini," bantered Helen as she got up and put her arms around Rodger. "Now, will you invite them to dinner?"

* * *

The rain ran its course by mid afternoon and Rodger and Bilgee set out for a walk around the marina. Passing Kitchen Pass, Rodger knocked on the side of the hull to see if Art and Gertrude were aboard. After a moment Art appeared at the hatch opening. “Hello Rodger, I see you weathered the storm. What`s up?”

“Helen and I want to invite you and your first Mate to dinner tonight. The menu is clam linguine.”

“Hey, that`s great; we`ll be there. What can we bring?”

“Just yourselves; how does six o`clock sound? We`ll eat at six-thirty.”

“We`ll be there and Gertrude will be thrilled to be eating someone else`s cooking.”

Rodger waved goodbye and proceeded down the dock behind an impatient dog looking for the first shrub or tree. The air was fresh after the storm and seagulls were making up for lost time looking for food on the far beach beyond the riprap jetty. With a ten-knot wind from the southwest, it put a chill to the air that encouraged a quick pace.

When they reached the top of the gangplank leading off the floating dock, Bilgee tugged at her leash. Rodger reached down unsnapping it to give her the freedom she craved. She soon claimed her territory and then ran after a flock of seabirds scanning for food on the open grassy field before them. Rodger lit his pipe, drawing deeply on the bowl of smoldering tobacco. Finally keeping it lit, he blew the gray smoke skyward sauntering along watching Bilgee play.

When Rodger finished his pipe, he realized it was time to return to the Sea Witch and prepare the dinner he was committed to cook. Bilgee came at his command and they quickly retraced their steps. Everything was still wet from the storm and Bilgee`s long hair lay a matted mess from her play in the wet grassy field. “Bilgee, I can`t take you on board that way. I`ll loop you’re your leash to the dock cleat until I can get a towel.”

Helen lay napping when Rodger went below, but soon awakened when he entered the salon searching for a towel. “What are you looking for?”

“We have one very wet dog and I don`t want to bring her aboard that way.”

“Take a towel out of the dirty clothes, it`ll have to be washed anyway.”

Doing so, Rodger returned on deck, but Bilgee was nowhere in sight. Rodger, momentarily stunned, called out, “Bilgee.” Getting no response, he started down the dock calling and searching for her. *Where is that dog?*

Having determined she wasn`t on the floating dock or walkway, Rodger quickly strode up the gangplank to the open field beyond the parking lot. There she was trailing her leash and joyfully chasing the seabirds that had joined in the game of tag with her.

"Bilgee, get over here; I`m really angry with you. I don`t have time for this foolishness."

Bilgee, recognizing the harsh tone of Rodger`s voice, left her play and quickly ran to his side. Rodger picked up the end of the leash, and without an additional word walked Bilgee back to the boat. There was no play or gentleness in Rodger`s manner and Bilgee was smart enough to accompany her master with no further resistance or detours.

Upon arriving at the boat Rodger picked up the towel he had lain on the deck, uncoupled Bilgee`s leash from the collar and gave her a brisk rub down with no conversation. Bilgee, subdued and chastised by Rodger`s silence, moved toward the stairway and waited for Rodger to carry her down into the salon. As he picked her up, she seemed to melt into the crook of his arm; comforted with the closeness she felt touching her master.

"Where have you two been? I went topside and didn`t see a sign of you."

"This dog took French leave and was chasing seabirds up in the field. I`m not very happy with her right now."

"How did she get away?" Helen put aside the book she was reading and got up from the divan.

"I guess I didn`t do a good job tying her up. I can understand her need to romp with the seabirds after being on board ship for several days, but she knew she was supposed to stay put."

"She looks contrite, if a dog can look contrite," chuckled Helen as she reached out to take Bilgee from Rodger.

"I`ll let her think about it for awhile. She has to know, that`s not acceptable behavior," said Rodger as he turned his back to her and started dinner.

* * *

Art and Gertrude arrived on time and accepted the cocktail Helen offered. "I hope you like a dry martini; if not I can get you something else."

"Oh no, this will be fine," said both eagerly.

They continued to stand as Rodger offered a toast to friendship and happy sailing. The four touched glasses and sipped their drink, "Wow," gasped Gertrude, "That is a very dry martini, but good. How much vermouth do you use, Helen?" All four sat down.

"I put a small amount in a chilled martini glass, swirl it a bit and then throw it out. What sticks on the inside of each chilled glass is all it gets, and I use a high quality gin."

"Well Art," said Gertrude, "I just learned how to make our martinis from now on."

Rodger received compliments for his Clam Linguine, and Gertrude asked him for the secret to his successful entrée. He replied, "I always have Helen ply my guests with a very dry martini first." This brought laughter and set the tone of the foursome for the evening.

After several hours of good companionship and good food they said their goodbyes. Rodger and Helen reflected on the evening while sharing the job of cleaning up and doing the dishes. "That was fun, Rodg, I like the Kaylors."

"I do too; they may be just what we need for a successful voyage to Tahiti."

"Gertrude certainly seems to be taken with you. I`ll have to watch her," teased Helen.

"I can understand that…after all, my Clam Linguine is breathtaking."

"Okay smart guy, it`s time for bed."

* * *

Helen sat at the radio listening to the weather report. They had mutually agreed with the Kaylors to leave for San Francisco at slack tide if the weather was favorable. "It looks like a go, Rodg. We`re looking at winds out of the south to 15 knots, and slack tide is at ten o`clock. Call the Kaylors on your cell phone and let them know we`re prepared to leave this morning."

"Okay, we`ll want to leave together and let them lead the way, at least until we get to open water."

Rodger called and found they, too, were preparing to travel today. Mutually agreeing to a ten o`clock departure, Art said he would call when they were ready to cast off. Rodger then took Bilgee for a morning walk before checking out at the marina office.

Helen busied herself with charting a route that took them to a marina in San Francisco Bay at Sausalito. The distance, two hundred miles, would be a forty-eight hour sail, and standing four-hour watches would be necessary. This would be a good test for them and the Sea Witch. It would also test the advantages and disadvantages of sailing with a companion boat.

When Rodger and Bilgee returned, he prepared breakfast while Helen walked over to the Kaylor`s for final sailing preparations. Art met Helen on the dock next to Kitchen Pass, "Any questions about our start today?" he asked.

"I`m assuming you`ll lead and when we hit open water, we`ll sail side-by-side. How much distance should we try to maintain between the boats?"

"That works for me; and I think a three hundred yards should gives us enough room for any unexpected maneuvers. We can put up comparable sails and see how our hull speeds match. Then adjust sails, if we need to. The goal will be to stay within sight at dusk."

"Sounds good, Art. We`ll be ready for your call at ten o`clock." Helen returned to the Sea Witch just in time to sit down to breakfast. Bilgee snuggled close to Rodger on the divan; happy to be back in his good graces. Helen filled Rodger in on the plans for the day and the excitement of departure began to build for each of them.

Helen did the dishes and straightened the salon while Rodger went topside to remove the sail covers. He then took the jib out of the sail bag and hanked it to the forestay and then the halyard and left it crumpled on the foredeck.

At ten o`clock Art called on the radio and both boats started their auxiliary engine. After a few minutes running at idle, they both ran satisfactorily and the two skippers signaled their first mates to cast off. Rodger and Gertrude worked in unison and both boats pulled slowly away from their moorage with Kitchen Pass in the lead. The two crews waved to each other starting their two-day sail to San Francisco Bay.

As they cleared the entrance to Eureka, two-foot waves came directly at them. Clearing land by a half mile with the Sea Witch following by three hundred meters, Art jibed and swung his boat to a southerly heading of 200 degrees. This would clear Cape Mendocino; Helen followed his lead.

After setting the autopilot in sync with the GPS, she and Rodger settled into the routine of sailing and being on watch. Soon Humboldt Bay and Eureka were far behind them, and both boats moved along in unison.

"Rodger, would you stand by the Tiller? I want to go below and contact Art on the radio to see if everything is okay regarding hull speed and compass setting."

"Sure, Skipper."

Helen returned in a few minutes with a smile on her face and thumbs up signal. "Everything is fine, and Gertrude says hello. Art said we`ll make a course change off Cape Mendocino."

With the wind out of the southwest at 10 knots, the gentle roll of the water surface became like a child`s slide. The Sea Witch charged forward, seemingly happy to be back in her element, with the waves breaking gently at her quarter. The temperature, in the 60`s and the gray cloud cover eventually gave way to patches of blue and white. Helen and Rodger snuggled side-by-side enjoying once again the thrill of sailing.

"When do we start the first four-hour watch procedure, Skipper?"

"After lunch. I`ll take a nap, and you can have the helm watch for four hours."

"What do you want for lunch?"

"How about a bologna sandwich and an Old English 800?"

"I can do that." Rodger removed his arm from around Helen`s shoulders and made his way forward to the companionway and down to the salon and galley. Soon he had the tray prepared and returned to the cockpit. "I threw in a few chips to round out the meal."

"Of course you did; I was counting on that." Rodger put the tray between them as they sat facing each other enjoying their first picnic at sea for a while. "This is the life, Rodg." Helen saluted him with her opened bottle of beer.

"It`s different having a companion boat running beside you," said Rodger looking over at Kitchen Pass. Art and Gertrude had followed suit regarding lunch in the cockpit as they each held a beer high in the air saluting Rodger and Helen. They returned the salute, but wind and distance prevented voice communication.

After lunch, Helen retreated to the salon to take a nap in preparation for an interrupted night`s sleep standing watches. Rodger checked the course and settled in for his watch. This consisted of watching the sails for maximum performance and the pathway ahead for obstacles to avoid. Bilgee lay beside him content to spend most of her time sleeping; only stirring when he moved about tightening a winch or letting out a sail sheet.

Kitchen Pass looked to be running well, with Gertrude alone in the cockpit, Rodger determined they were on the same watch schedule as he and Helen. *The U.S. Coast Pilot warns of reefs and obstacles within a half- mile of shore,* Rodger thought to himself, *so skippers chose well to lay a course beyond this. The coastline is low with sandy beaches and Cape Mendocino is ten miles ahead.*

Rodger grew stiff sitting in one position so he connected his harness to the tether and moved to the bow to stand, holding on to the forward halyard surveying the water ahead. The wind held at ten knots and now a cloud layer blotted out the sun. The waves came at them in rolling swells lifting the Sea Witch gently upward; then downward like a slow-gaited horse.

Seabirds occasionally swooped in using a flyer`s chandelle maneuver to skim past the boat on the waves of the wind. Satisfied there was no food to be had, they continued on their journey north in search of their next meal. Looking to starboard Rodger waved to Gertrude who had moved forward to sit on the cabin roof. Now bundled in a jacket, she returned his wave. Rodger realized he was cold and scrambled back to the cockpit to retrieve his jacket from Bilgee, who was using it as a mattress.

Grudgingly giving it up, Bilgee went forward to her assigned spot on the foredeck to relieve herself. Returning, she took her place by Rodger. He determined it was time to change course as they now lay off Cape Mendocino. Signaling Gertrude, she waited for him to set the new heading on the GPS, thus avoiding turning in to him. Rodger made the necessary adjustment and tended the sails to accommodate the change in direction. With the heading now at 140 degrees, Gertrude immediately followed suit.

At four o`clock Helen stuck her head out of the companionway and smiled because of the scene before her; Rodger holding Bilgee, and both of them intently scanning the water ahead. "Ahoy crew; is everything shipshape?"

"Aye, aye, Skipper. It`s steady as she goes, but the weather`s changing."

Helen turned to face the wind direction. "That looks like a front ahead; I`d better check the barometer. The wind`s stronger now and driving the waves higher since I went below. Stay topside until I check the barometer, get a weather report, and contact Kitchen Pass."

"Aye, aye, Skipper." Rodger put Bilgee down on the bench seat next to the tiller and stood to check the tell-tail on the mainsail. He pointed the bow a little closer to the wind to bring the tell-tail back to parallel. Sitting down, he returned Bilgee to his lap and waited for Helen`s instructions.

She stood in the open companionway with concern showing on her face. "It looks like we`re in for a bit of a blow. The weather report states winds to forty knots and rain."

"I guess our work`s cut out for us. What did Kitchen Pass have to say?"

"They`re going to double reef their main and put on a storm jib to start with. I guess we`d better do the same and as soon as possible. Doing it later with 40 knots of wind would be a wet and dangerous job."

"Where do you want me to start?" he asked.

"I`ll take the tiller, overpower the GPS, and bring her into the wind. Then I`ll tie the tiller down and help you with reefing the main. We can put the double reef in. When we finish, drop the jib and substitute it with the smaller storm jib; it`ll still give us steerage. If push comes to shove, we`ll use the engine for more steerage."

Working side-by-side, Helen and Rodger tied in a double reef, which reduced its sail area by half. Rodger than went below and retrieved the storm jib from the sail locker. Dropping the large jib, he quickly replaced it with the storm jib. Helen untied the tiller and let the Sea Witch drop off to the wind to pick up its course according to the GPS. The jib and main sheets were slackened a bit to get the Sea Witch on a close reach and bring the rail up, that was now running under the surface of the water. Helen and Rodger did a high five, and then he went below to bring Helen her heavy weather gear including her 8-inch high boots.

Upon returning, he handed her the gear and stood by while she put it on. The wind had stayed steady at 15 knots, but the front was rapidly moving toward them. Looking to starboard, Helen could see Art and Gertrude also had finished preparing for the approaching front. Art signaled he was going to call them on the ship-to-shore radio, so Helen went below and took a distressed Bilgee with her.

Returning a few minutes later she reported, "They hope we`ll enjoy the ride, and we can watch out for each other. Art sounds confident that the storm should blow itself out by midnight."

"That must be quite a storm front to have that kind of strength," replied Rodger. "Well, we`re prepared for it, but how does he know that?"

"He has Weatherfax."

"What`s that?"

"Weatherfax is a report of weather conditions for the entire Pacific Ocean. He gets four print-outs a day."

"Should we have that information?" Rodger asked settling down on the bench seat beside the tiller.

"Not if we travel with them across the Pacific. It`s expensive; you need a computer, printer, monitor and the program to install in the computer. The program itself costs about two hundred dollars. Oh yes, and you have to have a single-line radio set-up, which is the most expensive part of the whole operation."

"That makes traveling with them all the more attractive, doesn`t it?"

Helen sat down on the other side of the tiller facing Rodger. "It does, for a fact. We`d probably be looking at a couple of thousand dollars to install it. Well… we`ll cross that bridge when we come to it."

"Should I bring Bilgee topside? Maybe some fresh air and companionship would be good for her before the storm hits."

"Why don`t you hand her to me and then try to get a nap; it may be a long night."

"I am tired and I would welcome a nap about now." Rodger went below and soon returned with Bilgee in hand. Giving her to Helen he offered, "If you need me, don`t hesitate to wake me up."

"You can count on it," said Helen as she snuggled to Bilgee beside her on the seat and gave Rodger a friendly smile of dismissal.

* * *

A few minutes before sunset the lull before the storm occurred, and the wind followed immediately at 40 knots out of the southeast. Helen looked over at Kitchen Pass and saw Gertrude had come topside. Both Gertrude and Art were in their yellow foul weather gear. Helen called down to Rodger, who appeared in the companionway. "Put on your gear and come up, Rodg, so I can call Art on the ship-to-shore radio."

Rodger appeared in a few minutes with an expectant look as he approached Helen who sat holding Bilgee tucked under one arm. "What do you think, Skipper?"

"I think we`ve really got our work cut out for us. I`ll leave Bilgee below and join you as soon as I contact Kitchen Pass." Helen retreated to the salon, going immediately to the radio to call kitchen pass.

Art replied, "I`m falling off a bit to quarter the building waves better. I`ll wait for you to change course first so we won`t get into trouble turning in to you."

Helen affirmed she understood, ended the conversation, and returned topside. She relayed the message to Rodger who stepped aside so she could override the GPS and autopilot with the tiller and swing the bow directly through the wind and fall off a bit. Rodger slakened the sails slightly so the boat wasn`t driving so hard into the waves. He then turned to Helen for approval and further instructions.

She gave him thumbs up and patted the seat beside her inviting him to sit. The waves were no longer breaking gently on the quarter as before, and they were taking some water, which sloshed around in the cockpit. Even though the cockpit was self-bailing, as they sat there, the water rose half way up their boots, and the pelting rain stung their faces as they looked into the storm. The waves were coming steady at five feet, but they were quartering them nicely, and for the time being everything was under control.

"There seems to be a double wave pattern," said Rodger half-shouting into Helen`s ear. "How can that be?"

"In the ocean there is a constant wave pattern that increases or decreases according to what`s going on in all parts of the ocean. That`s how earthquakes in Japan end up as tsunamis on the west coast of the United States. The second pattern is formed by the winds in a local region, so one can have five foot rollers with a three foot chop on top."

"No wonder on calm days I've still experienced a rolling sea."

"Now you've got it, Rodg. Did you notice how quickly the wind rose from 15 knots to forty?"

"Yes."

"That's not unusual when passing through a weather front. It can change from 15 to 40 knots in as little as thirty seconds."

"Wow! Do you think it will stay at this velocity for the next six hours if we go by what Art says?"

"He has the weatherfax, so he`s probably right."

"In that case, we better take turns eating below and there`s cold stew left over from last night`s dinner. I don`t think I could cook under these conditions."

"That`s fine, Rodg. After I eat, you can go below until I need you." Rodger disappeared below deck leaving Helen to study the waves, wind and the feel of the Sea Witch as it responds to the helm. She knew she would be more responsive to emergencies than the autopilot.

Entering the salon, Rodger slipped out of his rain gear and lay down on the divan. Bilgee snuggled up beside him. Watching the swaying, gimbaled light above him didn`t put him to sleep as usual. The movement of the boat was rhythmic except for an occasional shudder from a larger-than-usual wave. His thoughts drifted back to the storm last year that nearly cost him his life. *I hope we don`t run into another rogue wave like that one,* he thought. He knew waves had an irregular pattern and about every hundredth wave had the makings of a rogue wave, but usually they were just a little larger than the rest; t*his time we`re better prepared for an ocean storm.*

Bilgee let out a groan, as if she was having a bad dream. Rodger patted her for a while and eventually they both fell asleep. He awakened to the sound of a pounding on the cabin roof over his head. Startled, he quickly darted up the companionway and slid the cover back to look at Helen. "Rodg, you`d better come up here with me; this weather isn`t getting any better and I`m bone-tired."

He returned to the salon to the wide-eyed stare of Bilgee. Slipping into his raingear he returned topside. Helen gave him a thumb up, and patted the seat beside her for Rodger to sit down. Looking over at Helen he shouted, "Are we having fun yet?"

"Almost," replied Helen as she offered him the tiller. "I need to go below for awhile. It`s about your time for the watch, and I`m so tired. Can I bring you up anything to eat or drink before I lie down?"

"An Old English would hit the spot."

"A storm doesn`t slacken your thirst, does it Rodg?"

"If anything, it increases it, and I have to admit… this is exciting, isn`t it?"

Helen rolled her eyes and went below.

* * *

Bilgee lay on the divan and showed her pleasure on seeing Helen. "Hi girl, I`ll be right back to snuggle with you as soon as I ply your master with sustenance," she said. Quickly she opened a beer and headed up the companionway. On her return she lay beside Bilgee, who gratefully snuggled up to her. The Sea Witch, being a heavy weather boat, was breaking into the waves nicely with not too much pitch or yaw. The choice of reefing the mainsail and using the storm jib had been a good one… at least for the time being.

Rodger looked over at Kitchen Pass where Gertrude and Art were both in the cockpit. They waved a hello and settled back in to a hunkered down position at the back of their cockpit. Their helm was the wheel-type common to newer and larger boats with a binnacle standing before it containing gauges including a compass. Art was standing at the wheel, so Rodger knew they were not on autopilot.

Lightening, striking far off to starboard, was more constant, the rain continued torrential, and the wind had more force. *If this gets worse,* thought Rodger, *we may have to drop the sails, and run bare poles down wind.*

After an hour with fatigue setting in, Rodger stood and stretched. Holding the tiller between his legs, he made circles with his arms, bent from his waist in a bowing motion, and rolled his head around on its axis to loosen the muscles that were stiff. Glancing over at Kitchen Pass, Art was in the cockpit alone.

Occasionally the Sea Witch would be required to climb an extra large wave and start yawing down the backside as Rodger fought the tiller to correct it before they entered the trough. Turning sideways in the trough would mean a knock down. As they ascended the next wave, they broke through near the top of the wave to start the descent, and on and on.

The water reflected the sky, dark and ominous. White spindrift blew off the top of the breaking waves occasionally splatting against the windshield of the dodger. Rodger found himself ducking automatically when he saw it coming. The cockpit always had about three inches of water, but the self-bailing feature kept it at that level; at least for the time being. *Eight-inch boots are really a godsend,* thought Rodger.

The rain, wind, and lightening suddenly increased as they entered a squall within the storm. This caused the wave action to rise from five foot to eight-foot waves. Glancing over to Kitchen Pass, Rodger determined he`d better signal Helen to come topside and both skipper and first mate could drop their main and mizzen and dump the jib. He doubled his fist and banged on the cabin roof.

Helen stuck her head out of the companionway, "What`s up, Rodg?"

"I think we should drop the sails as Kitchen Pass has and go bare poles."

"Gertrude just called and said they were going to go down wind on bare poles. I`ll take the tiller and bring the bow into the wind while you drop the sails."

After starting the engine and returning topside, Rodger quickly moved forward to loosen the halyard that was cleated on at the side of the main mast. He suddenly realized the sail wasn`t dropping. He glanced up the mast and saw the halyard had fouled in the track that ran up the mast. Helen was watching this drama and signaled Rodger to come to her.

"I've got to climb the shrouds and untangle it," she shouted.

"No way," shouted Rodger as he clipped on his harness and moved to ascend the shrouds. Using the shroud slats, like rungs of a ladder, enabled him to reach farther upward to the fouled halyard. The wind, determined to blow him off the shrouds, forced him to hold on with all his strength as he continued upward. Finally, by extending his arm to full length, he was able to release the fouled halyard, and the mainsail dropped.

Helen`s look of concern changed to a broad smile as he made his way back to her. "Normally the first Mate obeys what the Skipper says, but I`ll overlook it this time."

Helen watched as Rodger wrapped up the fallen mainsail and flaked it to the boom. Having accomplished this, Rodger made his way to the cockpit and collapsed on the bench seat exhausted. Helen looked over at Rodger and grinned, "Now you`re having fun."

* * *

At four o`clock in the morning the storm blew itself out and the dawn came up to clearing skies and lighter winds. Rodger relieved Helen at the helm as they shared a cup of hot coffee and a sea biscuit to sustain them until breakfast at eight o`clock. It had been a rough twelve hours for both of them; they were beat, but they had weathered the storm and after a brief radio conversation with Kitchen Pass, Art and Gertrude had also.

"It`s comforting to have a companion boat, isn`t it Rodg?"

"Yes, it is. I followed their lead in running bare poles downwind. It turned out to be the right decision at the right time. I might have waited longer and had higher seas and stronger winds to deal with. That squall in the middle of the storm front was a surprise to us, but not to Art and Gertrude. Their weatherfax showed it was going to cross our path, giving us time to prepare for it."

"That information helped both of us. Art says we should be in Sausalito by tomorrow afternoon," said Helen. "He also added this should be a good sailing day, according to his weatherfax, with winds to ten knots and a light chop. After I check the gear, I`m going below and get a few hours sleep. However, you look like you need the rest more than I."

"I`m okay, Skipper."

"I`ll hand Bilgee up and she can keep you company."

"Do that, Bilgee and I need a little R and R together. Helen soon returned with Bilgee squirming to get down and immediately went to her designated spot forward of the cabin. Rodger followed her with a bucket of seawater for a quick wash down and then they sat together by the tiller and enjoyed each other`s company.

* * *

The next twenty-four hours passed without incident and it was pleasant watching the California coast change from higher mountains of the coast range to foothills as the two boats plied their way south to San Francisco. They held their course about a mile off shore, and because of the warmer weather the wind shifted to come from the northwest.

This put the wind over their stern and allowed wing-and-wing sailing with the Genoa jib out to port held with a whisker pole holding it out like a mainsail`s boom and the mainsail out to starboard.

Helen and Rodger kept to the four-hour watch schedule even during the daylight hours to enable them to get the rest they needed. Bilge spent most of her time topside during the day doing her assigned role as companion to whoever was at the helm. She had learned to walk about the deck without mishap, and seemed to never tire of chasing seabirds that came too close. Helen and Rodger made sure her toenails were clipped short for better traction and they bought a tether and harness system for her, which she wore with pride.

Rodger became aware of erratic currents as they approached Pt Arena. According to the United States Coast Pilot book there were deep submarine valleys that caused them, but the wind held steady and the currents aided them on their journey adding to their speed. Navigation was made simple by watching the landmarks on the coastline as long as the sunny weather held out. However, Rodger knew this same area in the fog would be extremely difficult due to the currents and the submarine valleys that would eliminate the use of a depth sounder.

Helen spent less time with the charts now as they depended on Kitchen Pass and her weatherfax to give them course changes and weather patterns. Rodger did most of the cooking, and they ate most of their meals in the cockpit as they were now cruising in the shipping lanes. Art and Gertrude followed a similar watch system and the wing-and-wing sail pattern allowed them to sail closer together. Being only fifty yards apart, they could shout to each other adding to the feeling of camaraderie.

Rodger appeared in the cockpit with a tray at lunchtime of sandwiches, chips and beer. "Ready for lunch, Skipper?"

"You`ve been reading my mind." Helen slide over on the bench seat for Rodger to sit beside her. This closeness allowed them to snuggle together as they ate.

"I`ll be glad when we get to Sausalito so we can spend some quality time together," said Rodger as he put his arm around Helen`s shoulders.

"What do you have in mind, Rodg…as if I didn`t know."

"I guess you've answered your own question. These four hour watches are for the birds."

Helen went below after lunch to get about three hours sleep before her next watch. Rodger stood at the tiller with Bilgee beside him looking shoreward to pick out the landmarks using the Pacific Coast Pilot & Chart. Approaching Point Reyes in the distance he saw the coast change to a broad white sandy beach about ten miles long backed by high grassy sand dunes.

Point Reyes appeared to be a dark rocky headland about six hundred feet high. It became apparent it was the higher extremity of a ridge running in an easterly direction for about three miles. Rodger estimated they were twenty-five miles north of the Golden Gate Bridge. This would put them in Sausalito after dark, so they probably would follow Kitchen Pass under the Bridge, and on to moorage at a marina in Sausalito, the homeport for Kitchen Pass.

Rodger walked forward to stand at the shrouds and stretch his stiffening body. He tired sooner on watch now and decided his years were catching up with him. Helen seemed to stand up better on watch, but he wrote off his lack of endurance to the time fighting tuberculosis. He knew his lungs had been damaged causing him to occasionally use an inhaler. Helen, aware of this, questioned him about it and suggested he give up his evening pipe. However, she didn`t make an issue of it, and therefore he didn`t do it.

Looking ahead he could make out Point Bonita, the northern headland at the entrance to the Golden Gate. The coast had several lagoons that emptied into Drakes Bay on the way to Point Bonita. The Pilot indicated the Bay had been named after Sir Francis Drake who anchored there in 1579 because it is good protection from northwesterly weather.

Helen appeared in the companionway letting the gentle wind lightly blow her tussled hair. "How`re we doing, mate?"

"Everything`s shipshape, Skipper, and we`re about two hours from the Golden Gate Bridge. We`ll lose our daylight there, so I suggest we follow Kitchen Pass in after we round Point Bonita as this is their home turf."

"Good idea, Rodg. I`ll take over now, so call Art and confirm this before you start dinner. You were going to start dinner, weren't you?"

"Of course, Skipper. Corned beef hash and a lettuce and tomato salad okay?"

"It`ll do."

* * *

Kitchen Pass swung into the lead as they rounded Point Bonita using the northern channel that hugged the land, because the weather was good. Art had previously informed them over the radio if it had been otherwise they would have set a course from Point Reyes to the lightship and then approach San Francisco Bay from there. Rodger came on deck with dinner on a tray and sat beside Helen on the cockpit bench seat. "Now you can say you've dined while going under the Golden Gate Bridge."

"Isn`t it magnificent?"

"Dinner or the Bridge?"

"The Bridge, silly. I liked dinner, but I could never say corned beef hash was magnificent under any circumstances."

"Point well taken. Art said we lucked out on the tide as it`s beginning to flood about the time we get to the bridge."

"Would there be a problem otherwise?"

"On ebb tide we`d buck a 6 knot current on the Sausalito side of the bridge."

"We`re lucky. We might have had to lay off and wait for a tide change," said Helen as she stood to view the water before them. "Art`s clipping right along and we`re probably doing nine knots with the aid of the current."

"I`ll take the tray below and call Art for any further instructions."

"Good idea, Rodg. Ask him for our E.T.A. while you're at it as I`m disconnecting the auto pilot."

"Rodger Wilco," snapped Rodger as he stood and gave Helen a brisk military salute.

"Will you stop fooling around, and just do it?"

* * *

Rodger returned with a cup of coffee for each of them. "Art says we should be at the Sausalito marina about nine o`clock, if all goes well. Look at San Francisco Bay; so impressive with all its boat traffic and the night-lights of the city coming on now. A lot of the smaller boats seem to be headed the same direction as we."

"I`m glad Art has permanent moorage. He said it`s a popular marina for small boats and we could raft up to him if transient space was a problem," said Helen as she turned the tiller over to Rodger. "I need to go below and talk to Art on the radio and freshen up a bit. Do you want me to bring you a jacket?

"Yes, the temperature sure dropped when the sun went down."

Helen returned and handed Rodger his jacket as she took over the tiller. "Art says to shorten the distance between us as we approach Sausalito and drop the sails now and power in. They`re turning into the wind now to drop their sails, so we`ll do the same. Get ready to come about."

"Aye, aye Skipper." Rodger moved forward to drop the jib and mainsail. After securing them, he dropped the mizzen sail and flaked it on its boom as he had the mainsail. Helen turned the boat back on course after having Rodger go below to start the auxiliary engine.

"Good job, Mate. I`m moving closer to them now as Gertrude doesn`t work as fast as you and they`re still pointed into the wind." Helen pulled up within shouting distance of Kitchen Pass. "Everything okay?"

Art had Gertrude trade places with him at the helm while he flaked the mainsail and tied it down with the line. "We`re ready to go and should be there in half an hour." Art returned to the helm, and then turned Kitchen Pass toward Sausalito and signled to follow them as they moved away into the night.

Rodger settled down with Bilgee in his arms to share the night voyage. She looked up adoringly as if to say, *Thanks, Boss.*

"There`s the marina ahead and it looks crowded. We`ll follow them to the harbormaster `s office; as Art said they`d stand off while we talked to the harbormaster. If no space is available, we`ll both go to their moorage and raft together."

Helen brought the Sea Witch up to the transient dock while Rodger set Bilgee aside and hurried to the harbormaster`s office. Returning shortly smiling, he said there was a space for them. After being signaled off by Rodger, Kitchen Pass immediately backed out of the transient area to go to their space. Art and Gertrude promised to find the Sea Witch as soon as they had Kitchen Pass secured for the night.

With bumpers out and all lines tied to their transient slip, Rodger came topside with a beer for each of them. Raising his bottle to Helen he said, "It`s been a great day hasn`t it Skipper?"

"Yes Mate, it`s been a great day, and here come Art and Gertrude down the dock. I hope we have two more beers."

After Art and Gertrude asked permission to come aboard, Art said, "How was that for a storm yesterday?"

"All I wanted," replied Helen. "Rodg is below getting you a beer, if that`s your choice of drink."

"That would be appreciated," replied Art. "I work up quite a thirst after a day of sailing." Art sat down on the gunnel with his feet dangling into the cockpit.

Stepping aboard, Gertrude gave Helen a hug, and then held her at arms length saying, "You're quite a Skipper. I admire the way you handle this boat, Helen."

"Thanks, Gertrude. However, I have to admit I have some apprehension when I think of crossing the Pacific. Rodg and I are seriously considering your offer of letting us go with you and cross over to Tahiti from here."

Rodger appeared with two more beers for Art and Gertrude. Rodger proposed a toast, "To friendship." The bottles were touched together as if they were the finest of crystal wine glasses and each person echoed the toast.

Sitting silently, the two couples faced each other enjoying the moment as they let their tired bodies relax. The evening was pleasant with stars vying for prominence, competing with the night-lights of the cities surrounding San Francisco Bay. The tall slender buildings of San Francisco marching up Telegraph Hill dominated the scene across the Bay. "I`m glad we`re on this side of the bay, as San Francisco is breathtaking at night from this perspective."

"You`re right, Helen," said Gertrude. "We`ve always been happy we chose this marina in Sausalito. It gives us this view, but it`s also an easy exit to the Pacific Ocean, and if the weather is bad out there we can usually sail inside San Francisco Bay as it`s large."

Art interjected, "We`ve had a lot of good day-sails because of the bay`s size and being protected from the ocean weather. Actually there are two bays here touching each other. San Paolo Bay lies to the north and is on the northern edge of San Francisco Bay and the southern edge of the wine country. The wine tour is something we`d like to take you on while we lay over and prepare for our crossing."

"I`ll drink to that," laughed Rodger as he saluted them with his bottle of beer. "When do you plan to leave for Tahiti?"

"We`re going home for a week to take care of household tasks. Then another week to get Kitchen Pass ready and take on supplies," replied Art.

"What do you have to do to Kitchen Pass?" asked Helen.

"We want a mechanic to go over our engine. If we run into doldrums and we need to do some extensive motor sailing, we want to be sure we have a reliable engine," replied Art.

"And I have a grocery list as long as your arm," quipt Gertrude.

"That`s probably something we should consider," said Rodger. "I don`t think John`s mechanic checked our engine last month, but if he did, a second opinion would be money and time well spent."

"Maybe we could ask your mechanic to check it after he finishes your engine," said Helen. "Halfway across the Pacific is no place to have engine trouble."

"He works here at the marina, so we`ll make arrangements tomorrow," said Art. "I`m sure he can work you in."

"Would you two like to come home with us when we leave tomorrow?" asked Gertrude. "We`d love to entertain you in our home in Sonoma, we`re just fifty miles north in Napa Valley`s wine country."

"Let us talk this over and first decide what we`re going to do regarding the crossing to Tahiti. We`ll let you know in the morning."

"Speaking of morning," said Art. "I`m exhausted and I`m sure we all are. We`ll say goodnight and thanks for the beer." They said their goodbyes with hugs all around and went their separate ways to settle in for the night.

Rodger and Helen headed for the marina's shower facilities to wash off two days of being at sea. Returning to the Sea Witch, Rodger inspected the lines and bumpers before turning in. Helen was in bed by the time he came below. Quickly joining her, they snuggled together becoming aware of the gentle rocking of the boat. "This is the life, isn`t it, Sweetie?"

"Yes, Rodg, but...kiss me goodnight and I`ll see you in the morning."

"You are tired, aren`t you," said Rodg.

"Right," murmured Helen rolling over on her side ending the conversation, and the day.

Bilgee climbed onto the bed and snuggled beside Rodger... who welcomed her.

* * *

Helen awakened the next morning and smiled to herself as she watched Rodger and Bilgee lying together. *I guess I`d better be more responsive* *to Rodg after this or I could be replaced as a bed companion,* she mused. Her getting out of bed woke Bilgee who jumped down and ran to the companionway.

"Okay, Bilgee, I get the picture." Helen put on her robe and opened the hatch for Bilgee, then busied herself making coffee waiting for the dog`s return. Rodger remained asleep throughout this activity, but awakened to the smell of roasting coffee.

"How luxurious to wake up this way," he yawned. "This must be heaven."

"I don`t know… I was hoping for more," Helen replied.

"Why don`t you climb back in bed and wait for the coffee to perk, or whatever."

"It`s the what-ever that I`m not ready for. I`m not a morning person."

"You weren`t an evening person last night, either. What`s the problem?"

"I guess I`m just tired. Maybe we need a little time off the boat or at least some rest. I`m just not there physically or mentally."

"Maybe you need a little time away from me," replied Rodger. "You could go with Art and Gertrude to their place in Sonoma and I could stay here and supervise the engine inspection, or I could go home and see my family."

"Let`s think about it; either option has merit."

After a quiet breakfast and while Helen cleaned up the interior of the boat, Rodger took their laundry to the Harbormaster`s building that housed a bathroom, showers, and laundry facilities. With Bilgee on a leash, the two of them took a short walk while waiting for the laundry to be finished.

It was good for Bilgee to be on dry land again and able to stake out new territory. The marina was bustling with sailors and their guests preparing for a day on the water. This was an active marina with a much larger local population to serve than any they had experienced since their starting point at the Des Moines Marina in Washington State. It too served a large population around Seattle plus the neighboring towns of Des Moines, Burien, and Federal Way.

Rodger gathered up the folded laundry and, with Bilgee in tow, headed back to the Sea Witch. When he returned, Art and Gertrude were standing on the dock next to the Sea Witch talking to Helen. They waved hello and continued their conversation , which appeared to be agitated.

Rodger was the first to speak. "Hi, you two, what`s up?"

Art said, "Our mechanic tells us we need a new engine. It`s old and is no longer being made, so there are no replacement parts available."

"Bummer!" Rodger exclaimed, "Do you have an option?"

"No. It would be foolhardy not to have it replaced, he tells us. We told him to go ahead, but we`re looking at two weeks at least for it to be done."

Gertrude stood beside Helen who had a comforting arm around her. "Helen and Rodger," interjected Gertrude, "Why don`t you come home with us while we wait this out? We could show you the wine country and have such a good time together."

"It sounds like fun, but Rodg and I still have to talk over our decision on the point of departure for Tahiti. We`ll let you know this afternoon on both counts."

"Good," said Gertrude. As they started to leave to return to their boat Art suggested, "Why don`t you join us for dinner at that restaurant on the hillside over there?. It`s called the *Castaways* and has a great chef. We can talk about your decision then.

Helen and Rodger looked at each other and nodded agreement. Helen responded, "Sounds good; what time will you be by?"

"Seven o`clock," replied Gertrude after a short interchange with Art. "It`s only a ten-minute walk from here to the restaurant and the view is terrific."

They said their goodbyes and the two couples parted. Aboard the Sea Witch Rodger led Helen aft to the cockpit. "What do you want to do about our discussion this morning?".

"I don`t want you to leave for home unless you really want to. I think I just need what Art and Gertrude are offering us. You know me; I get these moods occasionally. I love you, Rodg, and I want to be with you."

"Okay, that`s all I needed to hear. We`ll take them up on their offer. What about joining them for the crossing to Tahiti?"

"I`m all for it. It`s a big ocean."

"I`m with you, Skipper; all the way. Now let`s go below and work on a to do list and a grocery list for our crossing. It takes some mind altering to grasp the idea we`ll be on our way across the Pacific in two weeks."

* * *

At seven o`clock Art and Gertrude arrived and the four of them walked out of the marina, across the street and up a long flight of cement steps leading to the restaurant tucked into the side of the hillside. Another set of steps led up and around the outside of the restaurant to the front entrance. Art and Gertrude led Helen and Rodger inside to the reservation desk. Art gave his last name and stated their 7:15 reservation time. The woman bent over the reservation list looked up and instantly let out a loud shrieke. "Helen, Rodger, what are you doing here?"

"Silvia," blurted out Rodger and Helen in unison. "What are you doing here?"

"I work here and Wolfgang has just replaced the head chef," she exclaimed excitedly. "Oh, wait until Wolfgang sees you. We have a lot to talk about; so much has happened."

"That`s for sure," said Rodger.

Art and Gertrude stepped aside and took in the scene, wide-eyed with wonder. "You obviously know our matre` d," stammered Art. "You`ve been here before?"

"We know Sylvia and her husband, Wolfgang, from Coos Bay Oregon," replied Helen. "They left town without saying goodbye and have some explaining to do."

Silvia said, "Let me seat you and I`ll tell Wolfgang you're here. Oh, he`ll be so excited; he`ll want to talk to you as soon as he can leave the kitchen."

Silvia led the foursome to a window table and the view of the city across the bay was everything Gertrude had promised. After leaving them with menus, Sylvia disappeared into the kitchen. A few minutes later she returned with a smiling Wolfgang donned in a high, white chef`s hat, chef`s coat and a big smile.

"My friends," he boomed. "Oh, it`s so good to see you. What miracle brought you here to us?"

"It is a miracle isn`t it." Rodger replied, "We`re moored in the marina," pointing out the window and down. "We`re here with our friends, Art and Gertrude, and we`ll soon be leaving to cross the Pacific from here to Tahiti."

"Oh, my," said Wolfgang. "Give us your slip number in the marina and we`ll show up for breakfast, we have so much to talk about."

"That`s our friend, Wolfgang," laughed Helen. "Everything centers around food." We`re in slip number 47 at the transient dock and breakfast is at 9:00. Can you make it?"

Wolfgang spoke for both he and Silvia, "We`ll be there. Now I've got to get back to work, we have a good crowd tonight." He and Silvia offered lavish goodbyes with hugs and kisses on the cheeks for Helen and Rodger and a friendly handshake for Art and Gertrude. Looking at Helen and Rodger he added, "We do have a lot to talk about."

The four diners sat quietly in their chairs stunned by the turn of events. Helen was the first to speak. "Let`s order a cocktail and do we have a story to tell you."

The drinks arrived and after a toast Rodger took the lead on the story telling. "Wolfgang and Silvia arrived in Coos Bay shortly after we did. He took a job, as part-time chef in a small café owned by Nelda, a friend of ours. Nelda, her boyfriend, John, Wolfgang, Silvia, Helen and I became close friends and the six of us went dancing each Saturday night. A stranger entered the picture and seemed to be primarily interested in Silvia and asked her to dance occasionally. As they danced he usually asked a lot of questions about her life.

When Wolfgang didn`t show up for work one morning; we immediately went to his rental on the beach only to discovered they had moved out in the middle of the night without a word to anyone, including the landlord. We later discovered the stranger at the dance was a bounty hunter and Silvia was a wanted alien by the immigration authorities."

"Wow!" exclaimed Gertrude, "this is exciting. Imagine your friends being chased by a bounty hunter."

"I wonder if that`s still the case?" asked Art.

Helen said, "I think we can assume they`re not, or they wouldn`t be working in such a prominent place as this."

"If Wolfgang is cooking," interrupted Rodger, "I recommend the Vienerschnitzal; it`s out-of-this-world."

"I love Vienerschnitzal," gushed Gertrude. "That`s what I`ll have."

"I`d order his roast duck, but that would take too long to cook," said Helen.

The food, conversation, and the ambience were superb and on their way out of the restaurant they said goodbye to Silvia. She assured them she and Wolfgang would be at the Sea Witch at nine o`clock tomorrow morning. The evening air was still a little cool so they didn`t linger when they returned to the marina. After affectionate goodbyes, went their separate ways.

* * *

By nine o`clock the next morning Rodger and Helen had showered, straightened up the interior of the Sea Witch and had the table set for four. While Rodger prepared breakfast, Helen took Bilgee for her morning walk. When she returned she put her arms around Rodger and gave him a kiss. "What`s that for?" he asked.

"Just for being you…you are a catch, you know."

"Really! I thought I`d already been caught." Rodger smiled at their word game.

"I think I hear Wolfgang and Silvia now; let`s go topside and greet them."

Wolfgang and Sylvia were standing next to the Sea Witch and just about to knock on the cabin roof when Helen and Rodger appeared in the companion way. "Ah, my dear friends," said Wolfgang. "Do we have permission to come aboard?"

"Permission granted," said Helen. As the four met and embraced, Bilgee joined in barking excitedly, as if to say, *Give me some attention, I`m part of this crew, too, you know.*

Everyone looked at her and broke into laughter. "Okay, Bilgee," said Rodger as he scooped her up in his arms, "We get the message." After everyone had greeted her in turn, they went below, and all but Rodger sat at the table. Rodger turned to the galley and started the bacon and eggs cooking and turned on the waffle iron, as everyone settled in for breakfast. They saluted with their glasses of orange juice and drank as they waited for breakfast to be served.

"I guess you`d like an update since last we saw you," said Wolfgang lightheartedly.

"We sure would," Helen and Rodger said in unison. Helen went on to say, "We didn`t ask any questions at the restaurant because Gertrude and Art were strangers to you."

"We appreciate that," said Wolfgang. "We solved Sylvia`s immigration problem by proving to them we had married six months ago. They told us we hadn`t followed the proper procedure, but they acknowledged the fact that we weren`t a couple of kids on a lark and let us fill out the proper paper work after the fact. We proved to them Silvia wasn`t a foreign woman who was simply marrying me for my money and a way to get U.S. citizenship. That was easy because we proved Sylvia has more worldly goods than I back in Switzerland. She had overstayed her visa after she married me, and we didn`t know what to do. When we realized Silvia was being sought by the authorities she turned herself in when we reached San Francisco and that also helped her case."

"Well, we`re so happy for the two of you," said Helen.

Rodger added, "We`re pleased because you are no longer on the run."

"It`s unbelievable," said Silvia. "I`m married to my wonderful Wolfgang, I have my green card, and I will get my citizenship as soon as I am eligible."

"How did it feel being an illegal alien on the run?" asked Rodger.

"Actually," said Silvia, "it was exciting, but I`m glad it`s over."

"Me too," said Wolfgang. "I now can work at my trade as a chef in the better-known restaurants. I had my own place in Washington D.C. once, but that is too much work for a guy like me who has to run everything. It`s better I stick to what I love to do, cooking, and leave the business end of the restaurant to someone else."

"I work," said Silvia, "because I want to be near Wolfgang. In Switzerland I was the buyer of fine art for a wealthy man. He wants me to come back, but I want to live here in America and be with my Wolfie."

"Wolfie?" said Helen. "Is that what she calls you?"

"Actually," said Wolfgang, "lots of girls have called me Wolfie, but I`m limiting that to only Silvia now. I've had my day in the sun, and now I`m ready to settle down and be Wolfie only to Sylvia."

Rodger returned to his cooking and soon had satisfied the appetites of all, including Bilgee. After breakfast they decided to take a walk over to Art and Gertrude`s boat to see what was going on with them. Helen and Rodger had told them at dinner they would be happy to join them when they drove to their home in Sonoma. However, they wanted to spend some time with Silvia and Wolfgang, too, and hoped they could do both.

Art and Gertrude had been busy packing a couple of bags for their trip home and planned to leave that afternoon. When Rodger and Helen told them of their dilemma about wanting to be in two places at the same time, they understood and suggested Helen and Rodger spend the first week with Wolfgang and Sylvia. They would return in a week to check on the motor replacement for Kitchen Pass and the four of them could then return to Sonoma. This was agreeable to all and the perfect solution to Rodger and Helen`s dilemma.

Chapter Thirty-Four

After Silvia and Wolfgang left, Helen and Rodger saw Art and Gertrude off on their trip home as rain-laden clouds hung low over the bay area, darkening the sky. Returning to the Sea Witch they busied themselves doing the necessary chores to keep their floating home shipshape. When finished they put Bilgee on her leash and headed for the Laundromat next to the harbormaster`s office.

"Let`s call Wolfgang and Silvia," suggested Rodger, "and see about getting together before they have to go to work this afternoon."

"I was just going to suggest that. Maybe we can meet for lunch somewhere."

"I`ll use the pay phone here, as my cell phone is back at the boat charging." Rodger pulled out the slip of paper from his wallet on which he`d written their phone number. After a brief, but animated, conversation with Wolfgang he turned to Helen and chuckled, "Leave it to Wolfgang. He and Silvia are bringing over a picnic lunch for us to eat aboard or somewhere close and they`ll be here in an hour."

"Great! I`m glad we cleaned up the Sea Witch. We`ll have the laundry done by then and have the rest of the day to devote to our friends."

Silvia and Wolfgang arrived with a picnic basket; greetings included the usual hugs and a light kiss on each cheek. "Ah, my good friends," said Wolfgang with his rich German overtones, "There is a little park within walking distance where we could eat, if you`d like to get off the boat for awhile. Either way, the choice is yours."

Helen looked at Rodger questioningly, "What do you want to do, Rodg?"

"I`m for a walk to the park; it looks like the weather is improving and the weatherman promises a warm afternoon."

"Wonderful," gushed Silvia. "It`s such a pretty place and with unbelievable flower gardens."

The four with Bilgee on her leash walked the two blocks to the park enjoying each other`s company. Silvia and Helen led the way while Rodger and Wolfgang sauntered along behind, satisfied to let Bilgee explore as they walked. The gardens were fenced and on the perimeter of the park with paths leading through from all four sides to converge at a gazebo on a knoll in the middle. An empty picnic table was visible in the center of the gazebo, so they quickened their pace to take possession of it.

"What a perfect place for a picnic. It`s unbelievable," gushed Silvia.

Wolfgang, Rodger, and Helen broke into laughter at Silvia`s remark as it`s a phrase she often uses. Being new to America, she expressed her delight with all the things new to her.

Wolfgang laid out the contents of the picnic basket consisting of two sticks of sausage-type meat, several interesting cheeses, a loaf of uncut, thick-crusted bread, a plastic baggy of pickles and olives, and a cube of butter. Also included is a bottle of a California Merlot with paper cups instead of wine glasses.

Rows of rose bushes fanned out from the gazebo like the spokes of a huge wheel. Gardeners had done a good job tending the flowerbeds, so the total effect was breathtaking. From their vantage point they could look beyond to a walkway arched over with climbing roses that led to a quaint oriental garden. Beyond all of this lay San Francisco Harbor in the foreground with the tall skyscrapers of the city completing the scene for the far view.

The four friends quietly ate their picnic lunch absorbed in the scene before them until Wolfgang broke the silence. "Wouldn`t this be a great place for a wedding?"

"Wolfie," exclaimed Silvia, "Are you suggesting we get married again?"

"No, silly girl. I`m suggesting it`s something for Helen and Rodger to think about."

"Hold it, Wolfgang," replied a startled Helen. "Rodg and I don`t need the legality of a marriage like you and Silvia do so she can stay in the country. We`ve talked about marriage and decided, at our age, we have the relationship we want without the encumbrances of the marriage laws."

Rodger sat back, smiling, as he listened to this exchange between Wolfgang and Helen. Finally, unable to contain laughter any longer, he blurted out, "Wolfgang, I never took you for a matchmaker. Silvia maybe… but not you."

"It`s obvious I believe in marriage," counters Wolfgang, "I've been married three times… that I know of?"

"What do you mean, `that you know of?" exclaimed Silvia.

Wolfgang raised his cup and smiled, "I was just kidding, Silvia."

Having finished lunch, the foursome walked along the many rows of roses identifying the different species by the convenient nameplates staked near their base. Many different fragrances permeated the air adding to the pleasure of the spring day. The two couples walked hand-in-hand as young lovers on a double date. The weatherman kept his promise making it an ideal day for their picnic.

Eventually Wolfgang looked at his watch and exclaimed, "I hate to say this, but it`s time to return to our apartment and get dressed for work. Our workday starts at three in the afternoon to prepare for our dinner customers."

"It`s been a lovely picnic," countered Helen. "Thanks so much for the invitation. Tomorrow, perhaps you`d like to take a cruise on San Francisco Bay. We can eat aboard and see this area from the water."

Sylvia clapped her hands, "Wouldn`t that be wonderful, Wolfie?"

"Of course," he replied, "if the wind isn`t too strong. You know, Silvia, I have a tendency to get sea sick."

"I didn`t know you had that problem," said Rodger as he turned and faced Wolfgang. "If the weather doesn`t cooperate, we`ll do something else."

Returning to the boat, the foursome parted after their usual goodbyes, with an agreement to meet the following day at ten o`clock.

* * *

The next morning a knocking on the side of the hull awakened them. "Ahoy, is anyone home?"

Rodger slid out of bed and opened the hatch to see who was interrupting his sleep. Glancing at the clock on the bulkhead he realized they had overslept. "Well hi, Art. What are you and Gertrude doing here? You weren`t supposed to be back until next week."

Art and Gertrude stood on the dock laughing at the tussled sight of Rodger with just his head appearing out of the cabin hatch way. "We received a call from our mechanic and they`re installing the new engine today and Kitchen Pass will be ready to be launched in a few days."

"That was fast," replied Rodger. "Does this mean you want to shove off sooner than two weeks from now as you originally planned, which would abort our trip to your house?"

"Yes," Art replied. "We`d like to leave as soon as possible, and we`ll give you a rain check on the trip to Sonoma. We can do it when we get back from Tahiti.."

Helen had joined Rodger in the companion way and replied, "The sooner the better. We`ve been a long time coming to this place in our voyage and we`re both looking forward to it."

"I couldn`t have said it better," Rodger added, enthusiastically. "I guess we`d better start shopping for the supplies we`ll need for the next seven weeks."

"Oh, this is getting exciting," joined in Gertrude; "I can hardly wait. We`ve got a motel just a short distance from here so we can store provisions there until Kitchen Pass is launched."

"Give us a few minutes to get dressed, and we`ll meet you at the marina restaurant for breakfast," said Rodger. "We`ve got a lot of planning to do."

"Right," replied Art. "We`ll see you there."

*   *   *

A half hour later, Helen and Rodger joined Art and Gertrude at the café for breakfast and a planning session. The morning crowd was boisterous, as boaters tend to be when they get together in a social setting. After breakfast, they sat enjoying their second cup of coffee and discussing the preparations and supplies needed for their crossing to Tahiti.

Art pulled a folded sheet of paper from his pocket and handed it to Helen. "This is a list of the food supplies that we`ll be purchasing for the trip. Look it over and make a copy if you`d like. It`ll give you an idea of what`s needed and how much for two people for seven weeks."

"Thanks Art, that`s a big help. Rodg and I are both new at buying for this length of a trip. Of course we`ll add to this list the supplies we need for Bilgee."

"She wasn`t very happy with us this morning, as all she got was a five minute walk," added Rodger. "We`ll make up for it this afternoon. Yikes, I just remembered. We`re supposed to see Wolfgang and Silvia this morning. I`d better call them on my cell phone right now."

*   *   *

After apologizing for the change in plans, Rodger suggested they come to the boat and join them for lunch. Art and Gertrude said their goodbyes, as they wanted to be in the boatyard when their new engine was installed. Helen had shopped the day before, so it was just a matter fixing lunch and eating at their slip rather than out sailing on San Francisco Bay. The day started out cooler than usual with a 15 knot wind blowing from the east, so Wolfgang was happy with the change of plans due to his tendency for motion sickness.

Wolfgang and Silvia arrived at the appointed hour laden with cut flowers they had purchased along the way. Silvia, beaming, thrust the bouquet into Helen`s arms, "For our two wonderful friends who will soon be leaving for their big adventure sailing to Tahiti."

"Oh, how beautiful," said Helen as she held them to her face inhaling the fragrance of the bouquet. "What are they? I don`t recognize them; they don`t have a fragrance I`m familiar with."

Rodger stood back with Wolfgang as they watched the two women enjoying the opportunity to be feminine, a trait not apparent in Helen until after the shipwreck. *Helen had been the no-nonsense ship`s captain,* Rodger thought to himself. *But when she thought she`d lost me forever, she lost that captain`s façade. Now, she`s my life`s-companion first, and captain of the Sea Witch second. It`s good seeing her allow the femininity trait to blossom.*

"They`re California Lupine," replied Wolfgang, happy to become a part of the dialogue. "Silvia never arrives at a friend`s residence, no matter what the occasion, without a gift of some kind."

Blushing, Silvia silently accepted the compliment from her husband. The four sat at the table in the saloon area of the Sea Witch to partake of the luncheon Helen and Rodger had prepared. Rodger proposed a toast to their friendship that had begun in Coos Bay, Oregon. They all laughed as he reminded them of Silvia`s flight from the long arm of the immigration law.

After touching glasses Rodger said, "Just think of the odds of us meeting in a restaurant four hundred and fifty miles south of Coos Bay."

"Unbelievable," replied Silvia. Soon it was time for Wolfgang and Silvia to leave to prepare for their jobs. Reluctantly departing, they promised to return the next day so they could spend as much time with Rodger and Helen as possible. Weather permitting; they would take the postponed boat ride and luncheon on San Francisco Bay. Wolfgang concluded with, "We`ll bring the lunch."

* * *

Art and Gertrude stopped by the Sea Witch late that afternoon after spending the day at the boatyard. Knocking on the side of the hull Art shouted, "Permission to come aboard?"

"Welcome aboard, you're just in time for cocktails. Today I`m serving vodka tonics," said Rodger answering from the companionway. "Have a seat in the cockpit; Helen and I will be up shortly.

"Vodka tonics sound heavenly," replied Gertrude to Art as they made their way on the narrow deck surrounding the cabin on the way to the rear cockpit. When Helen and Rodger arrived a few minutes later, each carrying an extra drink for their guest, Art and Gertrude were snuggled together on the bench seat clad in matching gray sweatsuits, as the day had remained cool. Rodger and Helen wore lightweight sailing jackets over their summer clothes.

Rodger spoke as they saluted each other with their glasses held high. "Here`s to a successful voyage." Turning to face Art, he asked, "How goes the motor exchange?"

"No problems," replied Art, "but it was sad to see our old engine being hoisted out. It was like saying goodbye to an old friend, as it`s taken us a lot of places in the past five years with only the usual maintenance, and little thanks."

"Art...you surprise me with your sentimentality," injected Helen.

"He is a softy," Gertrude replied. "That`s one of the things I love about him."

"Okay, you two, now that you have dissected my personality, I am what I am, but mainly, I`m the skipper of Kitchen Pass; she`s a good vessel that`ll take us to Tahiti and back; that`s for sure, the weather Gods permitting."

"You know, Helen," injected Rodger, "we`ve always talked about sailing to Tahiti, but never about sailing back."

"I assumed that was a given; what goes up, must come down, and what goes over, must come back."

"Not necessarily;" injected Rodger, "there are other options, Skipper. We could sell the Sea Witch and fly home, or we could fall in love with Tahiti and make it our home port."

"Okay, I see your point. I guess we make the return home decision after we`ve sailed there. I think we`ll know what we want to do at that time. Helen leaned back on the cockpit seat staring up at the top of the mast, the mottled sky beyond, and appeared to be deep in thought. "I suggest we call it a day; I can smell rain in the air."

"Right," replied Art. "We`re both tired and it`s time we settled in for the night."

Gertrude stood and put her arms around Art`s waist, "Our motel room is just like a little home with a kitchen, living room, bedroom and bath, and it sure beats commuting eighty miles each day to Sonoma while we`re getting ready for the crossing."

"How long do we have to get ready?" asked Rodger.

"Assuming there are no hitches at the boat yard, I`d say a week."

"Do you hear that, Helen?" I think we`d better get busy after we take Wolfgang and Silvia out on San Francisco Bay tomorrow."

"Yes, but right now all I want to do is enjoy the warm glow in my stomach from that vodka tonic."

Art smiled as he took Helen`s remark as a hint she wanted to be alone with Rodger. "We`ll see you tomorrow afternoon on our way home from the boatyard."

Rodger escorted them off the Sea Witch and returned to see Helen beckoning him to sit beside her in the cockpit. "Can I freshen your drink, Skipper?"

"That would be nice; we can stay out here and bundle together until it`s time to go below for dinner…or something."

"Your wish is my command. Should I bring out the comforter along with our drinks for bundling? It`s getting a bit chilly."

"Sounds good, Mate."

* * *

The next morning Helen was up first and immediately stuck her head out the companionway to check the weather. Satisfied the day was going to be good for a cruise, she awakened Rodger so they would be ready for Silvia and Wolfgang upon their arrival. A quick call on the cell phone confirmed the outing, and Wolfgang reminded them they were bringing the lunch and would arrive at ten o`clock.

"I`ll take Bilgee for a walk, if you`ll fix breakfast," offered Rodger.

"What do you have in mind?"

"I`m up for something simple, like oatmeal. Then we`ll be ready for a big lunch."

"You got it!'

"Bilgee! Settle down. Rodg is getting your leash."

Rodger, with Bilgee in the lead, headed down the dockway leading to the gangplank that took them to the pier fifteen feet above. A grassy field separated the marina service complex from the boater`s parking lot. Bilgee immediately began tugging at the leash seeing the open field beckoning her. Rodger quickly undid the leash allowing her to dash off much like a convict being released from prison.

Rodger stood on the pier waiting for Bilgee and surveying the large bay before him. The cities of Oakland and Richmond lay directly across from Sausalito with San Francisco in the background. *We can sail north by San Rafael to San Pablo Bay or south to the lower portion of San Francisco Bay* he thought. *Boaters already out on the water are being treated to a ten-knot wind blowing from the south.*

Releashing a reluctant Bilgee, they returned to the Sea Witch to find breakfast on the table. “Bilgee hated to give up that open field today,” said Rodger. “I can`t blame her, but she`ll have to learn to do without land to be a real sea dog to survive the trip across the ocean. Maybe we should cut a plug of grass and put it where she`s trained to go.”

“That`s something you can decide later. After breakfast we need to be ready to cast off, as soon as Wolfgang and Silvia arrive. You`ll need to take off the sail covers, clear the decks, and warm up the engine, Mate.”

“Aye, aye Skipper, right after breakfast; this oatmeal smells delicious.” Rodger filled his bowl from the pot on the stove and sat down at the table joining Heklen.

* * *

At ten o`clock Silvia and Wolfgang arrived and after a robust greeting they climbed aboard. Helen took the helm while Rodger untied the three lines and cast off. With a small chop on the bay, a sky clearing nicely, it looked like a wonderful day to be on the water. All four sat in the cockpit sharing the thrill of sailing. The only sounds were the gentle smacking of waves on the hull as it cut through the water, and the rustling sound of salt-laden wind as it came off the trailing edge of each of the three sails.

Sea birds soared past them, screeching as they bunched together on the water. It soon became apparent they were feeding on a huge ball of herring near the water`s surface. A few gulls shot touch-and-go landings, picking up a herring each time they swooped down to the water. Other sea birds in the area, noticing the excitement, quickly turned and headed toward the feeding frenzy below them.

“How are you doing, Wolfgang?” asked Helen.

"I`m okay. I took a Dramamine before we left the apartment, and I have several here in my pocket. If the water stays like this, I`ll be fine… and if not…fortunately, we`re not scheduled to work tonight."

"Good, but let me know if you start to feel ill."

"He will, believe me," injected Silvia. "Wolfie isn`t one to suffer in silence."

"Is the pot calling the kettle black, or what?" chided Wolfgang in retaliation as he gave Silvia`s shoulder a love pat.

Happy conversation filled the cockpit as the four joined in the verbal play. Even Bilgee got caught up in the moment and started a series of barks as if to say, *I`m here too, and I want to be a part of this.*

Helen chose to sail south into the wind for faster, more adventurous sailing. "This will hopefully put the wind at the stern for the return trip later in the day," she confided to the group, "and should be an easy sailing attitude and perhaps allow us to sail wing –and-wing."

They were always conscious of sailing in waters surrounded by heavily populated cities such as San Bruno, Burlingame, Redwood City, Hayward, Alameda, and Oakland. All being suburbs of San Francisco ringing the South Bay area. Being a good sailing day brought many sailors out to take advantage of the wind conditions.

"It`s obvious," said Helen, "a lot of people live in this part of the state of California, and I can see why, if this is a sample of their climate and water amenities. This is almost as good as sailing in Puget Sound in the state of Washington."

"I agree," said Rodger. "If you don`t need me topside, Skipper, Wolfgang and I will go below and put lunch together."

"Good idea, Rodg."

Rodger and Wolfgang reappeared twenty minutes later with Rodger carrying a tray of food, and Wolfgang carrying a bottle of wine tucked under one arm and a bottle of sparking cider for himself in his hand. The morning of sailing sharpened their appetites and soon all four were intent on making the food disappear.

The wind picked up in the late afternoon making the last part of the return sail thrilling. The four of them sat low in the cockpit and laughed and whooped when occasionally the spray would climb over the rail and give them an unexpected face washing. Unfortunately, true to prediction, Wolfgang`s tendency toward seasickness caught up with him and he excused himself to go below to lie down.

They pulled into the dock just as the lights were coming on around the bay, and once they were behind the breakwater, the water calmed and they motored in. Wolfgang made a return appearance on deck as soon as the Sea Witch`s hull nudged the finger pier. His facial color had returned to normal and his expression was one of thankful relief. "What a wonderful way to end a perfect day," he exclaimed.

"I guess I don`t understand your word wonderful, Wolfie," injected Silvia. "I thought wonderful meant good."

"My dear Silvia," continued Wolfgang. "This is an example of the feeling of sublime following difficulty, tragedy, or unpleasantness. I feel so good getting over the seasickness that in totality, it has been a wonderful day."

Silvia smiled at her husband`s explanation. "I guess I`ll never understand you or this English language."

Rodger tied the bow, stern, and spring line while the others gathered their gear. The four of them said their goodbyes with hugs all around and a promise to get together the next day. Rodger and Helen invited them to be a part of the shopping trip to put in stores for the pending departure to Tahiti.

After Helen and Rodger tended the sail covers and went below to settle in for the night, Bilgee scampered about indicating it was time for her evening walk. "How about if I walk Bilgee up to the café and bring back a couple of hamburgers for dinner?"

"Sounds fine, Rodg; how about some fries, too?"

"That goes without saying." Bilgee barked approval and danced around while Rodger stooped to put on the leash. "Okay, Miss Bilgewater, we`re off and running."

* * *

The next day was spent with Wolfgang and Silvia buying groceries and supplies for seven weeks at sea. Art and Gertrude stopped by the Sea Witch in the late afternoon and told Rodger and Helen to be ready for an early departure day after tomorrow. They agreed to join Rodger and

Helen for an early dinner tomorrow at the restaurant on the hillside above them in order to say goodbye to Wolfgang and Silvia.

After Art and Gertrude left, Rodger and Helen sat in the cockpit area enjoying the late afternoon sunshine sipping a Vodka tonic. “It`s almost show time,” said Rodger. “It`s hard to believe, after a year we`re on the last lap of our voyage to Tahiti.”

“I agree,” said Helen. “It`s excitement coupled with anxiety.”

“Are you anxious, Skipper?”

“Of course I am; as I said before, it`s a big ocean.”

“We don`t have to do it,” replied Rodger, as he moved closer to Helen.

“Of course we do. We`ve come too far and too much has happened to turn back now as long as we`re physically able.”

“I don`t agree.”

“I`ll be alright. I`ll get over my stage fright as soon as we shove off.”

“It`s odd we`re using the theatre as a metaphor for our voyage.”

“By gosh you're right, and you know what they say, Rodg; the show must go on.”

* * *

Rodger was first up the next morning, and after putting on the coffee pot, he carried Bilgee topside, snapped on her leash, and walked to the local bakery for fresh apple turnovers. Bilgee wanted to run free when they got to the grassy field, but Rodger was determined to go directly to the bakery and return to the Sea Witch by the time Helen awakened.

Helen was lying in bed staring at the ceiling when they returned. “What`s the matter Skipper? Are you still anxious about departing tomorrow?”

“Yes.”

“Is this a woman`s intuition thing?”

“I don`t know. I've never been much on intuition. I do know it`s like a dark cloud hanging over me. I can put it aside for awhile by keeping busy, but when I slow down and let my mind take its own course… there it is again.”

"We`ll talk to Art and Gertrude about your dark cloud before we go to the Castaway`s for dinner this afternoon; Art`s a pretty knowledgeable guy."

"Good idea! Now pour me a cup of coffee, and hand me one whatever you have in that sack that smells so intriguing."

"Aye, aye, Skipper."

* * *

Art and Gertrude arrived at the appointed time, and the four of them walked up the long stairway to the Castaway`s restaurant overlooking Sausalito and San Francisco Bay. On the way Rodger suggested they stop at a rest area to allow their breathing to catch up with them. Helen turned to Art and told him what she had been experiencing the past twelve hours.

"I understand your anxiety," said Art as he slipped an arm around her shoulder. "I think most people who skipper a boat across an ocean have second thoughts. Responsibility for another's life and your own is not to be taken lightly. I've experienced it too, but now that Gertrude and I have done this before, it`s not the problem it was the first time."

Gertrude added, "I've had those feelings, and I've never been the skipper. It`s all part of the adventure, Helen."

Relief spread across Helen`s face in knowing she wasn`t alone experiencing the feeling of anxiety. "Sharing your past feelings with me helps; I`m sure it will pass as soon as we get under way."

"Yes, it will."

Continuing up the stairway, they eventually walked around the building to the front door facing on the street that enabled most patrons to get to the restaraunt. Once inside Silvia met them with open arms hugging first Helen, then Rodger, Gertrude, and lastly Art. "Oh, my friends, it is sad you`re leaving tomorrow, but I know you must be on your way. Wolfgang is preparing the dinner, so I`ll let him know you`re here. I`m sure he`ll want to greet you and also later when we say goodbye."

Wolfgang soon appeared wearing his white chef`s outfit including a tall chef`s hat. "Ah, my friends, it`s been so good to be a part of your lives again. Silvia has reserved the best table in the house for you by the window and I have taken the liberty of preparing roast duck. I know it`s Helen and Rodger`s favorite."

Art and Gertrude assured him they were delighted to have roast duck. Silvia then led them to their table with Wolfgang following. Once seated, Silvia took their order for cocktails and disappeared. Wolfgang brought up a chair to sit with them.

After their drinks arrived they toasted the chef, which pleased Wolfgang immensely. Rodger reviewed his and Helen`s relationship with Silvia and Wolfgang from the time they first met in Coos Bay, for Art and Gertrude. A hearty laugh followed Rodger`s explanation of Silvia as an alien on the run from the authorities. Goodhearted banter followed until Wolfgang had to excuse himself to check on the roasting duck and the rest of the dinners to be served that night. Silvia stopped by, adding to the conversation when her duties allowed it.

"Oh my!" exclaimed Helen when she spotted Wolfgang bringing in the duck and its` accessories on a mobile carving table. "Wolfgang, you've outdone yourself."

"Nothing is too good for my friends," he replied as he deftly cut the string holding the legs in place. He then used his large chef`s carving knife and deftly divided the bird into four equal parts and ceremoniously placed a quarter of the deeply browned, succulent duck on each dinner plate. The side dishes were attractively served family style. Wolfgang stepped back from the table with a quick bow at the waist accompanied by spontaneous applause from the four diners. He stayed long enough to see and hear the comments after the first bite of this gastronomical delight. Being satisfied he had done well by his guests, he excused himself to resume his chef`s duties.

Silvia brought a bottle of St. Michael`s Merlot on one of her many stops at the table. They soon became aware of the envious glances of other diners obviously curious about what was so special about this group who received such lavish attention from the maitre de and the executive chef who had carved a magnificent bird at their table.

As the evening came to a close, Silvia appeared with Wolfgang to say their goodbyes and wishe for a safe voyage followed by warm embraces all around.

"Call us when you get to Tahiti," said Wolfgang with a poignant smile. "As Shakespeare so aptly wrote in his play Romeo and Juliet,

`Parting is such sweet sorrow.` We must keep in touch after your journey`s end."

Promising to call, they quickly departed concentrating on remembering the delicious food and loving friendship of Silvia and Wolfgang; the rest of the evening was anticlimactic. Once back at the dock the foursome said goodnight; agreeing that Art and Gertrude would bring their boat alongside the Sea Witch at nine o`clock the next morning. This would allow a ten o`clock departure in order to accommodate the strong outgoing tide beneath the Golden Gate Bridge.

* * *

After a restless sleep Helen and Rodger awakened early and went about preparing for departure. Bilgee seeming to sense something was up and was reluctant to leave the Sea Witch, as if fearing she might be left behind. Rodger carried her up the dock`s gangplank for a final romp in the open grassy field above. She needed no coaxing to return to the boat and anxiously sat watching Helen and Rodger`s every move in a state of anxiety.

The day had all the earmarks of being a good early summer day with the weather prediction for off shore winds from the south to fifteen knots by afternoon. The sky was overcast, but would burn off by noon. Kitchen Pass appeared on schedule with Art at the wheel waving a vigorous hello as they approached. Rodger had tied two bumpers to the side of the Sea Witch to enable them to raft alongside.

Gertrude appeared from below deck and handled the lines for the tie up. She set the bumpers, threw the bowline to Rodger as Kitchen Pass glided silently along side the Sea Witch. She then threw Helen the stern line and the two boats were quickly tied to one another. Gertrude and Art were all smiles as they greeted Helen and Rodger. "Are you ready for the big adventure?" asked Art.

"You bet we are," replied Helen and Rodger in unison. Then they stepped aboard Kitchen Pass and shared the second cup of coffee of the day with Art and Gertrude playing host and hostess below deck. After going over last minute details and sailing expectations for the day, Rodger and Helen returned to their boat and prepared to cast off.

Rodger untied Kitchen Pass`s bow and stern line while Art shifted into forward and moved ahead and away from the Sea Witch.

Rodger quickly followed suit with their lines and the two boats slowly moved from the transient dock into the channel behind the breakwater that led to San Francisco Bay. Tiburon and Angel Island lay to their port side as they moved forward powered only by their engines. As they turned to starboard to pass under the Golden Gate Bridge, the foursome turned back to face San Francisco to wave farewell to nobody in particular. They were officially on their way across the Pacific Ocean to Tahiti.

As Helen and Rodger turned to face the ocean, they looked upward to fully take in the majesty of the Golden Gate Bridge above them. The automobile lanes appeared to be a hundred feet above them to accommodate tall ships of all types.

Suddenly Helen felt a strong tug on the tiller. Looking down and ahead she suddenly realized she had steered on the edge of a large whirlpool at least fifty feet across created by the North tower of the suspension bridge. Looking farther to starboard and ahead, she was surprised to see that Kitchen Pass had veered further to starboard thus avoiding the swirling powerful phenomena. *I should never have taken my eyes off the course*, she thought.

Fortunately the Sea Witch, being on the cusp of the whirlpool and being a nine-ton vessel, used her weight, large rudder, and deep keel to avoid being sucked into the maelstrom. Rodger, realizing the gravity of the situation, put Bilge down and stepped forward to help Helen fight the tiller that wanted to turn them in to the center of the whirlpool. Rigid with determination, Helen stood pushing all her body weight against the tiller, and with Rodger`s help, held a steady course forward; thus they were able to stay on the edge of this demanding monster.

In a matter of minutes the situation was past as the Sea Witch broke out the far side of the malstrom. Looking back, Rodger marveled at the strength of the dark, swirling water that could move nine tons of boat, under power, towards its orifice. The hair stood up on his neck at the thought of being sucked into this boiling, churning mass.

"Good job Skipper," he shouted. "I've never seen anything like that before."

"Thanks, Mate, but it shouldn`t have happened. I was so enthralled admiring the bridge, I wasn`t paying attention to what lay ahead. You can believe I won`t do that again."

"Unfortunately, I was doing the same thing," said Rodger. "Look at Art and Gertrude waving to us. I`ll go below to the radio, and tell them we`re okay. I`ll take Bilgee with me as she looks like she could use a little tender loving care"

Helen waved to Art and Gertrude and gestured by wiping the back of her hand across her forehead implying she was glad the situation was over. Art and Gertrude returned the greeting staying ahead about three hundred yards and slightly to starboard. After Rodger made radio contact with them he returned topside with Bilgee who looked up at him with adoration as if to say, "Thanks, Boss."

Once they cleared the bridge and its currents, both boats raised their sails and were on their way.

*　　　*　　　*

As the day came to an end Helen decided Rodger would take the first watch from eight o`clock until midnight. The GPS and auto pilot had been set to match the course determined by Art and Gertrude aboard Kitchen Pass, which would keep them about 500 hundred meters apart. If the wind held, Helen speculated, they would be through the shipping lanes when she took the watch at midnight.

"It`s reassuring to see Kitchen Pass`s nightlight on top of her mast," said Rodger.

"I agree. I`m glad we hooked up with them instead of trying to do this solo."

Helen had the watch, but the autopilot actually had control of the Sea Witch. Rodger and Bilgee snuggled together under the dodger on the wrap-around bench seat, their backs to the cabin bulkhead to avoid the fifteen-knot wind directly on their nose. "Rodger, it`s getting cold; would you go below and get our jackets?"

"Aye, aye Skipper. I`ll put on a fresh pot of coffee to help me get through the next watch. Do you want some?"

"No, I`ll want to sleep in a little while, and I don`t want caffeine to keep me awake. It`s going to take a little getting used to sleeping in four-hour shifts, but that`s part of the game with blue water cruising."

Rodger handed Bilgee to Helen and went below to get the jackets and coffee. When he returned the setting sun had turned the far horizon into a mass of gold to red colors. "Wow, isn`t that magnificent?" he exclaimed. "According to Art and Gertrude, the sunsets will be even more dramatic as we near Tahiti."

Rodger helped Helen with her jacket and then slipped his arms around her holding her in a loving embrace. "Now comes the grand adventure, according to some," said Rodger as he planted a kiss on her forehead. "But to me, our love affair is really the grand adventure."

"I couldn`t agree more," sighed Helen.

* * *

The night went without incident and Helen came topside for her second watch to relieve Rodger at the helm at eight o`clock. The weatherman promised a pleasant early summer day with moderate winds to fifteen knots and temperatures in the low seventies. Rodger eagerly greeted Helen with a kiss and went directly to the salon to get a few hours sleep before his next watch. As usual, he entered the vital statistics in the log before retiring.

Helen held a cup of strong coffee in her hand as she studied the GPS and the chart that centered on their present location. Looking off to starboard she could see Kitchen Pass with Art at the helm. He had his large Genoa jib in place, but not winched down tightly in order to only stay abreast the Sea Witch, as this would be standard procedure being the faster boat. On the other hand, the Sea Witch handled heavy weather better than Kitchen Pass because of her heavier weight and deep keel.

Bilgee sat beside Helen seemingly content to be snuggled close to her. Bilgee wore a harness with a tether tied to it to avoid any overboard accidents. This sometimes proved a problem as she moved about the cockpit pulling her tether behind her and getting tangled with human legs. However, this was solved with a little patience on the part of both parties. Bilgee`s job was to keep whoever was on the four-hour watch company during the night hours. This made her an important part of the crew.

Bilgee`s dry food was easily stored without spoiling. Occasionally she was given scraps from the table, but this was the exception rather than the rule. Helen and Rodger had purchased a sweater and booties for her for extreme wet weather. Neither had been called into service yet. A first-aid kit had been put together to treat her for every emergency they could think of while at sea, as there would be no handy vet to consult. She seemed to enjoy the extra attention she was receiving in order to be a full-fledged sea dog.

*   *   *

At noon Rodger appeared carrying a tray of two sandwiches, and two cold beers. Helen smiled, "You`re a keeper."

"I know," he said, a wide grin on his face. "It`s something I've learned to live with." Handing her the tray, he took the tiller. "I see the wind has freshened since my early morning watch and is more on our port beam. This is better than the partial headwind we had coming out of San Francisco."

"I agree, and we`ve covered about a hundred miles since we left twenty-four hours ago. If we can average that on a daily basis, we`ll be in Tahiti in seven weeks."

"When we pick up the trade winds, that should be easy," replied Rodger, helping himself to a sandwich and beer before sitting down beside Helen and Bilgee, "It`s nice not to be glued to the tiller, thanks to the autopilot and the GPS."

"Yep, it`s like having another crew member who never tires or eats sandwiches and drinks beer."

"I guess I`ll have to watch my step, so I won`t be replaced," Rodger grinned.

"No, you have some attributes no mechanical device could ever replace,"

Helen said resisting a smile.

Finishing his sandwich, Rodger put an arm around drawing her close. "That`s good to know, Skipper, or should I say Sweetheart?"

"For the present time Skipper will do. However, as the sailing conditions warrant, there will be times when you can call me Sweetheart."

"I`m glad to hear that. Otherwise, this voyage to Tahiti would become a real drag. By the way, have you talked to Kitchen Pass this morning?"

"Yes, I called before I took the eight a.m. watch. Everything is okay with them and they said they`d drop back to us this afternoon for some close face-to-face talk."

"Good, I`d like that."

"Me too. It could get pretty lonely out here all by ourselves. I`m going below to chart the course, fill in the log, and take a nap before our meeting; sleeping in three or four hour segments takes some getting used to." Helen took the tray and disappeared below deck with Bilgee at her heels.

Rodger visually checked the set of the sails, the telltale near the top of the mainsail, and the lines running to the winches. Everything seemed to be in order. After scanning ahead for obstructions and finding none, Rodger settled down by the tiller and zipped his jacket to the top of his collar. *The wind has a little bit of a bite to it*, he thought.

* * *

Four hours later Helen stuck her head out the hatchway and called above the wind, "Art`s on the radio and he`s ready to drop back for a little togetherness."

"Okay, I`ll hold it steady on course and let him come to us." The ocean had a gentle three-foot roll as Kitchen Pass came within a dozen feet of the Sea Witch. Both crews had put bumpers out for protection in case they actually did come together. Helen was at the tiller of the Sea Witch and Art stood at the helm of Kitchen Pass, as the two skippers should be. Gertrude and Rodger, as the deck hands, stood on the gunnels ready with a boat hook to fend off the two boats if necessary. As the two crews got used to riding the swells together and holding a straight course ahead, each relaxed in their individual roles.

Art called out, "Ahoy, Sea Witch. Do you have a cup of sugar we could borrow?" This broke the tension that had subtly built doing something for the first time; all laughed spontaneously.

"As a matter-of-fact, we do, if you're serious," called out Helen.

"Oh, he`s just being silly," said Gertrude. "The kind of sugar we need is just the sweetness of your conversation. I`m already tired of a monologue from Art. By the way, do you have any Tabasco sauce aboard? I forgot to get some and Art and I like to start our day with a Bloody Mary, which, with tomato juice and a shot of vodka, requires a few drops of Tabasco sauce and a little Worchester sauce to get your attention."

"Yes, we do. Hold on and I`ll get it for you."

Soon Rodger reappeared at the rail and prepared to throw the small bottle he held in his hand. "I hope you're a good catcher, Gertrude, as this is our total supply. I`d better put it in a small bag and tie a line to it, just in case."

"That`s a good idea," shouted Art. "While you're doing that, Gertrude and I can change places as I`m the former ball player in this family."

Rodger came back to the rail with a canvas bag in his hand and a light line attached to it. He twirled it around his head, like a Gaucho throwing a bolo at a moving target, and while holding on to the other end of the line, gave it a fling. The sack landed in Art`s outstretched hands.

"Good throw, Rodg. I`ll take some and return the bottle to you in a few minutes."

As the boats moved along together, the wind suddenly picked up causing the gentle rolling swells to become five-foot waves that curled at the top of each surge, throwing bits of spindrift into the air. The temperature dropped ten degrees and a wall of gray replaced white puffy clouds. Art cupped his hands and shouted to Helen and Rodger, "We`re going to have to move away from you as we may be in for some heavy weather. We`ll take good care of the Tabasco."

"Okay," shouted Helen, "but wouldn`t you know, all of a sudden I want a Bloody Mary. That`s life I guess; see you later!"

Rodger came to the helm after waving off Art and Gertrude. "What do you want me to do, Skipper?"

"Slack off the mainsheet and be prepared for a change of course for a few minutes. Then we`ll resume our original heading, that should put a safe distance between the boats."

"Aye, aye, Skipper."

The farther west they traveled, the stronger the wind increased until the wind gauge registered twenty knots. Because it was still hitting them on their port beam, Helen had to constantly adjust the winches to let out line in order to keep the Sea Witch from running with the rail underwater. Rodger, struggling against the swaying, pitching boat, fixed a dinner of gourmet hamburger patties, canned vegetables and lettuce wedge.

Once he completed dinner Rodger came topside to take Helen`s place at the helm. "Wow! This weather is kicking up," he exclaimed. "Go below and eat dinner with Bilgee, and I`ll stay close to the tiller."

When Helen finished eating she returned to the cockpit leaving Bilgee below to be a dinner companion for Rodger. Bilgee showed her pleasure of double dinner duty with a series of staccato barks.

After dinner, Rodger cleaned up the galley and joined Helen topside. "I see things are still pretty much the same," he shouted above the wailing wind. "How long do you think this blow will hold?"

"We should see a slacking as the sun nears the far horizon; at least I hope so."

As Helen predicted, the wind died down to five knots just before sunset. After watching the beauty of the setting sun disappear below the horizon, Rodger said, "I can see Kitchen Pass off to starboard and three hundred yards ahead; that`s reassuring. It`s time for my watch, Skipper; go get some rest, and I`ll see you at midnight."

* * *

Coming off his second watch at eight a.m., Rodger held his arms out to Helen, silently asking for an embrace. "That`s a long, lonely four hours. Bilgee is some help, but she has her limitations. I need some together time with you."

"I've just talked to Art on the radio and everything is running smoothly, so I think we could spend a little time together while Bilgee occupies the cockpit in our place. I`m in need of some togetherness too and actually the bed is still warm. I`ll meet you in the middle of it in five minutes."

Rodger grabbed Bilgee in his arms and sat back down by the tiller watching the water ahead. The wind held steady at five knots from the south and the telltales were parallel, showing the hull and sails were trimmed nicely. With the GPS running the auto steering, vacating the helm for a little while was only slightly risky. It would take an object in the water to cause a problem, as a change in weather would be immediately felt no matter where one was on the boat. Rodger glanced at his watch and sat Bilgee down next to the tiller. "You're in charge Bilg; don`t run us aground." With that command, Rodger disappeared below deck.

* * *

A half hour later, Helen appeared and took her place beside the tiller. Bilgee awoke from a nap and seemed pleased she was no longer alone. Helen reached over, picked up the dog, holding her out at arm`s length said, "Don`t you know sleeping on watch is a Captain's mast offense?" Then drawing a bewildered looking Bilgee to her, she hugged the dog for a long time.

Three hours later, Rodger came topside with a tray of sandwiches and two beers ready to take his watch at noon. "I`m a little early so we could have lunch together, Skipper."

"I like that. Did you get some sleep?"

"I had a little trouble settling down, but… yes, I did. I`m looking forward to the time when we can have eight hours of continuous sleep, I miss that."

"When I go below I`ll contact Art and Gertrude before I do the chart, write in the log, and take my nap. Last time I was off watch I didn`t get my full four hours sleep…but I`m not complaining."

Rodger and Helen sat close together and silently consumed their sandwiches and beer. Each seemed lost in their own thoughts as they idly watched the water pass by. Bilgee seemed content to lie at their feet and wait for the next offering of broken off sandwich. The sky, outlined with high cumulonimbus clouds, took many irregular shapes; their summits rising in formations of mountains or towers. Rodger broke the silence by pointing out the products of his imagination, as he looked skyward. "Doesn`t that cloud look like a bear? See the pear-shaped back side and prominent nose on the other end."

"If you say so, Rodg. To me it only looks like an irregularly shaped cloud. I guess I`m too much of a realist to play that game."

"That`s too bad. Letting your imagination loose occasionally expands your world. Let`s you go where you've never been and sometimes you get real surprises. You see and think things that make you ask, where did that come from?"

"I`m not pooh-poohing the use of the imagination," said Helen," I`m just not good at it."

"Look at the clouds and see if anything comes to mind other than the clouds just being clouds."

Helen lay against Rodger`s outstretched arm behind her and looked to the sky. After a moment of silence she said, "I see a contrail high above the clouds, which tells me there`s an airplane up there somewhere, and that`s not imagination, that`s real."

"You're right Skipper, you're not big on imagination, and yes, there has to be a plane up there somewhere. So much for cloud gazing; I guess it`s enough to know this type of cloud formation often is indicative of thunderstorm conditions."

"Really?" gasped Helen. "How do you know that?"

"I've always been interested in the world in which I live. Actually, I remember it from school days; some odd things just stick with you."

"Do you think we`re going to have a thunderstorm?"

Rodger sensed he was the source of information for a change. "Those clouds indicate it`s possible, we`ll have to wait and see. I`ll get the storm jib out in case we have to reduce our canvas, and we can be ready to reef the main if necessary."

Helen moved out of the comfort of Rodger`s embrace and stood looking at Kitchen Pass. "I`d better alert Art and Gertrude, just in case."

"Good idea. You might get on the weather channel too. I`ll monitor the sky, but it`ll be awhile, maybe towards late afternoon, if it happens at all"

"That`s one thing about sailing," said Helen. "There`s always something to do to the sails, or gear to keep everything shipshape."

Rodger replied, "I've noticed that, too."

Helen took the lunch tray and disappeared down the passageway to the salon in order to sit at the radio/ phone and contact Kitchen Pass. Gertrude answered immediately, and Helen relayed Rodger`s information to her.

"I`ll pass this on to Art so we`ll be prepared," said Gertrude. "Have you ever experienced a thunderstorm at sea, Helen?"

"Once, and I`m not looking forward to another."

"We have too, and it can be quite a show: with thunder, lightning, wind, and rain. It gave us a wild ride."

"When you talk to Art, ask him if and when he thinks the storm may break."

"I will; I`ll call back before you settle in for your off-watch nap," replied Gertrude.

"I`ll be here."

* * *

A few minutes later Helen saw the light on the radio/phone. Gertrude`s voice came through edged with excitement, "Art thinks it probably won`t happen until the temperature drops, around sunset or late afternoon; but if we`re lucky it`ll pass us by."

"On that happy note," said Helen, "I`ll give this information to Rodg and take my nap; it could be quite a night."

Helen, thrusting her head out of the passageway, relayed the information to Rodger who waved acknowledgement. Getting no verbal response from Rodger, she retreated to the salon for a much needed rest.

* * *

Four hours later Helen arrived on deck after slipping into a wool sweater. "It`s getting colder, isn`t it?"

"Yes, and the sky is dark with rain clouds in the near horizon. I`ll bet we`ll be in for it before dark."

"I`m not looking forward to that. You`d better get our foul weather gear out so it`ll be handy, and I`ll need you on deck with me for some sail work before it hits. Try to get a little rest, but when I call you, come up with your rain gear on so you can take over while I put mine on. I`ll try to allow time for you to have our sails ready for heavy weather before it overtakes us."

"Aye, aye Skipper."

* * *

It seemed to Rodger he had just dropped off to sleep when Helen, pounded on the cabin roof. It took a minute for him to collect his thoughts, and then he looked out the nearest porthole to assess the weather. A dark, threatening sky greeted him and the waves looked seven to eight feet high. After putting on his rain slicker, rubber boots, and sou`wester hat, he ascended the steep steps opening to the cockpit. Helen stood at the tiller facing the storm clouds ahead.

After putting on her foul weather gear she called out over the gusting wind, "I`ll stay at the helm while you put on the storm jib. When you`re finished I`ll help you reef the main and drop the mizzen. Then I`ll go below and make a fresh pot of coffee. We`ll have to settle for cold sandwiches for dinner tonight, but that`s sailing; everything changes when the weather changes."

* * *

After finishing the necessary chores, Rodger sat next to the tiller and anxiously watched the threatening sky. Thunderheads lined the horizon like toy soldiers standing in a line. Suddenly a crash of thunder, followed by a splash of lightning, zigzagged across the distant sky. The wind picked up and now rain pelted him steadily as he sat transfixed by the thunder and lightening show. Peals of thunder followed by sudden lightning illuminated the sky while the wind and rain intensified.

Helen stuck her head out of the companionway opening and shouted, "We`1l have to take turns eating; we`re in the middle of it now. I've finished, so come below and I`ll take the helm. We`ll keep

Bilgee below, at least for now. As long as one of us is with her, she`ll be okay."

"Aye, aye Skipper."

Rodger worked his way forward to the cabin as Helen made her way aft to the tiller. Backing down the stairs to the salon, Rodger was met by Bilgee jumping up to hold on to his leg. "Easy girl, it`ll be alright." In the galley he saw the plate of sandwiches Helen had made and nearby, a pot of coffee. He made short order of his dinner, then sat silently sipping a cup of hot coffee holding Bilgee in the crook of one arm. As he talked soothingly to her, it seemed to quiet her fears. After finishing his coffee, he sat Bilgee on the divan and gave her a hand signal and voice command to *wait* there. He then made his way up the companionway to join Helen.

Helen stood by the tiller looking forward; she had taken control of the helm. Smiling at Rodger, she motioned him to stand on the other side of the tiller. He complied, standing silently waiting for her to speak. The pelting of the wind-driven rain, the intermittent crashing sound of thunder, punctuated by sudden flashes of lightning filled their entire world. They had no need to talk; just look, listen, and feel all that`s going on about them.

Helen broke their silence, "Kitchen Pass seems to be riding out the storm okay. I can see Art alone at the helm, so Gertrude must be below fixing a simple meal like ours."

"It`ll be dark soon, and it`s going to be a big show if it keeps this up."

"I`m hoping it won`t last that long."

"If it doesn`t get any worse, well be okay. Sea Witch is handling these waves nicely, don`t you think?"

"Yes, she`s a very seaworthy vessel," replied Helen. "Being nine tons for only thirty-one feet of length, she handles the water better than Kitchen Pass."

"I see what you mean; I can see Kitchen Pass yawing as she rides down the backside of each wave."

"I`d guess the waves are about fifteen feet high now and Sea Witch plows into them with no yawing down the back side at all. It`s comforting to have a good ship beneath you at a time like this."

"I agree," replied Rodger as he reached across the tiller, put his arm around Helen, and gave her a reassuring squeeze. The throaty baying of Bilgee interrupted their moment of togetherness.

"You`d better go below and bring her topside. Poor little girl, I've never heard her sound like that."

"Aye aye, Skipper; she obviously wants to be with us."

Rodger returned in a few minutes holding a wide-eyed Bilgee who looked grateful to be received by Helen`s outstretched arms and immediately hid her head in Helen`s armpit, who then sat down turning the helm over to Rodger.

He smiled at them as they huddled together on the bench seat. The howling wind and torential rain continued to pelt them, as sheets of lightning struck the surface of the ocean intermittently; to be soon followed by the deep, resonant boom of thunder.

"Count the seconds between the flashes of lightning and the boom," said Rodger, "and you can tell how far we are from the center of the storm."

"Really?"

"Each second of time stands for a mile of distance." They sat together expectantly waiting for the next lightning flash to start their count. Suddenly lightning zigzagged across the sky and they started counting; one thousand one, one thousand two, when a peal of deafening thunder reverberated all about them.

"Wow!" exclaimed Helen, "I only got to two. Does that mean we`re only two miles from the center of the action?"

"You got it!"

"I don`t like this, Rodg," she frowned, "even if it is beautiful and exciting; we could take a direct hit. However, we have an extra long battery cable aboard for times like this that I almost forgot about. Go below and you`ll find it stowed on the port side of the engine compartment. Also bring a twelve inch crescent wrench from the tool box."

"Aye, aye, Skipper." Rodger went below and soon returned with a fifteen-foot long, rubber-coated battery cable with metal clips on both ends with slotted holes to receive a bolt. "Here it is Skipper."

"There`s a bolt with a nut on it on the starboard side of the mast just above the boom. Connect one end of the cable to it and then throw the other end overboard just ahead of the shrouds. If we`re struck by lightning it`ll travel down the mast to the cable and then follow it into the water."

Rodger had the cable bolted to the mast and the other end into the water in a matter of a few minutes. "There it is Skipper; the cable is long enough to get into the water," he shouted above the storm. Rodger made his way back to the cockpit grateful to be off his knees and into the protection of the dodger.

"Good job, Rodg, and thank goodness for the lightning-deflector strap." The two stood, arms around each other for a moment of reassurance, and then faced into the storm, as Bilgee lay huddled in her dog blanket under the dodger.

Kitchen Pass could be seen three hundred yards ahead and to starboard bursting through the tops of the curling waves throwing a spray of spindrift before it. To there horror they noticed each time Kitchen Pass started down the backside of a wave it veered sharply to port. However, just before it came to the bottom of the trough of the wave, the boat straightened out. They could see Art working hard at the wheel; Gertrude was nowhere to be seen.

Rodger, now held the tiller firmly in his hand. So far, the Sea Witch held a true course up to the top of the fifteen-foot waves and down the backside. "I feel sorry for Art and Gertrude, they`ve really got their hands full."

"Yes, but Art seems to have it under control. I can`t imagine Gertrude wanting to stay below deck, as it`s got to be a wild and crazy ride down there. I wonder if she always rides out a storm below deck?" Helen stood now with Bilgee snuggled tightly in the crook of her arm, "I think I`ll go below and call Gertrude on the radio/phone and see if she`s all right."

"Good idea. I`m in control here; I`ll pound on the roof if that changes."

As Helen went down the steps to the salon, she immediately felt comfort in the warmth of the cabin. Even though there was a steady rhythmic surge and roll to the hull, being below deck wasn`t as punishing as being out in the weather. Gertrude answered the phone immediately and seemed relieved to be talking to someone.

"Are you alright?" asked Helen.

"I`m as alright as you can be when you feel like you're in a washing machine. How about you?"

"We`re okay. I notice Kitchen Pass is yawing as it goes down the backside of the wave; is that normal for her in these conditions?"

"Yes, doesn`t the Sea Witch do that?"

"No, being a heavier boat, I guess, makes the difference. Why aren`t you on deck with Art?"

"He says I make him nervous; he`s used to this problem, and I really can`t be of any help, except to stay out of his way. I don`t mind being below deck, if it helps him."

"I just wanted to know you're alright; if anything changes, give us a call. We`ll monitor the radio/phone every half hour; that`ll keep us in touch and give one of us here a break from the storm."

Helen quickly drank a cup of coffee and took one to Rodger as she made her way forward with Bilgee again tucked under her arm. Rodger saw her plight and stepped forward to take the extended cup. Helen sat down on the bench seat under the dodger for protection from the continuous driving wind and rain. "I`m glad we had this dodger installed. I`ll change places with you, so you can enjoy your coffee and get a little rest."

"Thanks, Skipper. I don`t suppose you put a shot of Drambui in this coffee?"

"No, Rodg." Helen stifled a laugh, "I think we both need all our faculties about us." Helen took Rodger`s place at the helm as he took Bilgee and sat where she had been. Looking to the stern, he watched Helen standing next to the tiller, smiling as she faced into the storm. With water, running off her sou`wester hat, down her slicker, onto her boots, and into the cockpit; the deck now stood several inches deep in water; the scuppers couldn`t keep up with the deluge. He thought, *what a woman I've got here for a Skipper and life's partner; she`s now running on pure adrenaline.*

* * *

Nightfall came suddenly, the storm allowed no hint of a setting sun. Darkness made the storm more foreboding and intense. Vivid lightning strikes now brighten the ink-black sky, and booming of thunder became more unnerving. The distance between lightning and thunder is now one second, and Rodger and Helen now take thirty-minute turns at the helm. Each in turn sat huddled under the protection of the dodger holding a terrified Bilgee who hid her face and shuddered with each peal of thunder.

Every half hour, found one of them below calling Gertrude. Kitchen Pass was weathering the storm and nothing had changed regarding the yawing problem. Gertrude said she spent most of the time below deck, but made a pilgrimage to the cockpit after each phone call from the Sea Witch to reassure Art all was well with them. At those times he would tie the wheel down and sit beneath the dodger for a respite from the storm, while Gertrude supplied him with food, drink, and companionship.

Suddenly a close lightening strike zigzagged across the immediate sky ending at the top of Kitchen Pass`s mast sending the boat shuddering and reeling sharply to port. The jarring strike lit up the immediate sky outlining Art standing gallantly at the wheel. However, the electricity was dissipated into the water as Art and Gertrude had attached a grounding strap to their mast, also.

Helen immediately went below and called Kitchen Pass on the radio/phone. After a brief moment Gertrude answered, "Yes?"

"Are you all right?"

"I am, but I am going topside to check on Art. What a blow! Fortunately I was in my bunk, or I could have been everywhere, but up. Stay by the phone and I`ll call you in a couple of minutes."

A few minutes later Gertrude called, "Art`s okay, and so is Kitchen Pass. Poor dear, Art`s worn out, but he won`t let me take the wheel. How did the strike look from your vantage point?"

"For a moment you lit up like a Christmas tree, but your battery strap did its job evidently. You didn`t lose your electronics, did you?"

"No, thank goodness for that. Can you imagine being out here without them?"

"I don`t want to think about it," said Helen. "I hate to say this but I`d guess the strike went to your mast rather than ours because you have the taller mast. There`s an old saying in the boating world, *the sailboat with the tallest mast in the marina will get the lightning strike.*"

“I`ll pass that on to Art, although there`s no consolation there. It`s the first time its ever happened to us, and I hope the last time. The storm isn`t over yet.”

“One of us will call back in a half hour, and if its any consolation there`s another old saying, *lightning doesn`t strike twice in the same place.*”

“Thanks for the encouragement dear, I`ll pass that on to Art, too.”

* * *

As the storm continued into the night, Rodger and Helen caught snatches of sleep out of sheer fatigue. Suddenly the storm seamed less intense. “Am I imagining it, or is this beast moderating?” Rodger asked.

“I think it is. I just counted five seconds between lightning and thunder.”

“Thank goodness! The rain and wind are definitely slacking off, so I guess it`s passed us by.” Rodger tied down the helm and joined Helen and Bilgee under the dodger. Putting his arms around Helen, he drew her close and kissed her wet, smiling, but tired-looking face.

“We made it,” said Helen, “but I don`t want anymore nights like that one; I`m worn out.”

“You don`t have a corner on that market, Skipper.” As the storm continued to slacken, the first streaks of light from the breaking dawn appeared. “Man, am I glad to see the dawn. I was beginning to wonder if we`d ever see another one.”

“Granted, it was bad, but we were never in danger of capsizing like we did off Oregon.”

“Maybe I`m a little gun-shy… I remember only too well how close I came to dying. The Sea Witch is a good boat, but we found it has limitations.”

“All boats have limitations, Rodger; so do people.”

“Yes, and we don`t want to test our limits, do we?”

“Not really. We want to know what we`re made of, but there is a point of no return and we don`t want to go there.” Rodger leaned over and took Bilgee into his arms. “Well, girl, you've been tested and survived. Now you're a real sea dog." Bilgee looked up at Rodger and gave a sharp bark, licking his face unexpectedly.

"Bilgee stole a kiss," teased Helen as she rose to take the helm watch. "She`s getting pretty good at that, I've noticed. It must be nice to have two women in love with you."

"You don`t hear me complaining, do you?" Rodger rose and started for the cabin hatch, "I`m going below to call Art and Gertrude again and make sure they`ve recovered from the horror of that lightning strike."

* * *

Within an hour the storm had moved on leaving a surprisingly normal, good-sailing day. Sea birds swooped low looking for a handout. When none was forthcoming, they moved on. The wind held steady at ten knots and life aboard the two vessels bound for Tahiti returned to normal. The boats came close to within shouting distance and shared their lives briefly on a more personal level with the lightning strike being the main topic of conversation. Both exhausted crews returned to four-hour watches so sleep could once again be a part of their lives. They saluted their success over the storm by toasting with Bloody Marys laced heavily with Vodka.

Rodger sat on the gunnels looking out to the vastness of the ocean about them. "I can`t help reflecting on Burke`s essay regarding the excitement of the mind. Remember we talked about it after our first storm off Washington`s coast?"

"Yes, I remember. You quoted him as saying the sublime was experienced not in a state of tranquility, but in a state of fear or terror… right?"

"Right! During the storm I watched as you stood at the helm facing the storm at its worst; you were smiling."

"You `re right, and so is Burke; I was really on an adrenaline high." Helen turned the helm over to the autopilot and the GPS; then sat next to Rodger on the gunnels.

Rodger turned to face her, "Burke talked about mounting precipices and wondering how he got there and how he would return. I see our precipice as this ocean crossing."

"Yes, I can buy into that."

"Burke went on to say he didn`t have the tranquility, but the horror of solitude, a kind of turbulence between fright and admiration."

"That`s true, isn`t it. One minute fear, the next exhilaration."

"I look out at the ocean about us as far as the eye can see and the vastness gives me the feeling Burke would have called this *the dreadful and the sublime.*"

"I can see what an extra dollop of Vodka does for you, Rodg. It`s your watch, but Genie is doing just fine, so why don`t you join me below and we can test out Burke`s dreadful and sublime theory."

"Skipper, you're my kind of woman; I could stand a little sublime right now."

Chapter Thirty-Five

"It`s been two days since the storm," said Helen, "and I've noticed the wind is lighter than usual and the temperature is warmer. I hope we`re not getting into the doldrums."

Rodger had brought a tray of sandwiches made of sea biscuits and peanut butter and warm beer topside for a picnic on deck. "Doldrums? Tell me about that."

They sat facing each other in the cockpit sharing the lunch. "Our eating fare has changed, hasn`t it? Oh, for a cold beer," said Helen. Responding to Rodger`s question, "The doldrums is a belt of calm or variable winds lying between the trade winds of the northern and southern hemispheres. It`s usually accompanied by warm temperature, as it`s within five degrees north or south of the equator."

"I've heard the word used medically when describing depression or stagnation. I guess the sailors would be in that state of mind if they were slowed down or becalmed for any length of time for lack of wind and also had to deal with excessive heat"

Helen turned to Rodger and looked deep into his eyes. "Not to change the subject, but whatever made you so determined to sail to Tahiti?"

"It`s funny you asked now, as I asked myself the same question when we were in the middle of the storm two days ago." Rodger stood as he put aside the lunch tray, "I guess two things come to mind as I consider my obsession to sail to Tahiti. One is that I love the water and have been a recreational power boater most of my life. The second is Tahiti has a romantic appeal as a paradise in the middle of nowhere with a laid-back life style. As I tired of my life`s roll as mortgage broker, husband, and the typical suburban life, I longed to escape to this fantasy island aboard a sailboat."

"Really! Why a sailboat when you weren`t even a sailor?"

"I could never afford a powerboat big enough to get me there, and sailing always looked to be fun and easy. Also, it would give me a new challenge, as I had achieved my former goals in life: I was financially stable; my three sons were independent with families of their own, and Irene and I were like two old shoes."

"Lots of older people fit that description, Rodg."

"I suppose so, but when I came down with tuberculosis and the doctor gave me only a year to live…somehow, I had to fight back. That`s when I remembered the goal I`d had as a middle-aged man… to escape by sailing to Tahiti."

Helen took Rodger`s hand and pulled him down beside her on the seat. "I remember you telling me Irene didn`t like boating, of any kind."

"Yes, that`s when I started planning to buy a sailboat and run away from my present life that had the prospect of a lingering death at home or in a hospital and a wife that wasn`t cut out to be a caregiver."

"I guess I can understand your desperation, but to sail across the largest ocean in the world when you didn`t even know how to sail… unbelievable!"

Rodger turned to face Helen as he sat beside her. "It does sound crazy, doesn`t it? However, I didn`t know sailing was so involved. I just thought you raised the sails and steered the boat."

Helen burst out laughing, "Now you know better… right?"

"That`s for sure. You know, if I hadn`t met you, I`d never have been able to pull this off."

"I agree, but we`re not there yet, Rodg."

Rodger took both of her hands in his and looked deep into her eyes. "I love you Helen, and the paradise I sought is right here… right now."

"I love you too, Rodg, and reaching Tahiti has become a secondary goal for both of us. The first goal is to survive this voyage so we can spend the rest of our lives together."

"Amen."

Chapter Thirty-Six

Rodger stood at the tiller looking to the sea ahead, while Helen sat holding Bilgee, her back leaning against the cabin bulkhead. "We`ll be crossing the equator tomorrow if this five knot wind holds," Helen offered. "It`s been lighter and warmer since we`ve come close to the equator and probably will be light and variable for another five degrees of latitude."

"It`s nice not to have the heavier rains we experienced further north in the horse latitudes. That`s a strange name for an area of the ocean. What does it mean, Skipper?"

"There are two definitions that I got when I asked that same question of Clyde. One is, the name came from the unhappy job of having to destroy the horses when ships caught in the calms, found their water supplies depleted."

"I guess a lot of horses were carried by ship in the old days when armies were being transported that way." Rodger left the tiller to the autopilot and the GPS and sat beside Helen.

She smiled and continued her explanation. "The other theory is that a `dead horse` was the seaman`s term for the first month at sea---a month for which they had already been paid and had spent the money very quickly afterwards. So it seemed to them, with the money all gone, that the first month was spent working for nothing. To mark the end of the `dead horse` month the crew made an effigy of a horse and paraded it around the deck. Then with great noise and celebration, the effigy would be hoisted to the end of a yardarm, cut down and dropped into the sea."

"Really! I like the second explanation best."

"Me too; I`d rather have a fake horse dropped into the sea than a real one."

"Where did you ever come up with explanations like that?" asked Rodger.

"Clyde was always interested in trivia regarding boating. I was subjected to all kinds of trivia information, whether I wanted it or not."

"I would have liked your husband. You said he died of a heart attack?"

"Yes, he was your age when he died two years ago."

"If he`d lived, he`d be the skipper of this boat and the two of you would probably be on your way to Tahiti."

"That was the plan."

Rodger moved closer to Helen and put his arm around her shoulder. "How are you doing on that score, Skipper?"

"I often think of Clyde as I`m sure you do Irene, your sons, and their families."

"Yes. They will always have a place in our thoughts."

Helen`s eyes smiled lovingly at Rodger "But that`s in the past and our reality is now and the future. We can honor and remember the past, but we don`t live there."

Rodger stood, taking Helen`s hand, and helped her to her feet. "I couldn`t agree more…now, let`s have lunch."

"Rodg, you're such a romantic."

* * *

It was the next day when Helen announced, "We`re at zero degrees latitude and finally crossing the equator."

Rodger appeared on deck awakening from a much-needed nap having stood two watches during the night. His hair tousled and eyes heavy with sleep as he mumbled,

"Shouldn`t we do something in the form of a celebration?"

"I talked with Art and Gertrude on the radio/phone; they will pull along side us shortly, as the wind has died. We can raft together and have a *crossing the equator* party."

Rodger immediately came to life, "Great! How are we going to celebrate?"

"Gertrude has fixed some hors d`oeuvres and chilled a bottle of champagne."

Rodger turned toward the hatchway leading down to the salon, "I`ll go below and clean up a bit, change clothes and maybe even shave."

"Good idea, Rodg, and while you're at it, check the larder and see if we have anything delectable we can add to the festivities. When you finish, I`ll clean up too, but remember we only have a half hour until party time."

* * *

As their companion boat approached, Rodger and Helen stood amidships to catch the thrown lines needed to tie the boats together. Rodger put out three bumpers on the starboard side to keep the boats from chaffing after being tied bow, amidships, and stern.

"Ahoy," called Art as he slowly guided Kitchen Pass next to Sea Witch like two old friends coming together to embrace. "Gertrude, throw Rodger the bowline," Art called out. He then put the transmission in neutral and stepped to the stern tossing the line to Helen, who quickly cleated it off. Then expertly setting a spring line to amidships, he stood back to check the tie-up. By this time Gertrude had stepped across the gunnels to the Sea Witch and had her arms around Helen saying, "Oh, it`s so good to see you up close and embrace you," she gushed.

Art, satisfied with the tie up, stepped across and extended his hand to Rodger. The two friends then bear hugged, as if they hadn`t seen each other for a long time. "It`s so good to be with you two where we can actually sit down and talk. Gertrude has some champagne chilled and hors d`oeuvres, so come aboard and we`ll celebrate not only crossing the equator, but just being together."

"We`re for that," said Helen. "We have some canned anchovies and baby smoked oysters to add to the celebration. It`s so good to just sit in the sun and do nothing for a change."

The two couples crossed back to Kitchen Pass, and suddenly Bilgee came alive barking as if she wanted to be a part of the celebration too. Rodger went back, scooped her up in his arms, and carried her over the two gunnels to the cockpit of Kitchen Pass where the festivities would be held. Setting her down, she immediately renewed her friendship with Art and Gertrude.

"Crossing the equator for the first time," said Art, "used to be a big deal on old-time sailing vessels. King Neptune presided over a kangaroo court and the first-timers were initiated. I don`t see us doing that today. Gertrude and I have been across the equator several times and initiations are passé. But celebrating isn`t…so, I raise my glass and propose a toast to our two wonderful friends with whom we have shared this adventurous journey, Helen and Rodger… and, oh yes, Bilgee. May you reach your long-sought destination, Tahiti, and we`ll be right behind you."

Gertrude, raising her glass, shouted "Here, here!" Helen and Rodger joined in raising their glasses and shouted "Here, here!" Bilgee barked a series of sharp staccato barks, her contribution to the festivities. They burst out laughing at her and then settled down to enjoy the tasty treats before them.

"You two look good," said Art. You're both tan as a nut, and lean and trim."

"Yes, you do," added Gertrude. "Sailing keeps you in pretty good shape and the meals aren`t that sumptuous at sea; I miss fresh vegetables and fruit the most."

"I do too," replied Helen. "Fish is about the only thing fresh now, and we`ve been able to catch fish when we tried. I've heard of some mariners who never caught even one fish while on a voyage.'

"We`ve caught all we`ve wanted," said Art. "How`s your water supply?"

"We`re okay," replied Helen. "We`ve taken advantage of the rain for drinking and bathing."

"Modesty goes by the wayside when you need a shower," injected Rodger.

"You can say that again," agreed Gertrude.

* * *

Before nightfall they untied the two boats to allow them to drift apart, not trusting the weather to remain calm through the night. After a few moments of slow drifting, Art started the engine and motored about four hundred yards ahead. Both crews left all sails down and went to bed to enjoy a full night`s sleep.

The next morning a fresh breeze rattled the halyards against the masts serving as an alarm clock. Both boats got underway in short order to take advantage of the wind. The sky remained void of clouds, and the sun shone hot, but the wind held steady all day long.

“We must have picked up the Southern Trade Winds,” said Helen as they sat together sharing the cockpit. Bilgee lay on the cabin roof next to the dingy and seemed to be enjoying the sun.

“Wasn`t it great being with Art and Gertrude, if only for a few hours?”

“Yes, in fact I almost hate the wind for bringing an end to it,” replied Helen.

“Maybe the wind will die again soon and we can raft again.”

“If this is the Trade Winds, we`re in for a long, steady sail.”

“Of course, that`s what`ll get us to Tahiti,” replied Rodger,” but we`re really missing close contact with other people, aren’t we?”

“Yes, but can you imagine what it would be like doing this single-handed?”

“Ugh!” replied Rodger, “I don`t want to even think about it.”

“I`m going below to get some sleep. Four-hour watches make for long nights.”

“Sweet dreams, Skipper. Bilgee and I will take care of things.”

Rodger took off his shirt to work on his tan even though it was late in the afternoon. Bilgee curled beside him on the bench seat as Rodger lie back and let his mind take inventory. *The barometer is holding steady at thirty-point four, the wind at fourteen knots, we`re making maximum hull speed of six and one half knots, and no sea birds are to be seen…too far from land. Dolphins come often and play in and ahead of the bow wake… such fun. Occasionally we`ve seen a basking gray whale lying on the surface or spanking the water with its tail, perhaps riding itself of barnacles, or maybe just for fun.*

I`d better put my shirt on; the sun has worked its way across the sky and is turning rich shades of apricot and purple. He smiled to himself as he thought of that old song, "*When the Blue of the Night Meets the Gold of the Day." The waves are four-feet high now…we rise and fall like a mustang galloping at sunset across the high plains of Oregon to their night feeding ground. Funny I thought of that after all these years. Usually the wild horses travel in a herd, while we`re alone in a monstrous ocean except for Kitchen Pass.*

At eight o`clock Helen stuck her head out of the companionway and shouted "Dinner is served… if you like clam chowder."

Rodger quickly came out of his reverie, "I`ll be right there, Skipper; I love clam chowder." Rodger checked the GPS, autopilot, and scanned the water ahead. There was nothing ahead, but water and more and more water. Grabbing Bilgee, he worked his way below to the comfort of the salon enhanced by the heady smell of fresh-made clam chowder."

"Boy, that looks and smells wonderful, Helen, even if it`s made with powdered milk, dehydrated vegetables, and canned clams. I`ll open a bottle of Chardonnay, even if it`s not chilled, and we`ll have a banquet."

"Good thinking, Rodg. I could use a little relaxer now before I go on watch. Bilgee is a good companion at night, but not much of a conversationalist."

"I've noticed that; she does speak a lot with her eyes, however."

"That`s true."

Chapter Thirty-Seven

The days were unusually warm and the non-existent wind caused the sails to hang limp, and progress in the water a standstill. Helen talked to Art on the radio/phone about his assessment of the weather.

"We`re in the doldrums," said Art, "and can expect light to non-existent wind until we moved through the area. The solution is to drop the sails and use our auxiliary engines to move across the area until we find wind. The only limitation is to save enough fuel to be able to be under power when we come to a port. The alternative, being under sail in port, could be dangerous with boat traffic."

Helen and Rodger did as suggested and followed Kitchen Pass by 300 meters. "It seems strange to be under power," said Rodger as he stood at the tiller looking up to bare masts.

"I agree; it takes some getting used to." Helen sat back on the bench seat in the cockpit with Bilgee on her lap.

"Can we expect any wind at all in the doldrums?" Rodger asked while checking the engine gauges.

"Occasionally we`ll get light and variable winds, but Art says it`s almost like sailing in a vacuum."

Rodger stared at the flat water all about them with the only movement the ground swells that started a long way away. "How long do you figure it will take us, if we continue under power, to get out of the doldrums?"

"I`ll have to ask Art. He`s been here before and this is all new to me. In fact, I`ll go down to the radio/phone and ask him now."

Helen set Bilgee on the seat near Rodger and descended down the passageway to the salon. Rodger, having turned the tiller over to Genie, lifted Bilgee to his lap. She looked up showing pleasure at being held. His free hand found the itchy spot on her back near her tail and ecstasy showed in those dark brown eyes as his fingers massaged her skin. The day remained warm and the sky had few clouds in it to shield them from the relentless sun.

Helen appeared in the companionway; her brow furrowed into a frown. "We`ve got a problem! Art asked our fuel capacity and our rate of use per hour at 6-knot hull speed. When I told him we had forty gallons of fuel and used one and a half gallons per hour, he did some quick math and determined we may have a problem."

"What did his math reveal?"

"He said we could only run for twenty-six hours at best and that may or may not get us through the doldrums. If it`s only a hundred and fifty miles wide, we`re okay. That will run us out of gas, but he can spare some."

"Wow! A hundred and fifty miles is a long way. Is the doldrums that wide a band?"

"He says it varies, and winds do come through, but usually light and variable." Helen sat down beside Rodger, putting her arm around his shoulder, "They have twice the cruising distance we have and they are there to help us, if we need them."

Rodger brightened at Helen`s remark and held Bilgee up at arms length saying, "Maybe we won`t have to swim after all." Turning back to Helen, "Are the doldrums always in the same place?"

"No, I heard they were to be reckoned with so I read up on them a long time ago when Clyde and I were planning the trip here. It`s an area around the equator located between the northeast and the southeast trade winds in the Pacific and the Atlantic Oceans. These are areas of calm or light sporadic winds, but also there can be thunderstorms, squalls, and heavy rainfall."

"What a hodge-podge of weather. Doesn`t Art`s Internet print-outs tell him where the light wind areas are?"

"I`ll ask him when I call after lunch."

"Speaking of lunch," said Rodger as he stood and handed Bilgee to Helen, "are you up for a sea biscuit sandwich, and beer?"

"You read my mind."

* * *

After lunch Helen contacted Kitchen Pass and ran through her list of questions about the Doldrums. She then made her way aft to share the information with Rodger, who sat staring at the nearly flat ocean surface. "What do you see, Mate?"

"Nothing," he replied. "This is boring, boring, boring; I guess that`s why they call it being in the doldrums when talking about a person`s depressed state of mind."

"Now you've got it! Art says he`s headed for an area that should give us some wind that is in our path to Tahiti. He suggests we shut down before sunset and raft for awhile, then drift apart and get a good night`s sleep."

"That sounds great; we could even have a party to break this monotony." Rodger turned to Bilgee sleeping beside him, "What do you think of that, Bilgee?" Opening one eye when hearing her name didn`t bring the response Rodger had expected. She lay her head down and immediately went back to sleep. "I guess the doldrums have got to her, too."

Helen sat down on the other side of Rodger and reached for his hand, "I guess you`re in need of some stimulating activity. Why not get your fishing pole and see if you can catch something for dinner?"

"If the fish feel like I do, they won`t have enough energy to take the lure."

Helen aroused Bilgee and lifted her gently into her arms. "Wake up sleepy head; we`ll go below and give Rodg full use of the cockpit for his fishing venture."

* * *

As Rodger sat at the stern, fish pole in hand and line trailing over the transom, he closely watched the tip of the pole for the least sign of action. Rodger thought, *sometimes fish mouth the lure without taking it to determine if this is what they want. With an artificial lure it`s hard to fool a fish when they do this, however, most fish aren`t that patient. They just strike, taking the lure and line until the fisherman sets the hooks. Then the fight begins.*

My line`s rigged with a slip-sinker, flasher, and eighteen inches of leader to a lure. If the fish strikes, the sinker will loosen and slide down to the flasher and I`ll set the hook. Most fish will fight to get away, but some warm-water fish don`t act that way; they just follow the course of least resistance. I`d sure like a fighting fish, but I`ll settle for anything just to have some activity and maybe something for dinner.

Rodger had heard about triggerfish in this area and didn`t want any part of them. If he recognized the black and red markings on a fish, he planned to cut his line, sacrificing the tackle. He had been told if they puncture your hand with their sharp spines, you`d feel like cutting your hand off. *That`ll be enough motivation to sacrifice my tackle for.*

As the afternoon wore on and Rodger was about to doze off from lack of activity, the warmth of the day, and the two beers he`d consumed during the past two hours, the tip of the pole dipped from a forty-five degree angle upward until it nearly touched the water, followed by steady downward tugs. Rodger reacted by a quick upward motion with the pole; with the hook set, the fight was on. He had set the drag on the reel, which now produced a sound that`s music to a fisherman`s ears. Its zing, zing, zing sent chills up Rodger`s spine as he attempted to reel in the line. This fish was angry and heavy.

Rodger`s body tensed as his adrenalin surged, but he knew better than to try to reel in the fish too soon. The fish had to be tired before he could safely take up line on the reel. For the time being, he was satisfied to let the fish pull line off with the drag giving resistance all the way. He figured he had about a hundred yards of line out and his reel held three hundred yards, therefore, he had line to sacrifice for the battle ahead. His only hazards were the shrouds that supported the mizzen and main mast. If he could keep the fish to the stern area, there would be little danger of shearing his line on the rigging.

Suddenly the fish broke through the surface of the water and stood on its tail thrashing violently in an attempt to shake the hook from its mouth. Not succeeding, it dropped on its side and disappeared beneath the water, but still near the top, as its dorsal fin was evident part of the time. Rodger reared back on the pole keeping the tip high to allow it to be effective in resisting the movement of the fish.

The steady glide of the boat under power moved the drama forward and the fish came out of the water every couple of minutes in its attempt to shake the hook. Twenty minutes had gone by before Rodger felt less pressure on the line. At that instant he started to reel slowly, but deliberately.

Eventually, after he had recovered fifty yards of line, it became apparent the fish had fought a heroic battle, but lost. Several times, as Rodger continued to add line on his reel, he`d have to stop and let the tired fish make futile dashes to one side of the battle field or the other, but as long as the line didn`t break, it was only a matter of time.

The fish came to the top of the water about twenty feet behind the boat and never dove again. When he had the fish alongside, Rodger took his gaff hook and slipped the sharp tip of the hook under the flared-out gills of the gallant fish. Hoisting it aboard took both hands on the gaff and most of his strength. As he carefully lifted the fish over the gunnels and into the cockpit it flopped repeatedly in its death throws until Rodger mercifully slipped the gaff hook out of its mouth and hit it on the head with the back of the gaff. There lay forty pounds of fish whose identity was a mystery to Rodger, but it was a beauty. *There`ll be fish for our party and then some,* he thought, *but am I ever tired.*

Helen stuck her head out of the companionway, "Any luck?" Then her eyes looked own to the deck of the cockpit. "Oh my, you have been busy. What is it?"

"I`ll have to ask Art. I`m not familiar with fish in this part of the world, however, it fought like a king salmon."

"We don`t have to wonder what to have for dinner for a few days. Art has a pretty good-sized barbeque and we shouldn`t lose any from spoilage." Helen sat down beside Rodger who appeared tired from his half-hour battle, "That took care of your boredom problem didn`t it?"

"Yes! What a fighter! I`ll keep it covered with a wet towel and in the shade until Art sees it, otherwise, I`d clean it now."

*   *   *

Helen got on the radio/phone and after telling about the fish, suggested they raft together right away so he could identify it before they cleaned it. Art said they were looking forward to the rafting and he`d be happy to barbeque it for the evening meal, which he offered to host aboard Kitchen Pass.

Helen relayed the offer from Art and Gertrude and waited for Art to shut down their engine so they could come broadside and tie together. Once this was accomplished Art and Gertrude came aboard to see the prize fish. Rodger uncovered it as it lay on the cockpit deck.

"Rodg, you've caught a Barracuda which is common to these waters although I've never caught one, nor have I tasted one, but it should be good eating as it`s an active fish, as you found out."

Once identified, Rodger cleaned the fish and cut it in pieces to accommodate the grill. Gertrude lit the barbeque and the briquettes were just turning gray when Rodger and Art each carried a portion of Rodger`s catch to Kitchen Pass and placed pieces on the aluminum foil-draped grill. Gertrude, added seasoning, lemon juice, and onion rings to the top of the fish, then wrapped the foil together at the top to seal the heat and moisture inside the aluminum cocoon. Now they sat back to enjoy the cocktails Art had made.

Helen asked Gertrude, "How long do you think it will take to cook tonight`s dinner?"

"About forty-five minutes," came her reply, "as I have the grill set to cook slowly. When it`s done we can eat and cook the rest for tomorrow. Once it`s cooked it should be good for several days."

Chapter Thirty-Eight

Motoring until they found wind, and because it held steady, Art determined it was the Southern Trade Winds and they were out of the doldrums. Now they were logging up to one hundred and twenty miles every twenty-four hours. Occasionally they would sight other vessels with a variety of configurations: container ships, recreational sailing ships, and occasionally military ships. They seldom had ships cross their path as the highways of the ocean usually followed the ocean currents and the wind paths. Life aboard had a routine, as long as the southern trade winds held steady.

On the fifth day out of the doldrums a rainsquall hit them from the stern. Rodger, on watch at the helm, spotted the sheets of rain and turbulence coming at them. He pounded loudly on the cabin roof to awaken Helen. Shortly, she stuck her head out of the companionway and asked, "What`s wrong?"

Rodger pointed aft. "That!"

Helen turned and sighed, "Oh, Boy." Disappearing below deck, she soon appeared in foul-weather gear. "I`ll take the helm while you get yours on; this looks like more than an opportunity-to-take-a-shower type of squall. Those black clouds look ominous."

"I hear you, Skipper."

Disappearing below deck, Rodger reappeared in his gear holding Bilgee in the crook of his arm. Her eyes questioning as if to say, "What`s up?"

Rodger handed Bilgee to Helen then took his place at the helm. Helen, sitting on the end of the bench seat under the dodger, looked back frequently to track the approaching squall. It became apparent they were directly in its path and no way to avoid it. Helen handed Bilgee to Rodger, "Take her below, and then tend the sails."

"Aye, aye, Skipper." Rodger dropped the mainsail partway and began tying reefing knots to shorten the sail for the pending heavy weather. Helen helped him as the tiller was still being controlled by the autopilot. Once reefed, Rodger dropped the mizzen and changed the Genoa to the storm jib; Helen took the helm and waited for the storm.

Within minutes, sheets of wind-driven rain followed the first raindrops as the squall overtook them. The sun, blotted out by the dark, heavy-laden rain clouds, caused the temperature to drop markedly. Sea Witch heeled sharply to starboard as the wind hit them from the port corner of the stern. The trailing sea climbed the stern, and the first wave broke into a shower of water hitting Helen full force in the back. Even with a firm grip on the tiller and lifeline attached, she staggered forward into the cockpit from her standing position.

Rodger immediately jumped to her rescue by sitting on the other side of the tiller and holding it with her. She quickly sat to reduce her exposure to the shrieking wind and sheets of rain that engulfed them. The short and choppy waves caused the Sea Witch to buck like a bronco smashing down into the backside of the waves as the squall raged, driving everything before it. The Sea Witch, all nine tons of her, was actually surfing as she was carried forward, still listing to starboard.

Helen screamed above the storm, "We`ve got to change course and put the stern directly in the path of the wind, drop the main, then put out a sea anchor to raise the rail out of the water. We could get a knock- down."

Rodger nodded and the two of them slowly forced the tiller to starboard causing the wind to hit them squarely in the middle of the stern instead of on the corner. As soon as they swung the tiller, causing their direction to change fifteen degrees, the rail came up, and they were now on an even keel. Rodger looked at Helen; they both smiled in relief. Relaxing a little as the boat continued to surf, but didn`t go over the wave due to the sea anchor

Alongside, the water seemed to boil, as the boat now at maximum hull speed moved with the waves. Suddenly the sky became brighter, the rain and wind velocity decreased in unison, and the Sea Witch stopped surfing. The squall had run its course with them and moved on across the top of the ocean to find another victim or die a natural death, either by spilling all of its water or from a change in air pressure.

Helen and Rodger sat quietly in a state of exhaustion watching the water in the cockpit slowly flow out the scuppers. She was first to break the silence, "Now wasn`t that fun, Rodg?"

"Now that it`s passed, it was thrilling. However, it`s a good thing we changed direction; I wonder how Kitchen Pass made out?"

"I see them about a half mile ahead; I`ll go below and give them a call." Helen stood stretching the stiffness from her arms and legs before disappearing below deck.

Rodger turned control of the Sea Witch over to the GPS and the autopilot so he could raise the main part way, unreef it, then raise it to its full height. He changed the jib to the Genoa and raised the mizzen. Laying his foul weather gear aside, he sat for a long time allowing his body to recover from the strenuous event of the storm. He was more tired than he wanted to admit and thankful for the normal sailing conditions of the Trades. .

Chapter Thirty-Nine

A week later Helen sat near the tiller on her midnight to four a.m. watch, looking at the night sky. A ceiling of stars lay above her head with the Southern Cross visible instead of the Big Dipper. *If all goes well,* she thought, *we`ll be sighting Nuku Hiva, which is the northernmost inhabited island in the Marquesas, then Tahiti and some of the outer islands tomorrow. It`s been a challenging journey, but Rodger will have succeeded in his life`s goal, to sail to Tahiti. It`s taken seven weeks of sailing to do what an airplane flying from California can do in eight hours, but what a different experience. In either case, it`s the same islands, actually one hundred and eighteen islands, but what a far different journey.*

I`m glad Art followed my suggestion and dropped behind us during the night so Rodger will have the opportunity to be the first to sight land during his morning watch from four to eight a.m.

Helen stepped forward to stretch after sitting so long at the tiller. Bilgee awakened and looked at her questioningly. "No girl, our watch isn`t over yet." Helen again sat down and stared upward at the night sky. Her thoughts returned to Rodger. *He started out as a sick man at death`s door with only a predicted year of life. Running away from his tired marriage and his grown family, he took one last fling at life even knowing it could kill him.*

That`s where I came in. Actually, I needed Rodger as much as he needed me. Living as a retired, middle-aged, widow with time on my hands wasn`t much of a life.

I remember when he showed up at my door answering my newspaper advertisement in my attempt to sell the Sea Witch. Looking all of his sixty years, but with an excitement in his voice as he talked about his dream of sailing to Tahiti. After listening to him talk of his past boating experience, I soon realized he was a boater but not a sailor and would surely fail in his venture. Then words came tumbling out of my mouth from God knows where, "You buy my boat, and I`ll skipper it for you and teach you how to sail."

We both had stood silent in a state of shock. Finally, he simply said, "Okay."

Helen poured a cup of coffee from the thermos, and Bilgee came to life as she heard the pouring of coffee. Sitting back drinking her coffee Helen thought, *It`s hard to believe I suggested sailing to Tahiti with a perfect stranger. I guess I didn`t realize how desperate I was to have some kind of a life after Clyde`s death. I loved sailing and Clyde had been a good teacher.*

Now that it's happened, now that we`re almost to Tahiti, I think Rodger and I were meant to be. Oh, how I love him. His divorce from Irene actually set both of them free. For him to follow his dream and for Irene to be the independent businesswoman she thought she craved to be.

Helen looked at her watch and realized it was time to awaken Rodger for his turn at the helm. Putting Bilgee in the crook of her arm, she went below.

"Okay sleepy head it`s your watch. Kitchen Pass is behind us now, so don`t be alarmed. I don`t think they wanted to upstage your arrival at Tahiti, as this is your dream."

"We`re that close?"

"Dawn is in an hour and the first island, Nuku Hiva, can`t be too far ahead of us."

"I've waited a long time for this moment," Rodger sighed. "Get to bed, Skipper, and I`ll wake you as soon as I see it."

"It may be several hours, but I`ll be here."

Rodger lovingly tucked Bilgee under his arm and took her topside where they sat side by side. The thermos still had some coffee in it so he emptied the contents into his cup. Looking up at the starry sky always gave him pleasure, as they always seemed so much brighter when viewed at sea away from city lights. *Dawn should be breaking soon,* he thought, *wouldn`t it be something if Nuku Hiva was in sight?*

According to Art, there are three families living there in Anaho Bay on the northeast end of the island; I wonder if we should spend the day and night there and go on to Tahiti tomorrow? It would be so good to be on land again and see and talk to others.

At the first morning light… there it was. A saw-tooth ridge of uplifted lava needles starting off shore, protruding out of the water and extending up a mountainside. The jagged spires of lava rock looked like the silhouette of a dragon crawling up a mountain, a mountain that was surrounded by jungle, then lower down, palm trees, white sandy beaches, edged with beautiful lines of breakers running shoreward.

At the sight, Rodger jumped to his feet, ran to the far side of the cockpit, and pounded like a mad man on the cabin roof, laughing and crying for joy. "Land Ho," he shouted. "Land Ho!"

Bilgee, barking hysterically, ran in circles around the deck as Helen stumbled up the steps from the salon, rubbing sleep from her eyes. "Oh, Rodg, you've done it," she laughed excitedly. "You've lived your dream!"

Smiling and crying he put his arms around Helen holding her tight, looked deep into her eyes, sighed a long sigh of relief and completion. "We`ve done it, Helen, we`ve done it; you, Bilgee, and me." Then with a sharp gasp, he slumped into her arms.

"Rodger, what`s wrong? Are you kidding, or what? If you are, it isn`t funny." She allowed his body to slump to the deck. Stepping back to look at him as he lay face down, then dropping to her knees she shouted, "Rodger, what`s wrong?" Shocked and trembling she gently rolled him over and bent her face close to his; he wasn`t breathing. Quickly she pinched his nose closed and placed her mouth over his open mouth to breath life-giving air into his lungs. There was no response.

"Rodger," she screamed, "answer me!" Bilgee started to bark loud and hysterically at Helen`s shouting. "Oh my god," Helen cried out, "this can`t be happening. Don`t leave me, Rodger." Again she attempted artificial respiration, but to no avail. Lifeless, Rodger lay on the deck facing upward with closed eyes, no grimace of pain on his face, instead a smile of satisfaction. Tears streamed down Helen`s face and Bilgee, who had stopped barking, now lay close to Rodger`s side in quiet resignation.

Jumping to her feet, Helen dashed below to call Art and Gertrude on the radio/phone. When Art answered she screamed, “Something has happened to Rodger.”

“What do you mean?”

Helen forced herself to say the words, “I think he`s dead.”

“What! How can that be? What happened?”

“We were standing together watching the islands near the entrance of Tahiti coming into view and he slumped to the deck; I think he`s had a heart attack.”

“Is there any pulse or breath?”

“Not that I can tell,” Helen sobbed. “Please help me.”

“Slacken your sails, and we`ll be right there.”

Helen, once again, checked Rodger for pulse or breathing. Finding neither, she set about dropping the sails. Art brought Kitchen Pass alongside and tied the two boats together while Gertrude dropped their sails. Art scampered aboard and quickly bent over Rodger on the cockpit deck. Checking for pulse and breathing, he leaned back and looked up at Helen who was anxiously standing by, “He`s gone Helen; it must have been a heart attack. Did he have a heart problem?”

“Not that I know of. Oh my God, what am I going to do without him?” She dropped to hold Rodger`s head in her lap. Burying her face in his shoulder, she whispered, “I guess the doctor was right after all, Sweetie, but my God, what a year it has been.”

Chapter Forty

The funeral procession made up of a black hearse and a dozen cars slowly moved single file into the National Military Cemetery in Covington, Washington. The cars stopped a short distance from an outside, open chapel as the hearse proceeded forward. The people left their cars and walked the short distance behind the hearse. A military chaplain with his back to a simple alter stood at attention waiting for the people to take the empty seats before him. It was a late summer day; the mild temperature and the arrangements of flowers gave an air of beauty to the open-sided enclosure.

Helen, holding Bilgee and accompanied by her family and Rodger`s family, took the front seats. Friends, gathering to pay their respects, filled the remaining seats with a few standing beyond the back row. In addition to the immediate families and old friends, were Wolfgang and Silvia, John and Nelda, and Art and Gertrude. As the casket was brought forward from the hearse, a group of eight military musicians played the Air Force hymn "Off We Go Into The Wild Blue Yonder." Rodger had answered his country`s call during wartime and had chosen the Air Force.

The sermon was given and the flag draping the casket was slowly, and deliberately folded into a triangle accompanied by a single bugler playing taps; then presented to Helen as she sat gently weeping holding a quiet, sad-eyed Bilgee. It was over. Rodger was laid to rest having accomplished what he had set out to do with the help of the woman and dog he loved and who loved him.

At that moment Helen remembered a conclusion Rodger had come to after he had regained his memory some months ago. He said, *the greatest adventure of all isn`t our voyage to Tahiti, it`s our love affair.*

THE END

Dedication

This book is dedicated to the loving memory of Bilgee, the dog in the story who really did exist. Unfortunately, she met an untimely death under the wheels of a car at about the time this book was being completed.